The Witches of Dark Root

Book 1 in The Daughters of Dark Root Series

BY

APRIL M. AASHEIM

THE WITCHES OF DARK ROOT
Copyright 2013
by April M. Aasheim

Published by Dark Root Press

First Edition

ISBN-13: 978-0615819327 (Dark Root Press)
ISBN-10: 061581932X

Cover Art & Design by April Aasheim

Printed in the United States of America

2013

ACKNOWLEDGEMENTS

I'd like to acknowledge the following people for their contributions towards the creation and publication of this book:

My husband: You have always been my biggest fan and my toughest critic and without your continued support and dedication this book never would have made it past the idea phase. I thank you for the countless hours you spent listening to my ideas on plot, story, and character, as well as the time you spent with your red pen, making corrections and adding suggestions until I got it just right. Thank you for your friendship and your love.

My mother: Thank you for teaching me about the many types of magic. And thank you for the continual reminder on how important family really is.

My writing group: As always, thanks for the suggestions, the rolled eyes, the laughs, and the companionship. You kept me motivated to continue my story even after I wanted to throw in the towel.

My children: You keep me laughing, guessing, searching, stumbling, digging, and trying to better myself every day. Writing a book is easy compared to being a parent and I appreciate the patience and love you have shown me.

My sisters: I absolutely could not have written this book had I not had you girls in my life. Writing this book and remembering our adventures together as children I smiled, and cried, most every day for a year. I am the luckiest woman in the world to have shared my childhood with you. Thank you.

My nieces and nephews: You continue to inspire me with your fearlessness and your love of life. Keep doing amazing things, the world needs you.

My editor: You can always figure out what I mean to say, even when I'm not sure. Your dedication to the art is inspiring. Thank you for paving the way.

My father, my aunt, and my grandmother: Though you all have gone I continue to think of you every day. You will always live on in my heart.

And to Casey: For her continued friendship and inspiration. Thank you for always being there for me.

OTHER WORKS BY THIS AUTHOR:
THE UNIVERSE IS A VERY BIG PLACE

Praise for The Universe is A Very Big Place ~
"The Universe is a Very Big Place by April Aasheim is a real laugh-out-loud novel, written with pace, humour and a whole lot of charm..." (BestChickLit.com)

This book is dedicated to Shawn,
who reaffirmed my belief in magick

PROLOGUE

MAGIC MAN

Miss Sasha's Magick Shoppe, Dark Root, Oregon
February, 2005

The shop was cold and dimly lit, musty and confining.
A spider web had attached itself to the archway that separated the main room from the back and I ducked each time I passed beneath it, not bothering to sweep it down. Shelves lined every wall of Mother's Magick shop, displaying the hundreds of candles, masks, figurines, and baubles that made Miss Sasha's the most popular attraction in all of Dark Root.

While the oddities fascinated tourists, I hardly noticed them anymore as I went about my work. I hardly noticed anything anymore, except the clock that ticked down the minutes until I was released from my daily servitude.

"Excuse me," said a woman who had been meandering near the book section for the last hour. "Where is your restroom?"

I responded by opening the front door.

She looked like she was going to protest but decided against it. My apathy for the shop was notorious. She would probably lodge a complaint with my mother instead.

"You need to order more peppermint," my sister Eve said, emerging from the back room and sucking on a piece of candy. "We've been out

1

for almost a week."

"You order it," I responded.

If she was going to eat the supplies, she could order them as well.

Eve launched into a series of reasons why I should perform the task——I was practically a boy and therefore, better at math, I had no social life and thus had far more time for work, etc. I was about to tell her that it wouldn't bother me if we ran out of everything, that the whole place could implode for all I cared, when a crystal figurine on a low shelf caught my eye. It was an owl, an ugly thing with eyes that bulged and a beak that hooked. I wasn't sure who had ordered it but I was certain it would never find a buyer.

"Bet I beat you out of this town," I said, tapping its beak.

A losing bet, I realized. It had wings. I didn't even have a car.

I checked the clock again——five minutes 'til closing time——and glanced around the shop. It wasn't as clean as my mother would have wanted, but then again my mother wasn't here.

"I say we call it done," I said, tossing my apron on the counter.

"Maggie, come take a look."

Eve stood by the window. Her fingers twitched as she pointed to a man I had never seen before, seated by the window in Delilah's Deli across the street.

"Who is he?" she asked. "I don't recognize him."

I moved to get a better view, nudging her out of the way. "Well, he isn't from around here."

Eve clucked her tongue. Of course, he wasn't from around here. His sophisticated clothing identified him as a city person, not a man who spent much time slinking around a small town in Central Oregon.

"He's handsome," she said and I silently agreed. Though it was getting dark I could still make out his thick mane of wavy brown hair and the strong line of his jaw. He was leaning forward, talking to a gaunt young man who hung on his every word.

"We have to find out what he's doing here," Eve said. "It's just not natural." Though the town festered with tourists during the fall months when we held the Haunted Dark Root Festival, it was rare to see anyone arrive after November and before May.

"Probably just passing through on his way to Salem or Portland. Blew out a tire or had to use the bathroom."

"You have no imagination."

Eve chattered on about how he was probably a famous Hollywood producer. She couldn't allow anyone a normal life; she always reached for the dramatic.

But she was right. There was something special about the stranger. He had an energy that popped and sparkled.

As if he knew he was being watched, he turned in our direction. Eve ducked but I held my position, staring back. His eyes were as grey and stormy as the Oregon coastline. He knew things...secrets and mysteries.

I felt jolted awake after a long sleep.

"We should bring him over." Eve's dark eyes flashed as she pushed a step-stool across the floor to gather oils and vials from the top shelf. Next, she collected an assortment of herbs from bins beneath the counter. "... Candles. I need purple candles."

Like a fly to a spider, I thought as I watched her. She was driven when she had a mission, not the same dreamy girl who stared out the window all day talking about the life she was missing out on while she ignored customers.

"We could just walk across the street and talk to him," I said, moving away from the window.

"Just because you're too good for magic, doesn't mean some of us don't respect the craft."

"I never said I was against magic."

"Just practicing it. We can't all be Wilders, you know?" Eve placed her stack onto the counter and arranged the objects into neat piles.

I felt my face redden. Wilder was a slang word, used to describe a witch who had no control over her magic. The light above us flickered.

Besides," Eve grinned, as if she had said nothing wrong. "This is far more fun. Now, where's the book?" She scanned the room for our mother's spell book.

I shrugged. If she wanted to lure a man here against his will that was her business, but I wasn't going to help.

"Here it is!" She held up a small, leather-bound journal in her hands. It was a rare book, Mother claimed, filled with spells and incantations that would have been lost to time were they not carefully preserved on these pages. As a result, only Mother's direct descendants could remove the book from her store without suffering a terrible curse.

What the curse was, nobody knew, but Miss Sasha's magick was formidable, and no one in Dark Root wanted to risk it.

Eve went to work creating a concoction of vanilla, rose petals and thyme, hardly glancing at the open book beside her. She had probably committed her man-luring spell to heart.

"Wouldn't it be exciting if we fell in love and he took me away from this horrible town? Now that Merry is gone, there's nothing to keep me here."

I felt a dagger in my heart at the mention of our older sister's name. Merry had left three years ago to marry some guy she barely knew and nothing had been the same since.

"You really think you're going to get out of here before me?" I asked.

"Someone's got to take care of Mom. Besides," Eve looked at the clock on the far wall then back to me, "I *have* to get out of here. I'm going to be a famous actress one day. A psychic told me."

I snorted, peeking out the window again. The curtains to Delilah's Deli were shut now, indicating that the cafe was closed. I glanced up and down the street, hoping to see a sign of him or his car, but the street was empty. "Even if your spell does work and you get him to wander over here, what makes you think he's going to fall in love with you?"

"The travel spell is only part of it," she said. "One sip of my special tea and he'll treat me like the goddess I am." Eve retreated into the back room, returning with a white porcelain cup and matching teapot. "You might not have dreams, Maggie, but I do. God forbid that three years from now when I'm your age, I'm still working as a sales girl in this dump." She dropped her apron on the floor and kicked it under the counter.

Without warning the door opened, startling us both.

The stranger entered, removing his grey felt hat. He looked around the shop, taking it in. I glanced at Eve, wondering how her travel spell could have worked so quickly.

She shrugged in response.

"Well, hello there," she said, regaining her composure "Our shop is closed but we were just making tea. You are welcome to join us." She slinked towards the man, offering him the teacup.

The stranger blinked uncertainly, declining the tea with a wave of his hand. He strode past my sister and stood before me.

"Actually," he said, staring at me with mystical eyes. "Maggie Maddock, I'm here for you."

ONE

SISTER GOLDENHAIR

Woodhaven Compound, Humboldt County, California
September, 2013

IF I WERE A REAL WITCH, the kind you read about in story books
with black cauldrons and pet frogs, I might have put a curse on Leah
for bursting through the door and interrupting us like she did. Not
a big curse––according to Michael I already have enough karmic
repercussions to atone for––just a little something to teach her to knock
before entering someone's bedroom.

This wasn't the first time I had wished ill on Leah.

Ever since she had come to Woodhaven Compound two months
earlier, I had spent many afternoons daydreaming about what I could do
to her: bucked teeth, crossed eyes, thunder thighs. Gout. My fantasies had
gotten me through those long days when she was running after Michael,
listening to his every word, praising him, pretending to *get* what he was
teaching. She wasn't smart enough to *get* anything but Michael ate it up.
Men were so gullible.

Not that any of this mattered.

I wasn't a witch––not anymore. I had turned in my hat and broom
seven years ago when I had followed Michael out of Dark Root, Oregon,
and into Woodhaven. Here, witchery wasn't allowed. The only good

7

magic, Michael claimed, came from God, and unless God had a curse clause I didn't know about, I was out of luck.

On this particular morning I heard Leah trounce down the corridor outside our bedroom. Clitter-clat. Clitter-clat. Her sandals, one size too big, slapped on the wooden floors as she raced through the hallway.

The urgency of her steps didn't worry me. Leah never walked anywhere; she scurried. I ignored her, thinking she would move on to one of the other bedrooms in the large house. After all, Michael and I were the leaders here at Woodhaven and she was just a new recruit. She wouldn't dare intrude upon us in the sanctuary of our private room; that is, if she knew what was good for her.

Michael was sleeping, oblivious to her footsteps.

Perched on elbows, I hovered naked above his body, watching the rise and fall of his chest. I needed him. Badly. It had been three weeks since our last physical encounter and I was starting to feel the hole that comes from a relationship without sex grow into a deep, widening chasm. He had been so preoccupied lately, focused on the issues of Woodhaven, that physical intimacy had taken a backseat to more pressing matters. But even as his desires lessened with his worries, mine had grown exponentially. I wasn't sure if it was PMS or the Lifetime movies I had been watching on the sly, but something had revved up my estrogen level to DEFCON 1.

Wake Up!

I willed my thoughts into his brain, boring my eyes so deeply into his skull that I was sure I had developed an aneurysm.

Wake up! I thought again, louder this time, more commanding. I watched for the flickering of his eyes, the change in his breath. I raised a hopeful eyebrow.

He snored in response.

I sighed, slumping down upon his chest. Mind control wasn't one of my gifts.

But I was a woman of many talents.

Grasping a hair on his chest——a lone, gray straggler lost in a thicket of black curls—–I pulled it taut until his eyelids fluttered open. *Bingo!*

"Good morning, sleepy boy," I purred, running my fingers down his arms until our hands met and fingers locked. "Did you have a good nap?"

Michael responded with a soft grunt and kissed the top of my head, wrapping his free arm around me. His guard was down when he first woke up, his mind less full of worries. I nuzzled closer, tilting my chin up and finding his mouth. His breath was warm and his lips were salty. He didn't resist.

And that's when Leah tumbled into the room.

"Maggie, it's for you," she said, thrusting a cell phone in my direction as she turned her head away.

After eight weeks at Woodhaven, she still wasn't used to nudity. This was not unusual. It took most women three months to lose their clothes.

It took most men three hours.

"You should learn to knock," I said, feeling Michael's desire wilt beneath me.

He gave me a consolatory pat on my back, a pat that said we would try again later, but there would be no later. His time would be sucked up in workshops, politics, and council meetings. Being the leader of a great new religion required all of his time, as he often reminded me.

I blinked, squinting against the soft pink light that shone through the bare window.

Though I had not had a personal call in a very long time, my first thought was not 'who would be calling?' but rather, 'what time is it?'

The tracking of time was frowned upon in Woodhaven, and there was neither clock nor calendar anywhere on the property. Even sundials were taboo. "Do not make time your master," Michael proclaimed as he gathered up watches, phones and day planners at each initiation ceremony. "The Enlightened Soul lives only in the now." Rituals like meditating, bathing and eating were done in accordance with hunger pangs, body odors and a crude version of follow-the-leader.

Luckily we had the seasons to guide us in our planting schedules, though here in Northern California, the seasons could at times be non-existent.

"Maggie," Leah fidgeted, just inches inside the doorway. "It sounds important."

She shuffled from one foot to the next, dancing like she had to go to the bathroom.

I took my time rising, stretching my arms overhead and dropping the white sheet that had covered me. Michael snatched it up and tucked it around his waist. He believed in weaning newcomers slowly. My approach was different. Leah didn't need to be *weaned*. She needed shock therapy. Though my red hair fell nearly to my waist, long enough to provide some cover, I flung it back and marched, proud as Godiva herself, to take the call.

Leah tossed me the phone and fumbled out the door.

"Hello?" I said, looking for the hole where you were supposed to talk.

I had used the phone only once in the last seven years and that had required considerable assistance from our one-man tech department, Jason.

"Hello?" I said louder, turning the phone upside down. "This is Maggie."

There was silence at the other end and I wondered if I had accidentally shut it off. I pulled it back to inspect it.

"Maggie! Oh, Maggie. Thank God, I found you."

"Merry?"

I don't think I spoke the word out loud.

I looked to Michael for confirmation but he stared blank-faced back at me. I hadn't talked to my sister Merry since she had left Dark Root to marry Frank, almost a decade earlier. I had let go of the idea of ever hearing from her again.

And here she was calling me. It was almost like hearing from a ghost.

"Merry," I said, this time out loud. "Is everything okay?"

As much as I wanted to believe that she had found and called me just to talk, I knew better.

Michael sat upright, mouthing the word *speaker-phone* to me.

Even if I knew how to operate the speaker-phone, I wasn't about to turn it on. I yanked the sheet from him and covered my body, certain Merry could see me across the miles.

Michael pointed to the phone again indicating that he wanted to hear our conversation.

I shook my head and he fell backwards onto the mattress, covering his face with his arms. I heard Merry gasp on the other end, trying to catch her breath. I licked my lips and said very slowly, "I'm listening, Merry. Please tell me what's going on."

"Maggie, you need to come home, right away. It's Mama. We need you."

"I don't want to go home," I said, racing our white van towards Brunsville, twenty-eight miles north of the Woodhaven property line and the closest thing to a town we had.

Michael sat unbuckled beside me, his window rolled down as the wind blew through his thinning hair. His right foot hit an imaginary brake with each car I passed or curve in the road. He hated my driving, but not enough to take the wheel. In the seven or so years I had known him I had never seen him drive anywhere.

He claimed he could, but I had my doubts.

"It can't be that bad," Michael said, fiddling with the radio dial as he tried to locate the classic rock station.

I cringed. Having been raised in a house where every song was circa 1970-something I'd had quite enough of that music. Songs from bands like Fleetwood Mac and The Eagles were "the only good songs," according to my mother. Conversely, Michael had grown up in a quiet home where anything other than Bach and Beethoven was considered an assault on the ears.

Lucky for me all he found was static and turned the radio off.

"As I recall," he continued undeterred. "Dark Root was quite charming."

We passed small trees in all stages of color transformation. Yellow, orange, red, and brown leaves clung uncertainly to thick branches. I turned sharply off the main road and we fell into a forest––a shortcut of mine. The trees were larger here, mighty redwoods with upturned boughs, reaching for the last rays of sunshine before succumbing to another soggy winter. We opened into a clearing, jouncing along a gravel path until we merged again with the main road. The semi-darkness that had swallowed us in the woods was replaced by the white light of morning.

I pushed a pair of cheap sunglasses onto my face, not slowing my speed.

"Don't ignore me, Maggie," Michael said. "I hate it when you ignore me."

I gave him a sideways glance and tightened my hands on the wheel.

Michael had been in Dark Root an entire twelve hours––long enough to use the public restroom, eat a sandwich, and charm me into coming with him. In all the time we had known each other since then, he had never once asked about my family or the town where I had spent the first twenty years of my life.

"Is something burning?" Michael sniffed at the air through the open window.

I inhaled and nodded, uncertain if it were coming from the tires or the engine. Either way, I was not stopping to find out. I rolled up the windows with the button on my door, one of the few gadgets that actually worked in this rolling pressure cooker.

Michael fanned himself but didn't say anything. Unless he wanted to change a tire he knew better than to complain about the heat.

Finally, our exit came into view and I swerved onto it, kicking up dust and rocks around us.

"You could go for just a few days," Michael continued as I skidded into a parking space at the grocery store. "...Go help your family and come back."

I stormed out, trying to slam my door shut, but it wouldn't catch the latch. I wrestled with it until it clamped shut and then stomped inside. Michael followed, calling for me to wait.

"...Are you trying to get rid of me?" I said.

I turned to him once I was safely inside Grocery World. Cool air blasted over my body, peeling the damp hair away from my face. The foliage might be declaring that it was fall, but the temperature outside indicated otherwise.

I stood for a moment, wondering once again why we weren't allowed to have air conditioning at Woodhaven. Open windows and ceiling fans were our only reprieves from the heat.

Thank God we lived in California. Michael had originally wanted to settle in the Southwest, where he was certain 'The Greys' would make contact with us prior to the end times coming. It took me awhile to convince him that if there really was an intelligent alien race sent to warn us of an impending doomsday, they could just as easily find us in Northern California as they could in New Mexico.

"Why would you think I'm trying to get rid of you?" Michael asked, picking up a sales flier from the bin by the door. He looked it over, folded it, and returned it to its bin. "I'm trying to be supportive."

"Well, I don't get it," I said. "You have a lot of good qualities, but being *supportive* of me being around anyone other than fellow members isn't one of them. You never let me go anywhere without an escort. I have to take a body guard to go to Wal-Mart. And now you want me to go home? It's just not adding up."

"First of all, Jason isn't a bodyguard," Michael said. "...He's your friend, and there are quite a few young ladies who would gladly trade places with you for that privilege. Secondly, who would ever want to get rid of you? You're far too agreeable." Michael smiled, his dimples poking through his sculpted cheeks. Dark stubble covered his jaw line and the two top buttons on his denim shirt were left undone.

He looked rugged and uncivilized. And unfairly sexy.

I turned my head before I fell prey to his charms.

I grabbed a shopping cart for myself and shoved one in his direction. He caught it and immediately wiped the handle off with one of the complimentary moist wipes from a nearby dispenser. He grabbed another to clean his hands, and then tossed both into a trash bin.

I left mine dirty just to irritate him.

We scanned the store together, our eyes moving from the produce aisle on the left to the bakery on the right.

A sample table filled with cookies was set up straight ahead of us and I bolted for it. I could feel Michael's eyes on me as I devoured two cookies and pocketed a third. Michael didn't approve of us indulging in things like sex, alcohol, or sugar in public. He said it gave people the wrong idea about our tribe.

I argued that it showed people we knew how to have fun.

As I wiped the crumbs from my hands, I watched Michael mentally plan our route.

He was systematic in his shopping, preferring to hit each aisle in numerical order to ensure that nothing was forgotten. He even wrote the grocery list in the order the food appeared. Though his methods bored me, I'd usually go along with it.

But not today, not after his *agreeable* comment earlier.

I aimed my cart towards the center aisle and pushed forward, almost knocking over a pyramid of creamed corn on the end cap. Michael followed, attempting to keep pace as he threw sacks of pinto beans, rice, potatoes, and flour into his cart.

If he wanted to be difficult, so could I.

"We should really get a Costco membership," he muttered, checking the price on a gallon of soy milk. He handed me several cartons of free-range eggs, twice as expensive as the normal eggs, and I wondered if anyone would notice if I swapped them out.

At last, every item was crossed from his list, and our carts were so full I could hardly push mine. Feeding an entire community was difficult, especially our group, with their diverse food preferences. Many were vegetarian, some were vegan, and a scant few were normal eaters like me. We grew some of our own food, but without the help of a calendar or an almanac it was tough. I thought about bringing this up for perhaps the hundredth time, but held my tongue.

I had another agenda.

"My turn," I said, smiling sweetly as I maneuvered my cart towards the one aisle that never found a place on Michael's list.

Aisle 13––the snack food section.

I stood at the edge of it, like a queen surveying her lands.

An amazing array of boxes, bags, and cans in orange and pink packaging glimmered before me. I checked my cart, wondering how many Keebler Elves I could shove inside before it exploded. I managed to find room for two boxes of Zingers, five bags of Potato Chips, and a case of Diet Coke. A lone package of double-stuffed Oreos balanced atop my hoard.

Satisfied, I gave Michael a thumb's up.

He bristled but said nothing.

He had learned years ago that low blood sugar and a Welsh temper weren't a good mix.

I drummed my fingers across the handle of my cart, trying to figure out how I could smuggle my stash into the house. Michael refused to participate in my addiction, but Jason could probably be bribed with an Oreo or two.

"They call it junk food for a reason," Michael said, pushing his hand through his hair, then checking his palm to see if any strands had come loose. He grimaced at the two dark hairs that no longer lived on his head. He flicked them from his hand, glancing briefly at a Rogaine display we just happened to pass.

"You know you want one," I said, tapping the box of Zingers. "Delicious and nutritious!"

When he didn't respond I removed one of the cakes, opened the wrapper, and shoved the entire thing into my mouth.

"...I really don't see how eating these will delay my transcendence," I added. "If anything, it makes me feel closer to God."

Michael gave me his disgusted look, and I knew I had crossed a line. When it came to GOD Michael had no sense of humor.

"I'm sorry," I said. "I just miss being able to eat a donut without feeling like I were committing a mortal sin."

"It's okay," Michael said, his voice softening. "I miss things, too."

This was news to me. Michael never seemed to want for anything. If he indulged in a Pringle it was breaking news.

"Really? Like what?"

"Sugared cereal. I used to eat Cocoa Puffs by the box when I was a kid. Now I can't remember what it tastes like. Kind of sad, I think."

I normally had a comment for everything, but this caught me off guard. This felt like an intimate moment, something I wasn't used to, since coming to live with Michael. In Woodhaven there were no secrets. Everything, including thoughts, was community property.

I wanted to reach out and take his hand, but I stopped myself; it would be like pointing out his weakness. I changed the subject, instead.

"I don't like the new girl," I said. "She bugs me." My hand reached for the Zingers box again.

"Leah? I thought you guys would hit it off, since you both hail from Oregon." He stretched out the last syllable of the word, making it sound like Or-eh-gone.

"Another good reason to stay out of Or-eh-*gun*," I corrected him, pushing my cart in the direction of the checkout stand. "There are a lot of Leah-types there."

"I'm not sure what a *Leah-type* is, but she seems okay. I think she may even be gifted."

I stopped the cart. "She's not gifted! She's boring! She doesn't do anything except run around kissing your butt."

"Well, I can't count on you to do that," Michael said, spreading one of his hands and grinning. He stared at me, leaning against his shopping cart, smiling until I relaxed.

The pendulum had swung, and though I was angry with him for wanting me to go home to Dark Root, and for not agreeing with me about Leah, I loved him, and I smiled back.

In the last few months, as more and more members left Woodhaven, Michael's spirit, once dynamic and commanding, had begun to fade. He was quieter now, less inclined to spar with me when we disagreed. His interest in the things he loved––reading, walking, praying––had waned. He spent his free time alone, worrying endlessly about 'the end.' Not the real end he had once prophesied––that beautiful end that would transform all of us into dazzling rays of light before a grand ascension into the heavens––but the end of something else.

This was the first real grin I had seen from him in a long time. I fumbled for something to say but he rescued me.

"Don't worry, darling," he said. "Leah might be gifted, but you are special. You are the most special girl I have ever met."

"For the first time in a long time," I said, still smiling. "We agree on something."

Michael removed a wad of money from his wallet and began counting it out by twenties.

"But I need you at one-hundred percent," he said. "Lately, you seem...disengaged. I think its hurting morale. Woodhaven might be mine in name, but you are the backbone. I need you to get back to the basics. Meditate more. Stop filling your body with crap." He pointed his chin towards my Zingers. "...Make friends with the new recruits."

"You know I don't do well with strangers."

"They are only strangers until you get to know them," he said. "Then they become...what's that magic word again?" He slanted his lips in a sideways smile, toying with me like he was a birthday magician about to pull a quarter from my ear.

"I will never be *friends* with Leah."

"She's not the only new member. The younger ones need to meet you. Show them how special you are. Let them see the power of God. You can do that, Maggie. My little Maggie Magic, remember?"

"I can't turn things on and off at will."

I stopped the cart, my face warming. He had no idea what was involved in it, what currents I needed to pull from. If I didn't know, he sure as hell didn't.

"You used to be able to."

"It comes and goes. I can't control it."

"Clearing your mind and centering would help." Michael reached into his front shirt pocket and pulled out a shiny glass object on a long brown cord. He took my right hand and placed the object in my palm. "Take this. It will help."

I furrowed my brow. "Your crystal? Why?"

"You need the help. Please."

I ran my fingers over the crystal, feeling its long smooth edges that came to an abrupt point. "I don't need any help, Michael. I can still pull it out when it matters."

Michael sighed, searching for the right words. "Flickering light bulbs and setting off fire alarms? Cheap parlor tricks, Mags. We need more than that. You are capable of more than that. You are capable of *great* things."

I felt the heat well up inside of me. "I'm trying, Michael!"

I was about to lob the crystal back at him when the music on the loudspeaker was suddenly replaced by loud, crackling static.

Michael's face lit up. "Maggie Magic. See? The crystal is helping already. That's the most I've seen from you in a long time."

I stared at the crystal, letting its energy warm my hands.

My mother was a witch——a coven leader, at that. I had been raised to believe in magic. I also believed in coincidences, however. Static over the radio was not an indication that there were other forces at work. But Michael would believe what he wanted to believe, and if it made him happy I could go along with it. For now.

I put the cord around my neck and tucked the crystal under my T-shirt, feeling it dangle between the gap of my small breasts. I walked, in a daze, to the checkout line with Michael tailing closely behind.

"Maybe if you went home you'd get some perspective on things," Michael said as the cashier scanned our groceries.

I glanced at a woman's magazine and a smiling jack-o-lantern stared back at me. Halloween would be here shortly. My favorite holiday and one of the few things I missed most about the outside world. My hometown's tourist season revolved around Halloween and we spent the entire year preparing for October.

I flipped through the pages of the magazine as Michael slid our groceries onto the conveyor belt. I could buy it and he probably wouldn't say a word, but when he stuffed the cash back into his wallet and wrote a check instead, I changed my mind.

"I don't need perspective," I said, pushing my cart towards the van.

Michael didn't hear me.

He was talking to the bag girl about the glories of God and the joys of communal life. "The only man you'll be working for at Woodhaven is the big one," he told her.

I unloaded the groceries while he finished his pitch.

"Any luck?" I asked, as we climbed inside. "Will she be joining our loving cult?"

"Maggie, you know I hate that word. It makes us sound weird."

"I know, but it's funny."

"To answer your question, no, she will not be joining us." He sighed, buckling up. "It's hard these days, unless you have a website."

I laughed and started up the engine.

"Let me think about it, Michael," I said. "I know you'd like to think me leaving Dark Root was entirely because of you, but there were other reasons." I stared out the window, watching as mothers and their children filed inside Grocery World.

My life at Woodhaven wasn't ideal, but I was free here.

As free as I could be, anyway.

"I wished I had been given another chance to see my family," he said. His fingers clawed at his knee as he struggled to keep his voice steady.

"Yeah," was all I could say.

"We need you, Mags. Go see your family and come back stronger and recharged. If you can't get it together, Woodhaven isn't going to last much longer."

I thought about his words as I drove us home.

TWO

STAIRWAY TO HEAVEN

MY MOTHER HAS A DISDAIN FOR WARLOCKS.

Though she admits they have *some* power, she argues that a warlock's capabilities will never match the creative, life-giving magic of his female counterpart. In order for a warlock to balance this upset in the spiritual scales, he must siphon energy from a woman, typically through sex.

A nice girl will do, for a while, but if her life force is weak she may crumble under the frequency of his need.

Bad girls provide him with a stronger manna but it can be a tainted energy, which may eventually destroy them both.

A dark warlock will continue down this path, seizing small bites of power through sexual vampirism, yet never knowing real power of his own. An enlightened warlock, however, will eventually seek out a more powerful woman––a witch.

It is through her that he will learn to submit, to both take *and* give, and consequently come into the full powers of his birthright.

Though the word *warlock* was banished from my vernacular soon after Michael recruited me––*there are no witches and warlocks Maggie, just energies, male and female, yin and yang*––old lessons die hard, and the message remains the same.

Men need women to accomplish great things.

And so I waited––perched restlessly in the window seat of my bedroom––for Michael to come for me.

Time moved miserably slow.

I fiddled my thumbs and tapped my bare feet against the bamboo floor.

Where was he?

It was our Fall Revival, and Michael always spent the hour before each session with me, making love and going over his speech as he got dressed.

Then we'd make our way out to the assembly room––a converted grange hall––across the property. Arms intertwined, we'd enter the auditorium, finding our seats at the front of the room, the Prophet and Prophetess of Woodhaven. In the years since we had founded Woodhaven, the routine had always been the same; yet tonight, I sat alone, watching the sun go down and the shadows in my room grown longer.

I considered looking for him, but the thought of Leah's smug, rodent face asking me if everything was 'okay' as I frantically searched for my boyfriend kept me in my room.

I slid from my window seat onto the floor, pushing my back against the wall and wrapping my arms around my knees. I had never been good at meditation––sitting still for long periods of time without having interesting thoughts was difficult––but Michael claimed it led to inner peace.

I tried to clear my mind, but my imagination was especially active this evening, so I decided to follow it along for the ride instead. I was engrossed in a fantasy about Leah and some alien probes, when a knock on the door brought me back.

"Mags? Can I come in? I'm supposed to make copies of your report for the Council Meeting," Jason said, cautiously opening the door. When he saw me *meditating*, his face broke into a wide smile. "I know that look, Mags. You're thinking of Leah and the evil aliens again, aren't you?"

I loved Jason.

We had met the day Michael found me in Dark Root, the first two disciples of Michael's *New World Religion*. Over the last seven years, we had developed a special friendship, listening to each other's ideas and making fun of the strange new people Michael was forced to recruit to keep Woodhaven going. Jason got me, and didn't chastise me the way Michael did when my mind went dark.

I smiled innocently at his Leah statement as I rummaged through a stack of notebook paper on my desk.

"Here it is," I said, handing him the report. "Michael's not going to like it."

Jason looked over my report and nodded his head thoughtfully. "Well, he wanted the truth." He gave me a quick wink and turned to go. "It's starting to get dark, so be careful on the way to the meeting. I can come grab you, if you want?"

"I'll be okay. You haven't seen Michael, have you?" I steadied my face, hoping Jason wouldn't see my anxiousness.

Jason licked his lips. "No, sorry Mags."

I could feel the pity in his voice.

I gritted my teeth and pretended I was okay. "I was just wondering what he thought I should wear? I'm torn between two different dresses tonight."

Jason was a gentleman and nodded as he left my room, but he knew that I was lying.

He also knew that I only had one good dress.

I played with a strand of my hair, looming the red curl through my fingers as I tried to puzzle things out.

Maybe Michael had already peeked at my report and wasn't happy with me. If so, this wasn't fair. Michael had charged me with the task of determining why we were losing so many members, and gaining even fewer. It took me several weeks but I did my best, collecting data from interviews, surveys, and CNN. We were supposed to go over it together before the meeting, and then review it with the other Council Members after the Fall Revival.

But if Michael had already seen it, maybe he wanted some time alone to digest it. He was never one to show real emotion in front of anyone, even me.

Suddenly, I felt bad for what I had written. Maybe I should have softened it a bit. I went to my desk and pulled out a piece of crumpled paper. It wasn't the official report, just the notes I had made while conducting my research.

1. *Too Many Men.* The male to female ratio at Woodhaven is approximately 3 to 1. Women are harder to recruit. It's more difficult for them to give up friends, family, and community to start a new life with a group of strangers than it is for men. Add to that the bad press we were inadvertently getting from Nancy Grace——a few young women come up missing in the Caribbean, and the world thinks everyone is in the trafficking business. Without females, the guys at Woodhaven flee to pastures where the cows are more plentiful.

2. *Family Member Retrieval (FTR).* We have little contact with the outside world. This includes letters, phone calls, and visitations. After extended time without contact, loved ones can freak out. Some even come to 'break out' their family members. This is especially true after some suicide cult makes the news. When that happens we get bombarded by panicky loved ones convinced we are hacking off genitalia and dressing our members up as chickens to sacrifice to the Thunder Gods.

3. *Technological Impotence.* We don't allow our members to use computers, cell phones, or even calculators. Not to mention watches or clocks. Most people are not willing to give up their gadgets just to get closer to God.

4. *We just don't care anymore.* A long time ago we had a

vision: The old world would die, and a new one would be reborn. We were the chosen people, who would help others attain enlightenment after the cataclysm hit. But Michael's dates have come and gone many times. We made excuses at first. Mixed up numbers. Misinterpreted prophecies. Leap Year. With each wrong Armageddon prediction, we lost a few members. And when the last date––the really big one, that Michael was so certain of he had even gone to the news to warn the rest of the world about it––left us still intact, we lost members in droves. We should have been happy that the world hadn't ended. Instead, we became depressed. Or in my case, apathetic. I reminded Michael that time wasn't relevant, but he didn't see it that way. All he saw was his failures.

Ouch.

I grimaced when I read number four, and tried to remember how I had phrased it in my official report. Perhaps I had been more diplomatic, but tact wasn't one of my strong suits. Oh, God! If Michael read this, of course he was going to avoid me.

I peeked out the window, hoping to catch a glimpse of Michael coming up the walkway.

There was no sign of him. Jason was right. Night was coming early.

I went to my closet and pushed aside the few clothes I owned, to reveal a shelving unit. It was my private world, probably the only place on the entire compound that no one else was privy to. Shoved in between my collection of Yankee Candles and Mr. Bubble, was my package of Oreos. The wrapper looked like it had been tinkered with and I counted cookies. There were four missing. My sugar-is-sin boyfriend had been dipping into my stash.

I ate three cookies and put the package back on the shelf. If Michael was going to be stealing from me, he had better not complain when I doubled up on my next trip.

I pushed my clothes back into place and shut the closet door.

The room had darkened and that meant that our meeting was about to begin. Michael always held revivals 'at dusk.'

I slid out of my beige, knee-length skirt and large, blue T-shirt and dropped them to the floor, toying with the idea of leaving them there for Michael to pick up. Michael couldn't stand for things to be out of place, and I enjoyed riling him up.

Then I remembered the last time I had left my clothes on the ground. Michael didn't even scold me; he just gave me a disappointed look as he scooped them up and dropped them into the laundry basket. It was fun turning David Banner into The Hulk, but not so entertaining when he morphed into Eyore the Sad Donkey instead.

I kicked my clothes towards the hamper in the bathroom, catching site of my naked reflection in the mirror.

It had been a long time since I had really looked in a mirror.

Vanity was another in a long list of sins we were supposed to check at the door. But unlike junk food, giving up a mirror hadn't been hard for me. I had never been one of those women who found themselves beautiful, had never been in love with her own reflection. My skin was pale, my hair red and unruly, and my cheeks were marred by a dusting of beige-brown freckles that could not be scrubbed away.

But seeing myself in the mirror now, under the unforgiving honesty of our new fluorescent light bulbs, I was surprised to see that the person staring back at me was no longer 'interesting looking' but plain. My face was fleshy, and my high cheekbones, once my best feature, had disappeared. There were dark circles beneath my eyes and my skin looked more like chalk than the butter cream Aunt Dora proclaimed it to be when I was a kid.

Worst of all, my belly, which had always been flat, protruded out an inch beyond my hips. Age and junk food were catching up to me, and I wanted to hide it all, before anyone else saw. I sucked in my gut as I slid my white dress over my head. It hugged my waist and hips a little too tightly, straining the material.

26

I would start dieting tomorrow, I promised myself.

And do more yoga. Maybe even take walks around the garden.

Both my mother and my Aunt Dora were large women, and I hoped it wasn't genetic.

I pushed the thoughts out of my head as I worked my hair into a long braid. Braving one final peek into the mirror, I sighed. In my long white dress I looked like The Michelin Man or a well-fed ghost.

There were voices outside, ambling towards the meeting hall. I had spent the last several weeks creating and posting fliers in and around Brunsville and the surrounding towns. It looked like our advertising was paying off.

But still, no sign of Michael.

Finally, I could wait no more.

I left my room and made my way outside, picking my way across the paved road that led to the old grange hall. I passed the smaller buildings that lined the road, recently constructed shacks where some of our married couples lived. The lights in their windows were turned off, evidence that they were already at the revival. When I was within a few feet of the grange hall, I heard Michael's unmistakable voice coming from inside.

I stopped in the doorway, collecting myself.

Something had felt wrong all night, and now I knew why. Michael was sitting in his appointed chair at the center of the table. But lounging next to him—in my spot!—was Leah. They didn't notice me and I watched as she laughed, touching his arm whenever he spoke. Her hair was pinned back, accentuating her rodent-esque features, and she wore a short, toga-style dress that made my own look Amish.

"Sister Maggie," Michael said, rising as I stomped towards the Council table. He smiled easily, as if everything were normal. "Ready to make some magic?"

"What is she doing here?" I demanded, turning my gaze on Leah. "She's not a Council member. And that's my seat."

Michael wiped invisible crumbs off the table with the tips of his fingers.

"She is going to be my assistant, Maggie. She's taking notes and giving us feedback on how things go tonight. Your report was quite... disconcerting...to say the least. She thought we might need an outside perspective on things."

"The Council met without me?" I stared at him, mouth open.

One of the fluorescent lights flickered overhead and everyone around our table shifted uneasily.

"You can't have a Council meeting without me!" I said. "I'm a Senior Council member and it was my report! I waited for you in *our* bedroom."

"I apologize," Michael said. "I must have misunderstood. I thought you were just delivering the bad news. If I had known that you wanted to be more involved, we would have waited. We can talk it over after, okay?"

His voice was calm. Pragmatic.

I turned my eyes on Leah. Outside perspective, my ass. I had been raised in a family of women. I knew what she was doing, even if Michael didn't. I stepped forward, ready to pounce. She looked down like a dog that had been caught peeing on a rug.

"She can't have my seat!" I hissed.

Leah scrambled out of the way and I took my spot.

"...This is my chair, not hers," I repeated.

Michael motioned to a fold-up chair at the end of the table and Leah took it.

She pulled a pen and a notebook out of her bag and gripped them in her nervous little hands. It took every ounce of dignity I could muster to keep myself from yanking the notebook away from her and using it as a weasel swatter.

"Save that energy for the meeting, babe." Michael slid back into his seat and patted my hand, which I yanked away.

At this moment, I wasn't his *babe*. At this particular moment I was Maggie Maddock, the *only* woman on the Council of Five, and second only to the bastard leader of Woodhaven. I wasn't about to let him

28

pretend to control me, so that his cronies would know I was 'in check.' My teeth chattered, though I wasn't cold.

Jason appeared, taking his seat next to me, offering me a sympathetic look.

The hall filled with members who positioned themselves strategically around the room and strangers who shuffled in, taking up the remaining seats. I counted twenty newcomers and willed a serene look onto my face. It wasn't easy. I had a lot to say to Michael and Leah, but we had all worked too hard for this night for me to lose it now.

"Good haul," Jason whispered, and I nodded.

If we recruited even one person, this event was a success.

I leaned back, lacing my fingers behind my head. Michael gave me his 'please-don't-do-that-look,' which I ignored. It was my marketing campaign that had brought them all in. I deserved to be smug.

Someone coughed, our cue that the revival was about to begin.

The overhead lights dimmed, replaced by a solitary yellow spotlight that landed on Brother Robert, a large, doughy man at the rear of the room. He wore a grey suit that was too tight in the chest and too short in the legs. He was sweating already, and the spotlight amplified the liquid beads that were forming across his forehead. He stood quietly, waiting until every eye was upon him, before raising his stubby fingers to the sky. Tiny sparks shot from his fingertips that no one else seemed to see.

"Are you ready?" he asked the crowd, hands still raised as he squinted against the spotlight. "Are you ready to change your lives?"

At first, his voice was so low that the audience leaned forward, straining to hear him.

This was rehearsed, a script he never strayed from.

Brother Robert repeated his question, "Are you ready to change your lives?" louder this time. Several people, mostly Woodhaven members, nodded. The remainder sat quietly, unsure of what to do.

Brother Robert was undeterred by the silence.

He took one lumbering step forward, and then another, the spotlight never leaving him as he made his way towards our table at the front of the room.

"Are you ready..." He stopped halfway through his march, scanning the crowd. "...To witness a miracle?"

There were some enthusiastic affirmations from the crowd, as well as a few snickers.

Along with the curious and the 'I-want-to-believe'-ers, there were always those who came just to mock us. These were the people who got my ire up. Even if I thought the stuff was crazy at times, I didn't like anyone else making fun of us.

Michael insisted I keep my composure, and use the anger for my part in the presentation later. Sometimes I wondered if he planted them there.

Brother Robert ignored the chuckles and resumed his walk.

The rumble of his footsteps, made possible by his passion and considerable size, grew with each stride. He pointed fingers at various faces, accusing them of sinning without saying a word. They shuffled uncomfortably in their seats, but no one made a move to leave. When he was within a few feet of our table, he quickly swerved back towards the crowd, his face arranging itself into an expression of excitement.

"We are told that we are all entitled to the *pursuit* of happiness, a job we take seriously. Am I right?" Several people nodded and laughed. "We work 40, 50, 60 hours a week to make the money to buy this *happiness*. We spend our paychecks on restaurants, new clothes, vacations. We tell ourselves we deserve these things. And when that doesn't work, when we still aren't happy after spending all our money on what we are *supposed* to want, we spend our money on things to fix us, like prescription pills and therapy. And yet, happiness still eludes us..."

He paused dramatically.

"...No matter how many hours we work or things we buy," he continued. "Happiness keeps slipping through our fingers. Why? Because, despite everything you've been spoon-fed since childhood, working and spending isn't what makes a person happy. It's a trick. A diversion *away* from happiness. Real happiness comes through faith.

Faith in yourself. Faith in your neighbor. Faith in a higher power..."

"Amen!" someone hollered.

"You came here to change your lives because you knew that there was something fundamentally missing from it...a huge void in the soul. So let's start. Stand up now. Get on your feet." Brother Robert gestured for everyone to rise. "Stand up if you're ready to leave behind the tribulations of this earthly world. Stand up if you are ready to get off the treadmill of work and spending. Stand up if you're ready to begin anew!"

Even though I wasn't on 'the treadmill,' I had to resist the urge to stand up.

Brother Robert had a way about him; under the right circumstances, he could move mountains. Michael had found him preaching in a small, non-denominational church in Alabama, and though it cost us a small fortune to feed him, Michael had never regretted his decision. Robert's power was short-lived, however, as he tired quickly, and could never run a full service.

But he was one hell of an opening act.

One by one, the audience took to their feet as Brother Robert continued speaking——clapping, stomping, cheering, and nodding. Even those who had been reluctant in the beginning joined in, caught in the fervor of Brother Robert's charisma. An energy ran through the room, touching one person and ricocheting onto the next.

I wanted to squeeze Michael's leg, to show him that Woodhaven was going to be okay, but I was still mad at him. I tightened my hand into a fist to prevent it from slipping onto his thigh.

Eventually, Brother Robert lowered his hands, gesturing for the crowd to take their seats.

Hesitantly, they obliged.

Robert leaned a heavy hand onto our table as sweat rolled down his face. He inhaled deeply, catching his breath.

"...But friends," he said, wiping his brow with the back of his free arm. "It's not me you've come to see. I am here only as a messenger. Without further hesitation, I bring to you the true Master of Miracles, a dear friend and the man who saved me...Brother Michael."

Robert backed away, sneaking into the sidelines, as the spotlight fell quietly on Michael.

The audience clapped uneasily, unwilling to trade Brother Robert for the unremarkable-looking man who didn't raise his eyes, but sat silently doodling with his index finger on the table. People shuffled in their seats and asked each other if there was some mistake, but Michael appeared unaware.

At last the crowd grew quiet. Only the scritch-scritch of Michael's fingertips on the plastic table could be heard.

My knees began to shake and my fingers tingled. Michael was gathering energy; I could feel him pulling it from the crowd. Nervous energy, collected, bundled, and stored for the main event. The hairs on his arms rose, indicating that he was almost full. It was trickling into my space but I pushed it away. Nervous energy made me sick.

The spotlight faded, replaced by the main overhead lights and we adjusted our eyes to accommodate the brightness.

Michael lingered in his chair, as if contemplating whether or not we were worthy of his message. At last he rose, gradually sliding his lean body into full view of the audience, his ascension a meticulous and calculated event. The table shook, hardly enough to cause a waver in a cup of coffee, but I noticed. My body trembled along with it.

It had been a long time since Michael had exhibited such power, and I was awed.

A weary smile crept across Michael's face as he surveyed the room.

Despite the theatrics, Michael's heart was in the right place: He really did want to save the world. I felt a wave of love for him; I couldn't help it. When he applied himself, Michael had this ability to make you feel love. For him, for yourself, for the entire fucking universe. I would follow him off a goddamned cliff, if he said that's what I needed to do right now.

I closed my eyes to block it, determined to stay angry. The crystal he had given me in the grocery store pulsed against my chest. I clenched it, breathing in and out, calming us both.

Everyone sat spellbound, feeding off of Michael's calm, loving energy.

Only Jason seemed to have his wits. He looked at me, checking in. I nodded back, sure that no one else would notice. Michael, in his element, was hard to ignore.

Then, with a practiced, ethereal voice, he spoke, looking and sounding just like a prophet.

"I was lost once," he began, his face and arms tanned and perfect against his white, button-down shirt. "But then..." His eyes moved to something far away and invisible. "...But then, I was given a message... from God. And God said..."

He stopped. Pausing for effect.

"God said, 'Michael, you cannot keep living like this. You cannot keep filling your body with junk and expecting it to function as it should. You cannot keep plugging into the technical 'necessities' of life, and not expect your body to suffer power shock. You cannot keep stock piling material items to make your life meaningful...'"

"Amen," said a woman. "Preach it!"

Michael continued speaking as he wandered through the aisles.

"You cannot keep having sex with women you feel nothing for. In fact..." Michael turned, his eyes resting on a stranger. "...You need to change *everything* about your life, if you hope to sit with me one day. Enlightenment comes only with sacrifice."

Michael straightened, lifting his chin, showing his full height.

"All of you *must* make changes. The day of reckoning is coming, and if you don't get right now, you are surely damned. God sent me to help with your transformations. I will show you what to do..."

For the next thirty minutes, Michael spoke about God, spiritual evolution and reincarnation.

My hands stopped shaking. His channeling was done.

My mind drifted back, lost in memories of how it used to be when I first met Michael. He was amazing then, so filled with passion and life.

His charisma was contagious. Seeing his performance tonight reminded me of those days.

A pinch on my right thigh brought me back.

Jason nudged me, his eyes darting from me to Michael. *Was I up already?* I licked the front of my teeth and stood, almost tripping over the legs of my chair in the process.

This part of the ceremony always made me nervous.

Making miracles wasn't easy, especially miracles on demand, and I was never sure what would happen. A light might flicker or even go out, an unexpected noise might startle the audience, or if I was really lucky, a chair might tip over. Once our little grange hall had been hit by lightning, but I was premenstrual that night.

You just never knew.

"I feel," I said, scratching my head and glancing around the room. "...A miracle coming!"

Normally, I would have cleared my mind and focused my energy into a specific location before it was my turn, but I had been so caught up in my memories of Michael, that I had forgotten to prepare. The only things I felt coming on now were a migraine and an anxiety attack.

I could sense Leah's eyes on me. She had heard about the 'Great Maggie Magic,' but had never seen me in action.

My palms grew sweaty and I wiped them onto my skirt. I straightened, pushing my shoulders back and tilting my chin upwards, hoping to portray a look of confidence.

"There," I said, pointing to a random spot in the room. "A miracle will happen there."

I waited, like everyone else, hoping against hope that whoever was in charge out there loved me enough to show itself, or at the very least send out a minion.

I bit my bottom lip. *Come on. Come on.*

Leah's eyes gleamed, like a rat looking out of her hole.

I swallowed, though I knew my mouth was dry. I knew that I was a poor excuse for a disciple and I promised to pay that penance later. For now, I needed a miracle. I squeezed my eyes shut and asked for help.

Please, please, please. God. Universe. Allah. Intelligent Alien Race. Please.

Nothing happened.

Though my eyes were closed, I could feel everyone watching me, including Michael. Just an hour ago I had been so angry I didn't want to talk to him, and now all I could think about was how I didn't want to disappoint him. Maybe I shouldn't have specified the exact location of the miracle. I wondered if I could redirect it to the tract lighting.

There was a shriek to my right.

I opened my eyes, turning to see Leah, her hands in the air. "He talked to me!"

I blinked, confused. Was this a new part of the show?

Leah placed one hand on her forehead and pointed upwards with the other. "God spoke to me! He wants you to know that there is still time for your salvation..."

My face burned.

This was an act. It had to be. God didn't speak to weasels.

I was about to say so, out loud, when a loud *Boom,* like a clap of thunder, emanated from the spot above Leah's head. All eyes looked up, startled. Even the Council Members seemed confused. There was excited talk from around the table, as a few of our elders and some of the visitors left the building to check the immediate surroundings, including a quick glance at the roof. They returned, shaking their heads.

Leah's thin lips formed into a taut smile. She fanned herself, and then flung her body into her chair, as if the whole thing was just too much for her.

"The voice of God," she said, lifting her head as Michael rushed to attend her.

"A testament to the faith of a true believer," Michael nodded approvingly.

Leah appeared to blush and look down at her lap. Michael praised God for making his presence known, and spoke at length on the powers of faith. Jason patted my leg but I shrugged him off. I didn't need his charity sympathy right now. I wanted to be alone.

We completed the service, everyone asking questions of Michael and Leah while I sat closed-mouthed and stewing. When it was over, Leah was surrounded by newfound admirers. Hoax or not, she was the star of tonight's show.

She said 'God' was going to help her lead others into the light.

No one noticed as I slipped out of my seat, along the back wall, and out the rear door. The walk to the main house was a dark, lonely one. I took a final glance back, watching silhouettes celebrate in the windows, as I slunk towards my bedroom.

THREE

HOTEL CALIFORNIA

WOODHAVEN WASN'T OUR FIRST HOME.

We had taken other stabs at residential permanency in places like Nevada, New Mexico, and Kansas, but none of these locations worked out. Nevada was too expensive, New Mexico was too hot, and Kansas was too Kansas.

But the Woodhaven Compound was just right. It sat nestled in the heart of Humboldt County where the California climate was mild and the citizens tolerant.

At first, no one understood my fascination with the house and the accompanying grange hall. We had seen the property several times as we journeyed along the lonely highway that connected Northern California with Southern Oregon, and I convinced Michael to use it as a squat. I took this opportunity to wander its endless halls and corridors while the rest of the group slept huddled in the living room.

It was a dilapidated, sad sack of a building, large and rectangular with rooms added on willy-nilly. The ceilings sagged and the carpet was soiled so badly that it was impossible to make out its original color. But I fell in love with it, boarded windows and all. Though it wasn't as beautiful as the Victorian houses I had grown up with in Dark Root, its vastness reminded me of home. And, though I would never admit this to Michael, since *the enlightened soul holds no attachments,* what I really longed for was a home.

By the time we discovered the house, with our travel-weary band of refugees, we had been on the road for two years, and porta-potties had long ago lost their charm. I set my mind to getting it. Michael resisted at first, thinking the desert might be better-suited for our tribe, but I wore him down, and once he was in, he was in.

It was easier, he said, to buy the house than to war with Maggie.

Michael rallied the troops and we became worker ants, pawning our possessions, taking on odd jobs and selling flowers to raise the cash needed to buy the property. It took us almost a year, but it was finally ours––the place that would give us stability *and* credibility.

The house was christened with champagne from Trader Joe's and I named it 'Woodhaven,' a tradition carried over from my time in Dark Root, where all homes were said to be alive and should thus be named. And though Michael doesn't believe in marriage, he presented me with a silver ring and carried me over the threshold to commemorate the event.

We all changed during that first year in our new home.

Before Woodhaven, we had been a group of philosophers who would rather talk about the end of the world than wash a dirty dish, but Woodhaven demanded our sweat. We worked together to hammer, nail, strip, and saw the place into something beautiful. Bonds were formed under the strains of physical labor, followed by late night, bullshitting sessions. Step by step, stone by stone, we moved from a mild wilderness into a mini-civilization.

Through Woodhaven, we were a family at last.

And now, after all this time and work, I was in danger of losing it all.

Back inside I drew a bath, hoping to drown Leah out of my mind, but lying in warm water, chin deep in bubbles, I could still hear the hullabaloo outside. It was dying now. Excited chatter began to be replaced by quiet conversations and closing doors as people found their way inside the main house.

All this commotion for one boom? You would have thought that she had turned water into wine the way everyone was carrying on. It was as if the compound were under a spell.

My stomach worked itself into a knot.

Everything was changing so quickly and suddenly. One moment I was queen of this castle, the next a stranger. I closed my eyes, sucking in deep breaths, but all I kept seeing were Leah's beady eyes and Michael looking at her the way he used to look at me.

I tightened my fists, squishing sudsy water through my fingers. *Clarity. Grant me clarity.* I breathed in again, slowly this time, allowing the fragrance of the Lavender-Vanilla candle to bypass all the jumble of my emotions, to that calming station in my brain.

At last, my mind began to clear and Leah's face melted like wax.

I noticed the limbs of my body growing heavy, submitting to the water. I was tired. God, I was tired. I allowed my head to roll to the side as I focused on the nothingness, a cool dark void where problems didn't exist. But before I could fully settle into that world, a nagging parade of thoughts clawed their way back into my consciousness.

I was losing Michael. I was losing Woodhaven. I was losing my family. I was losing my home.

My eyes flew open.

The image of Leah returned. Leah patting Michael's arm, laughing at his jokes. She meant to take him from me. But she wasn't going to win. Not on my watch.

I was going to fight.

I sat up, my chin set with a new resolve.

It was true, in the past year I hadn't been as involved in running this place as I should have been, and my miracles were sub-par, even on the good days. And, truth be told, after that last big prophecy when nothing happened, I had lost a little respect for Michael, and though I never said anything, he must have sensed it.

But I could change things. I could help him rebuild. Michael was still mine. Woodhaven was still ours. The terrible stomach knot unfurled itself.

"Mags!" Michael burst into the bathroom, his face flushed with excitement.

"Hi," I said almost shyly, wringing the water from my hair. I climbed out of the bath, sucking in my gut as I reached for a towel. I was still embarrassed about slinking out of the grange hall like that, but tomorrow was another day and I was going to make some changes. I was going to clean house. "I'm so glad you're here. I missed you."

I reached over to kiss him and he offered me his cheek.

"Sorry hon, you're wet."

I used the corner of the towel to dab the water from my face. "Good night, huh?" I said with a broad smile, attempting to mirror his excitement.

"The best!" He rubbed his hands together and I escorted him into our bedroom. He buzzed around the room, inspecting things as if seeing them for the first time. He stopped to pick up a photo of us taken by a sign that read, "Welcome to Wichita." He looked at it for a moment, then placed it back on the shelf before moving on to one of my women's magazines. He flipped quickly through the pages then dropped it onto the bed.

"Three new members! Three!" he said.

"Three? That's amazing! Congratulations." I secured the towel around my chest as Michael continued pacing. He zipped from one side of the room to the other, wringing his fingers in that way he did when he was making plans. He hadn't taken his shoes off, and he was leaving mud tracks on our floor. I half-expected him to grab a towel to clean it up, but he didn't seem to notice.

"...And two more that said they were really interested. I think they were telling the truth. They even gave me phone numbers. That's the best recruitment we've had in years."

"I'm glad. That was a lucky coincidence with Leah and that crash, huh? Good timing."

Michael stopped pacing, swiveling his head in my direction.

He said, "Mags, you know as well as I do that there are no coincidences." He laughed but his laughter was different. Mad, maniacal.

The laughter of a man who has just discovered he can bring dead things to life. "...I think we got a winner with Leah."

The stomach pain returned. "Michael, that was a coincidence or a set up or something. There's no way that *secretary* has any gifts at all."

He looked at me like I had just committed heresy, but someone had to talk sense into him.

I plopped myself onto the bed and repeated, "Well, she doesn't."

"Maggie..." His voice softened as he joined me on the bed. He brushed through my hair with his fingers, starting at the scalp and working his way to the ends. It was wet and tangled but he skillfully plowed through the knots.

"I'm sorry," I said. Warring with him wasn't going to help anything. When I was done with my transformation, he would remember why he fell in love with me and see Leah for the pitiful weasel that she really was. I cracked an apologetic smile. "...I'm just upset with myself. I haven't been performing lately. But I'm gonna try harder, I promise. Eat less junk food and meditate more and really focus. I'm so sorry, Michael. I promise to do better."

Michael put his head on my shoulder. He smelled like soap and sweat. His scent always drove me crazy and I wanted to bury myself in him.

"Maggie, remember the early days when we were first starting out? You were on fire then. You walked into a room and things just... happened. Remember that?" I was about to comment that we were both different then, but he continued before I could speak. "...Remember that time when that cop was trying to arrest us for vagrancy? Suddenly his sirens go off and his radio goes crazy. He looked like he had just seen a ghost! You did that. We got two new people, James and Beth, when they witnessed that..."

I brushed Michael's hair with my fingertips and smiled. "Well, it didn't hurt that you told the cop the Lord wasn't going to be happy if we got arrested for preaching the Good News."

Michael took my free hand in his lap and squeezed it, then released it, finger by finger, unwrapping himself from me. He stood and went to our dresser, removing the flannel nightgown that I had owned since I left Oregon. It was the warmest, most comfortable nightgown in the universe, one of the few things he allowed me to keep from my old life.

Without saying a word he helped me get dressed, pulling the nightgown over my arms and head like my mother did when I was a little girl. Then he kissed me on the lips and I felt that familiar wave of love rush through me. I leaned back, pulling him with me, wanting him to take me, to remove any distance left between us.

He smiled, but nodded a gentle no.

"You, my dear," he said. "...Need to go to sleep. I don't think you've been getting enough rest lately." He covered me up and tucked the sheet under my chin. "I love you, Mags," he said, stroking my cheek. "I love you so much, in fact, that I won't even wake you up for morning meditation tomorrow. Sleep in as long as you want, okay? Then we can spend some time together."

I nodded, my chin disappearing under the sheet, and yawned. The bath and Michael's hands had left me exhausted. I would talk to Michael tomorrow, when things were calmer. We would work everything out and life would be good again.

"What are you going to do now?" I asked, rolling onto my sleeping side and adjusting the pillow.

"Going to meet with our new recruits," he said, standing to leave. "I will introduce you in the morning. Get some rest, sleepy girl." He walked to the door and flipped the light when he heard my little yelp. "Oops, sorry Mags. You haven't gone to bed before me in so long I forgot. Closet light okay?"

I nodded yes and he cracked the closet door, reaching for the pull rope inside. A flicker of light fell into the room. Just enough light to keep the dark at bay. I smiled and closed my eyes as the door shut behind him.

FOUR

DREAMS

SISTER HOUSE, DARK ROOT, OREGON
NOVEMBER, 1989

"*GET OUT!*" MISS SASHA'S VOICE WAS FIERCE, *as her long finger pointed towards the door. The red-haired man shook his head, spittle forming at the corner of his lips.*

"You're a stubborn woman, Sasha. That will be your downfall." He took a hat from the table and hugged it to his chest, pausing. Then he looked at the other grownups in the room. "I'll be back." He said the words quietly, but Maggie, though only three, could tell that it was more than a promise, it was a vow.

He placed his hat on his head and walked out the door.

"Anyone else going with him?" Miss Sasha eyeballed her friends.

They shook their heads in response.

"What's happening?" Maggie whispered to her sisters, Ruth Anne and Merry. They were huddled together, spying on the scene from their secret spot under the staircase. Her two sisters shrugged, saying nothing.

"I'm going, too," spoke a skinny woman with long brown hair and glasses. "We don't have to stay here," she said, addressing the others. "I know a spot where we can ride it out, be safe. Dark Root isn't the only

stronghold in this part of the world."

Maggie heard commotion on the far side of the room. People talking, chairs scuffling, voices raised. She tried to step out for a better look but Ruth Anne pulled her in.

"No, Maggie, patience."

In the dark, Maggie could feel her sister Merry shiver beside her.

"Then it's settled." Miss Sasha's voice was easily recognizable. "You go, too. We don't need that here. But..." she said, her voice taking on a threatening tone. "...Mark my words. Your self-preservation will be your undoing."

"We'll see," said the brown-haired woman, gathering her coat and heading towards the door. "You squander your gifts, Sasha."

"Git outta here, den!" Aunt Dora said, shooing the woman towards the door.

A few others followed her out, and the house grew suddenly quiet.

WOODHAVEN COMPOUND, HUMBOLDT COUNTY, CALIFORNIA
SEPTEMBER, 2013

It was a dream. I've always dreamed in third person. Michael says it's my way of protecting myself *even though I'm safe and sound here at Woodhaven.* In the past, my dreams had all been run-of-the-mill, images of daily life mixed with the incredible––like walking a dog that suddenly turns into a banana––but nothing real, nothing noteworthy.

Since Merry called however, I've been treated to a nightly hodgepodge of clips from my childhood, more memory than dream, with every detail perfect and magnified for my viewing pleasure. But this was the first full-length clip I'd gotten, and I was surprised by how far back it went. I couldn't remember myself at the age of three, but my subconscious did, and it offered me up to me for further study.

Eyes still closed, I groaned, pulling the covers over my head, trying to shake the unease of being back in Dark Root. In my dreams, I was a powerless kid again, small, squashed and suffocated. Too young to understand, ask questions, or rebel. The world unfurled around me and I had no choice but to be part of that story. My mother's story.

I willed my mind to replace the dream with images of things I loved: Oreos, Jack-O-Lanterns, Michael. The last image didn't help. Leah quickly joined him in my neurotic brain, smiling at me while she stroked his arm. My blood pressure rose and I changed tactics, trying an exercise Uncle Joe taught me when I was six, Find Maggie's Happy Place.

I did a quick mental scan and settled on the garden of my childhood home, a great floral wilderness surrounded by weeds. I smelled the earth, dampened by rain, felt the point of a thousand blades of grass as they stabbed at my bare legs, and saw the tree that Aunt Dora had planted in a far corner, hardly more than a seedling now, but that would one day give us the apples we candied in the fall.

I willed myself into the picture, bringing my sisters with me: Ruth Anne, Merry, Eve.

We ran through the garden playing tag, Eve's eyes bright as she ran towards me, Merry pulling away just as I caught a tuft of her fine, white hair, Ruth Anne watching from the bench, an open book on her lap. We laughed as the rain came down on us, lifting our chins to the sky and taking in large gulps of water.

"Ye'll catch yer death o' cold!" Aunt Dora hollered from the doorway and we screamed with glee in response. A clap of thunder in the distance sent us scurrying home, through the iron gates and onto the sanctuary of the porch.

I smiled and the image dissolved into confetti.

It was ironic, I thought, that the one place I ran to for comfort was the one place I needed to escape from. Home.

I rolled onto my side, wanting to wake Michael and tell him about the dream, but there was a large gap on the mattress where his body should have been. He had not come to bed yet. I pulled the sheet down and opened my eyes. And that's when I noticed it.

The light in the closet had gone out.

I was completely and utterly in the dark.

I stared into the black void of the closet, trying to justify the reason. Probably just a burned out bulb, I thought.

But what if it wasn't?

I threw the sheet from my body and felt my way towards the closet, using my hands as a guide. My fingers found the edge of the half-opened door. I pulled it open and stepped inside, measuring the space with my feet. I reached for the pull cord, took a deep breath, and tugged at it. The room flooded with light.

I stood frozen, trying to figure out what had happened. Maybe Michael had turned it off while I was sleeping. But why? To save a few pennies on electricity? That didn't make sense. He knew about my phobia and though he liked to tease me, he wasn't cruel.

I stepped back into my bedroom and looked around.

Everything was in its place. There were no new mud tracks on the floor. If Michael had come in, he left no evidence.

I was about to climb back into bed, chalking it up as a strange 'coincidence' that I would ask Michael about later, when one of the closet shelves crashed to the floor.

In an instant I was racing to my bedroom door. I twisted the knob and fell into the hall, my heart beating so loudly, I could hear it in my ears. The corridor was dark but flickering lights beneath doorways assured me that others were still awake. I ran for the stairs that would take me down to the common room where Michael would be meeting with the new members.

"You okay?" Jason asked as I bolted past him in the hallway. He was in a white t-shirt and gym shorts, carrying a glass back to his bedroom.

I shook my head in some sort of yes/no combination and kept going.

The common room was dark and quiet. I flipped the light switch on to see if Michael had fallen asleep on one of the couches, but he was not there. I shot a glance at the kitchen behind me but the lights were off there as well. I felt an urgency to find Michael. I needed him to comfort me and tell me that it was all in my imagination and that everything was okay.

I raced across the living room, through the dining area, and into the library, Michael's personal retreat. It was empty.

Maybe he was back at the grange hall?

It was possible. Whatever had caused that 'boom' earlier may have been something breaking, something that needed his immediate attention. I didn't want to make the trek out there in the dark alone. I could ask Jason to escort me but I couldn't bring myself to let him see me like this. I bit my lip, wondering how I should proceed.

I was starting to feel silly as I wandered around the house in my nightgown, looking for my lost boyfriend, all because of a dislodged shelf and a dark room. I decided to return to my bedroom where I would turn on all of the lights, leave the door open, and wait for him in private. It was bad enough that he knew about my fear of the dark. I didn't want everyone else at Woodhaven––especially Leah––having that kind of power, as well.

I crept back upstairs and down the hall, hoping no one would notice my return. I should have grabbed a biscuit or a cup of tea, some tangible excuse to prove that I had a reason for roaming about at this time of night. Something to prove that I wasn't crazy.

On the way to my bedroom I passed *her* door.

The very dimmest of twinkling lights shone beneath it and the scent of pure lavender wafted out, a heady fragrance. Leah was burning candles. I paused at the door, listening, but there was only silence. Lavender was a well-known sleep-inducer, I told myself, an ancient remedy for insomnia that many were familiar with, not just those who practiced magick.

I turned to leave. And that's when I heard her giggle.

Leah was a lot of things––a lot of wretched things––but she wasn't a giggler.

I started to panic but caught myself. Maybe she was on the phone, or reading a book? Or watching sitcoms on a smuggled-in TV? If I burst in now, she would know my insecurities.

Another laugh—no longer a girlish giggle but a deep, throaty laugh—forced my hand to the knob. Before I could talk myself out of it, I pushed open the door.

Leah stood in the middle of the room, her thin body draped in a long, sheer nightgown. She was surrounded by pink, red, and purple candles of all shapes and sizes, placed on shelves and dressers around the bedroom. Though she was facing me, her eyes were closed, her arms wrapped sensuously around Michael.

"What...?"

At the sound of my voice, Michael pushed Leah away and spun towards me.

"Maggie!" he said, as Leah's eyes turned to daggers. He made a grab for me, but I stepped back. "What's the matter, baby?" he asked coolly, smiling and licking his lips as he continued to advance. "Couldn't sleep?"

I shook my head in disbelief.

This couldn't be real. Not Michael. Not with Leah. We had our problems but he had never given me a reason to distrust him. I felt sick, sick like I could throw up, right then and there. I swallowed, hoping to stave back the bile that was working its way up my throat.

"How long?" was all I could manage to choke out.

"Maggie, come on. You know me." Michael took another step forward. His calm, smiling face filled me with rage. A red candle from a high shelf toppled to the floor. Leah let out a small yelp and jumped to grab it, swatting at the spot where the flame singed the carpet.

"Maggie, stop! It's not what it looks like."

"Now I know why you won't touch me."

Another candle—larger than the last—plunged to the floor, like a swimmer from a diving board. The carpet hissed as the flame licked it.

"Maggie, please..." His eyes were desperate. Leah crouched beside him, ready to grab any other candles that might fall. "We've just been talking shop. She has some great ideas for this place." He opened his arms at his side. "...That's all."

"I bet she does. I hope you take them all to heart too, Michael. You will need all the help you can get."

"Can't we just talk...?"

"Unless you want this whole fucking place to burn down, you will never speak to me again, *Brother*."

I ran down the hall, holding back the moan that was threatening to escape me. When I got to my room––our room––I slammed the door shut and turned the lock.

Michael was right behind me, knocking, quietly at first, then louder, more insistent. He knocked for such a long time that I was sure his knuckles bled and that everyone in Woodhaven was now awake. After what felt like hours, he stopped, the knocking replaced by whimpers.

"Please, Maggie, please open the door. I'm begging you. I was stupid. I love you. Please."

I had been a fool, but not again. Not this night.

When he finally left, I fell asleep, slumped against the bedroom door, the light in the closet still burning.

FIVE

TURN THE PAGE

I FELT SO MANY EMOTIONS DURING THOSE FIRST HOURS after discovering Michael and Leah together. Rage, jealousy, betrayal, hurt. I stayed locked in my room for two days, living on tap water and Oreos as my heart ran its emotional obstacle course.

True, Michael had never married me, but he knew I would never share him. I had told him so, on many occasions after making love. He'd stroked my hair and told me I would never need to. We were soul mates, he assured me, an indestructible match forged by God himself.

Fucking liar.

I pulled his ring from my finger, shredding my knuckle in the process, and tried to melt it in a candle. I watched it sink deep into the votive, floundering in the wax as it made its descent, but it refused to dissolve. When the candle liquefied, I removed the ring and pressed it into my palm, searing my skin. The pain was excruciating, but it offered me a reprieve from the inner reel that played in my head of Michael embracing Leah, telling me I had gotten it wrong, crying at my door. It was my own little horror movie and it looped endlessly, without commercial breaks.

Sometimes the scenes changed just a little, freeze-framing on Leah as she snatched at falling candles, or Michael, arms open as he moved towards me, but the ending remained the same and I was stuck through the closing credits.

I opened my hand and surveyed the damage.

The ring wasn't hot enough to leave a mark.

Too bad. I wanted a permanent reminder of his betrayal.

Through the parade of emotions, I felt there was one that led the charge, refusing to go away no matter how many cookies I shoved down my throat. Humiliation. I couldn't live in this house anymore, not amongst the people who had seen me played the fool. I imagined them whispering, mocking me, or worse, feeling sorry for me.

I was leaving Michael, and Woodhaven, behind.

On day three I emerged, with wild hair and hollow eyes, dressed in my white assembly gown.

Michael was sitting by the door, looking thinner than I had ever seen him. "Maggie. Oh, God. I am so sorry."

He didn't stand. He just sat there, crying. It was pathetic.

"I'm going." I announced simply.

"Please, no."

He had spent the last two days shoving notes under my door and shouting out promises of what would change. He would kick Leah out of Woodhaven. We would start over, run off, leaving everyone else and this damned house behind.

I was tempted to accept his offer, run away with him and then desert him in the middle of the night in some town in Godforsaken nowhere. Leave him, just as he left me. But it didn't matter. There was nothing I could do that would hurt him the way he had hurt me.

His tactics changed the next day as I packed.

"You won't make it in the outside world," he said. "You're institutionalized now."

I ignored him, throwing candles, magazines, a hair brush, and my clothes into a Goodwill suitcase.

"You forgot your crystal," he said, opening his hand to reveal the necklace I had left on the side of the bathtub the night he tucked me into bed. "If you do nothing else, take this. It will help channel your energy, and if anyone needs help with that, it's you."

He smiled sadly, pressing his lips together.

I stared at the necklace like it was poisoned, but I took it, shoving it into my skirt pocket, and then slammed the suitcase closed.

"I did love you," he said, his hand lightly grazing my wrist.

I wrenched my arm away and stood on tiptoes so that we were eye to eye. "Michael. You never loved anybody but yourself."

"Ready, Sister?" Jason asked, peeking into my bedroom.

I nodded, relieved that he would be the one driving me to the bus station. He offered to take my bags but I shook my head. I wanted to drag it down the stairs myself, listening to the satisfying thump-thump as it hit each step. There were several members gathered by the open front door. I wasn't sure if they were there to see me off, or to witness a final confrontation between me and Michael. I hugged a few, the long-term members I had practically grown up with, and nodded at the others. I didn't cry, even as the goodbyes wrenched at my heart.

They would never see me cry.

Leah stood on the second floor, looking over the railing like she was bidding bon voyage on a cruise ship. It took every ounce of willpower I could muster to keep from willing that banister to break. Having Michael would be punishment enough. Let them burn.

I took a last glance at the place I had come to call home and said a silent goodbye. I wasn't sure what waited for me out there, but there was nothing left for me here.

Jason grabbed my bag, placed it in the back of the van, and opened the passenger door to let me know the time had come. I closed the door to Woodhaven and slid into the passenger seat.

I could feel Michael's energy emanating from my seat and I almost asked Jason if I could drive instead, but I changed my mind. Though I hated Michael now, there were memories of love intermingled in that energy, and for some odd reason I felt it was important to hold onto that, too. I was full of bad at the moment, and an ounce of good, even if it no longer existed, was my only salvation. I might be grasping at dead straws, but it was all I had.

I removed the crystal from my pocket and placed it around my neck, tucking it inside my shirt. We pulled out of the driveway.

I could see Michael's silhouette in our bedroom window.

He caught me looking and moved away.

"You're going to love again," Jason said as he drove, never taking his eyes off the road. "I promise."

"I can't. I won't go through this again. Ever."

Jason removed one hand from the wheel and touched my arm reassuringly. I smiled, pulling my lips into an expression they hadn't experienced in days. But in that smile, I felt a ray of hope. Not for love, but for my life.

"Where will you go?" he asked, Woodhaven becoming a speck behind us.

"I guess I'm going home for now." It was a temporary stop, but the only place I could think of at the moment. And Merry was there. My beloved Merry had come home, too. Surely, I could handle Dark Root for a few days, just until my head cleared.

I had never seen a bus station. Not up close, anyway.

We had passed a few during our road travels, but we had never slowed down long enough for me to get a good look at one. Michael said that people who traveled by bus were transients with no real goal of settling, so he preferred the pickings at airports.

As Jason heaved my suitcase out of the van, heavy under the weight of too many Yankee Candles, I stopped a moment to take it in. The building was old, probably built at least sixty years before. The stucco was chipping and the color of urine. A skinny, smiling dog on the billboard announced that this was his vehicle of choice, although a sign above the automatic doors read, 'Service Dogs Only.'

Dozens of people descended upon the station, a few moving hyper-speed while the rest sauntered along zombie-style through the double doors, carrying suitcases, duffel bags, boxes secured with electrical tape, and babies. A frighteningly thin man appeared out of nowhere and offered me assistance with my bag. I politely refused, but he picked it up and made away with it. Before I could react, Jason was on him, pulling it back, daring him to try something like that again.

The man backed off, shaggy and apologetic, and vanished into the throngs.

I shivered, rubbing my arms to fight off the goose bumps.

I had been thinking more of comfort than warmth when dressing, and I wore only a t-shirt, a skirt, and a pair of combat boots. I thought briefly of rifling through my suitcase to locate a sweater, but I had barely been able to close the suitcase the first time. I wasn't sure if I could do it again.

"No one's forcing you to go," Jason said as we stood in line for a ticket.

There was a family ahead of us, a young woman with a baby in her arms and two crying children tugging at her blouse. She cooed at the baby and hissed at the children, trying to quiet them all.

"...Nobody wants you to go," he said.

I smiled at him. We had known each other since Michael found me in Dark Root seven years ago. For the first several months, it was just the three of us and the Battlestar Gasholica, the name Jason lovingly gave to our van. I was suddenly seized by memories of arguing with Jason over who would get to use the pile of dirty laundry for a pillow, or who got to drive while the other read maps. While Michael had been the closest thing I ever had to a boyfriend, Jason had been the closest thing to a brother.

"Woodhaven is Michael's place," I answered. "Not mine."

I stared through a large, open window as number 721 pulled in, the bus that matched the ticket in my hand.

"That's not true." Jason tossed my suitcase onto the luggage cart and walked me to my terminal. "I was there when it was just Michael, remember? We were nothing then. It might be his in name but it was your magic, Maggie. Before you came, we were just a couple of kids talking bullshit philosophies. You made it real."

He looked down at the linoleum floor as we moved up in line, avoiding the gum and cigarette butts.

"...I still remember when you predicted that earthquake a few years back in LA," he said. "Made us all get up in the middle of the night and leave town. I gotta admit, I thought you were crazy, but sure enough, the next day...well, I'm just glad we weren't there. What you call witchery, I call God, and he moves through you. Believe that, okay?" Jason flushed and looked at the door as the line before us disappeared into the bus. "You are one of the most special women I've ever met."

I felt my face change color. "Thank you, Jason. That's the sweetest thing anyone has said to me in a long time."

"It's true. I hope whoever is getting you recognizes that."

"I doubt it," I said, looking past him. "In Dark Root, Sasha Shantay is the star of the show. We're all just extras."

"Sasha? Your mom, right? Sorry, you don't talk about her much."

I nodded. "She never liked for us to call her mom. Said it made her feel old." I had to laugh. My mother seemed to have been born old, and no amount of witchcraft or Mary Kay could change that. Although she claimed to be not a day older than thirty-five, her gray roots and loose bosom gave her away.

"That's what families are for, right? To make you crazy."

"I should have asked you years ago, Jason. Where is your family?" I felt guilty. I had known this man for a quarter of my life and I knew so little about him. But all of us at Woodhaven, those who stayed anyway, were running from something.

Jason's eyes softened. "They're all gone, Mags. It's just me." He spread his hands and smiled. "Family is important, even if they do make you a little nuts."

For the first time in years, I took a good look at him. He was not

56

the thin, acne-ridden twenty-three-year-old I remembered from the past. He was tanned and muscular and when he smiled, devastatingly handsome. I cursed Michael for making me love him when there were men like Jason on this earth.

"You ready for this?" he asked. There were just a few people ahead of me, but the woman and her three children were taking awhile to board. "We've sheltered you. I feel bad now, protecting you like we did. You were so sweet and innocent when we found you, the kid sister I never had. Now I feel like you are entering the world completely unprepared." He thrust his hands into his pockets, the mop of his hair falling across his face.

"I'm not sure what I'm ready for, to be honest," I admitted. "But life's an adventure, right?"

He nodded. "Mags...two things. Don't trust men. Any of us, okay? We all want one thing and that's all. Once we get it, we change." He grinned. "Well, except for me, of course."

"Men suck. Got it. And might I add that you don't need to worry. I've already learned my lesson on that one. What's the second thing?"

Jason removed a hand from his pocket and produced a wad of money and an electronic gadget. "I *acquisitioned* these for you. A thousand dollars and a cell phone, courtesy of a generous new donor." Jason chuckled and produced another phone from his pocket, winked, and returned it. "The other one is mine. I programmed in my number. Call if you need anything, okay?"

I was about to object when he stopped me.

"The outside world is expensive *and* dangerous, Mags. You're gonna need a bit of help." He pushed the items into my palm and tightened his fist around mine in a *this is non-negotiable* sort of way. I gave him a tight-lipped smile and accepted his gifts.

"Thanks, Jason. You've been a good friend. I love you."

We gave each other one final hug and for the first time since making my decision to leave Woodhaven, I almost turned back.

"I love you too," he whispered in my ear.

Fucking Michael.

"721 departing for Salem, Oregon," said the man at the door, giving me a warning look.

I nodded a goodbye to Jason and went through the portal that would take me to my new life...the old life I had left behind.

SIX

WILD WORLD

DARK ROOT, OREGON
JANUARY, 1990

"*SHE'S HERE! SHE'S HERE!*" *Maggie's sister Merry screeched, scrambling from her window seat and knocking off two flowered cushions in the process.*

She ran for the door, a blur of blond hair and pink crinoline.

"Well," she said to Maggie, who laid tucked under a pile of blankets on the sofa. "...Aren't you coming?" Maggie shrugged, popping her thumb into her mouth as she stared at the cartoons on the TV. Shaggy and Scooby had gobbled up their Scooby Snacks and Maggie giggled, almost biting her thumb.

"Can't we just get a puppy?" Maggie asked, removing her thumb from her mouth to speak. She examined a blister on the tip of it where she had sucked too hard, and then rubbed it across the satin edge of her blanket. She thought about asking Merry to kiss it better, but decided against it. Merry might kiss it, but she would also lecture her.

"Miss Maggie," said Aunt Dora, waddling in from the kitchen and flipping off the television. "Git ready to greet yer mother, will ya? An' don' go tellin' her I let ya watch cartoons. I promised her I wouldn'..." Aunt Dora gave Maggie a little wink.

Maggie yawned, smoothed down her unruly, cherry-colored hair, and made her way towards the door to stand with Merry.

"Ruth Anne!" Aunt Dora hollered up the staircase.

When her niece didn't respond, Aunt Dora cupped her hands together and bellowed again. She hated climbing the stairs, claiming age and bad knees made it impossible, especially steps as steep as the ones in Sister House.

"Ruth Anne! Yer mother's here! Git down here, girl."

"I hope it's a boy!" Merry squealed, rubbing her hands together and bouncing on the balls of her feet. "I think we have enough girls."

"Why do we have to have another baby, anyways?" Maggie asked, reaching for Merry's hand. There had been nothing but baby talk since before Christmas and Maggie was tired of hearing it. Though she was almost four, and just eighteen months younger than Merry, she enjoyed being the youngest of the house. "...I like our family the way it is." Maggie strained her ears to listen to the sounds outside. She could hear her mother's voice, saying goodbye to Uncle Joe who had dropped her off.

"It's not our choice. Yer mother wanted another baby and she had one." Aunt Dora turned her gaze on Maggie. "I don' know why she wants another rug rat runnin' around, neither. Ya three are enough to make a young woman ol' and put an ol' woman in her grave."

And then, turning to Merry,

"Ya'll love it, whether it's a boy or girl. Ya love e'ryone, Miss Merry."

Merry giggled and turned towards Maggie. "You're going to be a big girl now, like me and Ruth Anne. Isn't that exciting?"

Merry twirled on tiptoes, yellow hair and tutu spinning out around her.

"How long has Mama been gone?" Maggie asked, popping her thumb back into her mouth. Merry gave her a disapproving look and Maggie removed it. "I don't remember what she looks like."

"Oh, you'll remember her. No doubt about it." Her sister Ruth Anne trudged down the stairs carrying the largest book Maggie had ever seen. She was wearing a pair of jeans with holes in the knees and a *baggy t-shirt their mother hated. Her long, brown hair was fastened in a loose braid that hung over her shoulder. "No one forgets Sasha Shantay..."*

Ruth Anne posed dramatically at the bottom of the staircase, letting the book fall from her hands and land on the wooden floor with a noisy thump. Merry and Maggie laughed in response.

"Be good girls, will ya? Yer mama's not gonna let me sit wit' ya anymore if she see the way yer acting." Aunt Dora removed the apron she was wearing, and placed it on the breakfast table. "Okay, now. I think I hear her comin' in. E'eryone smile pretty."

Ruth Anne removed a pair of glasses from the front pocket of her jeans, deposited them on her face, and joined her younger sisters. The girls lined up according to age, youngest to oldest––Maggie, Merry, and Ruth Anne.

At last, the door opened and their mother burst in, wearing a purple-feathered boa around her neck and an infant carrier draped across her arm like a very large purse.

"Mama!" Maggie and Merry hollered in unison as Ruth Anne reached forward to give her mother a quick hug.

"My girls!"

Their mother sat the carrier on the ground and scooped her three daughters into her arms. They allowed it for a second, then wiggled free to see their new sibling. The baby was pink and round with a dark patch of fuzz on the top of its head. It was dressed in a rose-colored nightgown that was tied at the bottom like a birthday present.

"It's a girl!" Merry exclaimed, leaning in to smell the baby. She inhaled deeply and grinned. "Oh. Babies smell wonderful."

"Just wait," Ruth Anne said, after a brief glance at the new family member before going to retrieve her fallen book. "They don't smell that way for long. Trust me." Ruth Anne plopped herself down in a voluminous recliner and began reading.

Their mother ignored Ruth Anne's lack of interest.

"You three have a new sister, born on New Year's Eve, exactly one

week after Merry's birthday. Isn't that special? We have two holiday babies now!" Miss Sasha reached into the carrier and covered the baby up with a soft-looking, pink blanket that had been wadded up by her feet.

"Well, what's da child's name, for mercy's sake?" Aunt Dora asked, working her way in. "Or have ya even thought of that, yet?"

"Eve." Their mother smiled tiredly, stretching her arms overhead. She removed her feathered boa and her fur coat and placed them on hooks by the door. "It's drafty in here. Dora, are you trying to freeze us all?" She rubbed her arms to prove her point.

"Are ya kiddin? It's hot as Hades in dis house, at least in the downstairs. Upstairs, it's so cold I didn't wan' the girls sleeping up there. Ya should git someone out to check the thermostat. These old house are full o' weird air pockets." Aunt Dora meandered into the kitchen.

"Don't mind her, girls," their mother whispered, loud enough for her sister in the next room to hear. "She's a Grumpy Gus, lately. That's what happens when you go through the change."

Aunt Dora appeared in the kitchen entryway, wielding a rolling pin and waving it overhead. "If I'm gettin' old, I'm draggin' ya along wit' me," she said, then disappeared back into the other room.

"Maybe Eve can be my birthday present?" Merry asked. She was crouched down, peering intently into the carrier. "We never did have a party for me."

"We will have a birthday for you, Merry," her mother apologized. "And you can be my special helper with the baby, okay?" She picked up the carrier and walked to the breakfast nook, placing the baby on the table. Then she settled herself into one of their mismatched wooden chairs and called Aunt Dora to bring her some tea.

"Does it hurt to sit?" Ruth Anne asked, her eyes frozen on her book. "I heard popping out kiddos makes it hard to sit."

Their mother threw her head back and laughed, long brown waves shimmying around her face. "Ruth Anne, you are such a funny girl. Are you sure you're only eight?" She caught her reflection in the brass *framed mirror on the opposite wall. She studied it, pursed her lips together, then pushed her finger into one of the deeper lines around her mouth. "Dora," she called into the kitchen. "While you're at it, can you find me my aloe cream? My skin's a little dry."*

Aunt Dora muttered an indecipherable answer and Miss Sasha returned her attention to her daughters.

"To answer your question, Ruth Anne, I am fine. Fine as wine, in fact."

Maggie crossed her arms, her chin jutting out defiantly. "Can't we take Eve back? I don't want another baby."

"No, darling. She is ours forever now. You'll get used to her, I promise"

"She going to sleep in the sitting room? There's nothing in there but junk, anyways," Ruth Anne said, moving her eyes from the book she was reading to the locked door on the side of the living room.

The color of their mother's eyes changed from violet to black.

"Nobody goes into the sitting room but me, do you understand?" Her jaw tightened and the thin, blue veins in her neck pulsed. Merry, Maggie, and Ruth Anne tensed up at the look on their mother's face and remained quiet, waiting for her storm to pass. Finally, her face softened. "I'm sorry," she said, closing her eyes and opening them quickly. "I'm just tired. Having a baby takes a lot out of you."

She poured herself a cup of tea from the pot Aunt Dora had produced, took a long sip, then swallowed, turning her eyes on Maggie. "She is going to sleep with you in the nursery. You'll be four soon, much too old for a crib. We'll get you a big girl's bed. Won't you like that?"

Maggie panicked.

She had thought the baby would be sleeping in her room but not in her bed, too. She knew that she had gotten too old for the crib long ago, but she had always felt safe inside the little cage, with her stuffed animals and her night light. It was her own private fortress and at night, when everyone was asleep, she would cover it in blankets and stay hidden until morning.

It had kept things...away.

"No!"

Her voice was strong and angry, surprising even her. Mother's tea cup trembled on it's saucer. Aunt Dora's eyes widened but her mother just nodded.

"I know you have nightmares, Maggie," her mother said softly, "With Eve in the room with you, they might just go away."

Maggie knew the argument was over and that she had lost.

Maybe there were other safe places in the room. The closet or under the crib. She would scout them out later, when she was alone.

Or maybe, if she was lucky, the 'thing' that was looking for her, would go after Eve instead.

SOMEWHERE IN CENTRAL OREGON

SEPTEMBER, 2013

It was another dream. I rubbed at my eyes trying to push back the past. It was bad enough that I was forced to return home. I didn't need the constant reminders of why I left.

I tried to wiggle my legs but they were locked in between the seat and my suitcase on the floor of the bus. Our last bus had broken down, and a new one had been sent for us. Unfortunately, the luggage compartment was already full, and so I had to finish the ride with nowhere to put my feet. But I didn't dare let it out of my sight; a man across the row had been eyeballing it since I boarded, licking his lips and twitching his eyes.

The rest of me was achy too, courtesy of the potholes and poor road skills of our new driver, who I was sure was out to get me ever since I demanded he pull over and let me use a real bathroom because I wasn't going to pee in their courtesy cesspool.

"If yer too good for our facilities, you can piss yer pants for all I care," he growled, purposely aiming the bus into every hole and divot in the road thereafter.

I glared at the back of his head from my seat. He glared back through the rear view mirror.

It was a standoff and he was winning.

"Piss break," he finally hollered as we rolled into the parking lot of a run-down, roadside bar. I watched my fellow passengers—an old couple with a squawking bird, three teenaged boys who kept referring to my rack, and a young man who kept his face buried in a book—slush past me on their quest to find a real, working toilet. The twitchy man across from me rubbed his greasy palms through his even greasier hair and offered to sit with my suitcase if I needed a break.

I dislodged it from its spot and hefted it out of the bus, giving the driver a dirty look.

"Where are we?" I asked one of the teen-aged boys, who shrugged in response. I then asked the book-reading man, who informed me that if I had kept my paper itinerary, as he had, I would know exactly where I was.

I should have taken a plane, I thought, then dismissed the idea.

I had never flown anywhere in my life, and as much as I now hated traveling by bus, the thought of sitting in a metallic floating machine made my knees weak. No matter how many people explained the *science* of it to me, it didn't seem possible.

And at least the scenery had been pretty. I had spent hours leaned up against the cool glass window, watching as California faded into Oregon. The landscape was lush, green, rolling, straight out of a portrait. A man I sat next to for awhile had been tracking Big Foot, he said. Looking out the window, staring at an endless horizon of nothing but trees, it was hard to discount his beliefs.

Anything might live in these woods. Fairies, elves, even a Sasquatch.

"Twenty minutes," the driver called to us, shutting the double glass doors behind him. I was near the last in line for the bathroom, slowed down by my over-sized suitcase. The twitchy man leered at me through the bus window.

I looked around as I waited my turn.

A neon sign announced that we were at the Fat Chance Bar. Only a few beat-up cars and trucks dotted the parking lot. A wooden door led into the main bar. The *busser's* bathroom, according to a crudely-written sign, was located on the side of the building.

I grabbed a Pay Day bar out of my purse and gnawed on it while waiting my turn. A gust of wind caught my skirt, sending it floating above my thighs and the teen-aged boys elbowed one another.

I was startled by the ringing of my newly-acquired phone.

I removed it from my bag and answered it.

"Hello?"

"Maggie! Are you okay? I heard you were coming home by bus."

I was surprised to hear Merry's voice. I wasn't sure how she had gotten this number, but I could only guess that Jason had something to do with it. I turned my body away from the crowd and cuffed the mouthpiece with my hand.

"I'm fine. Almost home, I think. Ready for me?" I laughed nervously. When she said nothing I continued. "...Where're we meeting? Not Mom's, I hope? I don't think I can handle jumping right into things without getting my feet wet first." My fingers tightened around the phone. What would come would come...but hopefully not tonight.

"No. We are meeting at Harvest Home, if that's okay? I just got here this morning." Merry paused, sucking in her breath. "Maggie, Mom's not good. I had heard things were bad, but I didn't know they were this bad. I think we all need a good night's sleep before seeing her."

She laughed, a nervous laugh, and it took me aback. Merry never got anxious.

"You reach our sisters?" I asked casually, grabbing the handle of my suitcase and moving up in line.

"I tried. I can't find she-who-shall-not-be-named at all. I even looked her up on the Internet and tried to email someone with that name. No response."

"Email? They still doing that?"

Merry laughed. "Maggie, you are so funny sometimes. I miss that."

I smiled, feeling the distance between us melt away. We may not have seen each other for eight years, but we were still sisters. "And Eve?" My eyes turned upwards, towards the darkening sky. "Aunt Dora told me she had moved to New York a few years ago. Acting, right? If I know Eve, she's too busy leading her glamorous life to come back to Dark Root."

"Well..." Merry's voice tightened. "Eve will be here late tonight. She's catching a ride from a *friend*." She tilted the word like she were trying to push it down. She had never approved of Eve's *friends*. Bad news, the lot of them, but that didn't stop Eve from collecting them.

"Well, I should beat her there, then," I said, relieved. "If all goes well."

"I can't wait to see you, Maggie. I miss you so much. We've been apart too long." The words slid from her throat and wrenched my heart. "I've got a surprise for you," she said, her tone light again.

"A surprise? Is he six-foot-tall and rich?" I teased, leaning against the wall of the Fat Chance Bar.

"Nope. But I think you will like it, just the same. Can't wait to show you."

The excitement in her voice warmed me, and for the first time, I couldn't wait to be home. If only to see my Merry.

"Okay, enough Hallmark talk," I said. "See you on the flip side." Merry knew this was my cue to leave. I hung up, not letting her say goodbye. I hated goodbyes.

I turned towards the restroom when a young man in a blue t-shirt and faded jeans stopped me. "Excuse me miss, I couldn't help but overhear. Did you say you were going to Dark Root?" He grinned, his white teeth almost glowing in the near dark. He was clean cut, lean, and muscular. And he smelled too good to have been riding the bus.

I narrowed my eyes, trying to get a read on him, but I came up empty.

"Yes," I finally answered, pointing to the bus to let him know I wasn't alone. There was a big, hairy driver manning the wheel who might not like it if one of his passengers, albeit an annoying one in his words, came up missing.

"You from Dark Root? Or just visiting?" His shaggy brown hair flopped into his face, obscuring one of his grey eyes.

I shook my head, confused. I wasn't used to people being interested in my personal life.

"...Sorry, this must seem weird," he continued. "I don't meet many people going to Dark Root, anymore. Name's Shane. I own a little cafe there on Main Street." He reached into his back pocket and pulled out a little, white card with the words *Dip Stix Cafe* written in red font across the front.

I blinked at him, still not quite understanding.

"Yeah, I get that look from women a lot." He laughed, pushing his hair out of his face. "I'm from Montana, where there's more deer than people. I may not be good at talking to girls, but if you ever needed an Elk whisperer, I'm your man."

I handed him back his card, but he shook his head, indicating that I should keep it.

"Wait a second," he said, his eyes flickering with recognition. "I know who you are! You're Evie's sister! Maggie!" He leaned his head back and laughed, like it was the funniest thing he had ever seen. "Well, I'll be. Imagine me meeting Evie's older sister out here in the boondocks. What are the odds?"

I tilted my head to the side in a questioning manner.

He continued, undeterred.

"...You don't remember me, do you? We played together when we were kids. Well, I played with Eve, while you made fun of us."

I snorted. "That could be anyone," I said, smiling at the memories. I had never really been able to rattle Eve or her friends, but I spent much of my childhood trying.

"Same old Maggie," he said, grinning again. "I guess you heard what happened to your ma, then? Sorry about that."

I bit my bottom lip. "Yes," I lied. Merry had not yet filled me in, but I wasn't going to let this stranger know that. "...And we are handling this privately, as a family."

"That's good," he nodded. "Family's important."

He looked towards a white, extended-cab pickup that sat at the rear of the lot.

"Well, you have my number," he said. "I have to get going. There's a restaurant about thirty minutes south that's going out of business. I'm seeing if they have anything I could use, for cheap. Call me if you need anything. And look me up once you get to town."

"Yeah," I said.

"Unless," he said, turning back. "...You want to ride along? It might put another few hours in your trip, but you wouldn't have to ride that thing." He jutted his chin towards my bus.

I considered it, briefly.

Although I very much wanted to get off of the bus, I really wanted to see Merry before Eve got there. I couldn't afford a two hour delay.

"No thanks." The line before me had cleared out, and I stood in front of the restroom door. The driver started up the bus, indicating that we were leaving soon. "I better go."

"Yeah. I got you. Say..." he said, scratching his head. "Is Eve going to be in town? I'd love to catch up with her too."

I shrugged and twisted the knob on the door.

He smiled. "Bye, Maggie Maddock. We'll be seeing each other soon." He waved and went back to his pick up.

I pushed my way through the heavy bathroom door, turned on the flickering, fluorescent light, and finally peed. I had held it in so long that it almost hurt to go. After washing my hands I looked at his business card again. Shane Doler.

I still couldn't place him, but the name sounded familiar.

I plugged the number into my phone——a trick I had learned from one of the teenaged boys on the bus——and put the card back in my pocket. I then left the bathroom, suitcase in tow. It was darker now, like someone had flipped a light switch to the world during the few minutes I was inside.

I was all alone. The bus had gone.

FAT CHANCE BAR, CENTRAL OREGON
SEPTEMBER, 2013

I stood for a moment, like the proverbial deer in headlights, except that, instead of a headlight, there was a neon sign blinking *Fat Chance Bar*.

My head was foggy, refusing to accept what had happened. My bus was coming back for me. I knew it. The driver was just trying to teach me a lesson. I raced into the parking lot, looking down the road. The bus was nowhere in sight.

I still had my cell phone. I could call Jason. I knew that he would drop everything to rescue me. But the idea of Michael answering instead stopped me cold.

I had Shane's number too, now. He might turn around and get me. It was partly his fault I was in this mess, anyway. If he hadn't stood there yammering on, I would have had plenty of time to get back on my bus. Even so, I couldn't bring myself to dial his number, either. I was too embarrassed about my predicament.

I glanced at the door, wondering if I should go in.

In all honesty, I hadn't been in many bars. Dark Root had only one corner tavern and I was twenty when I left, too young to have gotten in without a report being sent back to my mother. And Michael didn't believe in drinking, so there was no chance after that. The only thing I knew about bars was what I had seen in the movies––dark, vile places that smelled like vomit and were frequented by rogues and smugglers. Sometimes there were shootouts, sometimes light saber fights. Either way, I wasn't sure I'd fare well.

I swallowed, summoning my courage. I could wait inside while I figured out who to call to turn my bus around.

I dragged my suitcase to the front entrance. It hit every rock in the asphalt, twisting and tipping and being generally unmanageable. I tried picking it up, but it was too heavy. As I wrestled with it, a car raced into the parking lot, kicking up sand and gravel as it performed donuts. Two young men whooped through open windows before braking abruptly, just a few yards away from me.

I watched them emerge, all flannel shirts and shiny hair, smiling at me.

"Hey baby," said the first one, advancing in my direction. His blond hair was slicked back and his jeans were tight. I took a step back, pulling my suitcase with me. "I haven't seen you before. You new in town?" He continued towards me.

The other man hung back, grinning, his front tooth chipped.

"Don't be scared, darling. I just want to know your name." His step quickened. "Maybe we can have a drink together. I'm parched."

I dropped my bag and ran for the door.

"Look at her run!" The one in back said, slapping his thigh. "I don't think she likes us."

"Quiet, Johnny," the first man ordered, chasing me.

The door wasn't far, maybe less than a hundred feet, but it was dark and I tripped on something, sending me sprawling face-forward, onto the ground. I could feel the greasy man behind me and I struggled to get up, but he was on me, yanking me by the wrist and knocking the cell phone out of my hand. I tried to pull away but he tightened his grip.

"Looks like we got us a fighter," he said, grabbing at my other wrist and securing them both in one of his large hands. "God, I love redheads."

He shoved me backwards and I felt my head smash against the building as his friend hollered and howled behind him. With his free hand, he grabbed my chin, tilted it back and forced me to look into his dark eyes.

"Kiss me," he ordered.

His breath smelled like bubble gum and alcohol. I screamed, a blast so loud I couldn't believe it was coming out of me. It was cut short with another forceful shove into the wall.

"Shut the fuck up!" He covered my mouth and nose with a hand as he wrenched my legs open with his knees. He turned slightly, beckoning for Johnny.

In an instant, his friend was by our side.

"Listen, girlie. We can make this enjoyable for all three of us, or we can make it enjoyable for two of us, and pretty fuckin' miserable for the other. You understand?" He released his grip on my hands and reached to touch my breast.

I wriggled, freeing a leg. I lifted my knee and thrust it into his groin.

He gasped, doubling over.

When he stood again, his eyes were dark, crazy orbs. Johnny unzipped his pants, ignoring his injured friend.

"Not yet, dummy," the first man said, leading me away from the wall by pulling my hair. I went to scream again but he had his free hand back over my mouth. "Help me get her into the car." He turned to me. "You get one more chance. Be a good girl and we all go our merry ways. Be a bad girl and we take a drive. Understand?"

I pushed my lips together and nodded, my eyes darting towards the door a few feet away. I prayed that someone inside had seen or heard me.

"She's shy," Johnny said, opening the door to the back seat of their car. "Or maybe a virgin. A virgin would be fun, huh, Steve?"

"You fucking dumb ass," said Steve, shooting Johnny a dirty look. "I told you never to call me by name." Steve did a quick glance around the parking lot to make sure that we were still alone. Satisfied, he pushed me into the back seat and followed, closing the door behind him. Johnny got in the front and turned on the engine, leaning over the seat to watch us. His eyes glittered like a rat's. Steve pushed me backwards, flattening his body onto mine.

Once I was secured he began removing his belt.

I was sick with fear and unsure of what to do. One wrong move could be my last. I couldn't allow myself to give in to that fear. I had to stay rational, focused. My life depended on it. *Think. Think.* A memory came to me, Michael giving me a self-defense lesson before sending me out to recruit new members. I remembered his words.

It's easier for someone to hurt you if they don't see you as a person. Put a name to your face.

I heard a clicking sound. Steve unsnapped his jeans.

"Please, don't do this, *Steve*. Please." I looked into his eyes, trying to force a connection. "My name is Maggie. Magdalene. I'm twenty-seven-years old. I grew up in Oregon. I have three sisters and a mother and an aunt and they are all waiting for me right now."

Johnny hammered his fist on the upholstery, but Steve didn't answer. His face was stone as he stared back at me.

"...They are waiting for me to come home."

I noticed a ring on Steve's left hand and I took a chance. "Do you have a wife, Steve? A daughter?" I looked into his eyes, trying to calm my shaking body. "How would they feel if they knew you were doing this? You're a good guy, I can tell."

Steve's face softened for a moment, and I wondered if I was reaching him. Then his eyes turned to dark slits.

"Don't you *ever* mention my daughter again," he whispered, pushing his pants down around his knees, but his underwear was still on and I wondered if he was having second thoughts. I opened my mouth and Steve snapped his fingers at Johnny, pointing at the stereo on the dashboard. "Play something to drown this bitch out."

Johnny nodded, his whole body rocking as his eyes darted from side to side.

"Got it," he said, hitting a button on the dash. 'For Those About to Rock, I Salute You' blasted through the vehicle. Steve tugged at my skirt and motioned for Johnny to keep watch outside, but Johnny just continued to leer at us. "I ain't gonna miss this," he said, pounding his hands on the passenger door in time to the music.

Realizing I had nothing to lose anymore, I fought back, twisting, turning, and biting at him like a feral cat. "Go for the nose, the eyes, and the throat," my self-defense teacher's voice came back to me, and I attacked Steve with a ferocity I didn't know I had.

But he was quicker and stronger, capturing my hands each time they slid from his grip, calling me names I had never heard before.

Johnny jumped around in the front seat muttering, "Oh man, oh man," and "For those about to rock I salute you." Steve told him to shut the fuck up and Johnny retorted with, "Who are you to tell me what to do? You can't even control one little girlie."

I gnashed my teeth, tearing into Steve's ear, ripping off a small piece. It tasted like iron and salt.

"Bitch!" He backhanded me, twisting my neck into an unnatural position. He kissed me hard and I spit blood back into his mouth.

"That's it!" he said, "I'm done with this!"

He covered my entire nose and mouth so that I couldn't breathe. I could feel myself losing consciousness as his hand reached for my breast. With my last ounce of strength I pushed his hand away and found Michael's crystal under my shirt. I gripped it as I slid into a long, dark tunnel.

Just as suddenly, I was back, gasping for air.

Steve's hand no longer covered my face.

The rear car door was open and a muscled arm thrust itself inside, pulling Steve's body across mine. He yelped as he was thrown into the parking lot. The front door opened and the arm returned, ripping Johnny out the door.

I sobbed as I pulled down my skirt and listened to the scuffling outside. At last I gathered myself and scrambled to the opposite door, away from my attackers.

"Wait!" A voice called out as I raced into the darkness of the trees that surrounded the parking lot. The forest was pitch black but I didn't care. I just ran, tripping and terrified through the woods. The sound of footsteps followed me. I looked right, then left, unsure of where to go.

Two strong hands seized my shoulders from behind and I screamed.

"Maggie. It's okay. It's all over."

I knew that voice and it wasn't Steve or Johnny's.

My knees buckled and I went limp in his arms. He pushed my wet hair away from my forehead, cradling me like a baby. When I was strong enough to stand on my own, he wiped my tears away then guided me out of the woods.

"We called the cops." He nodded towards two large men who had my two assailants slung over the back of an old Cadillac Eldorado. "... They will be here any moment."

I heard a siren in the distance, careening in our direction and I knew that he was right.

"I'm taking you home, Maggie," he said.

I nodded and followed Shane to the truck.

SEVEN

WITCHY WOMAN

*BUMP, BUMP, BUMP! The last jolt startled Maggie, practically sending
her spiraling over the side of the wagon and into the crowd.*

Luckily, Merry caught her by the arm and pulled her back.

*Maggie gave her an appreciative smile and returned to the task at
hand. She still had half a sack of Halloween candy to throw out, and the
parade was coming to a close.*

*Some younger kids propelled out of the crowds, running alongside
the wagon. "Candy!" they screamed, arms stretched overhead and
eager mouths open. Maggie reached into her bag to scoop out a
handful, but Eve was quicker, dumping the entire contents of her
own sack overboard. The children cheered. Eve stuck out her tongue
triumphantly.*

*Maggie moved to pinch her, but then caught sight of their mother.
Miss Sasha was waving to the crowd at the front of the wagon. If
Maggie did anything to ruin her special day, she would be in trouble.*

"Maggie, Eve, Merry!" Ruth Anne called to them.

*Maggie tottered to the other side of the wagon to catch a glimpse
of her sister. Ruth Anne stood with Aunt Dora by the entrance of Miss*

Sasha's Magick Shoppe, smiling and cheering the girls on. Maggie felt a small tug at her heart. This was the first year Ruth Anne wasn't accompanying her sisters on the parade route, and that his suited Miss Sasha fine.

Still, Maggie didn't like it. Ruth Anne was doing her own thing more often these days, and she could feel the chasm between Ruth Anne and her younger sisters growing deeper every day.

"We're almost done, girls," Miss Sasha said, turning in their direction.

Her black, pointed hat almost fell off her head as she spun around, but she caught it and pushed it firmly down over her ears. Maggie adjusted her own hat and straightened her simple, black dress. The 'Witches of Dark Root' were expected to play the part the entire day, and that meant staying in character, even if the costumes were itchy and a size too small.

Bump! Another sharp jolt as the wheels hit a crack in the road. Maggie looked ahead. There were three floats and a band in front of them, crossing the parade's finish line.

Just in time, Maggie thought. She needed to use the bathroom really badly and the jostling of the wagon didn't help.

"Do you have your candles?" Merry asked, as she produced her own white, tapered candle from the pocket of her dress. Maggie and Eve nodded, earning them a look of approval. "Good. Hold on to them for later, for the lighting ceremony..."

As the horses that pulled the cart proceeded towards their destination, Maggie caught sight of a woman with spiraling, dark hair weaving in and out of the crowd. She was speaking, her voice a deep growl as she kept pace with the wagon.

Maggie was used to seeing strangers during the Haunted Dark Root Festival, but there was something sinister about the woman that Maggie couldn't explain.

"Mother!" Maggie called.

Miss Sasha turned and Maggie pointed to the woman.

"Larinda!" her mother gasped. Miss Sasha hurdled the bench that separated her from her daughters. "...Girls, come close! Hurry! The circle cannot be broken!"

As the horses crossed the finish line, Miss Sasha swallowed her daughters into the folds of her black cape, and they vanished into the night.

SHANE DOLER'S PICKUP TRUCK, CENTRAL OREGON
SEPTEMBER, 2013

Bump!

Whatever we hit, startled me awake. For a moment, I forgot where I was, but as my eyes adjusted to the dark, I recognized the driver gripping the steering wheel and I remembered.

"Sorry about that," Shane said, glancing in my direction. "I think I dozed off a little there. I was fine until the radio lost reception. I'm glad you're awake now." He yawned and blinked several times. "Want to keep me company?"

I shrugged. After what I had been through, I wasn't in the mood to entertain anyone, even if it was my rescuer. I took a moment to study him. He wore a goofy grin and a large silver belt buckle. But at least he looked friendly. And safe.

I sighed and wedged myself back into my corner of the bench seat.

"What are you looking forward to the most?" he asked, cracking his window. The smell of moss and rain filled the cab of his pickup. "Seeing your sisters, I bet?"

I shrugged again, wishing he would stop talking. My body was heavy and achy and I wanted to sleep.

"You know your ma's shop closed up, don't you? About three years ago, I guess. Darn pity, too. There's a small college a few towns over and

I bet you, dollars to donuts, those students would swarm that store if it reopened. I know your ma isn't in any position to..." His voice trailed off and his eyes softened. "...I'm sorry. I'm being insensitive."

"Do you have any aspirin?" The pounding in my head was getting worse. I was starting to feel nauseous.

"I got some headache powder," he said, reaching into his console. He produced what looked like a Kool-Aid packet and ripped it open with his teeth. "It's powder, so works quick. Swallow it and chase it with a drink of my coke. Don't worry," he said smiling again. "I don't have cooties."

I looked at the packet. I had never heard of headache powder before, but I was willing to try anything. It tasted like chalk and I practically choked as I chugged down the soda to wash the taste out of my mouth.

"You don't do anything quietly, do you?" he laughed, as I wadded up the wrapper and threw it on the floor of the passenger seat. "When we were kids, you were always making noise, too."

I squeezed my eyes shut, hoping the medicine would kick in. I pushed my fingers to my temples, trying to squeeze out the pain.

"Do you remember when we used to play hide and seek?" he continued. "Whenever it was your turn to hide, we could always find you, because you would squeal whenever you thought we were close."

I opened my eyes and looked at him again, trying to dig up old memories of us playing hide and seek together. The process made my head hurt worse. "I'm sorry," I confessed when he began another *do you remember story*. "...I still have no idea who you are."

Shane's face tightened. He looked hurt.

I leaned my head back, pressing my neck into the headrest and wishing that I had said that a different way. "Sorry." I offered him a weak smile. "It's been a tough night."

Shane nodded and leaned forward, peering into the deep darkness that surrounded us.

Even with the high beams on, we moved sluggishly through the winding wilderness of central Oregon. The trees closed in around us, tall monstrous beasts that loomed even larger in the night. Their branches canopied us like long, twisted fingers. Through the crack in Shane's window, I could hear the sound of the restless wind moaning. We cut through the darkness like it was unexplored jungle, carefully hacking our way into the moonlight.

"I understand," he said, as we reached an area where the trees were less dense and we could finally see the moon. It hung in the sky, a sliver of gold punctuated by a few dim stars. But it was enough. We both relaxed.

Shane continued, "...I'm sure I look different, now. Do you remember Joe Garris?"

"Yes," I answered.

Uncle Joe, as he was called by all of us, had owned Delilah's Deli. He had been part of my mother's coven and had been responsible for helping me and my sisters with some of our *lessons*.

"Well, he was my Uncle. My biological Uncle. I would come down from Montana every year and spend the summers with him. I was that skinny boy with freckles and glasses. You girls used to come to the deli and we'd run around the tables after it closed."

A light of recognition hit my brain.

Shane Doler. The dorky kid who used to go frog-hunting with Eve.

I recalled how Eve had gotten him to kiss one of those frogs once, claiming that if he did, it would turn into a beautiful princess. It didn't, of course. Just because Eve practiced magick didn't mean she was any good at it.

After that event, I had nicknamed him Frog Frencher. I smiled at the memory, even though it hurt. "Yes, I remember you. Sorry about the nickname."

He laughed, bobbing his head. "I had it coming. Who kisses a frog?" He shook his head, and his brown hair shook with him. He had filled out since I had seen him last. He was still thin, but thin in a handsome sort of way.

Not that it mattered. I was done with men. Especially the handsome ones.

"So you work with Uncle Joe now?" I asked, remembering that he was on his way to buy restaurant equipment for his cafe. The headache powder was working and I could feel my temples relaxing. I took a deep, slow breath and let my shoulders settle, too.

"Well, after Uncle Joe passed, I..."

"What?" I stopped him. "Uncle Joe is dead? How? When?" I shook my head in disbelief.

Uncle Joe had been such a huge part of our childhood. After Mama closed her shop each night, we'd wander over to the cafe and he'd serve us a special dinner. Afterwards, he and Mother would talk 'business' while we played in the restaurant, hiding under tables and serving phantom customers. At the end of each night, he'd let us pick out one candy from a jar by the register. He had always been kind and patient, even with me.

People like kind, Uncle Joe weren't supposed to die. They were supposed to live on forever.

This day was only getting worse.

"Sorry, I thought you had heard." Shane took a sip of his coke, then passed it to me. I declined. "He died three years ago. Heart attack. People from all over came to say goodbye. Boy, I tell you, my Uncle Joe had some interesting friends." He chuckled softly at the memory and took another sip of his drink. "He was very popular."

"Yeah, he was very loved. I just can't believe he's gone." I could feel myself tearing up but I gritted my teeth and willed the feeling away. I had done enough crying lately.

We continued to jounce along in his pickup truck.

Shane talked enthusiastically about how he had taken over his uncle's cafe and was working it himself, but I was mostly tuning him out. The news about Uncle Joe, coupled with rest of this day, was too much. Going home seemed more depressing than ever.

"We're making good time," Shane said, glancing at the clock, but his voice sounded uncertain. "I've never driven this route this late at night, or this time of year."

There was only one road that led to Dark Root, he said, so we couldn't be lost, but we could be...absorbed? A small, wild creature with red eyes

82

darted out from the wilderness trees and was caught it in our headlights.

Shane slammed on the breaks, throwing us forward, and the animal scurried away unhurt.

"You're going to kill us," I said, the pain in my head returning.

"Did you want me to hit that raccoon instead?"

"No," I admitted, wriggling my legs, which were beginning to stiffen. "But now I have to pee."

Shane pulled to the side of the road and motioned towards the woods around us.

Reluctantly, I left the vehicle in search of a bush. Peeing in the woods wasn't new to me, but it certainly wasn't pleasant. Especially in the dark. When I returned, I fished around in my suitcase in the backseat, adding clothes to keep back the chill, while he politely shielded his eyes.

"Interesting outfit," Shane grinned, as he noticed my new ensemble, a tank top over three long-sleeved shirts, a skirt so long it covered my feet, and checkered socks.

"Just drive," I said.

He complied.

"Dark Root, Oregon. The most magical town in the Pacific Northwest..." Shane recited the town's slogan after a long silence. "Bet you are excited to get back."

I was leaned over the seat, rummaging through my open bag in the back of the cab.

It was less full now that I was wearing half my wardrobe. Finally, I found my package of Oreos and pulled them into the front. I hadn't eaten since morning and my stomach was not happy. Once I had scarfed down a half-dozen cookies, I responded to him.

"First of all," I said. "Towns can't be magical. Secondly, you are terrible at small talk. Thirdly, I'm not staying in Dark Root. It's just a stop until I figure things out."

"How can you say towns aren't magical? You of all people should believe in magic, considering your upbringing."

I snorted. "Why? Just because I am a supposed descendant of Juliana Benbridge, our town's first witch?"

"Well, yes."

"It's just lore. And lore isn't necessarily true," I said, offering him a cookie which he took. "Especially when a town's economy is based on it. Lore is used to sell postcards."

"Well then, Dark Root needs a new slogan," he laughed.

"Among other things," I said.

Shane flipped on the radio, settling on one of those sad, storytelling songs on the country station. It was sappy in all the wrong ways.

"No one has ever proved that magic exists," I argued, realizing I could have let it drop and wondering why I didn't.

"No one has disproved it either. And..." he added thoughtfully. "Sometimes people *want* to believe. Nothing wrong with that. Makes life more interesting."

"Doesn't mean they should." I thought of Michael, staring absently out the window, wondering why Woodhaven was failing. "When you get too locked into a set of beliefs, you can't see anything else."

I blew on the window, watching the fog cover it. I began to etch out my name, or at least the first few letters. The fog had lifted before I could write the letter 'g.'

"No magic, huh?" He opened his console and handed me my cell phone. "Well, how do you explain the fact that your phone called me, even though you had dropped it in the parking lot? Had I not gotten the call and heard you scream, well..." Shane scratched his head and blinked his eyes.

Was that how he had known I was in trouble? I had never asked.

"I had just programmed in your phone number," I replied, trying to come up with a logical answer. "When it hit the ground, it dialed you. Lucky coincidence on my part."

"Uncle Joe used to say there are no coincidences. He said there are forces in the world at work, whether we see them or not."

"That's the problem with coincidences," I said. "You can never prove them."

"You're jaded, Maggie. I'm not sure why, but it's kind of sad. I hope Eve hasn't become jaded, too."

Hearing him speak Eve's name darkened my mood. I turned the radio dial away from his hillbilly crying music. I found a station playing Metallica and I blasted it, mostly because I thought it would annoy him.

Instead, he started banging his head to the beat.

"I'm going to sleep," I said, closing my eyes.

Surprisingly, he kept the radio on the heavy metal station. We listened to songs from Van Halen and Motley Crew. Then 'For Those About to Rock I Salute You' came on. My eyes flipped open. Shane was drumming his fingers against the wheel.

"Please, turn this off," I said. But he didn't hear me. I sat up and repeated my request, this time louder. "Please, turn this off."

He gave me a curious look. "You picked the station."

"Turn this off now!"

Pop!

A spark shot from the radio and then it went quiet. Shane did a double take as he fiddled with the knobs. Nothing came on, not even static.

"You did this?" he asked, his face a mixture of fear and incredulousness.

I didn't respond.

"You *did* this," he repeated, a smile spreading across his face. "Maggie. What they say is true. You are––"

"Careful," I said, looking at him out of the corner of my eye.

"...Special," he concluded, shaking his head in disbelief. "I always knew Eve had 'something,' but it was never tangible. But this. I can't believe it."

"Coincidence."

"Yeah, right." He thought for a moment, scratching his head. "I've read about this on the internet. Electro-kinesis. You manipulate the energy of electrical devices like the radio and cell phone. It's a pretty rare gift..."

"The internet? Oh, then it has be true," I said dryly, pretending to bite on my nails.

I was angry at him, but I wasn't sure why. His references to Eve? His talk of Dark Root? His insistence that I was...*something?* And why was he so excited about me being special? Was he like Michael? Hoping to use my so-called powers for his own gain?

"I may be able to turn a radio off, or pop a light bulb once in a while," I snapped, my anger growing. "But I have no control over these things, they just happen. And maybe they really are all just coincidences. So no, Shane, I am not a *witch,* if that is the burning question you are dying to ask me..."

"I never called you a witch." He turned, giving me his full attention.

"Wilder, then."

He looked sorry for me and went to squeeze my hand, but I pulled back. No, he hadn't called me either of those things, but the words *wilder* and *witch* were my labels back in Dark Root. Labels I had tried to leave behind.

"I'm sorry," he said, staring back at the dark road before us. "I didn't mean anything by it."

I took a deep breath and nodded, accepting his apology. I knew I was being overly sensitive.

We had escaped the darkness of the forest, and had come to a large area where most of the trees had been cleared. Shane turned off his high-beams and we picked up our pace. Neither of us spoke, and with the radio off, the silence was painful.

Finally, our headlights caught a sign.

Welcome to Dark Root. Where Every Day Is Halloween.

Shane lifted his chin and hit the gas, ready to unload his troublesome cargo.

"Where we headed to?" Shane asked, as we drove down the back roads of Dark Root towards the downtown proper. He had a weariness to his voice, and I could tell he wanted to get home himself. We passed houses I recognized from my childhood, large Victorian structures, many dark and boarded over. Had they been that way before I left? Or had I been only one of many people who had fled the town?

"Do you know where Harvest Home is?" I asked.

Of course he had to know. Harvest Home was the largest house in Dark Root, and the only Bed and Breakfast in the area. At least it was seven years ago.

He nodded. "I kinda guessed you weren't going straight to your ma's. At least not until..."

He let his words trail off.

"...I have a few drinks," I finished for him.

He laughed at my joke, and I was glad. I knew that I had frustrated him on our ride and I was grateful for how he had saved me. I had a few triggers, namely magic and my mother, and he had pushed them. But I knew he hadn't meant to upset me.

"Bring back memories?" He relaxed as we headed onto Main Street. It was dark and hard to see, but I could feel that something wasn't right. The shops didn't look the same. I was going to ask him about that, but decided I could only take so much news in one sitting.

As we approached the intersection where Miss Sasha's Magick Shoppe sat, I looked down.

Shane had said Mother closed the shop, and I couldn't bear to look at it.

Shane relieved my guilt by pointing to the cafe across the street, where Delilah's Deli used to sit.

"There's my shop," he said. I could hear the pride in his voice. "...And my home. I have an apartment directly above it, in the attic."

Dip Stix Cafe sat quiet and unassuming, with only a hand-painted sign in front to let anyone know it existed at all.

I laughed, unable to help myself. "I've got to ask. Why did you name it Dip Stix?"

His eyes glowed mischievously in the dark. "That, my dear, is a secret. You will just have to come by and see for yourself."

I smiled. His enthusiasm was endearing, if a little dorky.

I squinted my eyes to get a better look. The building was the same, but the paint looked fresh and there were new, striped awnings over the windows and door. A welcome sight in rainy Oregon.

"Business good?" I asked, genuinely interested.

Shane's eyes took on a faraway look as he drove forward, leaving Main Street. "Could be better." He shrugged. "But I have the feeling my luck is about to change." He gave me a sideways look. "Next stop, Harvest Home."

He turned left onto a long, winding road.

"It will be a kick to have the gang together again," he said, bobbing his head. "I hope you do decide to stay. At least for awhile."

The road took a sharp right turn, and Shane followed it, turning smoothly. He must have driven this a few times. At the end of the road sat Harvest Home, the crown jewel of our town. It was supposedly built by Juliana Benbridge's sister, Corelia, in the early 1900's and still retained most of its original charms.

"My lady," he said, gesturing out the window as we pulled into the full view of the house.

Even in the dark, I could tell it was just as magnificent as I remembered. Painted an ocean blue that never seemed to fade, trimmed with white shingles and shudders, complete with a brick chimney and wraparound porch, it was a storybook house. It looked as pristine and out of place in Dark Root as I felt. Which made me love it all the more.

"Thanks," I said, wondering if he could sense the anxiety building inside of me.

I leaned forward, trying to peer through the windshield. It was late and everyone inside was probably sleeping. There were two cars in the driveway, a black Explorer and a maroon sedan. I wasn't sure which one was Merry's.

"Maybe I should come back in the morning," I said, though I had no idea where I would spend the night. Dark Root didn't have any motels.

"You should call someone," Shane said.

It was funny how easily I could forget about the benefits of technology after living in near seclusion for the last few years.

I was about to call Merry, when the front door opened and a figure emerged. Short, curvy, and bouncy. Merry.

She ran to me, giggling, pale hair flapping behind her like a curtain in the breeze. The flowers that lined the path perked up and the limbs of the trees bowed as she made her way down the cobblestone path. I thought about running to her, embracing her and spinning her around.

But I didn't. Instead, I stood at the car and waited for her to come to me.

"Maggie! Oh, Maggie, I missed you. I was so worried. We went to the bus station but you didn't come out when you were supposed to. Didn't you get my messages?"

I turned on my phone. Four new messages flashed across the screen.

"Sorry," I said, with a light shrug. "I like to be fashionably late."

"You are our mother's daughter," Merry said, grinning.

She took my hands, swinging them like she used to, when we played clapping games as children. Her hands were warm and I could feel that familiar tingle creep through my fingers, up my limbs, and course through my entire body. She was feeding me energy and probably taking in some of my exhaustion, as well.

I pulled my hands away before I poisoned her.

"This is Shane. He gave me a ride." I gave him a look that he hopefully caught. I didn't want anyone to know about the incident at the bar.

Shane extended a hand and Merry shook it gently. I watched with interest as he was jolted with her spark. I could almost see him glow.

"Pleasure's mine," he said, placing his other hand over the top of hers.

I resisted the urge to jump in. I had learned to stop saving my sister from vampires years ago. She didn't need me then. She certainly didn't need me now.

"We've met, Shane," she said, squeezing his hands. "When we were kids. You played with Eve."

"The geeky boy," I added.

Merry shot me a disapproving look and I flushed. Here I was, in her presence a mere three minutes, and already I was incurring things I would need to repent for.

"I remember you, too, Merry." Shane put his hands in his front pocket, then he turned to me. "You gonna be okay?"

He was looking for permission to go, so I let him off the hook.

"Yeah. I'll be fine."

"Okay, then. I'm off, ladies." He tipped an imaginary hat. "Dip Stix opens at nine in the morning, if you want to come by. I make a mean biscuits and gravy. Bring the whole family, of course." He turned, sauntering off to his vehicle.

"Cute." Merry said, as we watched him drive away. Her pale pink nightgown fluttered around her, though there was not a hint of wind. "Is he yours?"

I laughed. "Nope. Not even a little. I've sworn off men. All they do is break your heart and eat your junk food."

Merry looped her arm through mine and we practically skipped towards the house.

I had told Shane that there was no magic in Dark Root, but I was wrong. As long as Merry was here, there was magic. In my sister's presence, I was a kid again and I could believe in anything. My shield was falling, and by the time we got to the door, I was smiling so broadly my face hurt. I hadn't smiled like that in years.

"We going to wake Miss Rosa?" I asked, cautiously peeping in.

Miss Rosa, one of Mother's oldest friends and the owner of Harvest Home, had let us play here when we were children, but didn't like noise after 'certain hours.' Though I was glad to be here, I did wonder why Merry had chosen to stay here, instead of our own house or one of the motels in a neighboring town.

Most likely, it was as nostalgic for her as it was for me.

"Oh, Maggie, I thought you knew." Merry paused in the doorframe as the light from the stairwell cast a halo over her delicate face. "Miss Rosa is in a nursing home. The doctors don't give her long to live. Aunt Dora is looking after the place until they find a buyer. This might be the last chance we have to see Harvest Home before it's sold to a stranger."

Harvest Home sold? To a stranger?

The thought of Harvest Home being owned by someone other than Miss Rosa made me sick. Merry sensed my dismay and brightened.

"The good news is," she said, squeezing my hand. "We get to stay here for a few weeks, while we get Mom's place situated. One last trip down memory lane."

I nodded, not sharing in her enthusiasm.

Things were changing, and I didn't like it. I frowned, stepping into the house and closing the door behind me. Once inside, I looked around. It wasn't as dark as I had anticipated. Night-lights, lamps, and even an old candelabra helped to illuminate the main floor.

That was a relief. By day, Harvest Home was lovely.

By night, it was almost spooky.

The living room was huge, but not as large as I remembered. Maybe because my standards of *large* had changed since Woodhaven...or because childhood memories had a way of expanding places and people into giants in your mind.

But it was still pretty darn big.

To the right of the entrance was a set of ornate, red-velvet sofas that faced one another, accented by end tables covered in doilies and fake flowers in glass vases. A sleek, wooden, coffee table with lion's feet had been placed stoically between the sofas, speckled with glass coasters and a stack of Ladies' Home Journals. Built-in shelves covered the walls, stuffed with old books and the strange knick-knacks we had ogled as children, but were never allowed to touch. Miss Rosa claimed that most were antiques, some older than the house itself.

To the left, in a partially walled-off side room, was an elegant dining room table surrounded by thirteen high-backed chairs.

Three empty candelabras sat on the table and I remembered how they had once housed tall candles of various colors: reds, whites, violets, and blues. Merry and I had taken a few purple candles once and tried to conduct a fake séance.

Miss Rosa quickly reported our doings to our mother and we were forbidden from going to Harvest Home for an entire month.

"There are things out there," our mother chastised us. *"...That you children do not understand."*

Merry tapped my shoulder and pointed to a grand piano in the corner of the dining area.

I had been allowed to accompany Uncle Joe on the piano during holidays and special events, and though I knew I wasn't as good as he was, he always made a big deal about my talent. I felt a pang in my heart as I realized I would never play alongside him again.

"You still play?" Merry asked.

I shook my head. I had planned on playing at her wedding, but then she eloped.

There didn't seem to be much point after that.

The one new item in the room was a large, flat-screen TV. Two over-sized chairs were aimed in its direction, proof that Aunt Dora really did occupy this space now.

I could smell something delicious coming from the kitchen and my stomach growled in response.

Merry laughed, throwing her head back. "I saved you something from dinner. Come see."

She motioned for me to follow her into the kitchen, and I sat myself down at the small, round table. Merry removed a plate wrapped in foil from the oven. She pulled back the wrap to reveal two drumsticks covered in crumbs and fried in oil.

I was practically salivating. I hadn't had Aunt Dora's fried chicken since I was a kid. I picked up a leg, raised it in her honor, and took a big bite.

"With cooking like this, I can't believe our Aunt never married," I said.

Merry leaned over the table, propped up on elbows, and watched me finish every last bite. When I was done she gave me a warm smile.

"Good girl," she said, handing me a napkin.

"Want to talk now?" I asked, pushing the empty plate away. I was still in the dark about what had happened to our mother, and though I wasn't relishing this conversation, I knew it had to come.

"Not now," she said, lowering her eyes. "Let's rest up first and we can have a family conversation tomorrow. It's better that way." She came to me, practically pulling my limp body from the chair, and pushed me up the stairs.

"But I don't wanna go to bed, mommy," I teased, and she laughed. When we were kids, Eve and I called her mommy because she was always fussing after us. When we got a little older we dubbed her Mother Merry, a nickname she seemed to like.

Harvest Home had four themed bedrooms and I couldn't wait to see which one we were sleeping in.

"This is your room," she said, pointing towards a door that I remembered as the flora and fauna collection. An overly fluffy room in shades of powder pink and lilac purple. Not my favorite. I would have preferred the Midnight Oasis theme, but as long as I was there with Merry, I didn't care. I quietly opened the door and she gave me a quick hug.

"You're not sleeping here?" I asked, and she shook her head. I peered into the room and could see the silhouette of a sleeping body in the King-sized bed. "Eve got here before me?"

I should have known.

"Yes, several hours ago, in fact."

"What about her 'friend'? He's not sleeping in there, too?"

"His name is Paul, and I think he really is just a friend," Merry smiled. "...Much to Eve's chagrin. He seems like a nice guy, though. Drove her all the way here from New York. He's sleeping in the attic until we get a room cleaned up for him."

"The attic? That place gives me the heebie-jeebies."

"I was worried, too. But he just cleared out a space, blew up an air mattress, and went to bed. Acted like sleeping in an attic full of giant porcelain dolls was the most natural thing in the world. If Eve can hook this one, she should keep him. She might never find another guy who can put up with these sorts of eccentricities..."

"No kidding," I said.

That went for any of us, I supposed.

Merry brushed a strand of hair off of my shoulders. "We'll catch up tomorrow. I still have that surprise for you."

I smiled to reassure her. I would have relished snuggling under the covers with her all night, sharing secrets and catching up. Instead I was stuck with Eve.

I said goodnight to Merry and crept inside the bedroom.

Eve stirred under the blanket, but her steady breathing told me she was still asleep. I envied her. She could sleep through Armageddon if she needed to.

I quietly kicked off my shoes and wriggled out of my skirt, pulling off all of my long-sleeved shirts before crawling into bed. I should have brushed my teeth first, I thought, but I was too tired to find my toothbrush. A yucky mouth in the morning was a small price to play for a good night's sleep.

I slid under the blanket, mentally marked the invisible line that separated my side of the bed from hers, fluffed my pillow, and lay my head down for the night. I heard Eve take a deep breath beside me and I held still so I wouldn't wake her.

But it was too late.

"Sissy," she said, yawning. "You're late."

"Sorry about that."

"No problem. It gave me and Merry a chance to hang out."

She gave me a kiss on the shoulder and draped an arm across my waist. Her smell was familiar, an earthy scent.

I just laid there, still and unmoving, waiting for her to fall back to sleep.

At last, her breathing deepened.

I inched my way out from under her arm and onto the edge of the bed. Sleep hit me like a punch in the face and I succumbed to it, knowing I would need all my energy for the things still to come.

EIGHT

MAGGIE MAY

HARVEST HOME, DARK ROOT, OREGON
JUNE, 1994

MAGGIE SAT FROZEN IN THE UPSTAIRS HALLWAY, her head turning
robotically from one side to the other, trying to decide on her next move.
She could hear footsteps plodding up the wooden staircase behind her
and she cocked her head to determine if it was one set or two.

Her pursuer's breathing was excited and labored, and like her,
looking for a place to rest.

Maggie spotted Merry standing in the hallway and she ran for
her sister. Maggie took her hand, and the two girls moved through
the corridor together, passing doors with various words chiseled on
plaques. Some rooms Maggie was familiar with, while others were
forbidden.

"Where we going?" Merry asked, her face scrunching up in her
expression of seriousness. "I'm tired."

"We can't stop now," Maggie insisted, dragging her sister behind
her.

They opened each door as they passed, peeking in for possible
hiding places.

Each room presented its own set of challenges. Too small. Not enough furniture. No escape route. Occupied. Had they been back at their own house, they might have had an easier time figuring out a plan. Maggie knew every nook, corner and cranny of Sister House, but Harvest Home was still a foreign land.

"There!" Merry pointed to a string that dangled from the ceiling.

They looked up to see the rectangular outline of the attic door.

"That's not a good idea," Maggie said. She was afraid, but she didn't want her sister to know. "You might get hurt."

Merry clucked her tongue. "We never get hurt." She rubbed Maggie's arm and a warm, soothing energy crept through her body. Behind them, a set of wild, heavy footsteps let them know they were still being followed.

Feeling helpless, Maggie pulled the rope.

A heavy wooden door fell forward, unrolling itself, barely missing their heads as it dropped. The footsteps grew heavier, beating down upon them like a wild horse. Merry scrambled upwards and Maggie followed cautiously behind, keeping watch.

"It's dark," Merry said, surveying the room.

Maggie swallowed, allowing only her head and arms to enter the blackness. A tiny round window high up on the vaulted walls, obscured by cobwebs and dirt, was the only source of light.

"Help me get the ladder up," Maggie said, pulling herself fully into the attic. The footsteps had momentarily ceased, and Maggie realized the follower was probably scouring one of the rooms. Time was short. "Quick!"

The two girls wrestled with the ladder. "It's heavy," Merry said, her breathing deepening as her chubby fingers locked around the rungs.

Maggie nodded and wondered if it was too late.

But with one final tug the ladder acquiesced, folding itself as if by magic, and the girls whooped victoriously.

The moonlight from the window fell across a clump of figures near Maggie's right foot. She jumped back instinctively. Could that be a pile of bodies? Curiosity won out over fear and she touched one, expecting to feel something clammy and spongy, something decomposing. The object was dry and smooth.

She grinned. These were not bodies. They were giant, porcelain dolls.

A scuttling in the corner caused them to yelp.

"Probably just rats," Merry said.

Maggie grimaced. Her sister may love all animals, but she didn't. She sat down on the cold floor and covered her knees with her skirt, Merry following suit.

"Let's try and be quieter," Merry whispered.

Maggie looked around, trying to make out shadows in the dark. Long, formless shapes danced on the walls. "Do you think this room is haunted?"

Merry thought for a moment. "I don't think so. But even if it was, Mama says ghosts won't hurt anyone. They just want someone to talk to."

Of course, neither Mother nor Merry had probably been visited as Maggie had. The spirits came mostly when she slept, and only a scream or the flip of a light switch would send them away. She huddled closer to her sister.

"I think it's almost over," Merry said, nodding.

Maggie reached for her sister's hair, finding silver-yellow tresses so long they fell past her lap and splayed across the floor. She coiled them around her hand like spaghetti on a fork. They glittered in the darkness like the silken strands of a butterfly's cocoon. Maggie had just began to relax, when a loud, sudden noise made her jump.

The room flooded with light as the attic door fell open.

Maggie and Merry caught their breath, clinging to each other, small hands digging into each other's arms. They watched and waited as a figure emerged.

Maggie could hold it no longer and she let out a pitiful scream.

"Guys? Where are you?" It was Eve's voice.

Maggie could make out the silhouette of her sister's lithe body and *long, straight hair. She chastised herself for being silly.*

Merry stood up and beckoned. "Here we are, Eve! Come hide with us."

Eve scrambled to join them, not bothering to shut the hatch behind her. Maggie and Eve sat on either side of Merry like bookends.

"I was so scared you were caught!" Even in a whisper Merry's voice was a bundle of excitement.

"I almost was, but then I escaped." Eve explained.

Of course, she did, Maggie thought.

Eve always got away from everything unscathed.

The reunion was short-lived, however, as new sounds emerged— —a trampling of footsteps falling on the hallway below. Maggie could hear Merry suck in her breath as she grabbed her sister's hands. The three of them folded in on one another, waiting for their doom.

"Time's up," a voice said, as a short, slender figure made its way into the attic hideaway. "Mom says it's time to go..."

Ruth Anne stood before them, hand on hip.

"Shane's asleep on the couch," Ruth Anne said. "He gave up looking for you twenty minutes ago." She peered into the room and shook her head, an indication that she was not impressed. "Let's get out of here, before they open another bottle of wine."

"That was fun," Merry said, scampering down the ladder. "Ruth Anne always finds us, though."

Maggie agreed. Ruth Anne may not have any magic, but she had smarts.

In the hallway, the Counsel of Seven waited for the girls: Uncle Joe, Uncle Leo, Aunt Dora, Miss Rosa, Miss Narissa, Miss Lettie, and their mother.

"Darlings!" Miss Sasha said, running over and sweeping them up in her arms. "Mommy was so worried about you! Harvest Home is a big place and the spirits are restless here. But I'm glad you are safe..."

"We were just playing hide and seek," Eve explained. "Shane was supposed to find us."

Uncle Joe knelt down, producing three lollipops from his pocket. He took Maggie's hand and guided her down the stairs to the main room, while the others followed behind. Maggie spotted Shane snoring on one of the red couches. No boy could ever beat the Maddock girls. If he were awake she would stick her tongue out at him, but as it was, she would have to settle for teasing him about it later.

"Rosa," Miss Sasha said, taking the hand of her friend. "As always, I've had a marvelous time." Miss Sasha licked her index finger and held it up, pausing. "Looks like rain is coming. We must hurry home."

Uncle Joe cleared his throat and shot Sasha a look that said there was still unfinished business to attend to.

"Oh, all right, Joseph," their mother said, smiling at her daughters. "One more minute then. Girls, go say goodbye to Shane while you are waiting."

Eve and Merry proceeded to 'wake' Shane up by thumping him with throw pillows from one of the sofas. Ruth Anne plopped herself down in a chair and removed a paperback from her purse. Maggie stayed where she was, pretending to read a songbook while she eavesdropped on the adults.

"We've already had three sightings in the last year," Uncle Joe said.

"That doesn't mean she is stalking us, Joe. Really, I thought you people had more sense than that." Miss Sasha sounded amused.

"What type of people are you referring to?" Joe asked, less amused. "Gay people?"

"Now you really are being silly. I could care less about your orientation. I meant warlocks."

Joe accepted the answer and forced a laugh.

Miss Sasha continued. "Now, let's stop working ourselves up into a tizzy and relax. The Circle will not be broken."

"And you feel confident the girls are safe?" Uncle Leo asked.

Maggie stole a peek and saw both Aunt Dora and her mother nodding.

"I am their mother. Of course, they are safe. Neither Larinda nor any member of her tribe would be able to get past me."

The idea that they might be in danger made the hairs on Maggie's arm stand up. She turned to see if her sisters were hearing any of this, but they were preoccupied with their tasks.

"There are only four," Uncle Joe continued. "We need seven."

"Shall I hatch out a few more, then?" Miss Sasha tossed her hands into the air.

"Don't look at me," said Aunt Dora. "I said I would help with their care, not with the incubation. It's been a long time since my oven worked."

Aunt Dora's words were met with easy laughter, breaking the tension.

"We'll get there," Miss Sasha reassured them. "These things take time. Besides, we aren't even sure where Larinda is. I heard one of the women struck out on her own. That could be her."

"If that's the case, she's even more dangerous."

Maggie recognized Miss Lettie's deep voice.

"...She wants it, and badly," Miss Lettie went on. "As long as she is out there roaming around, we need to be extra careful. The girls are only half grown, and the circle is already beginning to crack."

"Well, no use worrying about it tonight," Miss Sasha said, reaching for her shawl. "Remember, the girls are safe, so long as the seven remain intact."

"Alright," Uncle Joe consented. "We've come too far now. And far be it from me to question a real...witch."

With that, Miss Sasha called for her daughters.

They gathered in the entry and said their goodbyes.

When they finally set out on the long walk home, it was approaching midnight. The dirt path was visible with the help of the moon, but it seemed to go on forever. There were things out there looking for us, Maggie thought, as she reflected on her mother's words.

She walked just behind her mother, listening to a tune Miss Sasha hummed which Maggie recognized as 'Maggie May.' Her sisters *followed, parade-style, with Ruth Anne dawdling far behind as she tried to read a book by the light of the moon.*

They didn't seem worried at all. Maybe Maggie wouldn't tell them about what she had heard. Maybe it was a secret she needed to keep.

"Girls," their mother said, when they finally reached their home. "Would you like a new baby sister?"

Eve and Merry clapped.

Maggie narrowed her eyes, and Ruth Anne shook her head and tromped up to her bedroom, slamming the door behind her.

HARVEST HOME, DARK ROOT, OREGON
SEPTEMBER, 2013

I awoke to a hazy sunlight that filtered through the rose-colored curtains of the Flora and Fauna room. It cast a majestic orange halo over my bed and for a moment I felt weightless and ethereal. I lay in bed and reflected on my latest dream. Shane was there, and Mother's friends, and once again the ominous Larinda had come up.

I rubbed my temples, trying to make sense of it all, but my thoughts were interrupted by the sound of a chair being pulled across a wooden floor.

I turned to see Eve sitting at the vanity, applying lipstick.

"Finally," she said, her eyes sparkling. I caught her reflection smiling in the mirror as she put on large hoop earrings. "We thought you'd never wake up, you lazy bones." Eve spun on her stool, placing her hands between her knees. "You have a visitor."

"I do?" I rubbed my eyes and sat up, glancing at the alarm clock on the nightstand. 9:55. I was surprised I had slept so long. I was usually up with the sunrise for morning meditation.

I became aware of a dull ache in my wrists and I rubbed them, noticing a red bruise forming around my right one. Images of my assault the night before rushed back, but I pushed them away. I had gotten out safely. That was all that mattered.

"It's so good to be home, isn't it?" Eve said, tilting her pointy chin in the direction of the sunbeam and closing her eyes. "I missed Oregon. I know I complained about the weather when we were young, but I would take the rain in place of a New York winter any day." She reached overhead, her t-shirt rising up with her, and I noticed that something about Eve was different.

She caught me gawking and smiled.

"You like?" she asked, pushing out her chest. "I got them done about three years ago. All the actresses in New York get boob jobs. You're practically shunned if you don't." She smiled easily, as if this was the most ordinary statement in the world. "Anyways, Shane Doler requests the presence of your company...if you can manage to get out of bed."

Eve returned to her primping, combing her hair, applying rouge, and painting her fingernails. I watched curiously. It had been a long time since I had seen a woman preen. I caught my own reflection in the mirror, pale-faced and wild-haired.

I needed a shower.

"I hardly know Shane. Why is he here?" I got out of bed and smoothed the comforter into place. I didn't have to do a good job. Aunt Dora would remake it anyways.

Eve shrugged. "You knew him pretty well when we were kids. Did they do a memory wipe on you, back at the cult?"

"No," I said, blinking slowly. "But I wish they would have."

Eve laughed, unperturbed. "Anyways, I thought he was here to see me, but it appears I was wrong." She shook her head at the absurdity of it. "Who knew?"

"Maybe he likes natural women," I said as Eve applied another coat of lacquer across her cheeks.

"No man likes natural women, Maggie. They just think they do. Give them the choice of two women, one who has taken the time to fix herself up, and one who looks like she just got done working on a farm, and he will chose the 'fixed up' one every time. It's called sexual selection."

"Then why are there so many farmers' wives?" I countered.

It was a weak point, but it did the job. She shook her head and let the conversation go.

"Anyways, are you coming down?" Eve pushed some things into her purse and went to the door.

"I need to shower first. Tell everyone I'll be down soon."

Eve winked and left the room.

Her long hair grazed her perfectly round bottom and I felt suddenly self-conscious. My mother swore that every woman was beautiful, but even as a kid I knew that some were more beautiful than others. I had seen the way every boy in town ran after Eve since the day she turned fourteen. The only time I had ever 'beaten' her was the day Michael walked into our mother's shop and chose me. And that turned out really well.

If she knew how that ended, I'd never hear the end of it.

I walked into the bathroom, undressed, and checked my body in the mirror. There were a few small bruises along the side of my neck and my back was red and purple. I searched through the cupboard and found a bag of Epson Salts. Aunt Dora swore by them, claiming they could cure just about any ailment that plagued you, inside or out.

I turned on the water, poured in some salt, then gingerly stepped into the tub. It stung at first but after a few minutes the salts did their job, relaxing and soothing my aches and pains.

After my bath I dressed in another long skirt and an over-sized sweater, something to hide all my bruises. I left my hair loose to cover up the marks on my neck, then applied a few drops of lotion to my face. Finally, I put on the crystal Michael had given me, tucking it into my shirt. I needed a reminder that once upon a time I had been somebody.

Once upon a time I wasn't just another daughter of Dark Root.

With nothing more to do, I went down the stairs to see what awaited me.

I passed through the living room and peeked into the kitchen. For such a big house, the room was quite small, nothing like the industrial-sized galley we had at Woodhaven. Even so, it was cozy and clean and there were fresh flowers in the windowsill. Blue-checkered curtains hung on the window that overlooked the garden. I could smell coffee brewing and bacon sizzling. And I could hear a steady stream of pleasant conversations as I entered the room.

Around the breakfast table sat a gathering of people I recognized: Eve, Merry, Aunt Dora and Shane. There was also a new face, a young male who sat opposite Eve. That must be her 'friend.' He was tapping on the table with his fork and staring absently out the window.

"Der she is." Aunt Dora dropped her dish cloth and charged towards me. "My Maggie girl! Yer Auntie missed ya so much."

She hugged me and I sunk into the heavy folds of her flesh. It was like climbing into a soft bed after a long day.

"Yer pretty as ever," she said, taking a step back to inspect me. "Still got da red hair I see. That's the Celt comin' out in ya."

"You told me before that it was Irish."

"Celt, Irish, Portuguese. It's all da same."

Everyone laughed and I gave my aunt a warm smile. It was as if no time at all had passed between us.

"Good morning, Maggie," Shane said. He was holding a coffee cup to his chin, letting the steam waft up to his nose. "I'm glad you woke up. I was about to go check on you."

I looked at him, hoping he hadn't told anyone about the previous evening. He smiled and almost imperceptibly shook his head, letting me know that my secret was still safe.

I gave him a grateful smile, which Eve caught.

"She's filled out, hasn't she?" Eve said, her eyes resting on my waist. "Soy milk must be agreeing with you."

"Not as much as ya have, Missy," Aunt Dora said, nodding towards Eve's new bosom. Eve surprised me by blushing and covering her chest with her arms. Aunt Dora winked at me, then went to stir something on

106

the stove.

"We've all changed," Merry said, handing us each a plate with a biscuit.

Aunt Dora followed, ladling out globs of sticky white gravy over the top.

I took a bite, wondering how many of Michael's food laws I was breaking. A surge of sadness hit me as I realized it didn't matter anymore. I was no longer a member of Woodhaven.

Fuck Michael, I thought, sinking my teeth deep into the biscuit. I was a free woman now. I could eat anything I wanted.

"Mmmm," I moaned. "Aunt Dora, this is so good." I devoured it.

Merry refilled my plate.

"I can' take credit fer dem," Aunt Dora said. "Der's yer man." She pointed to Shane who was quietly watching me with a smile on his face.

"I told you I make a mean biscuits and gravy," he said, folding his hands together. "These were left over from the breakfast rush. Was hoping you ladies would have made it over on your own, but I see I have to entice you. Now you know what you're missing."

"You have a rush?" I asked, surprised.

"I get a construction crowd around 5:30 in the morning on weekdays. On the weekends its mostly older people passing through town on their way to church. Then they magically disappear and I have the rest of the day to ponder my place in the universe."

"These are amazing," I admitted, finishing my second biscuit and looking around for more. When I realized they were gone my mouth formed a pout.

"I usually only serve them on Sundays." Shane stood and pushed in his chair. "But if you give me some advance notice, I'd be happy to whip them up any morning of your choosing. Gives me something to do."

Merry wiped her hands on a dish towel and gave him a sisterly hug. "If I'm right," she said, looking up at him with her big, blue eyes. "That's Uncle Joe's recipe, but tweaked. What have you done differently?"

"That, my dear," he said with a grin. "...Is a secret. If I told you, then you might open a competing business. With all the talent and beauty in this room, I'd be out of work in a week." He spread his palms apologetically.

"Okay, be that way," Merry laughed, gathering up the plates on the table. "Far be it from me to deprive a man of his livelihood. I will just go back to being a lowly dishwasher."

I jumped up to help her and Eve followed suit. Soon we had the whole table cleared while Aunt Dora directed, "Put dem on the top shelf, girls." "Careful, those plates are very old."

"Maggie," Eve said, when we had put away the last dish. "This is Paul." She walked over to the quiet man and put her hands on his shoulders, giving him a massage. "...Sorry, I forgot to introduce you. He's a friend from New York and an amazing musician. We met a few years ago and have been joined at the hip ever since."

I looked Paul over, giving him a more thorough appraisal.

He was young, maybe twenty-five, and thin. His dirty blonde hair was slicked back into something between a Mohawk and a pompadour. His eyes were so blue they were almost black. His cheeks were thin but chiseled. If you could get past the greasy hair, he was good-looking, almost handsome. He nodded a greeting at me but didn't speak.

"Care to accompany me around town?" Eve asked him, leaning over to wrap her arms around his chest.

Paul scratched at the back of his ear. "I don't know. I don't really do small towns well."

I laughed in agreement. "I hear you on that."

He locked his cobalt eyes onto mine and I felt suddenly warm.

Eve tightened her grip on him. "Oh, pretty please. I just have to show you around Dark Root."

Paul hesitated. "I'm not sure. Are you going, Maggie?"

I was so taken aback by his directness––especially in front of Eve–– that I didn't know what to say. Apparently, I wasn't the only one. Merry, Shane, and Eve all turned in my direction.

"I, um..." I responded, looking to Merry for help. She smiled ruefully, letting me know I was on my own for this one. I could feel Eve's eyes pierce me.

Luckily, Shane spoke up.

"We can all go," he said. "I wanted to show you guys Dip Stix, anyway. It's not much but I call it home."

We all agreed this was a good idea, except for Aunt Dora who wanted to catch up on her television. Eve's energy bristled as I made my way past her, but I ignored it. I was battle-weary from the evening before, and too tired to get tangled up in Eve's drama.

"Mommy, I'm hungry."

The small voice from the stairwell made me turn. It was a young girl, maybe five or six years old, with white-blonde hair and eyes a cornflower blue. She wore a yellow flowered nightgown and rubbed her eyes as she made her way to the table.

"I saved you a biscuit."

My mouth fell open when I realized it was Merry who answered. She caught my confused look and laughed.

"I told you I had something for you," she said. "This is my daughter, Mae. You're an auntie."

Mae looked at me with round eyes as she nibbled on her biscuit. No one else seemed surprised. I guess they had already met her.

"Your daughter? Mae?" I repeated, incredulous. "Spelled M-A-E?"

"Yes, silly. She's named after you." Merry turned towards Paul and Shane to explain. "Maggie's middle name is Mae. Mother was a huge Rod Stewart fan."

"'Maggie Mae,'" Paul said, bobbing his head and smiling. "Rod Stewart. I think I'm gonna like your mother."

Merry looked at me, waiting for a response. I had never been angry with her in my life, but I was upset now. She had never mentioned that I had a niece.

"Why didn't you tell me?" I demanded. "I could have made calls, sent Christmas cards...something." I looked at Mae again. Her hair was smooth and sleek, cascading over the back of her chair as she ate, a miniature version of her mother.

She was beautiful.

"Oh, Maggie, I tried," Merry explained. "But you were pretty much unreachable. And you never..." She let the words trail off, not wanting to hurt my feelings.

But I knew what she was going to say. She may have married Frank at eighteen, but it was me who had disappeared without a forwarding address. I looked down, suddenly ashamed.

A soft touch on the tips of my fingers brought me back. Mae placed her perfect, tiny hand in mine. In seconds, I felt calmer.

She had her mother's gift.

"I have a niece," I said, squeezing her hand. "A niece named Mae."

Mae made a face like she had just bitten into a lemon. "I don't like to be called Mae," she informed me, as she wiped the crumbs from her lap and onto the floor. "My dad calls me June Bug because that's the month I was born and..." She dashed from the kitchen and into the living room, returning with a jar filled with crawling insects. "...I collect bugs. Mostly lady bugs, but I like them all."

"We're hoping she'll outgrow it," Merry said, as June Bug placed her jar of critters in the kitchen windowsill next to the flowers. "Frank says that it's important that we encourage her hobbies, even if I don't like them."

I resisted rolling my eyes.

Frank was a 'child psychologist' and I had never had much regard for him. After all, how many child psychologists in their thirties marry girls just out of high school? The memory of him taking Merry away when she was barely eighteen angered me. I had told her that I was happy for her then, but I hadn't meant it. And I didn't like to hear his name now.

But it was her life and I was going to support her decisions, even if it killed me.

"Everyone got sweaters?" Merry asked, and we nodded like obedient children. My genuine alpaca sweater, a gift from the Woodhaven lost and found, was warm, if a bit grungy.

Eve scrutinized my outfit and wrinkled her nose but said nothing.

We lined up at the door and Aunt Dora called to us from her recliner. "Give me a call after ya visit yer mother."

I froze, having forgotten that visiting my mother was the real reason I was back in Dark Root, or at least my pretense. But it would have to be done.

Outside, we filed into two separate cars. Merry rode with Eve and Paul in his black Explorer, while June Bug squeezed in between myself and Shane in the front seat of his pickup truck.

"Can we have ice cream?" she asked, looking from me to him.

"Sure, we can," I said, hoping I wasn't stepping on Merry's toes. I knew how parents were about junk food, and Merry, who had never been a fan of processed foods, might be particularly strict.

"Just so happens I have some vanilla ice cream at Dip Stix." Shane started up the truck and we followed Paul's Explorer out of the driveway and over the bumps and cracks of a road that had seen better days.

"Yay!" June Bug squealed. "Mommy never lets me have ice cream."

"Oops." I looked at Shane and grimaced.

I was going to be in trouble with my older sister but it was worth it to feel June Bug put her head on my shoulder.

For a moment, life was good.

I had thought that Main Street looked different the night before, but without the cover of darkness to soften the blow, the town looked almost abandoned.

Many of the shops I had grown up with––the book store, the hardware store, the clothing store––were closed. Curtains were drawn, lights were off, doors were shut. And the businesses that remained opened––the Candy Corn, The Haunted Dark Root Tour Company, and Costumes Etc.––had few or no customers.

"Where is everyone?" I asked, turning my head from one side of the street to the other. "This is fall, the height of the tourist season. Dark Root looks like a ghost town...excuse the pun."

Shane's hands tightened around the wheel. "Sorry, Mags," he offered, but said no more.

June Bug sat between us, her mouth pursed in concentration as she took in the sights.

As we drove towards the apex of Main Street, I could see Dip Stix. Except for the name change and the new awnings, it looked like the restaurant I had grown up with. I took a deep breath, relieved. Not everything had changed.

"Is that Grandma's shop?" June Bug pointed to our left and my eyes followed, afraid of what I might see. My heart sank. The main window, the one I had spent many years of my life staring out of, was covered in sheets of paper, announcing that the shop permanently closed.

"What happened?" Though I had spent my youth trying to leave Dark Root, I never wanted the town to die. It should have been the one place in the world that time couldn't catch. "I feel like I'm in a parallel Universe. Surely all this couldn't have happened in just a few years?"

"It's turned into a regular Potterville," Shane said, pulling the truck into an empty parking spot in front of his diner. "I'm surprised Dip Stix gets any customers at all, but we have a few. Still..." His voice trailed off and I knew he wasn't convinced that Dip Stix was here for the long haul.

"Mama always talks about this town." June Bug looked at me, an expression on her face more adult than child, like she had access to knowledge the rest of us could never touch. "She tells me stories about it, about when she grew up here. She said that I would love it, too."

"Do you?" I asked, hopefully. Though I hadn't been around many children, I remembered from my own childhood that kids loved bizarro things, like leprechauns and giraffes.

"No. I want to go home."

I squeezed her hand. I couldn't blame her. This was the town that time forgot.

A ball of newspaper rolled before us, like a tumbleweed in a Western movie. I checked the streets again, noting all the litter on the ground. In my youth, I had never seen so much as a cigarette butt on the sidewalks.

"I'm not happy about this," I said, knowing I had no right to complain. Who was I to come back after seven years and be pissed off that things had changed?

We sat in the truck. I couldn't bring myself to open the door.

"It's like no one cares about this place anymore," I said.

"Well, Maggie Mae," Shane said, smiling. "It's not uncommon for small towns to fall apart once industry dies or its young people move away in search of better..." He gave me a wry look. "...Opportunities. It happens."

"But what about the tourists? Why aren't there people here?"

"From what I can gather, once you girls moved away, your mother just gave up and the rest of the town followed. You Maddocks were the cogs and gears that made this place run."

I looked down at my lap, ashamed. "I just can't believe the shop is closed."

Shane shrugged, trying to play diplomat. "Uncle Joe said your mother hired a girl to work there for a while, but it still fell apart. She couldn't bring in the customers like you girls did."

I laughed at the irony. "I think Eve and I scared off more customers than we brought in."

"Don't blame yourself, Maggie. Your mother got old and sick. Her health started going, along with her mind." He gave me a sympathetic look and pressed his lips together, saying no more. If his goal was to make me feel better, he was doing a terrible job.

June Bug yawned, unbuckled her seat belt, and curled up into my side. She closed her eyes and within minutes her breathing deepened. I lowered my voice.

"Why are you here Shane? What's in it for you?"

He closed his eyes briefly. When he reopened them I saw a spark that wasn't there before. "I'm an optimist. I loved this place when I was a kid. When Uncle Joe left me the diner in his will, I decided to give it a go. I didn't have much of a home growing up..." He choked, covering his mouth with this fist. "...This was always home."

He peered at the empty road ahead of us through the windshield.

"I know this sounds cliché," he said. "But if we all work together, we can turn things around. We just have to get your mother's shop up and running again, and start talking to some of the other business owners around here..."

June Bug was now snoring on my shoulder. I cupped my hand loosely over her ear, responding to him in a harsh whisper. "In case you've forgotten since last night, I'm not staying." I shook my head wildly. "This is only a temporary stop for me. Don't try and rope me into this."

"No, I haven't forgotten. Was just hoping you would change your mind when you saw all this. You could be of some real help."

"Listen, I spent my whole childhood trying to move away from this town. I'm not about to make it my permanent residence."

"Move away or run away?"

I shook my head. He was unbelievable. "Call it what you will, but I'm leaving in a few days. Don't get too attached."

"And where are you going? Back to California?"

I still hadn't formulated that plan yet. But it didn't matter. I had left once without knowing where I was going, and I could do it again. And this time I had close to a thousand bucks on me to make the trip.

"Not California. Maybe Texas or Arizona. Someplace warm."

"Will you stay for a while anyways? Just to see how things go?"

I slumped against the side of the door, depressed. My hand dropped away from June Bug's ear and she stirred next to me. "Again, I don't know. Can't we just take things one day at a time for now? I haven't even been back to my real home yet. God knows what waits for me there."

"Same old Maggie," Shane said, his face both incredulous and sad. He removed the key from the ignition and opened the door as Paul's car pulled in behind us.

"Took them long enough," I grumbled. "They must have taken the scenic route."

I opened my door and got out, then shook June Bug carefully awake. She yawned, smiled, and offered me her arms. I lifted her out of the vehicle and set her on the sidewalk.

"Well," Shane said, regaining his cheerful composure. "Ready to see my little contribution to Dark Root's booming economy?" He gave me a sideways grin as he made his way towards Dip Stix and unlocked the door.

It was dim inside. He flipped the light and June Bug and I followed him in.

Delilah's Deli, aka Dip Stix Cafe, looked exactly as it had ten years ago. Red and white checkered curtains, beige tablecloths, metal fold-up chairs and square tables topped with glass vases and real flowers. The wooden floor was worn, but clean enough to make out my reflection when I looked down. The small counter where the register and candy dish were located was fingerprint free. The room was immaculate, if dated, and I felt a wave of gratitude towards Shane for keeping up the place. Something from my childhood had remained intact.

"I see you kept the artwork," I teased, motioning towards the dozens of lacquered Elvis plaques and commemorative plates that covered the walls.

Uncle Joe had found the first two at a local estate sale and thought they would add some color to his otherwise sparse walls. But once he started putting them up, others contributed to the collection and soon the entire restaurant was covered in Elvis images in various stages of weight gain and age. It was a long-running joke in Dark Root that one needn't go to Graceland to see Elvis; you only had to go to Delilah's Deli.

"I'm thinking of taking them down." Shane scratched his head and looked around the room. "I'm beginning to feel like I'm being watched."

"Oh, you can't," I laughed. He was about to protest so I added, "At least keep a few. Promise?" I smiled sweetly and batted my eyelashes.

The result must have been comical rather than sultry because Shane burst out laughing like it was the funniest thing he had ever seen.

"Well, when you ask like that, I suppose I could keep a few up, to honor Uncle Joe. But I do think this place needs some updating. We won't attract many younger people here with this kind of décor. I was hoping you ladies might be able to assist with Feng Shui-ing up the place."

"Maybe," I said noncommittally. I did like to decorate. "I guess I could help out while I'm here."

June Bug, who had been holding my hand, slipped away to hide under one of the tables, just as her mother and I used to when we were kids.

Shane stroked his chin, considering. "I'll take what I can get. If you have any ideas at all for this place, I'm listening."

I glanced into the back room, just beyond the kitchen area, where there were boxes and bins shoved into every corner. The cleanliness of the place extended only throughout the main room.

"It would be easier to burn the place down and rebuild than to try and get rid of all this clutter," I observed.

"Maybe." Shane raised both eyebrows playfully. "How are your arson skills?"

The front door flew open and a sharp gust of cold wind hit my cheeks.

"We made it!" Eve entered the restaurant, arms overhead like she were arriving at a party. She had somehow changed clothes and was now wearing a pair of sleek, black leggings, knee-high boots, and a grey sweater with a fur-lined collar. Her dark hair looked extra shiny.

I must have been so preoccupied with her newly-enhanced cleavage earlier that I hadn't noticed she now had bangs.

"Mommy!" June Bug crawled out from under the table and raced towards her mother, who scooped her up in her arms and spun her around.

"Sorry for the delay," Merry said, after putting June Bug down and removing her brown leather gloves. "Our fashionista sister made us turn around so she could change clothes." Merry playfully rolled her eyes.

116

"You never know when you're going to run into a really cute guy." Eve smiled as Paul wandered in. He took off his knit beanie and immediately began inspecting the Elvis memorabilia.

"Cool," he said, pointing to a clock in the shape of Elvis's face. The clock wasn't working, and the small hand was permanently pointing up Elvis's nose. Paul made his way to the next in line, a wooden plaque depicting Elvis in a solid white jumpsuit. "Bad ass. This one's from *Viva Las Vegas*. Only Elvis could have pulled that look off..."

"You're into Elvis, huh?" I asked, the corner of my mouth curling up into a smile. Eve sure could pick them.

"Elvis was the king of rock and roll." Paul spoke with a confidence that said his statement was an irrefutable truth, one so infallible that the Universe would collapse in on itself if it was ever disproven.

I was about to argue that Elvis was a bloated, overrated, drug addict when Shane, sensing a confrontation, stepped in.

"Take the clock," he said to Paul. Then he turned to me. "Step one in the Feng Shui process."

"No fricken way!" Paul looked like he had just been told he'd won the lottery.

He carefully removed the clock from the wall and wrapped it in paper napkins, then dug a pen out of his back pocket and wrote PAUL on it in capital letters, just in case anyone else had designs on the artifact.

"Well, after that depressing tour of Dark Root, I'm happy to see this place hasn't changed much." Eve inspected the cafe, sniffing at the air. "Even smells the same." She peeked her nose into the kitchen. "Ah, the gravy vat."

I could hear her opening drawers and pulling out silverware and I followed her in. She was dipping a spoon in the gravy and eating it like soup. I took a spoon and joined her. Even without biscuits it was delicious.

"Girls!" Merry said, horrified. "That's disgusting. You're contaminating the whole pot."

Shane laughed. "Don't worry. That was from this morning. I was going to get rid of it, anyways."

"Yeah, Merry." I teased her. "It's from the morning. We are just making sure it doesn't go to waste."

Eve offered Merry a ladle of her own.

"What the hell," Merry said.

I imagined that Shane found the sight amusing, the three of us eating straight gravy out of his pot, but I didn't care. I realized I might be on the road soon, where gravy was hard to come by. I was going to get it while the getting was good.

Shane went to a sink full of dirty dishes and turned on the water, squeezing in a shot of dish soap. The water foamed and he tested the heat with his hand.

"Normally, I have this all cleaned up by now, but I was in a hurry to see you guys." He blushed and looked surprisingly like that dorky kid I was starting to remember from childhood. "Just don't tell the Health Department. They might take away my gravy card."

"Your secret is safe with us," I said, scraping what was left of the gravy from the bottom of the pot.

Merry dipped her hands in the dish water, then wiped them off with a paper towel. "I think the powers that be have bigger fish to fry than Dip Stix, Shane. Like harassing our family."

I gave Merry a quizzical look but she nodded towards June Bug who was playing near the kitchen entrance.

"Anyways," Merry said, changing the subject. "What else do you serve here, besides your amazing biscuits and gravy?"

Shane dried the last dish and put it away in a cupboard. He then opened a drawer and produced a stack of paper menus that he handed out to each of us.

"Everything on this menu." He stood taller, extending his chest like Superman.

In addition to biscuits, there were also chips, bread sticks, pretzels, french fries, and taquitos.

"This menu is a list of appetizers," I said. "No wonder you don't get

118

many customers."

"Not appetizers. These are all things you can dip. Hence the name, Dip Stix Cafe." He tapped the side of his temple twice. "Patrons get their choice of something to dip, and something to dip into. Read the back."

I flipped the menu and saw a list that read, *Dip Stix Famous Dipping Sauces: spinach, cheese, salsa, marinara, guacamole, and gravy.*

"I haven't added the bean dip yet," Shane said. "It's a new creation and my best so far. You're going to love it."

It was a nice idea, and in a city this might have gone over, but Dip Stix was the only restaurant in Dark Root. Hungry customers would probably want something more, like a hamburger or a sandwich. I almost mentioned this, but decided against it. I may have traveled a bit in the last few years, but I was hardly 'worldly.' This was Eve's domain.

I looked to her for backup, but she was too busy admiring the Elvis pictures with Paul. I wrinkled my nose. Eve had about as much love for Elvis as I did, which was none. I wondered how long she would be able to continue the ruse before she got busted.

"I hope you don't mind, but we promised this young lady some ice cream," Shane said, gathering our menus and looking from June Bug to Merry.

"That's fine," Merry laughed, a glimmer of her girlish self emerging through her layers of motherhood. "We've had a long few days and she's been a trooper. A little sugar never hurt anyone."

"Who are you?" I asked Merry. "And where's my sister, the health nut?"

"Hurray!" June Bug jumped and clapped, her blonde hair flouncing around her.

"Your mama never let us have sugar," I explained to June Bug. "Eve and I had to sneak it."

"Someone had to look after you two once..." Merry stopped, mid-sentence.

Eve and I turned towards her, wondering if she would say it.

We had made a pact long ago never to mention Ruth Anne's name aloud. Speaking about our missing sister had caused Mother to go into fits. It also brought up memories that were too painful to deal with when we were young.

But we were grownups now. Things should be different. Eve and I waited, but Merry didn't continue. She wasn't ready to go back yet. Maybe none of us were.

I placed my hand on the small of her back, letting her know it was okay.

Shane and Paul were oblivious to our discussion. They were busy with their tasks, serving ice cream and commenting on the many faces of Elvis, and the three of us soon joined them.

"Wow," June Bug said, as she tasted her first bite. "This is the best ice cream I ever ate."

"Thank you, little lady," Shane said. "I make that myself, too. Anyone else care for some?"

We nodded eagerly, even Paul, and gathered at one of the tables where we were treated to homemade ice cream and an assortment of toppings.

I had to agree with June Bug. It was amazing.

"Now," Merry said, wiping her chin as she finished her last spoonful. "I hate to be the party killer, but it's time."

"Time?" I asked. The ice cream was so good and I wanted more. "Time for what?"

"To see Mom."

"Oh." I put down my spoon, my appetite suddenly gone.

I could feel Eve grow tense beside me.

We had put this off too long.

NINE

GOODBYE YELLOW BRICK ROAD

WHAT IS IT ABOUT OUR CHILDHOOD that makes us want to run from it––and return to it––all in one breath? I had hated Dark Root in my teenage years, tried to escape from it like it was Alcatraz, yet now I was saddened because it no longer felt familiar and safe.

I had spent the night in Harvest Home, lulled into a deep sleep by the warmth of the blankets and the scent of lavender under my pillow, yet I tossed and turned all night with dreams of a past I had hoped to forget. I had been reunited with my sisters, the girls I had grown up with who were both my friends and my rivals. My body and mind were a jumble of emotions.

I was home. For better or worse.

There was one thing I was not ambivalent about––seeing my mother, Miss Sasha Shantay. The woman who had raised me, loved me, taught me, and brainwashed me.

I felt like a horrible human being for even thinking it, but I didn't want to see her. I wasn't ready. The thought left me with a chill that went deep into my bones.

I swallowed, scratching at an imaginary itch on my leg as I bumped along in the truck beside Eve and Shane. My sister stared straight ahead, lost in her own thoughts. I wanted to touch her hand, to show her that we were in this together, but we weren't. Eve would deal with it better than me. She was floaty, breezy, whimsical, shallow. Bad couldn't penetrate her, because there was nothing to penetrate. I was the one who sucked things in, letting them fester, holding on to them long after they should have been tossed away.

I recalled my conversation with Michael in the grocery store just a week ago.

I had told him that I 'left Dark Root for a reason.' Seven days ago I thought there were many reasons: because Ruth Anne had disappeared and nobody talked about her, because Merry had gotten married and not a soul objected, because Eve was going to leave at the first chance she got and I wanted to beat her to it.

But the truth was––and it was clear to me now, as we made our way back to Sister House––the truth was, I had run away from my mother.

My stomach sank as I wrestled with this revelation, braiding and unbraiding the ends of my hair until it was so gummy it held together by itself.

Who runs away from their mother?

Especially my mother, the beloved toast of the town, belle of the ball. People sought her out, flocked to her. I didn't remember a day going by when we didn't have a house full of visitors. There would be teas and brunches and salon style discussions. Sometimes we would be invited to join, dressed up like dolls, as Mother and her friends chatted about the weather, the economy, witchery, and their views on men.

"If you want to cast a love spell, all the power to you," Mother would say, taking a sip from her teacup. "I will point you in the direction, but I won't participate."

While she invoked the craft for many reasons, love wasn't on that list.

"Love is overrated," she'd say. "Love makes you give up everything, and for what? To be an unappreciated, overworked house-*frau*, with no life of your own. Just look at what it did to poor Julia." With that, she would point to the picture of Julia Benbridge, dressed all in black, which hung over our mantle.

"If you ask me," Mother would continue. "She was much better off after that man passed. Then, and only then, was she free to pursue her real life. No ladies, love has no place in this world. Men are only good for one thing, and when that's done, you need to move on..."

This didn't dissuade Merry, who fell madly in love with Frank after just three dates, or Eve, who practiced love spells on her own, in the middle of the night. Pity none of the men she ever cast her spells on were worth the rat's tails used for the invocations.

As for me, I wanted to believe in love. Despite Mother's warnings, I had this sense that when your soul finds someone, that right someone, there is a magic created in the universe more powerful than any incantation.

I had thought I found that with Michael, but after catching him and Leah...

"This trip is longer than I remember," Eve finally spoke, tearing me from my thoughts.

I nodded in agreement. We had traversed this road many times as kids, when we were young and untroubled. Was it so brambly and overgrown back then? I didn't think so. The world was full of possibilities then, and the road was clear. At least for us.

Eve chewed her nails and complained about the lack of decent radio stations in *Bumpkinville.*

Shane turned the dial, trying to locate anything that wasn't public broadcasting as he navigated the holes and weeds that had taken over the road. Ahead of us, Paul, Merry, and June Bug led the way, their car kicking up rocks into our windshield.

"I'm surprised you let Merry ride with Paul," I said, purposely antagonizing Eve. I was feeling the need to be confrontational and she was the nearest target.

"Oh, she's safe," Eve laughed, blowing it off. "Merry's married and she's got a kid. Way too much baggage for a free spirit like Paul."

"Well, you never know, do you?" I shrugged, hoping to make her uncomfortable. Eve raised an eyebrow, but didn't respond. She was too preoccupied to take my bait.

Shane must have sensed that I was looking for something else to throw at her, so he jumped in. "Your ma is going to be happy to see you girls. She talks about you a lot."

I looked at him, studying his face as he drove. He was younger than me, but seemed to have a grasp on everything that was going on in the world, or at least in Dark Root.

"How often do you see our mother?" Eve asked, flicking a bitten fingernail into the ashtray.

"Whenever she comes into town." Shane laughed, but it wasn't an easy laugh. I could tell he was withholding information. "Just don't be... shocked," he added, following the curve in the road.

I expected the sky to darken at his words, but it stayed the same grey-blue it did for most of the year. Partly cloudy, rarely sunny, dreary but not ominous.

The closer we got to Sister House, the more I wished I hadn't come.

Back at Woodhaven, there was Michael and Leah, but I could battle with them. Here, I wasn't sure what to expect. Would Mother be bedridden? Starved? Covered in festering wounds? I had no idea. The Miss Sasha I had known had always been hearty, vibrant, and larger than life. It was hard to imagine her image fading.

It would violate every law of the universe.

I studied Sister House as we pulled into the long gravel driveway. It was an imposing structure with two stories and an attic, and looked nothing like the house I remembered. The white paint was chipping, the wrap-around porch sagging, and the window boxes were empty. It was standing, but barely.

We all parked and filed out. June Bug dashed around the barren yard, searching for bugs she could imprison in the iced-tea jars Shane had given her from his diner.

"Bring back memories?" Merry asked as we wandered up the half-buried cobblestone path that cut from the driveway to the front porch steps. She looked very grown-up in a tan blazer and dark, corduroy jeans, nothing like the girl I remembered who wore crinoline, Mother's over-sized heels, and a Burger King crown, even to school. "Who wants to go first?"

"I volunteer Maggie," Eve said, only half-joking.

When we were kids and there was a particularly nasty task that needed to be undertaken, like cleaning toilets or pulling weeds, Eve always volunteered me.

Merry gave me the once over, then decided against it. "No, I'd better," she said. "I was here yesterday morning. I know what we're dealing with."

She took June Bug's hand and the two strode towards the house while Eve and I trailed behind. The guys followed at a distance. I wasn't sure if it was to give us space or because they were afraid. Probably both.

Merry grabbed the brass knocker and rapped on the door three times. It felt odd knocking. Though we were grown and had gone our separate ways, I still thought of it as our house.

There was no answer and I shifted on my feet, about to suggest that we just go inside, when the door creaked painfully open.

An old woman peeked out, her hair the color of cotton. Long, knotted fingers curled around the door. "Who's there?" she asked, not seeming to see us as she blinked against the sunlight.

"Mama," Merry said gently, peering at the crinkled face. "It's me. Merry. And I brought Eve and Maggie."

Eve and I exchanged looks. That couldn't be our mother.

How had she gotten so frail? And so old?

The door opened fully, revealing a tiny woman in a sheer, house dress. She was so thin that the crystal band she had worn forever looked as if it might slip from her wrist at any moment. Except for her piercing blue eyes, I hardly recognized her.

She looked us over, stopping at each face before moving on to the next. At last, her eyes rested on me.

"Magdalene! You've come home

TEN

CAT'S IN THE CRADLE

W<small>HEN</small> I <small>WAS A KID</small> I <small>LIKED TO RUN</small>. When I felt stifled, bored, ignored, or lonely I would wait until everyone was asleep, slip out the front door, and bolt down the road as hard and fast as I could. I loved the feeling of the wind in my face, the soft mud beneath my sneakers, and the air in my lungs. I would run until I was exhausted, and then lumber home unnoticed.

Sometimes I ran to another house, sometimes I ran to town, sometimes deep into the woods. Once, by the light of a full moon, I ran so far into the forest that I found a clearing I had never seen before. It was a beautiful place and I stayed there all night, curled up on the grass, gazing at the stars. In that private little meadow, all my problems disappeared.

I must have drifted off because one moment I was staring at the stars and the next I was dazed and lost and wanted nothing more than my sisters and my bed. I cried in silence as I wandered, getting more lost with every turn.

"Maggie! Thank God I found you!"

It was Merry's voice and I ran towards it, ignoring the branches and shrubs that tore at my bare legs. She had Shane with her, who had been spending the week with us while Uncle Joe was away on business. They escorted me back.

"How did you know I was gone?" I asked as she tucked me into bed.

"Shane heard you leave. He woke me when you didn't come home." She pulled the blanket up to my chin. "You've got to stop running and learn to face things. You don't want to be a wild, wilder do you?" We giggled at the joke and she kissed me on the forehead and we promised to never run from each other. Ever.

I kept my promise and never left her.

But she left me.

I could run now, I thought, as I stood in the entryway feeling my mother's eyes boring into me as she screeched out my birth name. "Magdalene! Magdalene!"

It would be so easy. Just one little step in the opposite direction, followed by another, and I could disappear into the forests. I could leave Dark Root and Eve and my mother. I could leave them *all* behind.

I rubbed my fingers together as everyone turned to look at me, wondering what I would do.

"Magdalene! Magdalene!" my mother's voice continued to call out to me.

I could run.

I looked from Mother to Merry. I had never been good at keeping promises but I had to keep this one.

"Hello," I said softly, stepping forward to face her. "I'm home."

She reached a bony hand out to take mine, her skeletal fingers closing around my wrist. I willed my feet to move themselves, not backwards but forwards, over the threshold and into Sister House. My promise to Merry may have stopped me from running but it was pity for my mother that pulled me inside.

The living room was dark; the curtains were closed and the lights were off. Merry pushed past me and immediately began flipping on switches and opening windows. "It smells horrible in here, Mama," she said. "Remember, we talked about keeping the windows open to air this place out?"

She was right; the room reeked of urine, mildew, and dust. I turned my nose towards my shoulder to keep from inhaling the fumes.

Eve slithered in behind me, avoiding Mother's touch, and plopped herself onto the sofa. The upholstery had faded and was covered in dust and balls of fur. June Bug whizzed by, latching on to her mother's hand. Paul and Shane hung back in the entryway, watching the scene.

A sharp yowl made me jump. As my eyes adjusted I could make out small shapes moving about the corners of the room. Cats. Lots and lots of cats.

My mother had become the cat lady.

"My girls have all come back!" She spun in the living room, her night gown and white hair whipping around her. "The circle will *not* be undone!"

No, Mother, I thought, as she twirled through the living room. *Your girls have not all come back. Ruth Anne was still missing*.

"Still crazy as a Betsy bug," Eve said, not bothering to lower her voice.

"Sit down, Magdalene," Mother said, shooing two cats off a recliner that looked on the verge of collapse. I sat uneasily as several new cats emerged from the shadows to inspect their guests. They were a sickly lot, frail and coughing. They gathered at our feet, meowing and pawing at us expectantly. Eve and I kicked them away, but Merry was brave enough to pick one up. She petted the creature, cooing at it like it were a baby.

It sneezed in response and Merry didn't flinch.

I felt something scurry across my arm and I screamed, slapping it away. June Bug came to my rescue and placed the bug in one of her jars. I pulled my legs into my chest, trying to take up as little space as possible.

A new scent hit my nose.

A hefty bag, untied and overflowing with garbage, sat beside the end table. I had been so preoccupied with the cats that I hadn't noticed the rest of the house. The floor was covered in bins, newspapers, and stacks of empty cereal boxes. A mountain of clothing camouflaged the love seat. Shoes were stuffed into the crannies of the bookcase. The breakfast table——where I had once eaten cereal and biscuits on Saturday mornings——was piled high with dirty dishes.

My skin crawled again, but this time out of pure revulsion.

"Our first order of business is to figure out what to do with all these cats." Merry addressed us as if our mother wasn't in the room. "It's a major health code violation." She faced a window and a beam of sunlight caught her hair, causing it to glow a sunflower yellow. "I've been paying a nurse to stay with her, but it's expensive. I am going to put an ad out for someone to come and sit with her at nights. We can take turns with her during the day."

I was about to ask Merry how we could ever convince anyone to come spend the night in this place when Mother reached a hand into the pocket of her house dress and pulled out a handful of dry cat food.

"Here kitties!" she called out. "Look what mama has for you."

She flung the cat food to the floor. The tougher cats arched their backs and hissed away the competition, while the weaker ones timidly ran after stray bits that bounced under tables.

"That one..." Miss Sasha said, pointing to a fat, orange cat who looked like it couldn't be bothered to pry itself up from the kitchen table. "...is Maggie. Isn't she beautiful?"

"Lucky you." Eve gave me a sideways look, the right side of her mouth turning up in a caustic smile. "Getting a cat named after you."

"I'm sure there's an Eve cat around here somewhere," I retorted. "Just look for the one with the long stick up its butt."

Mother continued spraying out cat food as Merry spoke to her.

"We're here to help you, Mama." She placed a hand on Mother's back. "We are going to get you to the doctor, and get your kitties good homes, and clean this place up. Everything's going to be okay."

Mother looked at each of us in turn, her expression almost lucid.

"Welcome back, girls. Dark Root needs you."

"Well, that was creepy." Eve sipped her coffee, pulling her faux fur collar close around her.

Dip Stix was chilly but Shane didn't want to run up the heating bill so he made us all coffee to warm ourselves.

"*The Twilight Zone* is creepy," I said. "That was *Rosemary's Baby.*"

I wanted to shake the event from my head, but I couldn't erase the images and smells from my brain. It had only been seven years since I left. How had she fallen so far? I was prepared for my mother the 'crazy witch lady'; I was not prepared to see her so shattered and frail.

I wasn't going back, I decided, as I took a long sip of my coffee, emptying my cup. Maybe that made me evil. If it did, I would deal with that later. All I could think about now was that it had been a mistake coming here.

I had to get out of town, and fast.

"You think we should have left Merry and June Bug there with her?" Shane asked, refilling our cups. He wore a red apron and looked a bit like a bustling old lady.

"Mom's fine." Eve rolled her eyes.

I was about to say something, but it was Paul, of all people, who spoke up.

"Eve, you saw that place," he said. "That was definitely not fine. I've been in some dumps in my time, but that place was so awful I didn't even want to go inside. And I lived in a squat in Brooklyn."

Eve didn't argue, like I expected. Instead she shivered. "I suppose it was pretty bad. I just don't like thinking about it."

"Me, either," I agreed.

"At least she wasn't repeating things this time," Shane said.

He was wiping down a table, the same one he had just cleaned five minutes before.

"...I took her some food last week and she kept repeating the same words over and over again. Something about preparing for the dark." Shane paused and looked out the window. "My grandmother had dementia and did things like that. Kept saying things in a continual loop, like a skipped record."

"Isn't she too young to have dementia?" Eve's perfect nose peeped over the top of her large mug. She was still wearing the red cashmere mittens she had put on in the car.

"No one really knows how old Mother is," I said, pressing my hands to my cup for warmth.

Miss Sasha had never revealed her age or showed anyone her driver's license. I did the math in my head. If she had Eve as old as a woman could have a kid, maybe forty-five, and Eve was almost twenty-four that would put her near seventy.

Maybe she wasn't too young after all.

Shane finished his tasks and joined us.

"That's how we found out about her," he said, pulling up the chair beside me. "She was out driving that old car of hers in the country and got pulled over by a trooper. She had no license or insurance and wasn't sure where she was. I guess they did some detective work and figured out she belonged here. Thank God they did. I'm not for driving without a license and endangering the community, but if that cop hadn't pulled her over..." He pounded the side of his fist on the table. "...She might have starved to death in that house alone."

"She wouldn't have starved," Eve pointed out. "She has two thousand pounds of cat food to live on."

Paul gave my sister a disgusted look but Eve simply shrugged.

"Well, she does."

"You're a good guy to take her food," I said to Shane, a bit embarrassed that he had been taking care of our mother. "Thank you."

He smiled and nodded his head. "It's the least I could do. Miss Sasha was like a mother to me, when I visited during the summers. And Uncle Joe really loved her, despite their frequent quarrels. Besides..." Shane looked from me and then to Eve, his eyes lingering on her face. "She was the mother of you girls."

I checked to see if Paul had noticed, but his focus had shifted to a commemorative Elvis plate hanging on the wall. This time, the King was wearing a striped prisoner's onesie. Eve could have run through the restaurant buck naked and in that moment, Paul wouldn't have noticed.

"How do you think she got that way?" I asked, stirring a sugar cube into my coffee with my pinky finger.

Eve set her cup down and peeled the mittens from her hands. "She was already losing it when I left. Always talking about preparing for the End Times. That's when she started her cereal collection. Suddenly the house was filled with Captain Crunch. She wouldn't let us eat that stuff when we were kids and here she was, buying it by the crate. Then she moved on to the harder stuff like Frosted Flakes and Sugar Smacks. By the time I high-tailed it out of there, when I was eighteen, the dining room looked like the Kellogg's factory."

"And you left her like that?" I clenched my cup.

"Hey!" she fired back. "Don't put this all on me. At least I had the decency to say goodbye. I didn't sneak off in the middle of the night with some crazy cult leader and forget how to use the phone."

I felt the anger pulse through me, starting in my gut and working its way down into my fingers and toes. The overhead lights flickered off, then back on again.

"Still can't control it, I see." Eve stared blankly at me, like she expected no better. "I guess meditation camp didn't do you much good."

Shane put his hands on the center of the table, separating me from my sister.

"It's no one's fault," he said, looking at both of us. "These things just happen."

Eve and I stared at each other, neither speaking.

The silence was broken by the doorbell.

We all turned to see a pleasant looking woman of around fifty entering the cafe. She had short, dark hair, cut elegantly around her soft face, and wore a long, grey skirt and a purple sweater with a faux fur collar similar to Eve's.

"Hello," the woman said, smiling and looking around the restaurant. "Is this establishment open?" Her green eyes sparkled as she took in the décor.

Shane practically ran to greet his new guest. He moved to offer her a seat by the window but she waved her hands.

"If you don't mind," she said, nodding to us. "I'd like to join these lovely young people. That is, if you don't mind the company? I've been on the road a while and it would be great to have some conversation while I have my tea."

I thought this was strange, but Eve seemed eager to have her sit with us and offered her the chair between us. If the woman had been dressed in rags, instead of expensive-looking clothes, Eve wouldn't have given her the time of day.

"My name is Jillian," the woman said, shaking each of our hands.

On her right index finger she wore the largest diamond I had ever seen. I couldn't help but gawk.

"You like?" She smiled, holding her hand up for me to appraise. "A gift from an old admirer. It's a terrible thing to lug around but I can never bring myself to take it off." She gave it a look that let me know there was a story behind it, but she didn't offer to tell it.

"I'm Eve," my sister introduced herself. "And this is my friend Paul, my sister Maggie, and of course, the proprietor, Shane Doler.

Shane opened his arms wide. "*Mi* Dip Stix *es su* Dip Stix."

"Pleased to meet you all, and I love your name, Eve. Very biblical."

"Yes, Mother liked biblical names," Eve said. "But ironically wasn't a huge fan of the Bible. Said the only thing she could appreciate about Jesus was his hair. Anyways," she added. "Guess it's a good thing I wasn't born a boy, or I would have been stuck with a name like Ezekiel or Jebediah. And then I would have had no choice but to become a farmer."

Eve clicked her nails on the table while she pondered this and the rest of us laughed.

"Sounds like your mother is a colorful woman," Jillian said with twinkling eyes. Then she turned to peruse the paper menu Shane had offered her. "Now, let me see if I can't find something to tide me over until I get home..."

Jillian ran her finger down the list and finally decided on the waffle sticks, no syrup or butter, please, and a cup of hot tea.

I'm not sure why, but I felt an immediate liking for Jillian.

She was warm, personable, and unlike most of the other women of her generation I'd known, sane. She told us that she was from Linsburg, twenty-five miles away, and was out doing a little shopping in neighboring towns. She saw this quaint little place and 'just had to come in.'

"It reminds me of the diners from my high school days," she said, smoothing the paper napkin onto her lap.

I looked over at Shane and raised a wicked eyebrow. He really needed to update the joint.

"This your first time in Dark Root?" Eve asked, mirroring Jillian's way of drinking from her cup with her pinky finger up.

"No, dear, you caught me," she laughed, her voice like a tinkling of bells. "I used to come for the Haunted Dark Root Festivals years ago. I've been nostalgic lately and I was hoping to grab some fliers to take back to my nieces, but, by the looks of things, it doesn't seem to be happening this year. Too bad. They were always so much fun."

Shane frowned. "I wish it was still going on, too. Good for business, great for the town. But I can't seem to convince anyone it's worth the effort. The folks that used to run it are getting old and..." He looked at me apologetically. "...Sick. So..."

He spread his right hand, helplessly.

"I see." Jillian took another sip from her cup and set it carefully back into its saucer. "I don't mean to be a Meddling Merriweather, but it seems to me there's a new generation of young people who care about this town." She looked around at all of us. "Why not revive it? It could be fun."

Eve, who had spent more time watching Paul than listening, was suddenly interested. "What a great idea! We could put on plays, like historical reenactments of the town's history. I could write them *and* star in them."

"What if I wanted to star in them?" I asked.

Of course, I had no intention of being in anything Eve had written, but I didn't like the idea that she was making this all about her.

"Don't be silly, Maggie. I'm the logical choice. I've starred in many off-Broadway plays."

"Way, way off, I bet." I laughed, thinking about it. "...Like in Milwaukee."

"Now, ladies," Shane interrupted. "We can hammer out those details later, but since you both seem so eager to do this, I say we give it a shot."

"I didn't actually volunteer," I reminded him. "I was just trying to prove a point."

I was planning on leaving as soon as I figured out where I was going, and I couldn't get involved in something so silly as a Halloween carnival.

Shane just smiled. "Now, there's only six weeks before Halloween, so that means we need to work fast. We are going to have to work hard and get everyone, including the Mayor, on board. When he learns the Maddock girls are back and willing to do their parts, I'm sure he will jump at the chance."

"Whoa!" I placed both hands on the table. "One mention of reviving this thing and you all pounce on it? Isn't that a little crazy? And I never said I'd do my part or anyone's part."

"I'll take whatever I can get from you, Mags." Shane put a strong hand on my shoulder, pushing me deeper into the chair as if to say *you aren't going anywhere yet.*

Eve and Shane chatted excitedly about what needed to be done; they had more ideas than Thomas Jefferson and Benjamin Franklin combined. Shane would rally the shop owners. Eve would write her plays. Maggie would...well, they never figured out 'what Maggie could do.'

I stifled a sigh and looked out the window at the road that led out of Dark Root.

"Don't worry, dear," Jillian said, placing two hands over one of mine. She had a warm, soothing energy to her. "Things will work out. You will see."

"Yeah," I sighed.

Well, if Shane and Eve wanted to resurrect that old festival all the power to them. I would be long gone six weeks from now.

"Well, everyone." Jillian stood and pushed in her chair. "Sorry to rile up the hornets' nest and leave, but I must be going. Linsburg's Homecoming is tonight and I'm tailgating."

I wasn't sure what tailgating was, but I wished I were going with her. It seemed far preferable to what I would be doing the next few days.

"Maggie, do you mind walking me out to my car?" she asked.

It was another strange request, since it was still daylight and Dark Root was not known for its muggings, but I agreed. Just being around her lightened my mood.

When we got to her Lexus she handed me a card that read: *Jillian Lightheart ~ Psychic Medium*. There was an address and a map on the back.

"What's this for?"

"Maggie, dear," Jillian said. "I'm not sure you are aware of it, but you have something behind you. It's big and dark and hides whenever it thinks it's been spotted. It's kind of like a cloud behind the sun. I think this one is just a hitchhiker––most of them are––but some things attach themselves for a very long time. Even lifetimes. I think you are the sort of person who attracts...many things."

I looked over my shoulder but couldn't see anything.

She laughed and slid into her seat.

"I told you, he's sneaky. At any rate, I'd like to help you with it, if you decide you want to. Free, of course. It's not often I get to meet someone of your talents."

I gave her a quizzical look.

My only talents were in generating mild electrical surges and making predictions that sometimes came true. Nothing a professional psychic would be interested in. Before I could speak, she started the car and drove away.

I looked at the card again. Her address was in Linsburg. Not far, if

I had a car. Which I didn't. I walked back to Dip Stix and thought about what she had said. She claimed she was a psychic medium, someone who could speak with the dead. According to my mother, that was one of the rarest and most powerful gifts a person could have. I was intrigued.

I felt a touch of cold on my shoulder and looked behind me. Nothing. Maybe I *would* go see her before I left Dark Root behind forever.

"What was that about?" Eve asked, emerging from Dip Stix with Paul.

"Oh, you know, just another old, eccentric woman."

Eve laughed and slid into the front seat of the Explorer next to Paul. "As if we don't have enough of those in Dark Root already."

"So what did you think of Paul?" Eve plopped down on the bed as I rummaged through my suitcase for pajamas.

I removed my flannel nightgown and was seized by sadness, remembering the night Michael had dressed me for bed before returning to Leah. I shoved it back into the suitcase and pulled out an over-sized Berkley T-shirt instead.

"...Isn't he great?"

"Hmm?" I asked, stalling for time.

Considering the day we had, I was surprised she was focusing on Paul and even more surprised she thought he was great. Aside from his love of all things Elvis, he didn't seem to have a lot to contribute to conversations.

"Where did you two meet?" I shimmied out of my clothes and pulled the shirt over my head. Though it hung to my knees, it was snug in the waist and I silently cursed Michael for putting it in the dryer. Another good reason to get rid of him, I reminded myself.

Eve ran a comb through her long hair and I noticed that in addition to her bangs, she had piece-y layers that framed her face. I was fascinated and a bit envious. My own hair was far too unruly to pull off a stunt like that.

"We met at an audition for *Rock of Ages* on Broadway." Eve sighed dramatically, turning towards the mirror. She checked every angle of her head, smiled approvingly, and put the comb away. "We hit it off right away and have been hanging out ever since."

She stood and pulled off her shirt, giving me a glimpse of her newly-enhanced cleavage.

"Did you get the part?" I watched, fascinated as she searched through the dresser for something to wear. I was no stranger to nudity, but I had never seen anything like the giant, floating orbs that Eve was now sporting. She was lucky that she had a naturally curvy bottom to balance her out, or she might have toppled over.

I turned my head away so that I didn't stare.

"I got a call back," she said, pulling on a loose, white t-shirt. "Would have been my first Broadway gig, too, but I didn't take it. That same day, I got an offer to play the lead in a play, and I just couldn't refuse."

"It must have been a pretty big deal to give up Broadway. Which play?"

"*Romeo and Juliet*. If you want to be taken seriously as an actress, Shakespeare is the way to go." Eve shrugged, pulling her hair up into a ponytail and secured it with a scrunchie.

Even without makeup, she was still spotlessly beautiful.

She climbed into the bed, fluffed her pillows and rested her arms behind her head. "Paul's supposed to be going back to Seattle, but I'm trying to convince him to stick around for a bit. Lord knows this town could use a little more life in it."

"Seattle?" I was suddenly interested in Paul.

If he was going to Seattle, maybe I could go with him. Then move on from there. It was a small stepping stone, but it would be a first step in getting out of Dark Root.

"He has family there," Eve continued. "Says he misses them." Her lips puckered into a thoughtful pout.

"Why don't you give him one of your magical teas? That might keep him here."

Eve's dark eyes clouded over. "Don't think I haven't thought of that. I have one dose, just for him, made with herbs I spent weeks collecting. But..." she sighed. "I'm hoping it doesn't come to that. He's too..." I could see her wrestling for the right word. "...Special. Nope, I would like for him to fall in love with me, fair and square."

I had heard Eve declare her unbridled passion for many boys before, but there was something about the way she spoke of Paul that made me wonder if this was different.

"Think you're in love?" I said.

Eve rolled onto her side so that she could look at me.

"I have no idea, but it's something. Maybe it's just the challenge. He's the first guy I've ever met who wasn't tripping over himself to impress me." She shrugged as if it wasn't really important whether it was love or the challenge, so long as she won. "Enough about that. What about you? You still with that religious guy?"

My body tensed.

I wanted to tell her the truth, but I couldn't admit the way that things had turned out. It would give her too much leverage.

"We are on a break for the moment," I said. "I've been wanting it for some time, you know? Coming here was a good excuse to see how things would be without him. I was so young when we got together and I wonder if I missed out on life."

Eve nodded thoughtfully, but I wasn't sure she bought it.

"Ready for bed?" she asked, patting the space next to her. She was gooey and dreamy again and I couldn't stay here when she was happy while I was miserable. Though I had put Michael out of my head, he wouldn't stay out of my heart.

"I think I might sleep in Merry's room tonight. Seems a waste of a bed otherwise. You be alright?"

Eve nodded, lost in thoughts of conquering Paul.

I tiptoed out as she fell into an easy sleep.

I crept down the hall, hoping to not wake Paul or Aunt Dora. Merry's room was neat, except for a few stray toys on the floor. I crawled into bed, turned off the bedside lamp, and pulled the comforter up to my shoulders. The realization that this would be the first time I slept in a bed alone in years hit me and I snuggled in deeper.

Think good thoughts, Maggie.

The smell of Merry's scent on the pillows helped relax me, and I settled my mind on thoughts of her at six-years-old, pulling me in a wagon around the front yard.

"Faster, Merry!" I screamed as I held tight to the sides. "Faster!"

The memory warmed me like the sun and I melted into a puddle of sleep.

ELEVEN

PIANO MAN

HARVEST HOME, DARK ROOT, OREGON
OCTOBER, 1995

"*MAGGIE, WAKE UP.*" *Merry jostled her sister, rousing her from her nap on the couch.*

Maggie sat up, rubbed her eyes, and looked around. For a moment she forgot that she was in the living room of Harvest Home.

"Already?" Maggie asked, pushing herself onto elbows.

A loud chime coming from the grandfather clock confirmed that that it was midnight, time for the ritual. Maggie felt the chill from the open door and looked around for her sweater.

"We aren't supposed to wear anything other than our robes tonight," Merry cautioned, but helped Maggie into the sweater, anyways.

"Where's Eve?" Maggie asked. If she was going to have to wander the woods in the middle of the night for some crazy ritual, then Eve better be up, too. Maggie saw her standing by the door, jumping up and down, not tired at all.

Miss Sasha and six of her friends emerged from the dining room, talking excitedly and exchanging knowing glances.

"You girls ready?" Miss Sasha asked. This was to be their first grown up moon chant and Miss Sasha could hardly contain herself. She

noticed the sweater Maggie wore over her long blue robe and frowned but didn't mention it.

Merry, Maggie, Eve, and Ruth Anne followed their mother and her friends into the night.

It was cold and the sisters shivered as they wound their way along an old dirt road shrouded by trees to a circular clearing, a half-mile away. The girls had played in the clearing many times during the day, but this was the first time they had seen it beneath the light of a full moon. The grass looked dewy and lush as the soft light fell upon each blade, but the trees that surrounded the meadow looked foreboding and ominous, as if their long, twisted boughs were ready to snatch the girls, if given the chance.

"What are we doing here again?" Maggie asked, as they made their way towards the center of the circle. "...And how long do we have to stay out?"

The adults moved to a point in the very center of the clearing and the girls positioned themselves a few dozen feet behind them.

Ruth Anne surveyed the area and sat, cross-legged, on the moist grass. "We are rooting out the evil spirits that are trying to infest Dark Root." Her voice was as flat and informational as an encyclopedia entry.

She reached into the pocket of her dress and pulled out a key-chain flashlight and a comic book and started reading.

"How do we do that?" Maggie asked, watching as the elders––five women and two men––linked raised hands towards the sky.

They began singing, a soft melodic chant that Maggie had heard before.

Merry answered, "Every fall, the Council of Seven places a protective spell around our town. It must be done before the second half of the year begins, on November 1st. It keeps out the dark energies and ensures that the circle is strong."

Maggie hopped on one foot, and then the other, trying to find warmth in the chill of the night. "But why do we have to do it now?" she

144

moaned. "When it's so cold?"

Ruth Anne responded, never lifting her eyes from her book. "It's the witching hour. According to legend, the hours between twelve and three AM are when all things magical, including witches, are at their most powerful." She turned the page of her book and cracked a smile at one of the drawings. "...It's too bad we can't keep out the crazy."

Maggie widened her eyes. "But if witches are the most powerful now, won't the bad things be more powerful too?"

"I'm scared," Eve said, jumping in place as the elders continued their chant. Eve liked magick, but only the lighter arts, and those that yielded her a reward.

Merry took Eve's hand and kissed it, and Maggie latched onto Merry's other hand.

"I'm scared, too," Merry fibbed.

Merry wasn't afraid of anything.

There was a long silence, followed by the heavy beat of a loud drum. Miss Sasha looked over her shoulder at her daughters, letting them know that it was almost their turn. They had been practicing the spell for weeks now, and Maggie hoped she wouldn't forget the words.

Ruth Anne set down her comic book and the four girls clasped hands and waded towards the center of the circle.

Miss Sasha nodded and the girls began their incantation.

As the Witching Hour chimes
And the whole world sleeps and dreams
We join our hands in sisterhood
Staving back the darklings
The circle stands, its shape eternal
Though the darkness is still beckoning
Our light will ward back the infernal
And shield us from the doomsday reckoning

Maggie was still tired and stumbled on a few of the words, completely missing some of them; however, Merry spoke them as loud and clearly as she recited The Pledge of Allegiance at school. All the while, Eve played with her hair and hardly tried at all. For her part, Ruth Anne recited the words without emotion, anxious to get back to her comic book.

"Who wrote the spell?" Ruth Anne had asked their mother earlier that day while they were preparing. "It doesn't sound right."

"It doesn't matter if it sounds right or not," Miss Sasha had explained. "It's the power of words––especially when spoken in numbers––that matters. When we stand together, no enemy would dare traverse the boundaries of Dark Root."

Maggie caught a movement to her right. She thought she had seen a dark form take shape and then vanish. And then another. Were they coming or going? She couldn't tell.

The ritual continued for what felt to Maggie like an eternity.

Her feet hurt, her face was cold, and she was afraid of shadows that zipped past, seemingly unnoticed by anyone else. She squeezed Merry's hand until she was afraid she had hurt her sister, but Merry didn't protest.

At last, Miss Sasha declared the witching hour officially over and they were allowed to return to their homes.

"Well, girls," she said, rubbing her hands together as she escorted her daughters inside Sister House. "Wasn't that fun? And..." she continued, her eyes twinkling. "Because you were up so late, I'm not sending any of you to school tomorrow."

"Yay!" Eve and Merry said almost simultaneously.

Ruth Anne said she was going to school anyway.

Maggie said nothing.

She was too busy watching a small, dark shape slink into the shadows at the top of their staircase, proof that there was at least one 'darkling' the coven had not banished that night.

HARVEST HOME, DARK ROOT, OREGON
SEPTEMBER, 2013

"Wake up!"

The voice was deliberate, masculine. I shook my head, trying to come awake.

"Wake up!"

My eyes flew open.

Though the room was dark, practically pitch, I could make out a form on the right side of my bed, a black shadowy figure hovering beside me. It watched me, staring with cold eyes on a formless face. I tried to scream, but the only noise I could produce was a harsh rasping sound from my throat.

My first instinct was to run, but I was somehow pressed onto my bed, my arms and legs held down by an invisible force. I could only move my head, and I thrashed it from side to side, trying to loosen the rest of my body, but the force continued to hold me down.

My body was paralyzed.

I began praying, saying the words that Michael had taught me. "Please watch over me and protect me with your pure, white light..."

I repeated it in my brain, until my lips followed suit and I was verbally speaking the incantation. The form beside me vanished and I was free.

Words have power.

I flew from my bed, yanked open the door, and ran into the hallway.

Mercifully, there were several night lights in the corridor. The clock at the end of the hall announced that it was 12:15 AM. I wasn't going back to that room. Not yet. Not until the witching hour had come and gone.

Dazed, I stumbled down the stairs, into the living room. Turning on lights as I went, I made my way to the kitchen. I was startled to see Paul at the table, reading a book. He looked as surprised to see me as I was to see him.

He dropped his book like he had been caught doing something wrong. "I'm sorry. I didn't mean to be roaming around your house at night. I couldn't sleep."

I smiled and waved my hand. "It's not my house and you didn't wake me."

He stood, pulled out the chair next to his, and offered it to me. My hands were shaking as he poured me a cup of coffee. I almost confessed to him why I was here but it sounded too ridiculous, even for me. I took a sip of the coffee and felt immediately calmed.

"This is amazing," I said, drinking more. I intended to stay awake, at least for the next few hours. This would help.

"This is one thing I really missed about the Pacific Northwest when I was in New York...the coffee. The stuff here is not as good as the stuff you find in Seattle, but it's a hell of a lot better than what they serve on the East Coast."

"I grew up in the Pacific Northwest, too, and this coffee doesn't taste like any I've had."

"The secret," he said, leaning in and whispering. "Is to add in a squirt of chocolate syrup and a pinch of nutmeg. I'm kind of a junk food fiend, and I get it however I can."

I laughed and raised my mug. "Cheers, then. To junk food. May it serve us well."

We clinked cups, then sat in silence. I listened to the clock in the other room tick down the minutes. He rose and took our cups, rinsing them in the sink.

"Going to bed, then?" I asked hopefully. I didn't want him to see me waiting for the monsters in my closet to disappear; I felt foolish enough, as it was.

"Not quite," he said, casually walking towards the piano in the corner of the dining room. "I hear you play."

It was a statement, not a question. He sat down on the bench and very lightly hit a key. When I didn't respond, he hit another key, louder this time.

"Shhh," I said, rushing towards him. "You're going to get us into trouble."

"With who?" he asked, looking around. "Your Aunt Dora is almost deaf, and once Eve finally crashes there's not much that can wake her. The only things that can hear us down here are the rats and the ghosts, and I'm sure neither would object to some Paul McCartney." He ran his fingers along the keys, tapping out snippets of 'Let it Be,' and 'Band on the Run.'

"All we need," he said, patting the seat next to him. "...Is love."

I had to laugh, though it was an absurd joke.

But the absurdity of the whole situation––hiding from a ghost, sitting at the piano in the middle of the night, and having a conversation with a man who, up until now, hadn't said more than ten words to me–– made the whole thing hysterical.

My laugh turned into a chortle and before I knew it, I was doubled over the piano with tears streaming down my eyes repeating, "...All you need is love."

"I'd like to think I was that funny," he said, when I had finally calmed down. "But I think you are suffering from a bit of exhaustion. You should probably go to bed."

I shook my head no. That thing was probably still up there, waiting for me. For all I knew, it was in my bed, fluffing the pillows.

"I'm fine here, for now." I stretched my fingers to take a turn at the piano. It had been years since I had played. I had never fooled myself into thinking I was any good, but it didn't matter. It always felt good. Like very loud therapy.

I serenaded him with a crude version of a Steve Miller Band classic, 'Come On and Dance.' It was one of my mother's favorites and she had me play it at all our birthday parties. I couldn't remember all the notes but I think I hit most of them.

"Not bad," he said. "Do you know any others?"

"Um...see if you can guess what this one is." I played him another.

Admittedly, I totally screwed up the chorus but I think I nailed the bridge.

He scratched his head and I could see his brain working.

"Well?" I said, smiling semi-victoriously. It was a win but only because I couldn't play it right. Still, I'd take it. "Give up?"

At last, a smile of recognition crossed his face. "'Your Song!' By the great Elton John. Enjoying a mild resurrection now, thanks to the movie, *Moulin Rouge.*"

"Moulin what?"

Paul shook his head dismissively and began playing 'Your Song' from memory, much better than I had done. I watched for a minute, then joined in, his fingers moving gracefully along the keys while mine hunted and pecked for the right notes. When we hit the chorus we sang the words together. I remembered those too, surprisingly, all about how it is the listener's song, how wonderful life is, how the song's ending means they're now in the world. I'd never really thought about the words before, but they struck me as sort of nice.

When we finished, I squealed. This was the most fun I'd had in a long time.

"You're a surprising woman, Maggie Mae." He leaned back and folded his hands behind his head and stretched out his legs beneath the piano. "I'm surprised you know all these oldies. A lot of young people don't."

"You make it sound like you are a hundred years old," I said. "And my mother loved the 70's. Said they stopped making decent music once video came out. Maybe she was right."

"Well, the 70's was the decade of the story-telling artists. It's too bad that so many songs nowadays rely on images, rather than lyrics. Where are the Claptons and Joels of this generation?" Paul sighed, shaking his head, then lowered his voice. "And of course I'm not a hundred," he continued, a shadow falling across his face. "I just feel like it sometimes.

150

My mom says I'm a bit of an old soul." He shrugged his shoulders then let it go. "Anyway, I wouldn't quit your day job, but that was pretty darn good."

"What day job?" I asked, wiping the sweat off my forehead. "Maybe we should tackle The Eagles now? How about a little 'Desperado'?"

"How are you at singing harmony?" he asked.

I was about to answer him when a loud bump on the staircase caught my attention. We turned our heads to see Eve descending the stairs. Normally, Eve moved as stealthily as a cat.

She must have wanted to be heard.

"Looks like I'm missing the party," she said, her lips stretching across her face. She moved towards us, her hips swaying from side to side. Eve didn't walk, she slithered, and it was hypnotic...at least for me.

Paul was too busy scouring the old songbook on the piano to notice.

"I thought I heard something about The Eagles," she said, leaning seductively against the piano, offering a full view down her loose T-shirt. "Sounds like you two could use a little backup."

"Dammit," Paul said. "No Eagles in this *Popular Party Tunes* songbook. Let's try something else." He turned the pages and pointed to 'Luck Be a Lady Tonight,' a song I didn't know. I listened while he played it and Eve crooned along with him, flopping down on his lap and opening her arms wide on the final line.

When it was over, she stood and curtsied, and Paul clapped appropriately before turning back to me. "I can teach you that one. You will pick it up in no time."

Eve stood behind him, arms crossed, waiting for my response.

I shrugged like I didn't care if I learned it or not.

"Well, I better head to bed," Paul said. "I may be taking off for Seattle in the morning and I don't want to stay up too late. Good night, ladies."

"In the morning?" I asked, alarmed.

I was still hoping to hitch a ride with him, but I couldn't leave just yet. There was Merry, and June Bug and Mother and a dozen other things I needed to get closure on, first. I had to stall him for a few days.

"You aren't ready to go, are you? We need you."

"You do?" Paul and Eve asked simultaneously.

The wheels in my brain were turning. I had to think fast. "Yes. I mean the town needs you. To get The Haunted Dark Root Festival up and running. We could use someone like you to help with all sorts of things, including music."

"I thought you weren't interested in that," Eve said, one eyebrow arched.

"Oh, well, you know...if its important to the community its important to me."

"Since when?"

"Since I got back and saw what's happened to Dark Root." I spread my hands.

Eve lifted her chin and tilted her head to the side, trying to decide whether or not she believed me. She looked towards Paul who was hunched over the piano in thought. Whether she believed me or not, she decided to use it to her advantage.

"Maggie's right, we do need you," she cooed, placing a hand on Paul's shoulder. "Maybe you could hang for a few days? Maybe a week. Aunt Dora says you can sleep in the attic for as long as you like. Keeps the rats from wandering down here." She smiled playfully.

Paul scratched his chin. "I don't know. I already told you, small town festivals aren't my thing." He lifted his hands overhead to stretch and I noticed the muscles in his abdomen as his shirt came up. I turned quickly before either of them caught me staring.

"Oh, please. Just for a week or two? It could be fun. Dark Root needs you." Eve beamed at him with big, innocent, doe eyes. "I need you."

"What else is new?" he laughed. He lowered his eyes and played the first few notes of 'Your Song' on the piano. "What about you, Maggie? Do you need me?"

My heart raced a little and I stammered, unable to answer.

"Well?" Eve smirked. I felt like a mouse, being watched by a cat with very sharp claws. "Do you need him, Maggie?"

"I, uh..."

"Of course she does," my sister answered for me. "We all do. Please stay, Paul. Do it for Dark Root."

Paul wiped his hands on his jeans and thought for a moment. "I guess staying a few more days wouldn't hurt anything. It's not like I have anything to go back to." His eyes found me. "Or anyone." With that, he turned and made his way up the staircase, leaving Eve and I staring after him. "Good night, ladies. Don't let the bedbugs bite." He waved his hand in the air.

When he was gone, I felt the energy around Eve turn as hot as fire poker.

"He's not into redheads," Eve said, flipping her hair as she ascended the stairs after him. "If he showed any interest at all, it was only to get me jealous."

"Who said I cared?"

"We all want what we can't have, Maggie. And you can't have him."

Eve turned and her perfect bottom swayed confidently behind her.

TWELVE

BORN TO RUN

"I'M GLAD YOU DECIDED TO STAY," Shane said, one hand resting easily on the steering wheel, the other arm hanging out his window. Small raindrops splattered across the windshield and he flipped the wipers on periodically to clear them away.

I checked the sky, noticing the clouds that were gathering.

Some things may have changed while I was gone but the weather remained a constant––overcast and dreary, with a chance of gloom.

"I'm not staying for long." I fiddled with my seatbelt, releasing it from its snap. It was pressing against my belly and I needed to pee.

Shane gave me a quick glance, but said nothing.

We didn't have a police station in Dark Root; we barely had a fire department. There was not much chance of getting pulled over for a seat belt infraction.

"I appreciate your help in getting me the ticket," I continued.

We had spent the morning on the internet and Shane showed me how to purchase a bus pass that would take me from anywhere in the country to anywhere in the country for less than three hundred bucks. I hated parting with the money, not sure how I would get more, but a ticket meant freedom. And choice. I wasn't stuck here, though I still hoped to make the first leg of my journey with Paul to Seattle, then figure out the rest later.

155

"You only have five weeks to use it," he said.

He had told me this a dozen times already. The ticket was good only until November first. That was more than enough time for me to come up with an escape plan.

"I could use a hand around the cafe until you decide to leave," he continued, looking at me out of the corner of his eye. "If you are interested in making a few bucks."

"Doing what, pray tell?"

"Waiting tables and cleaning toilets."

"I can't think of anything more horrible."

"Suit yourself, but you're going to want a little cash for your trip, I presume."

"Can't you just pay me for other things?" I batted my eyelashes playfully.

"I can't afford you," he said, giving me a sideways grin. "I'm already paying Eve."

I punched him in the arm and threatened to tell her. He said he was kidding and I forgave him, though a small part of me was upset by his remark, and not because he had basically called my sister a member of the world's oldest profession.

A song came on the radio, something about a honky-tonk princess in pink cowboy boots. Shane turned up the volume. He tapped his index fingers against the steering wheel and sang along, missing a few words and making up others. The wind caught his hair, shoving it back away from his face, and he looked very much like the goofy kid I used to make fun of.

He caught me looking and laughed.

"I need a shave," he said, rubbing his chin with his free hand. "I've been letting myself go the last few months. Hardly even work out anymore."

"I don't think you have anything to worry about. Dark Root is hardly known for its beautiful people." It wasn't until I left town that I realized round and lumpy wasn't the standard of beauty. I looked down at my belly––which was protruding even more thanks to Aunt Dora's homemade muffins––and sucked it in self-consciously.

He must have noticed.

"Works both ways," he said, turning onto the dirt road that would take me to Sister House.

Merry had phoned earlier and asked if I could help her out. Mother was sleeping, she assured me, knocked out on drugs that the nurse had given her, and the cats had all been corralled. I didn't want to go, but knowing that I now possessed the bus pass and would have Merry to myself for a few hours made it tolerable.

"I don't have to be thin for Dark Root," I answered him. "But if I want to fit in, in Seattle, I better hit the gym."

"Seattle? What's in Seattle?" Shane rolled up his window. The drops had become globs making visibility difficult, even though the wipers were running at full speed. He slowed his pace as we sloshed through puddles and piles and bumps.

"I just always wanted to go to Seattle," I responded, turning down the radio. "Birthplace of grunge."

"Uh-huh." The tone of his voice let me know he didn't believe me. "You were grunge way before it was popular. You don't need to go to Seattle for that."

"Is that a compliment?"

"Take it how you like it."

I felt the need to explain. "Dark Root is like the Roach Motel, Shane. You check in and you don't check out. If I don't get away, and soon, I will be trapped here forever. Like..." I looked at him and stopped.

"Yes? Go on. Trapped like what?"

"Like my mother."

"I see. And has it ever occurred to you that people like *your mother* choose to stay here. That they aren't trapped at all?"

"Might as well be." I slumped against the passenger door. I didn't like the way this conversation had turned.

"So, will you stay in Seattle? Is that where you will make your new home?"

I shrugged. It might be my first stop. It might be my only stop. It wasn't like I had somewhere else to go. Unless...

Woodhaven.

I had dreamed of it the night after playing the piano with Paul, in those wee hours before dawn. In my dream I was with Michael. We were young again, kissing, laughing, hanging out. I recalled his chest, his arms, his legs, and his breath on my cheek. True, he eventually morphed into Paul, but it started out as Michael. I woke that morning in a sweat.

I squeezed my eyes shut, forcing up the image of Michael and Leah in her bedroom together. It worked. I was back to hating him again.

Still...maybe he had learned?

Maybe he felt that same aching separation that I felt and realized what a stupid fucking jerk he had been. Maybe he was remorseful and had changed. People changed. That's what Oprah and Dr. Phil said. My heart harbored hope. The rest of me did not. I squelched the thought as Shane made a sudden swerve to avoid an especially deep pit in the road.

"No one wants you to leave," he said softly.

"No one's asking me to stay either," I replied.

Neither Eve nor Merry had expressed any interest in my continued presence these last few days. In fact, Eve watched me so intently, especially when I was in the company of Paul, that I was sure she would have bought me the ticket herself if she thought it would get rid of me sooner. And Merry had been so busy at Sister House, caring for Mother, that she hardly noticed I existed.

"I would like you to stay." Shane turned his head to look at me, his gaze making me uncomfortable. I turned the radio volume back up, pretending to listen to a country song I had never heard. "...Just keep that in mind."

We pulled into the driveway of Sister House. June Bug sat on the front porch swing, oblivious to our presence as she inspected something in her cupped hands.

Shane unbuckled and turned towards me, switching off the radio. "I know you probably think I've been a bit insensitive. I haven't asked you how you've been. That night at the bar must have scared the hell out of you. I just didn't know what to say. Back where I'm from, a man would never do anything like that. We are raised to respect women."

I inhaled, eager to change the subject, but he raised a hand to stop me.

"I wish I had been there sooner to stop those assholes!" He banged a fist against the dashboard and the cab of the truck shook.

It startled me, the depth of his anger. He didn't seem like the kind that got angry easily, but something told me when he did, someone had better watch out.

"I am grateful for what you did." I stopped, then decided to ask him the question that had come into my head a dozen times since the assault. "How did you manage to pull both of them off me?"

Shane shrugged, a smile lighting his face. "Adrenaline, I guess."

"Well, it would have been much worse if you hadn't..." I didn't need to finish. We both knew what would have happened. I patted him on the knee. "You're a good egg," I teased.

He gave me a crooked smile and started the engine back up.

"And now back to our regularly scheduled program," I said, nodding to the white Victorian home that loomed before us. A shutter, hanging on one hinge, smacked against the side of the house as the wind caught it. June Bug jumped but continued her studies.

"I'm sorry you have to go through this." Shane scratched his chin thoughtfully. "I've been reading about dementia. It's a sad, sad thing and no family deserves this. The best thing you can do is to be yourself and try to keep some emotional distance."

"You read a lot," I said, opening the passenger door.

One of my feet fell into a deep puddle and I immediately withdrew it, searching the ground for a safe spot. I found a small mound a few inches from the truck and stepped onto it.

"I guess I do read quite a bit," Shane responded. "A habit I learned from Uncle Joe. Every summer when I'd come to visit he'd hand me a pile of books with a warning that if I didn't finish them by the end of August, I wasn't allowed back the next year. And he had ways of making sure I read them. I never had to do a book report in school as thoroughly as the ones Uncle Joe put me through."

Shane's face relaxed at the memory and I smiled. Uncle Joe had the largest private collection of books I had ever seen. Ruth Anne had dragged me to his house on many occasions just to peruse his library.

"I better run," Shane said. "Dip Stix opens for dinner in two hours and I've got a hot stove to slave over. Be safe."

He nodded and drove away.

I waited until he had completely disappeared before I turned towards Sister House. The shutter continued to flap against the wall, the window reminding me of a one-winged bat. I reached inside my skirt pocket, running my fingers over the ridge of my bus ticket. I was going to tell Merry today, when the time was right.

"Aunt Maggie!" June Bug called to me as I made my way up the path towards the porch. She dropped whatever critter she had been holding to wrap her arms around my legs. "I missed you so much!" She smelled like rose petals, baby powder, and dirt.

"I missed you too, June Bug," I said, lifting her up and carrying her inside.

And I meant it.

The house still smelled of urine, but it was getting better. Merry had been hard at work, vacuuming the floors, dusting the furniture, and caring for the cats who were now housed in small kennels. They meowed and hissed at their restriction, but they looked healthier; their eyes and noses were now mucus-free and their coats shiny and groomed.

"How did you do all this in just a week?" I asked, torn between feelings of guilt and awe as I wandered into the living room.

It was bright and airy inside. The newspapers and boxes had been cleared out and there was no longer any fur on the sofas.

"Just call me the miracle worker," Merry laughed, pulling her long blonde hair into a low ponytail.

Her manner was more relaxed, easier than I had seen since I had come to Dark Root. I sat across from her on the floor, helping her sort through a bin of photos she had discovered beneath several layers of Captain Crunch boxes.

"You always could work miracles." I found a scrap of newspaper in the bin and put it in one of the three piles she had created: keep, dump, and give away. So far the dump pile was winning by a landslide. Or more accurately, a landfill-slide.

"I'm just good at organizing. It's my gift."

"You have many gifts." I touched the foot of the Maggie cat who was kenneled beside me, poking her paws out. She, more so than any of the other cats, seemed especially upset about her newfound captivity. "Hey, remember when we were kids and you kept every single test you ever took?"

"Yes, I suppose I have a bit of a hoarding personality, too." Merry pursed her lips thoughtfully as she reached back into the bin. "Why do you bring that up?"

"Oh, just thought I'd let you know how grateful Eve and I were for that. Saved us many hours of actual studying," I winked.

Merry laughed, throwing her head back. The light from the window caught her eyes, turning them a cerulean blue.

"You weren't fooling anyone," she said. "I knew you two couldn't keep your paws off of my work. But that was one of the few things you were actually united in, so how could I put an end to it?"

I was a bit disappointed that she knew. It was one thing to confess, it was another to be caught. I wondered how many other things she knew. I didn't want to think about it, so I changed the subject back to our original conversation.

"You've done a great job, Merry. No one else could have done so much in so little time."

She blushed and shrugged her round shoulders. She was never one to accept praise.

"June Bug helped. I think she has some healing abilities too. She would pick up the cats and they would calm down enough for me to treat them. It was pretty sweet." Her face glowed with pride.

I couldn't blame her. June Bug was terrific. For a kid.

"Merry, there's something I've been meaning to ask…" I looked at a photo of her, myself, and Eve. We were young, grinning, and standing in front of a giant cauldron on Main Street during a Haunted Dark Root Festival. I turned the photo over to see the year. 1996. The year before Ruth Anne left.

"Yes?" Merry asked, taking the photo.

"Did you believe in this stuff? The whole coven, Haunted Dark Root, Juliana Benbridge, every day is Halloween stuff? Or did you ever feel like we were just…"

"Pawns?" Her dimples deepened, a knowing smile on her face.

I laughed. "Yes, I guess, pawns. I mean, the festival kept Dark Root's economy churning for the next eleven months. Mother dressed us up, paraded us around, and put our pictures in newspapers, the young descendants of Juliana Benbridge. We spent our whole childhoods being told how special we were but what if…"

"…What if it was one big farce?" Merry removed another picture from the box, a young Miss Sasha and Aunt Dora. They wore fitted lavender suits and pumps that showcased their slim figures. Merry checked the date: 1966. She wrinkled her brow, trying to determine how long ago the picture was taken, but gave up.

Math was never her strong suit.

"Ruth Anne didn't believe," I said, cautiously speaking the name of our eldest sister as I removed a picture of her from the bin. Ruth Anne was about twelve in this one, glaring defiantly at the camera. She didn't like to have her photo taken and it showed. "…She said the story of Juliana was made up by Mom and her friends, just to get attention."

"No, she sure didn't believe, but, then again, she was always the odd woman out." Merry inhaled and released it slowly. "I wish I knew where to find her––Ruth Anne––but some people never want to be found."

At least we are talking about her.

I didn't speak this out loud. I didn't want to jinx things.

Merry continued sorting through the photos, paying special attention to the pictures of Ruth Anne. As her dainty fingers pulled each photo from the bin and placed them lovingly in their own stack, I realized, for the first time, that she and Ruth Anne probably had a special relationship I wasn't aware of. After all, Merry was a year and a half older than me, and just three and a half years younger than Ruth Anne. I was gripped by a feeling of envy at their relationship, and pinched my leg to distract myself with the pain.

I wondered, not for the first time, why I felt the need to have Merry all to myself.

We sat in silence for several minutes, both lost in our own thoughts. Finally, Merry spoke.

"We could have been pawns," she said. "Yes. I have wondered that. But you can't deny that there is something special about this town. And us. It wasn't until I moved to Kansas and noticed that others couldn't do the things I––we––could do, that I really began to understand."

She removed a picture of a group of men and women standing in front of a large tree. I recognized many of them: Miss Sasha, Aunt Dora, Uncle Joe, and their friends. The men were decked out in bell bottom jeans and long side burns, while the women wore tube tops, short-shorts, and fake eyelashes. Except for my mother and Aunt Dora, who wore gigantic floral dresses and sun hats. It seemed their slenderness hadn't carried over into the 70s.

"My husband even admitted that I had *something,* especially after June Bug was born," Merry continued, placing the photo in a new pile and looking down at her ring.

"...Now," she said, standing and wiping invisible dust from her hands. "...Can you go to the nursery? I think I saw a stack of boxes in there. We can start looking through those."

She went to refill her coffee cup and I swallowed hard.

It had been many years since I had been in that room.

Could I go back?

THIRTEEN

DON'T FEAR THE REAPER

SISTER HOUSE, DARK ROOT, OREGON
DECEMBER, 1995

MAGGIE STOOD BEFORE HER MOTHER, KNEES SHAKING.

Miss Sasha had her firm face on, the expression she wore when there was no debating the matter. Maggie looked to her sisters for help. Ruth Anne and Merry were already pleading her case, while Eve twirled the ends of her hair nervously. Maggie glowered at Eve. It was her fault she was in this mess in the first place.

"Now, don't you think I'd know if there was something haunting my own house?" Miss Sasha put her hands on her ample hips and the layers of excess flesh caused a mild wave that rippled from buttocks to breasts. "Are you saying I'm not that talented? Is that what you are saying?"

"Leave da girl alone, Sasha," Aunt Dora chimed in. "She's jus' a kid wit an active imagination. As I recall ya had an imagination like dat when ya was little."

Miss Sasha turned towards her younger sister and narrowed her eyes. "Now, now, Dora. I'm not in the mood."

"But there is something in there," Maggie insisted, pointing to the nursery door. "Ask Eve." Maggie nudged her younger sister but Eve just

165

lowered her eyes and said nothing. She was probably more frightened of their mother than of anything that might live in her bedroom.

"I'm getting this out of you once and for all," Miss Sasha said, grabbing Maggie by the elbow. Maggie planted her heels into the carpet, trying to make herself immovable, but her mother outweighed her twice over. "You will stay in there until you're not afraid anymore. When you can tell me, honestly, that there is nothing inside the room I will let you out."

"No, Mother!" Maggie's eyes grew wide as Miss Sasha threw open the door.

Ruth Anne and Merry begged their mother to stop while Eve cowered behind Aunt Dora.

"It's just a room...you'll see. And you'll thank me for it later." Miss Sasha continued to drag Maggie into the nursery, past the crib, the toddler bed, and the old rocking chair. With one hand still on Maggie's arm, she partially unscrewed the light bulb overhead, so that, except for the light coming in from the hall, the room was dark.

Maggie could make out the shapes of the toys around her––dolls, teddy bears, and blocks. A clown doll on the top shelf seemed to smile at her, causing goose bumps to rise on her legs. Maggie dug her nails into her mother's arm and begged her to reconsider.

Miss Sasha shook her head. "It's for your own good."

With that, she marched out of the room and locked the door from the outside.

"What are you doing?" Maggie could hear Ruth Anne in the hall. "You're crazy."

"Please, Mama, let her out," Merry pleaded. "I'll talk to Maggie. She won't make up any more stories."

"I'm done discussing this. That child's imagination needs to be reigned in."

Maggie stood in the dark room, listening as her family's footsteps disappeared down the hall. She gasped as the temperature dropped, the cold air closing in around her.

"Maggie," Eve's voice said from the other side of the door.

Maggie rushed towards the door and lay down, peeking under the large gap. She was nose to nose with her sister. "Evie...please tell Mother I'm not lying. Please tell her about the voices you hear in the nursery. Or about how you wake up bruised sometimes."

"Mom says they are just nightmares," Eve said. "If I tell her again, I will get in trouble."

Maggie was exasperated.

She was here because she had been trying to convince her mother that Eve needed to be moved into the attic with the rest of them. There was something 'bad' in the nursery and it was getting worse since Maggie had moved out of the room. But under their mother's inquisition, Eve wasn't brave enough to back her up. And now Eve was free, while she was trapped.

Without warning, the room began to vibrate. Maggie could feel her cheeks rumble against the bedroom floor. She widened her eyes as she pushed her hands down to make it stop. Instead, the trembling increased, sending small waves across the room.

"Do you feel that?" Maggie whispered.

"Uh-huh."

"Eve, unlock the door. Please. Please." The entire room was shaking now, knocking toys onto the floor. Maggie could hear the crash of dolls and blocks around her and she covered her head with one hand to protect her face. "Unlock the door!"

Eve stood and Maggie could hear the jiggle of the doorknob. "Hurry, Eve, hurry."

A book bounced off the wall above her, dropping down just inches from Maggie's face. The jiggling on the handle continued, then suddenly stopped.

"Did you unlock it?"

Eve began to cry. "I can't. I'm afraid..."

Maggie's heart stopped as her sister's soft footsteps raced through the hallway, and down the staircase. The light in the hall suddenly went out, and except for a dim light coming in from the small, high window, Maggie was in the dark.

Maggie sat up, braced her back against the door, and folded her hands around her knees. The large dollhouse in the corner of the nursery fell forward, scattering small pieces of furniture across the floor. She pushed her face into her knees and cried, wondering why she had tried to help Eve in the first place.

It wasn't fair. None of this was fair.

The porcelain clown doll fell to the floor near Maggie's feet, its mocking glass eyes fixating on her.

"Leave me alone!" Maggie screamed, kicking the doll away from her.

It crashed into the far wall, its face shattering with the impact.

"Leave me alone!" she repeated, standing up and addressing whatever was in the room. "Leave me alone!"

The 'thing' in the nursery had never really been after Eve, Maggie now understood. It had wanted her all along. And now that it had her, it was going to do whatever it took to break her down and keep her here.

"You can't have me!" she screamed, stamping her foot as a book whizzed by her face and crashed against the door.

Maggie picked up the book and threw it across the room with all her might.

The light bulb flickered on. The tremors lessened from a roil to small waves and then ceased altogether.

Maggie crossed her arms, defying whatever had been in there with her to start up again. But it didn't. She knew the 'thing' wasn't gone, but it had given her the win.

This time.

Maggie advanced to the bedroom door and jiggled the handle. It opened easily.

She walked calmly through the hall, down the stairs, and into the living room, where her family was still arguing. Upon seeing her, they

all stopped, staring speechless. Maggie moved past the others and fell
into the arms of Merry, who stroked her hair and kissed her cheek.

Without saying a word, Miss Sasha marched upstairs. Aunt Dora
and Ruth Anne followed behind. When they returned Miss Sasha said,
"Well, I think you've learned your lesson." She looked at Maggie like
she wanted to ask something, but decided against it. Instead she said,
"What a mess you've made. I've a good mind to have you go in there
and clean it all up."

But she didn't.

Eve moved into the attic that night.

Their mother, Maggie learned, did not like to be wrong. About
anything.

Sister House, Dark Root, Oregon
September, 2013

It was just a door, an ordinary door.

The large brass knob was highly ornate, cut with the dramatic
circular-swirling patterns standard in Victorian houses. The door itself
was covered in the same, beige-white paint as the other doors in the
hallway. If you were a visitor to Sister House and just walking by, you
would think it was just an ordinary door leading to an ordinary room.
But I stood before it, paralyzed, as if it could burn me.

There was something on the other side of that door, I knew.

Something ancient and angry.

I shifted my weight from one foot to the other, remembering the
night I was locked inside alone. I had won that battle, or at least escaped.
But that had been years ago. Real monsters don't get smaller with time.
They grew.

And though I had seen other 'things' since that time, nothing evoked the same level of fear in me that the 'thing' that lived in the nursery evoked.

And now I had to face it again.

"I can do this," I told myself, wiping my sweating palms on my skirt before reaching for the knob. My fingers folded around it, but hesitated.

"It knows you are here," a voice said, making me jump.

I stepped backwards, looking up and down the hall, my eyes searching for shapes that hid in the shadows.

"June Bug?" I called out. "Merry?"

No answer.

"Mother?" I tried again.

The light bulb above me dimmed.

I could go downstairs, I thought. I could tell Merry I couldn't find the picture boxes and leave it at that. But the thought of Merry giving me that sympathetic look, and knowing that I was both a liar and a coward was worse than my fears. She had argued on my behalf when we were kids, but I don't think she ever believed me.

I came up with another plan.

I would rush in, grab the boxes, then jump out. Whatever was in there wouldn't have time to react; I could be that quick. As I reached for the handle again, I thought I heard a soft laugh from inside, a child's laugh. I could feel invisible tendrils slither out from beneath the door, wrapping themselves around my feet, winding up my legs and skirt. I couldn't see them, but I could feel them. They were darkness and ice.

I wasn't going in there. I couldn't go in there. I didn't care anymore what Merry thought. There was nothing in hell or on earth that could make me turn that doorknob.

The icy tendrils tightened their grip on my legs.

There was a scream––loud and guttural––but it wasn't mine.

I heard footsteps in the hall and the tendrils withdrew.

Merry rushed towards me. I thought she had come to my rescue, but she kept running towards Mother's room at the end of the hall.

"Maggie!" she called to me, her face white. "Quick! Call an

170

ambulance! We need to get Mama to the hospital."

The ambulance arrived ten minutes later, loading Mother on to a long blue gurney.

We watched helplessly as her eyes fluttered open and shut, her breathing labored and grasping. Merry hovered over her, reciting prayers and feeding Mama her healing energy as the paramedics loaded her into their red and white wagon.

Seeing her grandmother like this, June Bug began to cry. I took her in my arms and hugged her, telling her that everything was going to be okay.

"You promise?" she asked, looking up at me, her face soft and hopeful.

"Yes." I kissed the top of her head. "I promise."

"Someone has to ride along," one of the paramedics said.

My mother's face was ashy grey, her lips were blue and her skin transparent. If I couldn't be in the same room with her when she was awake and crazy, I sure couldn't be with her when she looked like she was about to die.

I tried to speak, to make up some excuse, but Merry volunteered instead. "Stay with June Bug. I will call you when I can."

The ambulance doors closed behind them.

June Bug and I stood in the rain, watching the car disappear around the winding road.

"How long will Mommy be gone?" June Bug asked, her hair soaked and sticking to her face.

"I don't know. But I'm here with you now. I won't let anything happen to you." I took her hand, wedging my fingers in between hers.

Lightning cracked, splitting off the branch of a nearby tree.

We jumped as it hit the ground.

"Let's get you back in the house before you get sick," I said.

June Bug nodded, her chin round yet stubborn. She pulled me inside.

The rain continued to dump on us, but June Bug and I were cozy as we huddled up in the living room, playing checkers.

She was surprisingly good, and I didn't have to cheat to let her win.

When she grew tired of board games, she played dress up, trying on some of Miss Sasha's old clothes. She sang and danced as she shimmied in boas and high-heeled shoes.

I clapped, whistling and begging for more.

It was a strange feeling, having a niece. I didn't know her really, but I loved her. There was something about her youthful innocence that charmed me, made me believe in things. Or perhaps it was because she reminded me so much of her mother.

At any rate, I was beginning to see why people had kids around.

"Want me to make you cocoa?" I asked, as she tried on sun hats.

I was having such a good time that I had almost forgotten that Mother and Merry were at the hospital. My cell phone rang and brought me back to reality.

"Maggie. Oh God, Maggie. They think Mama's had a stroke!" Merry was sobbing, trying to catch her breath.

"Want me to call Shane and have him bring us up?"

"No." She inhaled audibly, holding it. "There's nothing you can do here. I know it's a lot to ask, but please stay with June Bug and let her know I will be back as soon as I can."

Merry paused for so long I thought she had hung up the phone. Then she started crying again. I stayed with her, saying nothing.

Finally, she regained her composure. "Oh, Maggie. What if she...?"

I wouldn't let her finish the sentence.

"Merry, don't. It will be okay." I laughed, trying to lighten her mood. "Our mother's a tough old bird. It will take more than a stroke to take her down."

Merry sniffled and agreed, but I could tell she was really afraid. So was I.

"Don't worry about June Bug," I said. "I will keep her safe, okay? Stay with Mother and we will figure things out tomorrow."

"Thank you, Maggie. I know she's in good hands." Another pause. "I love you. I'm glad you're here."

"I love you too, Merry," I said, looking at my niece in the living room. "I won't let you down."

We hung up and I was left with the unsettling feeling of guilt, a feeling I was getting used to since coming home. Then the realization of what Merry said came back to me. Mother had a stroke? It didn't seem possible. She had gotten old in the last few years but her life force was still strong, if a bit unstable.

I searched the kitchen for something resembling alcohol and found a half-empty bottle of wine. I popped the cork and poured myself a glass. I needed something to jolt me from this funk. I almost tripped over June Bug, who was now sprawled out on the floor, arranging her teddy bears around a makeshift picnic blanket. She looked at me, all blue eyes and dimples. She was wearing one of Mother's shawls.

"Is the cocoa ready yet, Aunt Maggie?"

I turned, mid-step, towards the kitchen. "Yes, honey. I'm getting it now," I said, dumping the wine in the sink and heating water for cocoa.

FOURTEEN

WHO'LL STOP THE RAIN

DARKNESS DESCENDED ON US like a flock of wild ravens as the rain continued.

Sister House screeched and groaned, protesting the deluge that battered her old roof, a roof that had been patched over the years, but never properly repaired. As a result, a few small leaks sprung in the house, mostly in the attic.

June Bug and I gathered pots and bowls to collect water from the leaks, steering clear of the nursery. When we were done, we gathered up armfuls of blankets and pillows, intending to camp in the living room overnight.

"This will be fun," I assured her, and June Bug bobbed her head, eagerly following me as we made our preparations. For good measure we grabbed flashlights, candles, matches, marshmallows and Ruth Anne's old copy of *Little Women*.

Downstairs, the shutters rattled, the pipes knocked, and the furnace complained when we fired it up, but eventually the place was warm and cozy. The only thing that ruined the atmosphere was the smell and sound of cats, all meowing and yelping through their kennels.

And the thought of Merry and Mother in the hospital, my mind added.

June Bug was a steady stream of conversation, telling me about the bugs she collected, her home back in Kansas, and the things she liked about Dark Root. Merry had been a talker too, and when I looked at June Bug, sprawled out on a throw rug, concentrating on a picture she was coloring, I was transported back to the days when Merry and I would color pages while Eve danced and Mother played records. Ruth Anne and Aunt Dora would be huddled at the dining room table, discussing one of Aunt Dora's *Time-Life* books on ancient civilizations.

It didn't seem that long ago, but it had been almost twenty years.

I took a long sip of my cocoa and let the warmth of the memory wash over me. This was one of the first good memories I had of my childhood, and I didn't want to lose it.

"I think I'm going to sort through some more of these pictures," I said, grabbing a box.

June Bug nodded. She had seen her mother sort enough boxes to realize this was important––and boring––'grown up' work.

"Look. Here's your mama when she was about your age."

I showed June Bug a picture of a petite, blonde girl in a white dress and a big hat. She held a large cat in her arms as she leaned against one of the pillars on the porch. Aunt Dora sat on the swing behind her, crocheting.

June Bug inspected the picture. "Aunt Maggie, how come you have red hair and Mommy's is yellow?"

"I don't know," I said, putting the picture in one stack and removing another. "I guess that's just the way God made us."

"What's God?"

"You don't know who God is?"

"No."

"Well..." I began tentatively.

If Merry hadn't given her a spiritual upbringing, I wasn't sure it was my place. Especially when my own religious views were in question. But she had asked.

"Some people believe that there is someone called God who made the entire world and all the people in it," I said finally.

"And the dogs and cats and bugs?"

"Yes. All of it."

"Is God a boy or a girl?"

"I don't know that, either. God's invisible. Some people think he is a boy and some people think He––I mean, She––is a girl."

"Do you think God's a boy or a girl?"

"I hadn't really thought about it. A boy, I guess."

"Do you believe in God?"

I wanted to tell her that I wasn't sure what I believed anymore.

Twenty years with Mother, and seven with Michael, had given me the foundation to believe in *something*, but I wasn't sure what that something was. Their religions at times seemed twisted and convoluted and applicable only to certain people. But I had seen and experienced too much to think there was *nothing* out there. I answered as honestly as I could.

"Well, I talk to God sometimes, so I guess I do believe."

"Is God nice?"

"I think so. I hear God used to have a temper but got nicer once He––or She––had a kid."

I shrugged, never quite understanding that. Back in the days when we were building Woodhaven, we had discussed the nature of God at length, but had never come to a consensus. I thought about it a bit more before continuing.

"...When most people talk to God, they are usually asking for something, so I guess that means we think God is nice."

"That means God is a girl." June Bug grinned like she had won a game. "When I want something I always ask Mommy––not Daddy–– because girls are the nicest."

"Excellent logic," I agreed.

Something occurred to me.

"Aren't you supposed to be in school?" I removed a stack of Eve's baby photos and dumped them on the floor in a pile of their own. For some reason, there were more photos of Eve than of all the rest of us combined.

Even as a baby, Eve demanded the spotlight.

June Bug concentrated, thrusting her tongue out of the side of her mouth. "Daddy doesn't believe in the public education system and he says there are no good private schools in our town so Mommy home-schools me."

She finished her drawing, a simple picture of a little girl holding hands with a red-headed, stick-figure woman. It made me smile.

"Don't you want to go to school?" I said.

"Not really."

"Don't you want to make friends?"

"Mommy's my friend." June Bug placed all her Crayola's back in their package, arranging them in order of color, just like her mother used to. "...And you're my friend, too."

"I see," I said, continuing to sort through the latest box of pictures.

I wasn't sure why Merry was bothering with the task. There were a million other ways she could spend her time, but she took her role as the 'family keeper' seriously. She liked to have things neat, laid out, and... preserved.

"Besides," June Bug continued, putting her art supplies into the small purple tote beside her. "...When I get bigger, I am going to live with my daddy, anyways. He says there are nice schools in Daytona."

My jaw hit my chin at the same time her art tote hit the coffee table. I was about to resume my questioning but she plodded upstairs.

Go live with her daddy? In Daytona?

Merry hadn't mentioned a word about Frank being in Daytona. I knew children had big imaginations, but she was so matter-of-fact about it, I couldn't believe it was all made up.

June Bug returned, wearing large, dark sunglasses and a bright yellow boa this time.

"How do I look?" she asked, pretending to flick a fake cigarette. It was scary how well she had my mother down, considering she had not grown up with her. DNA was a powerful thing.

"Just like your grandmother."

She squealed. Apparently that was what she had been going for.

"June Bug," I continued cautiously. "You said your daddy is in Daytona? Is he on a business trip?"

"No." June Bug drew out the word as she uncoiled the boa from her neck and wrapped it around the banister. "He lives there with Missy."

"Missy?"

"My second mom. She's not as nice as my real mom, but..." June Bug shrugged and disappeared once again upstairs.

That son of a bitch!

I knew it! I knew he couldn't stay away from little girls. I'll bet the second Merry turned twenty-five he left for the first barely-legal, eighteen-year-old he could get his wrinkled hands on. I tightened my fists, trying to control my anger as lightning cracked outside.

How dare him?!

He was lucky he wasn't here or I would...I wasn't sure, but I would do something.

I put my hands on either side of my head, trying to remove the throbbing in my temple. Why hadn't Merry mentioned this to us––to me––that her jerk face husband wasn't in the picture anymore? No wonder my mother hadn't trusted men. They weren't worth trusting, not a one of them.

I was about call Merry and demand an explanation, when I noticed a picture lying on the top of the heap, one I hadn't seen before. It was a photo of our mother standing next to a familiar-looking woman. The woman had a pleasant face and piercing green eyes and looked pregnant. They gazed intently into the camera, expressionless.

I turned over the photo and saw that the year was 1985.

I studied the picture, racking my brain, trying to remember where I had seen the woman. Then it dawned on me. It was Jillian, the woman I had met at Dip Stix the other day, the psychic-medium who had given me her card. She was about a quarter of a century younger in the photo, but it was her. At some point, she had known my mother.

I looked at the picture again.

There was nothing in the background to indicate where they were. Mother wore a large muumuu to cover up her own pregnancy, but otherwise the picture offered no clues. They had probably met at some natural childbirth class. Or a psychic fair.

I put the photo into my skirt pocket.

I would show it to Merry. She would know how Jillian knew our mother. Somehow, I felt it wasn't sheer coincidence that Jillian had wandered into Dip Stix a few days ago.

My thoughts were broken by the loud slam of a door from upstairs.

"Aunt Maggie! Aunt Maggie! Help!"

Without having to be told, I knew that June Bug was in the nursery.

I wasn't sure how I would make it up the stairs; they stood before me like Mount Everest, foreboding and insurmountable. I fought through my fear, willing my feet upwards, all the while wanting to turn back.

"Help!" June Bug called again as she pulled on the doorknob.

"I'm coming!" I propelled myself forward by holding onto the banister.

My feet felt heavy, like I was walking through mud. The lights overhead flickered uneasily. Finally I reached the top, staring into the dark hallway ahead. I could hear June Bug's hands hammering on the nursery door, punctuated by small screams. I quickened my pace, flipping on the hallway light switch.

It didn't come on.

When I reached the nursery, I noticed a vile energy emanating from beneath the door. It smelled like garbage and made me gag.

"I'm here," I said, tugging and twisting on the knob, fighting back the urge to retch. "Don't worry, honey."

"Aunt Maggie!" she cried as something crashed into the door.

"Be brave." I tried another light switch. No luck. "...And cover your head."

"The floor's starting to shake!" June Bug's fingers clawed at the door.

I could feel the ripples at my feet.

"Stand back!" I ordered, realizing that I would have to break the door down to get inside. I backed up to the wall behind me. I paused, took three deep breaths, then rammed my body into the door. It cracked down the center with the impact but did not open.

June Bug screamed again.

"That was just me," I said, rubbing my shoulder and backing up. "I'm gonna try again."

"Hurry, Aunt Maggie! *Please.*"

I breathed through my nose, focusing on the thin crack that had formed with my last push. If I did this a few more times, I would break it down. I lowered my head like a bull and charged the door, closing my eyes as I hit.

Only I didn't hit. I flew.

The door had flung itself open and I sailed past, tumbling into the middle of the room. My head hit something hard on the ground and I almost lost my breath. I turned, ready to grab June Bug and bolt out, but the door snapped shut behind me.

"Aunt Maggie!"

June Bug was on me, shielding me from flying objects with her small arms. Though it was dark inside, I could still make out the shadows of toys swirling around us in a mini cyclone. I picked her up and moved back towards the door, fighting through the flying debris.

We pulled on the doorknob together, but it still wouldn't turn.

I ran my fingers over the door, searching for the crack, but it was smooth. I looked around for something big enough to use as a battering ram. Dodging objects, I felt my way to the nightstand in the far corner of the room. A hardcover book flew at me, hitting me in the eye.

Instinctively, I put both hands over my face to fight back the pain. *Fuck this.*

"No!" I yelled into the dark. "No!"

The objects continued to swirl around me.

I stamped my foot, just as I had done as a kid. "No!"

The quivering floor now erupted into heavy waves which popped nails from the floorboards, sending them flying like shrapnel. I could see June Bug crawling for cover behind the large dollhouse. I caught the shadow of another book flying at me, and I managed to catch it, ripping it out of the air.

I flung it back against the opposite wall and it crashed, falling like a dead bird.

"NO!" I repeated with more force.

"Aunt Maggie, something's on me!" June Bug shouted and I ran to her.

The whirlwind of toys intensified, picking up more objects as it whipped around us. I shielded her with my body, pulling her with me to the door to try again.

It was still locked.

I was angry, so fucking angry. How dare it trap us in here like animals in a zoo?

"Please, God," June Bug whispered. "Help Aunt Maggie..."

I reached for the crystal dangling around my neck. It was hot. I closed my eyes and tightened my fingers around it, searching for calmness.

I leapt into the mental realm of nothingness, breathing deeply, pushing all thoughts from my brain. I could sense June Bug's presence, but I was no longer there with her. I was somewhere else, watching...

"Is she going to be okay?" It was Merry.

"Yes, darlin'. She'll be fine," Aunt Dora said.

I squinted my eyes at the sleeping figure in the bed and realized it was me.

Ruth Anne dabbed my head with a cold cloth, while Mother opened the window, letting in a cool breeze.

"I'm scared, Mom." Eve said.

I groaned, turning over, throwing off the covers. There was light in the room, but I couldn't make out the time. I had been in and out of sleep for days, maybe weeks.

The voices faded, becoming background noise and then it was dark.

Everything hurt. I felt weak. My life force was slipping away. I wanted to cry, knowing that soon I might be gone, but I was beyond crying.

I felt someone slip in the bed behind me. Warm lips touched my cheek and a strong hand brushed damp hair away from my brow.

"Magdalene." My mother said the word and held my shivering body.

I thought I heard her cry and the sound prodded me through the pain. I had never heard my mother cry. I focused my awareness on her, listening.

"You can't take her," she said, her voice barely louder than a whisper. "I love her and she's mine." She wrapped her arms around me and though I was burning up, I took great comfort in her embrace.

I fell asleep.

When I awoke, it was midday. I was able to open my eyes.

I could feel my mother still lying in bed with me. I turned to face her. She was staring at me, smiling.

"Welcome back, Magdalene..."

My eyes flashed open.

I was back in the nursery with June Bug, surrounded by chaos.

The image of my mother returned, her arms wrapped around me while we fought back my illness. I had no recollection of that memory until today.

Another book hit me in the head. I ignored it. I was calm as I faced the dark.

"Let us go," I said, directing my words towards the door.

The door shuddered, but did not open.

"Let us go," I said again, not raising my voice as I marched towards

183

the door and tried the handle.

"You can't have her," I said, opening my arms. "Not today, not ever. I love her and I will do whatever it takes to get her out of here. You and I can fight another day, but I'm getting her out of this room. Now."

The crystal hummed around my neck. The floor ceased moving.

June Bug tried the door, and it opened in her hands.

Anger had saved me as a kid, but it was love that saved me as an adult.

I scooped June Bug up in my arms and carried her down the dark hallway and into the living room.

"You saved me," she said, still clinging to my neck.

"Of course I did, silly. I love you."

"Where are we going?" June Bug asked as I crammed her pajamas and art kit into a backpack.

The cats meowed loudly, as if they knew they were on their own for the night. I felt bad that no one would be there to change litter boxes, but I had left enough food in their kennels to keep them fed for a week.

"We are getting out of here," I said, inspecting the house one last time.

It felt normal again, like the last hour had been a bad dream. But I knew the 'thing' was still in there, gathering energy.

"Can we call Mommy?" June Bug asked, as she tied her shoelaces.

I shook my head. "We are going to spend the night at Harvest Home with Auntie Eve and Paul and Aunt Dora. Won't that be fun? I'll let your mommy know when we get there, okay?"

June Bug checked on her cats and critters then grabbed her coat. "Okay."

A horn outside let us know that Shane had arrived.

I took June Bug's hand and we hastily made our way outside, picking our way down the porch steps. I forgot to lock the door, and when I remembered I almost turned back, but stopped myself. Anyone crazy enough to break in deserved what they got, be it ghosts or cats.

"Sorry I couldn't get here faster," Shane said. "The road is really bad right now. These rains have taken their toll."

"What was trying to get me?" June Bug asked, as we piled into Shane's pickup.

He backed up, turning around to leave the driveway. The tree branches bobbed in the wind as if waving goodbye.

"I don't know what that 'thing' is," I said. "I wish I did." I stared out the steamed window.

Shane was right. The road had turned to slush.

"It said it was going to keep me there forever. It said it was lonely. At first, I felt bad for it."

"Listen, honey." I took her chin roughly in my hand and forced her to make eye contact. "Don't you ever feel sorry for that thing in there. Okay?"

June Bug started to cry and I released my grip on her.

Shane squared his jaw and punched the gas.

"I'm sorry," I said. "I've just never been that scared in my entire life."

"It's okay, Aunt Maggie." June Bug rested her head on my arm, nuzzling me. "I'll keep you safe."

I gave Shane a sideways look, but he didn't notice. He was lost in thoughts of his own.

FIFTEEN

NIGHT MOVES

By the time we reached Harvest Home, June Bug was fast asleep.

Shane carried her inside, placing her on the sofa in the den. He and I then gathered in the living room with Eve.

"What do you mean, something was trying to get her?" Eve stormed back and forth across the room, her hands balled up into fists. "Are you sure, Maggie? I mean, this isn't one of your fantasies, is it?"

"Of course I'm sure. June Bug was screaming and something was holding the door."

Shane nodded. "June Bug said the same thing to me when I picked them up." He looked across the room, his eyes resting on Aunt Dora who was sleeping in a recliner. "I know kids make up stories, but I believe her." His eyes fell on me. "...And Maggie."

I felt a wave of gratitude for him.

He believed me. Who cared what Eve thought?

"Merry trusted you with her daughter!" Eve said accusingly as she rushed towards a small black bag on the dining room table. "And you let this happen!"

"I didn't *let* this happen," I said. "It happened. And we got her out."

I remembered the night I was trapped in the room with the 'thing' myself as a kid and Eve was there, unwilling to help. Who was she to accuse me of anything?

Eve returned with her bag and removed a thin, rectangular device, hardly bigger than a book. "I say, we fight fire with fire. If this thing wants to mess with a little girl, he better be prepared for the big girls, too." She pushed a button on the machine and it turned on.

A Windows icon flashed across the top of it.

"What is that, and what are you doing?" I asked, watching her fingers slide frantically across the device, bringing up a series of pictures.

"I'm checking the internet on my tablet."

I was in awe as I watched her, and I wondered why Mother had placed so much stock in magic when there were things like this in the universe.

"For what?" I finally asked. "Things that go bump in the night? I thought you didn't want anything to do with that stuff?"

"Maybe I didn't before, but that's my niece up there. I'm not about to let the same thing happen to her that happened to..."

She stopped, pushing her lips tightly together.

I narrowed my eyes, wondering if I had missed a near-admission. Eve continued checking her tablet, groaning as the minutes ticked by.

"Maggie," Shane said, as I watched Eve work. "Do you remember anything about the original Council, before they became the Council of Seven?"

"What does that have to do with anything?" I asked him, confused.

"Just answer me."

"Okay," I said, trying to pull up a memory. "I do remember there being a few more people in Mother's 'group' when I was really young, including a couple of men. That's about it."

"Yes." Shane ran his palm through his hair, trying to pick the right words. "Uncle Joe and Leo were the only men left then, and that was only because they were..."

"Gay," Eve chimed in, not lifting her eyes from the screen. "Mom didn't trust straight men."

"Eve's right on that," I said.

At some point in my early childhood, our mother had taken to man-bashing, but she never said why.

"Well," Shane continued. "Uncle Joe told me some things shortly before he died. I wasn't supposed to say anything, because your mother might get angry, but..." He paused, checking to see if Aunt Dora was still asleep.

He didn't have to worry. Her snoring was almost as loud as the TV she slept in front of. She wouldn't hear a word we said. Even so, he lowered his voice.

"...The Council of Seven was originally the Council of Thirteen. There was a rift in the group because some members didn't think your mother was using their magick to its fullest potential. They thought they could be more powerful if they could just learn to control a few things."

"Like what?" I said. There was something about his tone that made me nervous.

He took a long time before answering.

"Demons."

"What the hell?" Eve stopped playing with her computer and looked up. "That's crazy, even for this town."

Shane said, "It's true, at least according to Uncle Joe, and I've never knew him to lie."

I nodded. Uncle Joe was the most honest person I had ever met.

"How do we know *you* aren't lying?" Eve crossed her arms and leaned back, appraising him.

Shane shrugged. "I have no reason to lie. I'm just repeating what I've heard."

"I don't doubt you," I said. "But what's this have to do with us?"

The temperature in the room seemed to be dropping. I looked around for my sweater. It was thrown across the back of a chair and I put it on. It smelled like wet alpaca.

"It was said that those strong enough to control a demon could gain access to unlimited power," Shane explained. "Think of it like the genie being let out of a bottle, then having to obey its master. Some of the members were growing weary of just doing rain dances and performing protection spells. They wanted more, and they thought having a demon do their bidding was the way to go. But, because there weren't many demons running around, in order to control one, they had to summon one..."

He let the words sink in and I pulled the sweater tighter around me.

Why would anyone think it was a good idea to try and control a demon? To use Shane's genie analogy, things never went right when someone was presented with absolute power. I had read Arabian Nights. The genies always won.

Shane continued after an appropriate silence.

"...A few of the men in the group actually tried their hand at summoning," he said. "Your mother, of course, was against it and became infuriated when she heard about it. She banished them and their supporters from the group."

My heart began to race and I felt like I was being watched. I looked over my shoulder just to be sure.

"You mean the 'things' I've been seeing may be more than just ghosts?" I said.

"Just ghosts?" Eve scoffed. "As if ghosts aren't bad enough!"

"Shut up, Eve!" I ordered her. "Take something seriously, for once."

Shane thrust his hand between us. "I didn't bring this up to start a war. I just wanted you to know that this may be bigger than what we got the guns for."

So this was why Mother distrusted men. It made more sense now.

As if reading my thoughts, Shane gave me a somber look but said nothing.

"Stupid internet," Eve complained, flicking the side of her tablet. "It keeps shutting down."

"The connection's terrible here," Paul said, coming in from the outside and shutting the door behind him. He had messy hair and red eyes. He had either been sleeping out there or smoking something. He rubbed his hands together for warmth. "...I already tried. If you hold your tablet just right, you might pick up the neighbor's connection for a few minutes, but then it goes dark. The World Wide Web seems to stop at Dark Root..."

"Dip Stix has internet," Shane spoke up. "Free Wi-Fi for customers, not that it draws them in. Come by tomorrow. You can use my computer." He took the keys out of his jeans pants pocket.

I knew it was late, but I didn't want him to leave.

After all that had happened today––watching Mother and Merry drive away in an ambulance, learning about Merry's cheating husband, and rescuing my niece from a possible demon attack, I wanted as many people around me as possible.

Especially someone as positive as Shane Doler.

"Stay," I said, hoping he didn't notice the fear in my voice. "We have extra rooms if you don't mind all the flowers and baskets everywhere." When he didn't answer I added, "Please?"

He nodded and put the keys back into his pocket.

"I need to get to bed then," he said, turning his head towards the staircase. "Dip Stix opens early and I need to be there, customers or not."

He said goodnight to Paul and Eve and I escorted him upstairs, turning on every light in the hallway as we made our way to the only masculine room in the house, The Huntsman Suite. It was a darkly-paneled room, with pictures of fish and deer hanging randomly on the walls. A bear rug lay in front of the four-poster bed.

"Paul not want this room?" he asked, his smile almost a smirk.

"He likes sleeping in the attic. Besides, he's a vegetarian. Says all the dead animals creep him out."

"Oh, really? I thought I saw him eating meat at the cafe."

"He just smells it. Says he gets his fix that way, but won't eat the stuff anymore. Something about spending a summer working on a farm one year."

"Weird guy."

"Not really."

Shane gave me a quizzical look then changed the subject. "There's something that's been bothering me. I'm as worried about June Bug as you are, but I do find it interesting that your mother went to the hospital today, yet neither you nor Eve brought it up this evening. It's none of my business, but..."

I pretended not to hear him as I went into the closet and pulled out some extra pillows and tossed them onto the bed. I grabbed a spare sheet as well.

"Maggie?" he pushed, waiting for an answer.

"That is interesting, isn't it?" I bit my bottom lip and considered. "Maybe Eve and I are more alike then I realized." *Both soulless?* "Anyways, thank you. For everything."

I felt myself blush. In the last week I had thanked him more than I had ever thanked anyone. I was sounding like a parrot.

"No problem. Anything I can do for any of you girls––ever––I will do. Got it?" He leaned back against the headboard, then removed his watch from his wrist and placed it on the nightstand.

I wasn't used to men being nice to me and I wondered what the catch was. I tilted my head to the right, trying to get a read on him, but I couldn't find any hidden agendas in his energy.

Odd. And nice.

"Guess I better get to bed, too," I said, pretending to admire a picture of a bear with a fish in its mouth.

"Okay." His voice was soft and his smile warm. He took the extra pillows I offered him, fluffed them up, and placed them by his side.

I turned towards the door, but didn't leave. "When I left Woodhaven, I felt like I lost not only my boyfriend, but my family." I bit my bottom lip to stop it from quivering. I could feel his eyes on my back. "There was this guy...Jason. He was so great. Cute and smart and always there for me. I think I miss him the most."

"Oh?"

"Yes. You remind me of him," I said, turning my head over my shoulder, aware of the heaviness of my hair as it slid down my back.

Shane sat up, his eyes unblinking. "Really? Now that is interesting.

Tell me more about *Jason*."

"He was always getting me out of trouble. I guess I have a way of getting into it."

"That you do. You say he was cute?"

"Very. All the girls liked him but he didn't seem to notice."

"You and Jason ever...?"

"Ever?" His question caught me off guard, and it took a moment to figure out what he was implying. "Oh, God no," I said. "He was like a brother to me. That would have been incestuous."

I almost added that I had stopped seeing Jason as a brother the day he took me to the bus stop, but it was a moot point now, so I remained silent.

"Great," Shane said, falling backwards as he rubbed his eyes. "Now, if you'll excuse me, I need some rest. Something tells me we have a big day tomorrow."

Sixteen

September

"I REALLY APPRECIATE YOU DRIVING ME," I said, as Shane pulled into the hospital parking lot just outside of Linsburg.

The lot was nearly empty, and we found a space close to the entrance. It was nothing like the enormous hospitals I'd been to with Michael in California, where you had to take shuttles from the parking lot to the main building. Not that I had been in many hospitals, but there were times, Michael said, when even God needed a hand in answering prayers.

"Again, no problem, and please stop thanking me. It's unbecoming of someone of your station." Shane offered me a tired, half-smile as we walked towards Guest Services.

The wind had a chill to it and I pulled my sweater tightly around me. If I stayed in Dark Root much longer, I would be forced to go clothes shopping. I wasn't prepared for the cold weather to come.

"Are you sure we should have left Scooby and Shaggy alone?" I asked, referring to Eve and Paul. They were back at Dip Stix, *conducting research* on the internet.

"I think they'll be okay. Paul seems to know his way around a kitchen, as does Eve. I feel confident that if someone comes in, they will be well taken care of."

The receptionist let us know that my mother was checked into room 212 on the second floor. As we made our way to the elevator I was starting to regret my decision. "You sure you don't want to go with me?" I smiled brightly, enticingly. "It will be fun!"

He shook his head as the elevator doors popped open. "No, my dear. I'm going to kill some time in the reception area. They have a fantastic selection of *O, The Oprah Magazine* I'm dying to get my hands on."

He winked and practically shoved me into the elevator, before disappearing behind the two steel doors.

I wasn't happy to be here, and I wasn't planning on stepping foot inside Mother's room. I was simply going to check on Merry, drop off a bag of her things, and leave. I took deep breaths as the elevator doors opened, reminding myself of the plan.

The hall was long, narrow, and overly bright. Vases filled with fresh flowers were set on tables outside every door. Old people in wheelchairs, pushed by tired-looking nurses, greeted me as I walked by. A brass number on the nearest door let me know that I had arrived at room 312. I spun around and walked quickly in the opposite direction.

"Maggie?"

It was Merry's voice.

I stopped, smiled, and turned back around. Upon seeing her I opened my arms and said, "There you are!" When she didn't call me on catching me mid-flight, I knew something was wrong. "Mother?"

Merry bobbed her head, sniffling, and I followed her to the room.

"She's gotten worse in the few hours since we talked on the phone," she choked, her red eyes tearing up. "I just don't know what to do."

I handed Merry her bag and pushed open the door to peek inside. The woman lying there hooked up to a series of tubes and machines couldn't be my mother. She had become so thin that the blue veins in her hands popped out like electrical wires. Her breathing was hoarse and intermittent, as if it might stop at any moment, puttering along like an old car.

"Oh, Maggie," Merry whispered.

She placed a hand on my shoulder and I could feel that her life energy, usually so vibrant and robust, was fading. She must have been feeding it to Mother.

"Do they still think it's a stroke?" I tried to drown out the whirring and buzzing of the machines emerging from her room.

Merry shrugged, allowing a lone tear to trail down her pale cheek. I wiped it away with the tip of my fingers. She looked like she was about to collapse.

Merry was an empath. Whatever feeling she was experiencing, she was able to reflect onto others. She usually radiated joy and we clamored to bask in that happiness with her. But her empathy worked both ways, allowing her to take on the emotions and illnesses of those around her. She was a kind soul and never complained as she went about her 'work,' but I could sense that attending to our mother had taken too much from her.

"Pull from me." I said, taking her hands. "Take my energy, Merry."

She shook her head but my hands tightened around hers, squeezing them hard. I didn't have Merry's kind spirit but I did have something that she lacked. Strength.

"Take it," I said.

Merry nodded and we closed our eyes and stood nose to nose, hands joined. She pushed her energy through me and I was overcome by feelings of her burden: sadness, helplessness, and desperation. When she was done feeding me hers, I offered her mine, hoping I wouldn't poison her. Merry was pure love and I...wasn't.

When the transfer was complete, we opened our eyes. Merry had regained color in her cheeks while I felt weak and unsteady. I placed one hand on the wall to keep from falling.

"Sorry to give you all that," she said. "...And thank you."

I noticed her round, almost angelic features. June Bug had her face. They possessed an ethereal beauty that even Eve couldn't touch.

"I hope Mother gets better soon," I said. My stomach roiled but I forced myself to stand upright. I knew the feeling would pass. "June Bug misses her mommy."

Merry brightened at the mention of her daughter. "Speaking of which, I talked to June Bug today. Thank you for looking after her."

I arched an eyebrow. "Did she say anything?" I hadn't told Merry about our encounter in Sister House several days ago. She could only handle one worry at a time.

"Just that she loves her aunties and that you guys are starting up the Haunted Dark Root Festival again. She is so excited." Merry's eyes took on a faraway look. "I told her stories about how much fun we had as kids. I'm just surprised."

"Surprised?"

"Yes. You are the last person I expected to help out with something like that. This means more to me than you will ever know."

I almost told her I wasn't sure how long I would be in town or how much I would actually help, but she looked so happy. We could talk later.

"I need to go the cafeteria." Merry glanced through the door at our mother. "Do you mind staying with Mama? You don't have to go in. Just stand out here. If anything changes, there's a button on her bed that will call the nurses. Don't worry," she added, sensing my nervousness. "There are always nurses buzzing around here. I haven't had to push that button yet."

"Okay." If she could stay here with Mother for days, I could survive a few minutes.

"I love you, Magdalene." Merry kissed my cheek, then left.

I was left feeling like a peeping tom as I watched Mother from the doorway. I regarded her thin, lined face, her slightly parted lips as she struggled for breath. Her hair was tangled and matted around her. I stood for a while, lulled into a semi-trance as I listened to the machines hum along reassuringly.

"She'd be a great decoration for Haunted Dark Root," Merry said, startling me.

I laughed at her joke. She wasn't usually one for dark humor.

"Yep. Put her in a haunted house."

"She used to scare the Bejeezus out of me when she would run around like a wild woman under the full moons," Merry admitted.

"Really? You never told me you were afraid of anything."

"Well, after awhile, it just became par for the course."

I took Merry's hand and we stood like ghosts outside her door, lost in memories of a shared childhood.

Suddenly, Mother jolted and her body began to convulse.

"Mama!" Merry dropped my hand and raced inside. Mother's head flopped violently from side to side. Her eyes opened, then rolled back into her head.

Merry jabbed her fingers at the call button. "Maggie, quick. Find a nurse!"

I sped up and down the hall, but the place was quiet. I came back to the room and Merry was holding our mother, trying to calm her.

"You must stop Larinda!" my mother said, her head turning in my direction. "You must stop her!"

"Where's the fucking nurse?" I took over Merry's job of punching the call button.

"Calm down, Mama," Merry said. "We are here. Everything will be okay."

"The circle will be broken!" Mother screeched, arching her back and aiming her chin towards the ceiling.

Three women in gray scrubs rushed in, pushing us aside. "Please step out," a nurse ordered me. I nodded, backing into the hallway.

Merry remained at Mother's side before being ushered out herself. The same nurse took a long needle and injected something into Mother's bony arm. She let out one final yowl and collapsed onto the bed.

"Larinda. She said the name a lot, that first day we arrived here. Who is that?" Merry asked.

Her face was wet and I couldn't tell if it was because of sweat or tears.

The memory of the dream I had several weeks ago came back at me: The spiral-haired woman chasing us through the parade and Mother calling her Larinda.

"I don't know," I admitted. "But I'm going to find out."

A nurse left the room and I caught her arm as she tried to pass. "Is she going to be all right?"

She gave me a solemn look but didn't respond.

"Go home and take care of my daughter," Merry directed me. "I've been here a few days now, I can stay here as long as I'm needed. Aunt Dora can relieve me if necessary."

I felt like a beaten dog as I slunk out of the hospital, but I couldn't go back. I would rather face that 'thing' in the nursery a dozen times then see Mother like this. I stood in the elevator pressing random buttons, letting the doors open and close as I decided what to do. I remembered the vision of my mother lying in bed with me, telling the Universe that she loved me.

Everything was so confusing.

I reached for the bus ticket in my pocket––the ticket that could take me away from this place.

I was a coward but I wasn't so low as to leave things the way they currently were. I might not be able to help with Mother, but I could do other things for a while, like help with June Bug and Shane's stupid idea to bring back Haunted Dark Root.

And maybe find out who Larinda was.

"Fucking guilt," I said, as a woman stepped inside the elevator.

She gave me an empathetic smile.

Maybe I wasn't the only one in the world who had difficult decisions to make.

"Are you sure you're up to this?" Shane asked, as I slid into the passenger seat. He had made his way back to the parking lot, blasting country music so loudly that I could find him with my eyes closed.

"I don't know what I'm up for, anymore," I sighed.

He gave me a concerned look but didn't start the car. This was his way of telling me to buckle up. I was getting used to his profound need to follow rules and I half-heartedly obliged.

"Well," he said, lowering the volume and starting the ignition. "Far be it from me to challenge the intuition of a witch."

I bristled at the word, but didn't take the bait.

He laughed. "No comment? Does that mean I actually won? The score is now Shane, one, Maggie, one hundred..."

"I wish I was a witch," I said. "A witch could at least be useful." I bit at a hangnail near my thumb.

"Don't sell yourself short, Mags. Witch or no witch, you are very useful." He gave me a tight-lipped smile as he pulled onto the freeway. Linsburg was two exits away. "Are you going to ask about your mother?"

I turned Jillian's card over in my hand. If she really was a psychic medium, someone who could predict the future *and* talk to the dead, I had many questions for her.

"Among other things," I said.

"You could ask her how to make our festival a success?" Shane put on his country boy grin.

I had to admire his dedication. He had been working so hard, including coming up with a new look and theme for Dip Stix.

"Fondue is all the rage in big cities," Eve had explained to him. "And...it's still in the dipping genre. You can use cheese, chocolates, wines, broths. There's no limit to what can be dipped."

With that, he was sold, and the two had been making plans to turn the cafe into a posh restaurant by the end of October.

"We don't need a psychic for that," I answered. "If you want the festival to be a success you have to advertise and get all those fogies in town to keep their shops open more than three hours a day."

"Advertising...yes. Brilliant idea! Signs, posters, Craigslist."

"Craig's what?"

"Never mind." He scratched the left side of his jaw. "What about your mother's shop? Think you gals will reopen?"

I scrunched my lips as I watched the scenery wiz by. When I had left

Dark Root I had vowed to never step foot in Miss Sasha's Magick Shoppe again. But then again, so many of my plans had changed. Besides, it was only for a few weeks and it might alleviate a bit of this guilt that was building up. "It's not on the top of my bucket list but we do need to open it if we are going to revive the festival. Without it, Haunted Dark Root would just be..."

"...mundane," Shane finished for me.

We passed a sign that read, 'Welcome to Linsburg. The Happiest Place in Oregon.'

"Who comes up with the town slogans?" I asked.

"That, my dear, is our tax money hard at work." Shane scratched his head and a flake of dandruff fell out. I resisted the urge to make a snow globe joke. If living with Michael had taught me anything, it was that men were big babies when it came to their hair.

Shane pulled into the lot of a yellow, cottage-like house on the outskirts of town. The flower boxes were empty and brown-green grass dotted the front lawn. The trim, pillars, and shutters were painted a dull white. The house had a certain charm but I could tell it had seen better days. A sign on the front door let us know that Jillian Lightheart was open for business until noon.

If she wasn't busy, that would give me a solid half hour.

"Want to come?" I asked, grabbing my purse from the floorboard. "I could use the moral support."

"I'll support you from afar and maybe at lunchtime if you are willing to try the spinach-cauliflower sauce I invented last night..."

I nodded––though not quite sure about his concoction––and made my way up the four cement steps to the door of the house.

I knocked politely, waited a moment, and turned the knob.

I had known many people who claimed to be psychics. Mother loved to chat with them in the parlor of our home––*"Oh, please tell me what the weather will be like for Spring. It's been such a wet season already." "So he's going to cheat on me? That son of a bitch!"*––but I had never consulted with one myself.

The interior was nothing like I expected.

For starters, it was clean, well lit, and organized. It looked more like an office than a place where people came to have their palms read and futures told. A desk and computer sat in the center of the room, facing two comfortable-looking chairs. To the right was a leather love seat. Built-in shelves lined the back wall, crammed with books about psychology, religion, spirituality, history, geology, archeology, astronomy, philosophy and astrology. I recognized several of the titles from Mother's shop, Uncle Joe's house and Michael's library. I was glad Shane hadn't come in after all. We might have been here all day.

"Hello there." Jillian's lyrical voice greeted me.

She emerged from a side room dressed in a two-piece suit and heels. She gave me a warm hug and took a seat at her desk.

"Hi," I said awkwardly, realizing she was probably about to leave. "I know I should have called, but I was in the neighborhood and thought..."

"...Thought you'd get your fortune told?" Jillian's eyes twinkled. "No worries, Maggie. I had a feeling you would be dropping by." She motioned for me to sit in the chair facing her. "I don't have much time, but the time I do have is yours. Just give me a moment."

She tapped on her keyboard and I shifted uneasily, pretending to be interested in a glass sculpture of a pyramid that sat on the table nearest me.

"There," she said, raising her hands and wiggling her fingers. "Just had to update my Facebook. Now what can I do for you?"

Jillian rolled her chair out so that she was sitting directly in front of me. I wasn't sure where to start. Larinda? The 'thing'? My sick mother? It all felt crazy.

Noting my hesitation, Jillian took the lead.

"Hmmm...so much going on with young Maggie." She reached for my hands, placed them on her knees, then covered them with her own. A warmth crept through me and I relaxed. "Maggie, dear, your mind is all over the place, but we will begin with the most pressing issues and we can talk in the future about the others...alright?"

I nodded dumbly and Jillian closed her eyes.

I could feel her energy searching me, poking through the holes and pits of my soul.

Finally, she opened her eyes and smiled. "The good news is that the 'thing' you had following you when we last met has gone. Just as I suspected, it was a hitchhiker. Probably scared you a little during the night, fed, then disappeared. Nothing serious. Just siphoning off a bit of your life force before bouncing on."

I thought about the 'thing' I had seen hovering over my bed the night I rushed out of my room and found Paul in the kitchen. I shivered, unnerved that it had 'fed,' but relieved that it was gone.

"But..." Jillian tilted her head as if we were conspirators in a secret. "There's something darker and more powerful that has manifested. At your house, correct?"

"The house I grew up in," I said, grateful I didn't have to explain.

Jillian squeezed my hands. "For some reason, it has attached itself to you. I'm afraid he is here to stay."

"Is it a ghost?" I asked hopefully.

Jillian bit her bottom lip thoughtfully. "I'm not sure. I can't get a good read on it. Let's hope so." She gave me a mysterious look. "There are some things in this world more frightening than ghosts."

"Like demons," I said, in a voice so low I didn't think she could hear me.

Jillian stood, moving towards the bookshelf.

"It's a very old male energy and it likes your house because of all the feminine energy there," she said. "Makes it feel strong, especially when it scares you. It also enjoys all the 'power' you girls put out. You have sisters, correct? And you all have gifts?"

Jillian said this in a way that let me know she didn't expect an answer. She grabbed a book and thumbed through it until she found the page she was looking for.

"And you, Maggie Magic..." she continued, catching me off guard by calling me by Michael's pet name for me. "...You are the most gifted of all. It knows this and wants some of that power. It feeds off it. But the good news is, this particular entity is *not* a demon...

"It's not so bad." Jillian smiled bemusedly when I didn't respond. "I've been seeing spirits since I was in the cradle, too." She opened the book on her desk and pointed to a picture, a photo of a woman in a rocking chair with a smoky haze behind her. Within the haze you could almost make out the shape of a face. "It happens."

Jillian flipped the pages of the book as she continued.

"So, the question is, if it's not a ghost and it's not a demon, what is it?" She found the picture she was looking for and pointed. "Something in between. A dark energy from another plane of existence who has decided he likes it here for one reason or another, and wants to stay."

"Was it summoned?" I swallowed hard, remembering what Shane had told me about the original Council of Thirteen.

"No, dear. There are many planes and planets and realities. This one happens to be ours. But sometimes, sometimes..." She tapped the page. "...Realities cross over." The picture was a painting of a dark mass with two red points of light where the eyes should be.

The picture was terrifying. "What does it want?" I said.

"Maggie, you are like a power outlet for these 'things' to plug into. Your emotions are so powerful they are almost tangible. Especially the darker ones: jealousy, envy, and anger. They gobble this stuff up."

"No wonder they hang out at my house."

"And fear. Especially fear."

"Why fear?"

"Fear has a lasting effect. It's like walking into a room after a fight. There might be no physical evidence of the fight, but you can still feel it. Fear leaves that type of imprint but it lingers longer and is easily digestible to certain types of entities. If they can make you afraid, they get to stick around longer."

My heart was racing. "What can I do?"

"For starters, keep a night light on. The dark is the birthplace of fear. But most importantly, learn to control your emotions. The 'thing' can't eat if you don't give it food."

I gave her a desperate look and she laughed.

"Easier said than done, huh?" Jillian closed the book and studied me. "You've always had visitors, Maggie. That is a gift, and one you've been running from, but an important one."

"Visitors." I repeated her word. "You make it sound fun. Like they come to have tea and crumpets with me on the veranda."

Jillian laughed, her voice light and airy again. "Well, I do with mine, sometimes. Maybe I need to get some friends on this plane." Then changing the subject. "Do you have a crystal?"

I reached under my shirt and showed her the crystal. She reached out to grab it, lifting it to the light. "This one is wonderful. Very powerful. But it's not really yours, is it? It has the energy of someone else on it. Someone who hasn't been entirely, shall we say, behaving himself."

"No, it was a gift." I almost choked on the memory of Michael giving it to me.

"Its previous owner did have a certain power. Not like yours, but a power nonetheless, and it's infused in this crystal. Get your own. The right crystal will help you center and clear your mind. Both of which are necessary to help you deal with these unwanted guests of yours."

"How do I find one?"

"You don't. Crystals find you. But for now, consider getting that one cleansed. The past owner's energy is inhibiting yours."

"That figures." Even miles away, Michael was still trying to control me. "There is something else..."

"Yes, go on."

"My mother had a stroke. She's in the hospital." I swallowed hard and felt a strange tingling in the tips of my fingers.

Jillian narrowed her eyes and looked past me. "Your mother's fate is still unknown. There are too many factors." She closed her eyes and inhaled. "The cards are not all drawn. The fate of many things, including her life, rests on the shoulders of her daughters."

"I don't understand. How does her life rest on my shoulders?"

Jillian opened her eyes and smiled knowingly. "There is another player. A woman. You will face her."

"Larinda?"

At the name, Jillian froze. After several moments she spoke, her voice soft but serious.

"Honey, I should have confessed something earlier," she said. "I hadn't come to Dark Root by accident. The truth is, I knew your mother and some of the others back in the day." She threw her head back, laughing. "They were a bunch, weren't they!"

"I know." I removed the picture of Jillian and my mother together from my purse. "How were you two acquainted?"

She took the picture from me, tracing her fingers along its time worn edges.

"I was one of the original members of The Council of Thirteen." Jillian paused, choosing her words with care. "I was young and though I had gifts, they were a bit, shall I say, unbridled." She smiled at the memory. "Your mother found me in a mall, of all places, and promptly recruited me. It was great fun playing coven and having friends who shared similar interests. For once, I didn't feel like a freak. At any rate, the Council of Thirteen lasted a few years before we succumbed to dissension. Seven stayed in Dark Root. Five moved to another town and reformed. I went rogue."

"I've heard that some of the members were trying to control demons. Is that true?"

"Yes, that's true. But to the best of my knowledge, that never happened. They were not nearly as powerful as they pretended to be."

"I was told the reason the group broke up was because the men were dabbling in the dark arts. If that wasn't the reason, then why?"

"Whether they were able to summon or not, your mother wanted nothing to do with it. So, that was definitely part of it. But the real reasons we split were far more mundane. Power struggles, too many chiefs and not enough Indians. Jealousy. Love."

"Love?"

"Love is the most powerful Magick of all, and sometimes, when misguided, the most destructive."

"That doesn't sound like love."

"Bingo! You're a bright young woman." Jillian smiled broadly in approval. "No Maggie, real love is self-sacrificing. It's a give, not a take. When somebody, or something, wants to take from you, use you, control you, that's obsession, not love."

"Was Larinda on the council?"

Jillian nodded. "Your mother and her clashed. Often. They each had their own way of doing things and come hell or high water, they were going to get their way. They couldn't plan a picnic without fighting over who would bring the potato salad."

"Mother liked to be in charge," I agreed.

"She certainly did. Miss Sasha was a firecracker, that's for sure. Still, I'm not certain what Larinda has to do with any of this now." Jillian pressed her lips together. "Well, I hoped that answered your question. Larinda might be a player in this game but it is the Maddock girls who will determine the outcome. To many things."

I didn't like what she was saying. It sounded like even more responsibilities, best left for someone else. I had never really accomplished anything. If my mother's fate partly rested in my hands, the universe had a cruel sense of humor.

"Will you come see us at the Haunted Dark Root Festival?" I asked, purposely changing the subject.

"I will do my best." Jillian patted my hand. "I know the festival doesn't seem very important to you, but in the grand scheme of things, this may be just what your mother needs to get well again. Now if you'll excuse me for just a moment, I have a present for you."

Jillian went into the adjoining room and returned with a bundle of sticks wrapped in string, which I recognized as a sage stick.

"Burn this in your house," she advised. "It's not strong enough to get rid of that 'thing', but it can lessen its power and keep out future hobgoblins," she winked. "Well, dear, I do have to run. Call me and come

208

see me again, okay? You're a wonderful young woman and the door is always open."

We stood and hugged. I felt a deep connection with her.

Maybe it was because we had similar 'gifts'.

I walked out to the car, mulling things over.

Larinda was a real person. Jillian had once been a friend of my mother's. The Council of Seven had once been the Council of Thirteen. There was something between a ghost and a demon inhabiting the nursery. And Mother's life was dependent on us.

I chewed on my lip as I sorted it out.

Shane was leaned up against his truck, headphones plugged into his Ipod, tapping his toes. He didn't see me and I noticed again how handsome he was, in that goofy sort of way of his. I touched him on the shoulders and he removed the earphones.

"Get any resolution?"

"Just more questions."

He pointed at my sage stick. "What's that?"

"A little something to push back the evil spirits."

"Don't point it at me then," he teased.

"Maybe Eve can be in charge of this sage stick. Evil doesn't seem to bother her and I'm not sure I can go back in Sister House again."

"I don't blame you." Shane looked at the sky. The clouds had parted and a small ray of light fell on his forehead like a target. "Let's go home, Maggie. I'm playing around with a new chocolate sauce that has your name written all over it."

"Is that in place of the cauliflower nightmare you were trying to push on me earlier?" I teased. We got in the truck and sat in our appointed spots. I even buckled.

"It's dessert," he said, once we were settled. "...You can have some if you are a good girl and eat all your vegetables."

"You do know how to woo a woman, don't you?"

"I try, but it's not as effective as one might think." He stretched an arm out of the window, turning his palm towards the sun.

It was the last day of September. We would likely not see the sun again for many months. My stomach growled and I realized I hadn't eaten yet today.

"I'm so hungry I'm willing to try any of your concoctions right now," I admitted.

"Perfect," he said, turning onto the road that led us back to Dark Root. "You are exactly the type of customer I'm hoping for."

"So, ya had a good visit wit' yer mother?" Aunt Dora was attempting to lift her considerable body from the old kitchen chair. There were loud creaking sounds and I wasn't sure if they were coming from my Aunt or the chair. I shot June Bug a knowing look and she covered her mouth to keep from laughing.

I motioned for Aunt Dora to sit back down and I took over the task or clearing the table.

June Bug sat opposite her, coloring with markers on a sheet of poster board. I'd check her progress every now and then, giving her suggestions as well as encouragement. Her tongue flicked excitedly out of the side of her mouth like a little frog grasping at flies.

"I wouldn't call it a visit," I said, taking a dish cloth to the table.

Aunt Dora shook her head and pointed to a dry cloth and spray in the windowsill instead. I took the bottle and spritzed it across the table.

"...It was more like a haunting," I added.

Aunt Dora took a sip of her tea, watching me over the top of her cup. Though her face was covered in lines, she was as mentally sharp as ever. I could tell she was waiting to see if I would continue, so I teased her by humming quietly to myself. It wasn't long before she couldn't handle it and broke the silence.

"Well, what happened then?" she grumbled. "Ya really want to keep an ol' lady in suspense? Then yer gonna have two relations in da hospital." Aunt Dora slammed her cup onto the saucer and June Bug couldn't contain her laughter any longer.

"Let's just say I'm no Merry," I said.

At the mention of her mother's name June Bug grew quiet, gathered her markers, and proceeded into the living room.

"Poor dear," Aunt Dora said, her eyes following her great-niece. "Sensitive, jus' like her mother."

I nodded and peeked around the corner, into the living room. June Bug was coloring again but the expression on her face had changed.

"I'm worried about Merry," I whispered, shaking my head. My hair fell into my face, creating a curtain of red between me and my aunt. I pulled it back into a loose knot at the nape of my neck. "...She seems drained. I feel so guilty being here while she is there."

"An' ya should!"

The tone of Aunt Dora's voice surprised me. I looked up.

She caught herself and lowered it.

"...We all should, for dat matter," she said. "Yer sister is a good woman and one o' da few people in dis family wit' genuine compassion, and we are takin' her for granted. It's too much for her, especially wit' her havin' a lil' one an' all." Aunt Dora's eyes drifted towards the kitchen window, at a blue bird sitting on the branch of a tree.

"...I will go tomorrow an' give her a break." Her eyes found mine. "Ya can help yer sister in other ways. I think ya already are."

"Thank you," I said, rinsing the cloth under the faucet, watching the water turn from brown to clear. "That makes me feel better."

"I know ya long enough ta know there's something else on yer mind. Spill it, missy."

I sighed, leaning my hands on the counter. "I keep thinking back to the mother I knew and the mother I have now. I just can't reconcile them." I wrung out the cloth, hanging it across the sink divider. I watched as small droplets clung stubbornly to the rag before submitting to the drain below.

Aunt Dora nodded. "It's a hard thing, watchin' yer parents grow ol'.

I remember my own mother. So sad at da end."

I had never heard Mother or Aunt Dora mention their parents. I didn't speak, hoping she would say more about my grandparents, but she changed the subject.

"Yer mother hasn' been herself fer many years. She started having some phys'cal diff'culties after ya girls left. Back problems. Knees. Complained o' pains in her chest. She tried ta work da store by herself. She was so used ta having ya girls aroun', I'm not sure she knew what ta do once ya were gone..."

"I thought she hired someone?"

"Oh, she did, a college girl. But yer mother's phys'cal condition got worse and den her mental state took a turn. I guess it was too much fer da two o' dem." Aunt Dora stirred her coffee with a small, silver spoon, clanking the edge of the porcelain cup. "The hired girl left an' yer mother took to stayin' in dat ol' house o' hers alone. Den she closed da shop down."

I sat down in June Bug's empty chair.

Aunt Dora lifted the teapot from the trivet and poured me a cup. The steam came up, wafting the scent of her special blend towards my nose. I inhaled and smiled. Aunt Dora claimed she didn't dabble in herb magic, but there was something special about her teas, something even Eve could not duplicate.

When she saw that I was relaxing, she continued.

"Don' go blamin' yerself, or any o' yer sisters for dis one. Kids get big. Dey grow up. Dey leave. Dat's da natural order o' things." Aunt Dora drummed her plump fingers across the table. "At least, dat's da way it's s'posed to be. But yer mother, she's a hard-head. She ne'er understood dat. When Ruth Anne left..."

Aunt Dora paused and I could hear the lump that settled in her throat.

Though we all loved Aunt Dora––and she, us––she had formed a special bond with Ruth Anne, long before the rest of us ever came into the world.

"Well, anyway," Aunt Dora went on. "Losin' Ruth Anne was hard on e'eryone. Not just yer mother." Aunt Dora pushed herself up with the help of the chair handle and immediately reached for a cane. She pulled herself to a walking position and went to the sink to rinse her cup.

"Why did Ruth Anne leave?" I asked.

I remembered the night she left. She had said she was going to live with her father, but had never given us a reason.

"It's not fer me ta say, Missy," Aunt Dora said, her body tensing. "An' it's not fer ya ta be askin'. Sometimes families think dey shoul' be privy to all sorts o' information jus' cuz they're family. But truth is, sometimes families know too much."

I took another sip of tea, then gently set my cup back down on the table, trying to decide if I should pursue the topic or move on to something else. Aunt Dora was as stubborn as my mother, if in a different way. If I wanted to know more about Ruth Anne, I would have to wait.

"There was one thing that happened in the hospital," I said, adding a drop of honey to my tea.

"Oh?"

"Mother spoke to us. She said something about the circle being broken, and stopping a woman named Larinda. You wouldn't know anything about that, would you?" I kept my eyes turned down, watching as the honey dissolved.

"Larinda? Ya sure, girl? She said Larinda?" Aunt Dora had somehow teleported back to the table, hovering over me with wide eyes.

I nodded and Aunt Dora let out a little gasp.

"But I thought...I mean, we all thought..."

"Thought what?" I said.

Aunt Dora made no motion to answer me and I repeated my question.

"What did you think?"

"Dat Larinda was dead. Many years ago. Yer mother must be delirious."

"Aunt Dora, I know that Larinda was part of the original Council, but why is Mother afraid of her?"

Aunt Dora's eyes were far away. She didn't seem to be hearing me.

I tried again. "I had a dream about a woman named Larinda. She had dark hair and appeared at the festival parade. Mother was scared and hid us. But I know it wasn't just a dream. It happened."

"Shhh!" Aunt Dora had an expression of fear on her face. "Der are some secrets darker den witchcraft."

"Why does everyone talk in these crazy riddles? What do you mean?"

"Larinda was a powerful witch. Secon' only to yer mother. But she wanted more, started playin' wit' da dark arts. Even fancied herself a summoner." Aunt Dora looked down at me, her eyes watering, her body quivering.

"A summoner, as in summoning...what?"

"All manner o' ungodly things." Aunt Dora laughed, but it was clear she didn't find it funny. "O' course," she added, cautiously. "Der hasn't been a successful summoner in many years. But she's a strong witch, e'en wit'out that ability." Aunt Dora shook her head, as if doing so would erase the thought from her brain. "Be careful, girl. Ya could be in serious trouble."

"I thought it was the men in the group who were trying to summon?"

"Dat's true. But yer mother wasn't worried about da men. Dey couldn' do much alone." Aunt Dora parted her lips, licking them. "But wit' a witch at his side! A warlock was capable o' mos' anything."

"I'm still lost," I said, shaking my head.

"Der was one warlock, good fella, at first...but like all men, he wanted ta do more. He made Larinda fall in love wit' him, den used her power to aid himself. But dey had no success. He wanted us ta help him wit' it, too." Aunt Dora lowered her eyes and I could tell she was deciding how much to tell me. "Dis is dark Magick, Maggie. An' yer mother would ha' none o' it! An' me, neither! Dark Magick is fast an' powerful. It may serve ya in da short run but it will eat yer soul in da process." She leaned forward, her razor-sharp eyes fixing on me. "An' once ya journey down dat road, it's a long walk back."

I tried to piece it all together. Everyone had their own version of the same story. It was confusing, but I knew it was also important.

"And that's why the Council broke up?" I said finally.

"Der were many reasons, but dat was da last straw, da real reason yer mother wouldn' let warlocks in after. Dey weaken women."

"Do you think Larinda has figured out how to summon? Is that why Mother's afraid?"

Aunt Dora tapped her fingers on the table. "It's been many years since I seen her. Who knows what she's been able ta do in dat time? Assumin' she's alive..."

An image came to me, an army of horrendous dark shapes standing over my body while I slept. I wanted nothing to do with summoners. I was going to run, I decided...right away. Everyone was okay before I had come home. They would be okay after I left. I was about to tell Aunt Dora where she could stuff all this witchery business, when a small voice from the doorway brought me back.

"Aunt Maggie," June Bug said, holding up her picture. "I'm done."

"Well, look der!" Aunt Dora clapped her hands and took the poster, holding it up for me to see. There were skeletons, jack-o'-lanterns and ghosts, surrounded by families eating ice cream and playing games. In the center of the picture, a blond girl smiled, holding a balloon.

"Dis is exactly what Haunted Dark Root looks like!" Aunt Dora said. "I think ya got some of yer Aunt Maggie's artistic abil'ties..."

June Bug beamed.

I patted my lap and June Bug raced towards me, jumping on my legs. I wrapped my arms around her and kissed the back of her neck.

"I think yer stayin' a while more," Aunt Dora said, smiling wryly. "Yer work here is not yet done."

SEVENTEEN

MAIN STREET

SISTER HOUSE, DARK ROOT, OREGON
JUNE, 1997

"*DON'T YOU TURN YOUR BACK ON ME!*"

Miss Sasha was in a frenzy, chasing after Ruth Anne in the kitchen. Maggie and Merry watched from the sofa, not sure if they should be worried or amused. The two went at it often now, Ruth Anne accusing Miss Sasha of being a bad mother and Miss Sasha accusing Ruth Anne of being an ungrateful daughter.

"There's knives in the kitchen," Merry whispered to Maggie, but neither girl was alarmed. For all the shouting and name calling, neither Miss Sasha nor Ruth Anne had resorted to physical violence.

"When will you tell them?" Ruth Anne stopped on one side of the kitchen table, facing her mother on the opposite side. "They deserve to know. If you don't tell them..." Her words stopped.

Tell them what? *Maggie wondered.*

"I don't know what you are talking about." Miss Sasha straightened herself, patting her hair back in place. "And if you care about them, you will shut your mouth and go back to your books."

Ruth Anne pulled open the junk drawer and removed a pair of sewing scissors. Maggie's hand tightened on Merry's arm and the two

217

girls caught their breath.

"Put those away," Miss Sasha ordered. "I'm not playing with you."

"I'm not putting anything away," Ruth Anne said, waving the scissors above her head.

"You're not being sane."

"Please! I'm the only sane person in this family." Ruth Anne glanced at her sisters, giving them an apologetic look.

"Ruth Anne! Don't..." Maggie and Merry begged, finally intervening.

Miss Sasha ran towards Ruth Anne, grabbing for the scissors, but Ruth Anne was quicker, backing away. In one, quick moment, the deed was done. Ruth Anne's brown hair fell to the floor as Miss Sasha's mouth dropped.

"She did it," Merry whispered, her eyes widening. "She cut her hair."

A witch never cuts her hair.

That had been one of the first lessons the girls had learned. The longer her hair, the more powerful the witch. And here, Ruth Anne had just done it. It was almost impossible to believe.

Eve bounded down the stairs, still in her pajamas.

"Go back to bed, Evie," Merry said. "Everything is okay."

But Maggie knew that everything wasn't okay. On the floor lay eighteen inches of brown hair, shorn from the head of her eldest sister. Maggie looked to the floor and then to Ruth Anne, who stood looking like a boy, grinning victoriously.

"What have you done?" Miss Sasha clenched the side of her face, staring at her eldest daughter in disbelief.

"What I should have done a long time ago. I'm ending this nonsense."

Miss Sasha scooped up the tresses, clenching them in her fist. "The circle is breaking," she said.

"It's too late for me, but please let them have some normalcy in what's left of their childhood." Ruth Anne sat down at the kitchen table, *her face changing from triumph to exhaustion. "My father's coming for me. Don't try to stop me."*

Miss Sasha stared at her daughter for a long time. Finally, she spoke.

"What we need is music," she said, lifting her chin. She then went to the side room––her private room––and unlocked the door. She returned moments later with a record player, placing it on the dining room table. She plugged it in and moved the needle over the record. Take it Easy *began to play.*

"One can never stay down long when there's music in the house," Miss Sasha said. "That's what I always say."

Maggie, Merry and Eve stood speechless as their mother danced through the living room, like the incident had never happened.

Ruth Anne turned towards her younger sisters. "I'm sorry girls," she said, heading for the stairs. "...I can't live like this anymore. I'm leaving tonight."

"Yes, of course I remember that night," Eve said, shaking back her long dark hair.

She was dressed in skinny jeans, a tight, red sweater, and black lace-up boots with thick heels. She looked out of place in her hometown as we made our way up and down Main Street, handing out fliers to the few pedestrians who were about.

"You are resurrecting Haunted Dark Root, huh?" a woman I didn't recognize asked, as we shoved a piece of paper in her hand. "Well, I guess we can participate. I gotta ask Albert though."

The woman slipped into the book shop and I turned my attention back to Eve.

"I dreamed about it. Every detail of that night."

"So?"

"I think Ruth Anne had information that Mother didn't want us to know."

"Yeah?" Eve faced me, crossing her arms. Her makeup was dramatic, overdone on anyone else, but it suited her. "No one can keep a secret in a town this size. You take a piss and everyone knows."

"Classy," I said, but she was right. Keeping secrets in Dark Root was hard. The whole town knew I had gotten my first period before I did.

I recalled how Ruth Anne had told Mother that she needed to 'tell them.' Did she mean us? And if so, tell us what? I tried to dredge back the dream but the more I focused on it, the more I lost it. I gave up before it was gone altogether.

"Maybe she knew who our father was?" I said.

"Yeah," Eve said, raising an eyebrow. "I guess there is that little secret. Sometimes I'm not even sure if Mother knows."

I smirked. Mother always bragged about all the men that were in love with her, but I had never seen any of them. The only evidence of a past romantic life was that she had four daughters.

"I used to envy Ruth Anne," Eve said, turning her head towards the end of Main Street. A van drove by and disappeared––the only vehicle we had seen in almost an hour.

"She was the only one of us who had known her dad." Eve's eyes seemed weighted, as if her fake eyelashes were too heavy. She filled her lungs with air and let it out. "Haven't you ever been curious about who our dad is?"

I bit my lip and nodded encouragingly. It was rare for Eve to talk about her feelings. She seemed more human to me now, and I wanted her to continue.

"I used to look at every man I ever met," Eve continued. "...Trying to determine if there was a family resemblance. The only one who looks remotely like any of us is Uncle Joe. You and him have the same hair. But we know Uncle Joe wasn't fond of women...and Mother, in particular."

She laughed at the absurdity of it and I laughed with her.

"Do you think he was a warlock?" I asked. "Our father?"

Ruth Anne's father wasn't. He was just some car salesman that Mother said she picked up and had her fun with for a few months, until he knocked her up.

"Probably not," Eve replied, thoughtfully. "Mother wouldn't want anyone she couldn't lord over. Warlocks gave her headaches."

"You're probably right." I kicked at a pebble that was caught in the crack of the sidewalk, sending it skittering into the road.

"I wish Ruth Anne had taken us with her." Eve's voice cracked. She released the grip on the flier in her hand and it slipped away, sent spiraling down the street by a small gust of wind.

I took her hand and held it, sharing the memory with my sister. Ruth Anne, her bags packed, disappearing into a grey sedan with a man she called father.

We never heard from her again.

"I miss her," I said.

"I used to envy you, too." Eve released my hand and stared at the ground, swallowing.

"Me? Why me?"

"You knew Ruth Anne better than I did. Both you and Merry did. I was still so young when she left and when she was gone, she was gone. We didn't even talk about her. I never got to know her. You never told stories about her..."

I could tell Eve was on the verge of crying. She covered her ears, like she was hearing something she didn't want to hear. I watched her quietly, not wanting to touch her because I knew she would shake me away. After a few minutes she regained her composure.

"I'm sorry," she said.

I stepped forward to hug her, something I had never done, ready to confess that I had envied her too––envied the way everyone doted on her, the way boys looked at her, the way she had taken Merry's attention away from me when she was born. As my arms reached for her, Eve stepped back, bending over to tie a lace on her boot that had not come undone.

"Yeah, whatevs," she said. "It is what it is. No big deal. Anyways, how many more of these do you have?" Eve opened her tote bag to show me that she was almost out of fliers.

I counted the stack in my hand. There were less than ten.

"Not a bad morning's work," Eve said. "Maybe we should tape the rest to the store windows that aren't occupied."

I agreed and we stuck the remaining posters onto every available surface.

At last we found ourselves at the end of Main Street, standing in front of Miss Sasha's Magick Shoppe. We looked at one another. We had come to the end of the trail.

"It's locked," I said, jiggling the doorknob. The windows were covered up with butcher paper from the inside, obstructing our view. "Oh, well."

Eve stared at me, unblinking. We both knew that there was a back window, one we used often when we had forgotten our keys.

"Shall we?" she said, pulling me by the arm into the alley behind the store, avoiding stones and broken glass.

We wrestled with the window until it gave way.

The opening was narrow and several feet above our heads. Eve managed to make it through easily, but I wrestled with the task. "If you stayed away from Aunt Dora's muffins, you wouldn't need help," she said as she took my hands, pulling me through.

When I reached the top, I halted for a moment before stepping into the darkness.

"It stinks in here," I said, covering my nose with my hand.

With the bins of exotic spices and herbs, as well as scented candles and incense, the shop had always had an interesting smell, but this new aroma was downright nauseating.

"...How long has this place been empty again?" I jumped as a furry black shape scuttled across the floor.

"I'm guessing about three years, judging from my conversations with Aunt Dora," Eve said, pulling out her cell phone and using it as a flashlight.

We stood in the back room where we used to store merchandise, conduct inventory, and take our breaks. Over the years, the boxes had accumulated and the room was a jumbled mess. I had to watch my step so that I wouldn't trip.

"This way," Eve said, guiding me towards a ray of light coming from the front room window.

"What do you think is in all those boxes?" I asked.

Eve walked towards the window and tore down the butcher paper, letting light fill the room.

"Just more of Mom's crap," she said. "She must have run out of hoarding space at the house and moved some of it here..."

The front room was in better shape. There were only a few random boxes strewn about and the scent wasn't nearly so strong.

"I suppose it's too much to ask for the electricity to work," I said.

Eve must have wondered the same thing, because she was already at the light switch, flipping it off and on with no success.

"We could reopen this shop, you know?" she said, scanning the store.

I was surprised by her remark. She had never enjoyed being at the shop when we were young, and here she was, suggesting we start it back up again.

"You serious?" I said.

"Uh-huh. It's not in that bad of shape. We clean the place up," Eve continued, charging towards the back room and returning with a broom. "...Dig through the boxes, order supplies. We could have this place up and running again in time for Haunted Dark Root."

Eve's eyes flashed and the energy changed around her.

She was serious.

I remembered that I had told Shane I would help. "I guess...I'm just not thrilled about working in Mother's sweat shop again."

I looked out the window; it was ghostly quiet on Main Street. I wasn't sure how we were going to accomplish everything in the next several weeks.

"That's just it, Maggie. Mom's in no position to run this place. This could be our place now. We could run it the way we want."

"What about New York? Won't you miss performing?" I fidgeted, uncomfortable with the way Eve had basically written Mother out of the picture. I turned my attention towards Dip Stix across the street, focusing on the table where I had first seen Michael seven years ago.

"I just finished up a really big show and I could use some time away," Eve said. "Performing takes its toll on you, if you don't learn to rest. Besides, my agent knows where to reach me if something important comes up."

She looked up and to the right, her lips moving as she silently counted. "...I could probably juggle a few things and stay long enough to get this place going again."

Eve removed a broom from the supply closet and began sweeping the floor, pushing up more dust than she collected. When she had gathered a sufficient amount, she opened the front door and let it roll out.

"I thought you were helping Shane open up Fondue Land?"

"This shop was the heart of Dark Root. If we can get it up and running, both the festival and Shane's restaurant are bound to be successful."

"Why does any of this matter to you?" I asked, genuinely interested.

"I don't know," she replied, pausing to think. "It just does."

As Eve resumed sweeping, I checked the bins beneath the glass counter. Once they had been filled with fresh herbs; now everything was brittle and dried up.

"I saw Mom and Merry today," Eve said casually, as she put the broom away.

"Oh?" This was news to me.

"Yeah. Paul drove me. Stayed and visited awhile. Mom's not looking so good."

I moved from the bins to the shelves, inspecting the assorted knick-knacks and items that were now coated in layers of dust. Some of the things I remembered, some were new.

"Had lunch with Merry while we were there," Eve continued. "I think it cheered her up."

"That's nice," I said, trying to sound like I didn't care. But I did care. Even though I didn't want to go to the hospital I cared that Eve had gone.

Eve wasn't going to drop the conversation. "I apologized for not bringing you, but Merry knows how you get about death and stuff. She understood."

If my sister wanted me to feel like crap, she was doing a good job. I was thinking of a way to defend myself when I noticed something on the chair near the front door. It was so covered in dust it was almost unrecognizable.

"Eve, look. *The book!*"

I had forgotten much about my time in Dark Root, including Mother's book of spells. But there it sat in the corner, quietly, unassumingly, as if it were just waiting, wanting to be picked up.

"So? It's just one more dusty artifact in this place. Why do you care?"

I didn't have an answer.

I had never cared about it before, but finding it now seemed monumental. I blew the dirt off the cover and read the title: *Prayers, Curses, and Incantations.* Opening it to a random page, I was surprised to see that the paper was yellow and crumbling.

I gingerly turned the pages, calling out names of spells that sounded particularly interesting as Eve wiped off the bookcases. "Changing the Weather. Finding Money. Warts. I could have used these back at Woodhaven. Hey, here's one for you––a love charm."

Eve pretended not to hear me.

"I'm taking this," I said.

Eve turned to me. "Aren't you worried about *The Curse?*"

"I figure if Mother could actually curse someone, we would know by now. That mailman she had a feud with when we were kids seems healthier now than ever. Besides," I added. "The curse specifies that its only non-family members who aren't allowed to remove the book. I am her daughter."

I turned the pages, wiping them carefully as I went. "...And it looks like someone has already tried. There are two pages missing."

Pages 32 and 78 had been ripped from the book. Maybe the curse only worked if you tried to take the book in its entirety? Someone may have found a loophole.

"Suit yourself," Eve said, reaching for something on one of the higher shelves. "Hey, Maggie, remember this ugly thing?"

Eve tossed me the object and I caught it, a small glass owl. I remembered the last time I had seen it, just a few minutes before Michael walked into our shop and changed my life forever.

"Take it," Eve said, watching me study it. "You'll need the company when you go."

I gave her a questioning look, wondering if she knew my intentions to escape once everything was 'done.' She offered me a wicked smile, but didn't speak. I placed the owl and spell book in my purse, next to the pocket that contained my bus pass out of here.

I was curled up in bed reading a book. June Bug was asleep beside me, tired from a full day of painting pictures and capturing caterpillars. The phone rang. It was Merry.

"How you holding up?" I asked.

"I'm exhausted, but Aunt Dora's been helping. How's my daughter?"

"Anxious to see her mommy." I stroked June Bug's hair, careful not to wake her. "When will you be coming to town?"

"Soon, maybe tomorrow."

"Good. I miss you." I stopped for a second, embarrassed to even ask. "How's Mother? Any news? Aunt Dora's been tight-lipped about her."

Merry's voice took on a heavier tone. "At first they thought she had a stroke, but now they aren't so sure. They have been testing and scanning her like crazy, but everything comes back clean. She just won't wake up."

I could tell she was on the verge of crying. "...I'm paying one of her old friends to sit with her at night so I can sleep at a motel down the road. God, I feel so guilty leaving Mom with someone I hardly know, but I just can't..."

"Don't feel bad Merry. You're a saint."

"Yeah, right," she said, deflecting, but I heard the smile in her voice at the compliment. "But thanks for saying so." She sniffled, blew her nose, and continued. "...The hospital says that if her condition stays the same, she can probably come home as long as she is monitored. That means paying for a nurse. I'm not sure how we can pull that off. I'm guessing Mom doesn't have great health insurance."

"Maybe we can take up a collection from the Witches Union?" I said, joking.

Merry laughed.

"You always make me smile," she said.

"Don't worry, Merry. We will figure it out." There were probably a million ways to raise money for Mother. We just had to put our heads together and come up with them. I had helped to buy a house in Northern California by selling flowers. Surely, I could conjure up a few bucks to help with a nurse.

"Even if we do come up with the money, Mama's social worker won't release her until her home is 'clean and safe'. I can't put this on Aunt Dora, so it means––"

"That we will be cleaning up our mother's mess."

"Yes."

I hadn't told Merry about the incident in the nursery a few weeks ago. It had seemed too much then, and I didn't want her to worry any more than she already was. Still, she needed to know, especially if we were going to get Mother's house ready for her return.

"Merry?" I began meekly. "There's something I need to tell you."

"Yes?"

"First, let me say I'm sorry for keeping this from you. I feel terrible about it." Then I told her everything––the attack on her daughter, breaking June Bug out of the nursery, taking her back to Harvest Home. By the end, I was crying.

"I see," she said, far too calmly. There was a strange clicking sound on the other end of the line, like she were tapping her fingernails against the phone. "It's come back then."

"Back?" I was startled by her response. "What do you mean, it's come back? I thought you didn't believe me?"

"There are some things I didn't want to believe in, but I always knew. Though I couldn't see it like you did, I could sense it. I just didn't want to scare you any more than you already were."

"It's horrible, Merry. Whatever *lives* in that room is just horrible. I haven't returned to Sister House since that night. I don't think I can ever go back."

"But Maggie," she replied, equally calmly. "We have to go back. We have to send that bastard back to where he came from."

EIGHTEEN

THE JOKER

THE PHONE VIBRATED ON MY CHEST, WAKING ME.

Somehow, I had fallen asleep with it still in my hand after my conversation with Merry. I rolled my head across the pillow, trying to focus my eyes. When I could finally see, I noticed Jason's name on the screen. It was 10:20 in the morning and June Bug was nowhere in sight.

How had I slept so long?

I dialed Jason's number. I had not called since I left Woodhaven and I hoped that he would forgive me. He was still very important to me, even if I had left him behind.

"Maggie!" His familiar voice on the other end made me smile.

"Hey there, sorry for not contacting you. Life's been crazy." I twirled the ends of my hair as I thought about what to tell him. So much had happened in such a short time.

"It's okay," Jason said hurriedly. "I'm sorry to be bothering you. I know we are the last people in the world you probably want to hear from."

I was about to assure him this wasn't true but he kept talking.

"...I wish I was calling just to catch up but I needed to warn you."

I sat up straight. "Warn me? About what?"

"Michael. He's on his way to Dark Root. He left in the van about two hours ago."

"Michael is coming for me?" I shook my head in disbelief. Michael didn't drive.

"Yeah, and he looks a bit crazy, too. He's been practically manic lately...yelling, cursing, throwing things. And he has this look in his eye. I tell you, it's almost feral. He figured out where you are--deductive reasoning, I guess." Jason snickered nervously. "He wants you back."

"I see," I said, trying to wrap my head around what he was saying. I had never seen Michael lose control. This new image didn't compute. "Are you sure he's coming...here?"

"Yes. Sorry, Mags. I tried to stop him, but he's developed this Hulkish strength. The last few weeks he's been difficult, running most everyone off."

"But not you."

"Not me," Jason sighed. Then his voice turned wistful. "Not yet."

"Is Leah still there?" I asked, catching my breath.

"Nope. She is gone too, left right after you did."

"She left on her own?"

"Yes, slunk back to whatever cellar she crawled out of."

"Ferret Village," I said.

"Weasel World," he added.

I felt my heart flutter as I recalled our goodbye at the bus station and I realized I missed him. "You always knew the way to a woman's heart."

"That's me. The Commune Casanova."

We both went silent. I could hear a heartbeat and I wasn't sure if it was mine or his. After several moments he spoke again.

"At any rate, not sure how long until he reaches you, assuming he knows how to get there." Jason laughed and I understood. Michael had an uncanny knack for getting lost.

"Thanks, Jason. You are good to me."

"All in a day's work. And now, I think it's time I head out, too. I'm in this big house alone and I'm starting to feel like I'm haunting the place." He paused. "I don't think this was the end that Michael predicted."

I looked over the top of my phone at the wall across from me, at a picture of a purple flower in a vast field. "No," I said. "This isn't how any of us thought it would end."

We said our goodbyes and I hung up the phone.

I let the realization that Woodhaven was no more sink in. I was filled with sadness, like I had just read the last page of a very long book. Only this time, there was no rereading that story whenever I wanted to go back.

I shook off the melancholy and focused on what Jason had told me.

Michael had taken the van and was on his way to Dark Root. I knew I should be alarmed, but I wasn't. It was Michael and I knew him better than I had known most anyone in my life. Surely he wouldn't act crazy around me. I fell back into my pillows and shut my eyes, wondering what I should do.

Images of Michael's face——young and perfect on that day we first met——amassed in my brain. I wanted to go back to that time when he came into our store on Main Street, back when I didn't have to worry about anyone but myself.

Back when someone had come to take me away from all my troubles.

Maybe I could.

Nineteen

House of the Rising Sun

Sister House, Dark Root, Oregon
October 31st, 1998

Miss Sasha raced through the house, *practically coming out of her slippers. Her hair was still in curlers and several of those curlers had come undone, dropping to the floor as she ran. Coming across her daughters in the living room, she suddenly stopped.*

"You girls have made me late!"

"It wasn't our fault." Merry tried to be diplomatic. She had been explaining to their mother all morning that the power had gone off in the house and that the alarm clocks hadn't worked.

"Maybe you should have used your witchcraft," Maggie said, defiantly crossing her arms. Merry gave Maggie a look, pleading with her to be quiet, but Maggie was done being quiet. "What good is having Magick, if you don't use it?"

"You." Their mother barreled towards the trio, pointing one long finger in Merry's face and ignoring Maggie. "...Are the oldest and responsible for your sisters. No excuses."

Merry's bottom lip began to tremble. She wasn't used to warring with her mother, but she stood her ground nonetheless.

"I'm not their mother. You are. If Ruth Anne were here..."

233

There was no spell in the girls' arsenal as powerful as the name of their missing sister. In the blink of an eye, Miss Sasha transformed from formidable monster to feeble mouse. She buried her face in her hands and slumped into a chair, sobbing.

Maggie and Eve looked at Merry with a combination of horror and respect. She had invoked the power of Ruth Anne's name and it had worked.

But Merry immediately regretted it. "Mama, I'm sorry," she said, rushing towards her mother. She folded her arms around her and they wept together.

Maggie checked the window, wondering what was taking Aunt Dora so long. She was supposed to have picked them up for the Haunted Dark Root Festival ten minutes ago.

"We've been studying." Merry attempted to pacify her mother as she slid into her lap. "Eve's been working on her enchantment spells and got a pig to follow her all the way home from the fields!"

Miss Sasha wiped her eyes with the back of her hand and offered up a weak smile.

"I think I'm getting the love spells down, too," Eve added. She moved behind her mother and began removing the rollers from her hair, letting the loose spirals slither down her back.

"You haven't been playing matchmaker again, have you?" Their mother raised mascara stained eyes to Eve.

"No, Mom," said Eve, combing through her mother's hair with her fingers, setting each curl in place.

"Your Aunt Dora could use some help in that department," Miss Sasha snorted. "Maybe you could fix her up with that pig that followed you?"

The three laughed as Maggie watched on, feeling like an outsider.

"What about you?" Miss Sasha directed her attention towards Maggie. "Have you been practicing too?"

Maggie lifted her shoulders then let them drop. She wanted to tell her mother that no, she hadn't been practicing her 'witchery' and that it was all stupid anyways, but Merry's eyes were round and begging. Since Ruth Anne had disappeared over a year ago their mother was a constant pendulum of craziness and neediness, leaving the eldest remaining daughter to play peacemaker. Maggie acquiesced––for Merry's sake.

"I practiced a little," she said.

Miss Sasha stood, shaking off her other daughters. "A little? A little?" Her blue eyes narrowed. "How are you going to take over the coven, if you just practice a little?"

Merry stepped forward but Maggie halted her with a hand.

Very calmly, Maggie answered, "Maybe I don't want to run your coven. Maybe I want to be something else."

"What?" Miss Sasha said. "Maggie, you are primed to take the center seat of the Council one day. You have to practice. Everything hinges on it."

"I don't think I'm going to be a witch. I'm leaving, just like Ruth Anne did." There was a small part of Maggie's heart that broke when she spoke these words, but she couldn't help it. If her mother really loved them, she'd let them be free to do what they wanted. She had already chased one daughter away. Did she want the others to follow?

"You're only twelve. You don't know what you want."

"I may be young but I know I don't want to become like you."

"You little ingrate! After all I've done for you!"

"You can't decide our lives for us," Maggie said, lowering her voice. "You have to accept that."

Miss Sasha stared, open-mouthed. Finally, she collected herself and rose to her full height, still six inches taller than Maggie. "You are not my daughter." She turned her head to look at Eve and Merry. "None of you are my daughters." Her mouth formed a snarl.

"Mama!" Merry ran towards her. "You don't mean that. You're just sick."

"I do too," Miss Sasha said. "I gave up everything for you all, and this is how you repay me."

"We need to take you to the doctor, Mama," Merry cried. "You're not well."

Miss Sasha covered her ears and looked right, then left. "The circle is breaking, crumbling all around us. Can't you see that?"

"I'm calling the doctor now," Merry said, reaching for the rotary phone on a nearby end table.

"No! No more doctors!" Miss Sasha grabbed Merry's arm and threw her to the ground. She stood over her, hand raised, ready to strike and Merry covered her head.

"Mother, stop!" Maggie's voice exploded as every light in the house went out, like a bolt of thunder had crashed down upon their home. There was only silence as everyone stared at Maggie, standing calmly in the center of the living room.

"...If you ever try to touch her again, you'll be sorry." Maggie reached down, pulling Merry to her feet.

Miss Sasha fell to the floor in a sobbing heap. After several minutes she looked up at Maggie with tear-stained eyes. "Maggie. You have too much of your father in you. Sometimes I wonder if I've raised the devil."

DIP STIX CAFE, DARK ROOT, OREGON
OCTOBER, 2013

"Any news on your mother?"

Shane's words jolted me from the memory. It wasn't enough that my childhood haunted my dreams; it was now infiltrating my daytime thoughts, as well.

"Maggie?" Shane said, waving a cloth in front of my eyes. I pushed it away.

"No word," I finally answered.

I wasn't in the mood to discuss my mother right now, a habit carried over from childhood. Once Miss Sasha started having her *episodes*, Merry had sworn us all to secrecy. Most of our early teenaged years were spent sequestered in Sister House, caring for our mentally fragile mother who could slip in and out of tantrums as easily as a toddler.

I chewed on my bottom lip as I watched Shane polish the sleek new tables that had come in on the delivery truck that morning. He seemed happy as he arranged them into symmetrical lines. Though I was wallowing in my own funk, I didn't want that to rub off on him. I put on my happy face.

"I have to admit this place is looking great," I said. "Eve's input is certainly helping."

He bobbed his head and surveyed the room.

New plantation blinds and awnings replaced the dingy, checkered curtains that had hung there since the diner's opening in the 1970's. A fresh coat of tan paint covered the walls, giving the room a more modern feel. And the Elvis memorabilia––much to Paul's chagrin––was all sold on *Ebay,* replaced by a few abstract paintings created by regional artists. The greatest change, however, was in the cookware. Most of the stock pots and cast iron frying pans had been upgraded to electric, stainless-steel fondue pots and matching skewers.

The cafe had become a Café.

"It's coming along," Shane agreed. "I only wish Uncle Joe were here to see this."

"I'm sure he's here in spirit." I inspected the red cloth napkin that I had folded into the shape of a swan. It had taken me the last thirty minutes to figure out how to make the wings. I placed it on my palm. "What do you think?"

"Looks great, if we are going for a T-Rex motif," Eve said, floating in from the kitchen wearing bell-bottom jeans, a white peasant blouse, and a red apron. She looked as if she were either getting ready for the Fourth of July or to board a ship full of sailors. "The kitchen is set up," she announced, motioning towards the next room.

"Nice job," Shane said, as we inspected her work.

Everything looked very organized. There were cork boards with dangling utensils, labeled canisters on the new shelving units, and copper pots hanging from an overhead rack. I crumpled up my swan napkin and tossed it on one of the tables.

"Nice job, yourself." Eve nodded towards the small, wooden stage on the far right dining room wall that he and Paul had spent the morning putting together.

There were so many changes to the restaurant that I wondered when Shane slept, but he seemed to thrive under the pressure. The closer we got to re-opening Haunted Dark Root, the harder he worked, always with a dopey smile on his face.

"Well," Shane said following Eve's eyes to the platform. "I had to give you a stage worthy of your talents."

"Then you should have built her a bed." I gathered up my pile of red napkins that lie in a swan-less heap and stormed into the kitchen. Ever since Eve had been helping Shane with his restaurant, he had been hovering over her like she was the prized pig at the county fair. I just couldn't watch.

"Need help?" I asked Paul who was busy counting silverware.

I watched as he counted out knives in stacks of four, and then placed them in the drawer. Next he moved on to the spoons.

"One, two, three, four, drawer..." Only when he had finished his task did he answer me. "Sorry, I like everything to be even. I'm a bit obsessive-compulsive."

"An OCD musician? Didn't know they went well together."

"On the contrary. Some of the greatest musicians must have been a bit obsessive-compulsive as well. You don't write songs like 'Stairway to Heaven' unless you are a perfectionist."

"Or on drugs," I added.

He smiled but didn't comment. We had discussed this before. Though Paul admitted that some musicians used recreational drugs, he didn't believe it enhanced their artistic abilities. True art, he claimed, came from nothing but talent and hard work.

"Hey guys." Eve poked her head into the kitchen. "Shane and I are going to Mom's shop for some candles. I'm thinking tea lights will really add to the atmosphere here." She smiled at Paul, deepening her dimples, but he didn't notice. He had moved on to counting forks. "Okay then," she said, giving him one last chance to object. "If we don't come back right away..."

She let the words trail off as Paul waved her dismissively goodbye.

"If you still want to help," Paul said, nodding towards a tray of stainless steel utensils on the counter. "...You can hang those on those hooks I installed."

I took the tray and made my way towards a set of steel beams by the stove. As I picked them up, I couldn't help but get my fingerprints on them. Paul noticed this and brought me a cloth, keeping one for himself.

"Eve says I'm a pain in the kitchen," he said, carefully removing my fingerprints from a long metal spoon. "I guess she's right. But it's one of the few places I feel like I'm in my element."

"Oh?" I was more than a little curious about the nature of his relationship with my sister. The way Eve talked, she and Paul were practically soul mates, but his actions towards her, at least in my presence, suggested otherwise.

"Whenever she called for an order and I took too long making sure everything was arranged just right, she would complain. Didn't seem to appreciate my dedication to the craft. Not that any of the Hooters' clientele are looking at the plates," Paul chuckled, stepping back to view his masterpiece of hanging spatulas. Satisfied, he put the cloth away and headed into the dining room with me following. "...I'm hoping I get a better gig in Seattle. I wasn't cut out to deep fry hot wings for men who are more interested in the waitresses than the food."

"You two worked at Hooters?" My sister had left out this little tidbit of her glamorous New York life.

"Yes, but Eve looked much better in her uniform." Paul pushed out his chest, batted his eyelashes, and puckered his lips.

So, Little Miss Off-Broadway was really slinging wings at Hooters!

This was getting good! I pretended to busy myself with wiping down the salt and paper shakers as Paul moved towards the stage. He picked up his guitar and sat on one of the stools Shane had purchased for the *live entertainers*.

"I thought you and Eve met in an audition," I said casually.

"Nope. We went on a few auditions but nothing really came of it. Most of my time in front of a New York audience occurred during open mic nights at local coffee houses." He strummed a few notes, playing a tune I tried to place, then stopped before I could bring it to full recall. "I realized it was time to cut my losses and move on."

"What about Eve? Didn't she have any success?" I wasn't even trying to hide my inquisition anymore.

Paul looked at me, his expression matter-of-fact. "Eve's a pretty girl with a decent voice and a nice set of legs, but New York will eat you alive." He paused for a moment to tune his guitar. "Everyone who goes there wants to be a star. I don't think either of us was prepared for the sheer number of people all vying for the same few parts. We were small fish in a pond the size of Lake Michigan."

He played a few notes from a Santana song, cocking his ear towards the guitar to listen for clarity. Satisfied, he continued talking.

"...I'm glad I can fall back on cooking, something I've always loved to do. Music is great, but at this stage in my life, it's just a hobby."

I was shocked as I listened to his confession. The picture he painted of their life in New York did not match up to what Eve had been telling me. She had been acting as if she were doing us all a giant favor by dropping her 'real' life to come help out for a few weeks. I couldn't wait to tell her that I knew her secret.

"Sing with me," he said, patting the seat beside him and breaking me out of the daydream where I was outing Eve in front of Shane.

"Me? No. You don't want to unleash this voice on anyone." I put the salt shaker I down and looked out the window. Shane and Eve's silhouettes were visible as they moved around Mother's shop. Then they disappeared into the back room.

"*Au contraire.* You have a great voice. Its husky and full of soul. Do you know 'House of the Rising Sun'?"

That was one of Michael's favorites. And my mother's. I nodded as I made my way towards the stage. Paul played the first few notes and then began to sing. Hesitantly I joined in. In a few minutes, I was lost––lost in the sound of the guitar behind me, lost in Paul's voice intertwining with my own, lost in the lyrics of the song, which reached me from somewhere far away. I sang about a house in New Orleans, and my mother being a tailor and my father a gambling man. I could feel my body swaying, as I sang closed-eyed into the microphone.

We came to the musical interlude where it was just him playing.

I opened my eyes again, watching his fingers strum across the strings of the guitar. It was beautiful and effortless. I caught my breath, spellbound.

"That was amazing!" I said when he had finished. "It's like magic."

The right side of his lip turned up as he considered this. "Music is a form of magic, I suppose," Paul said. "It can take you back in time, change your mood...and some even claim, calm the savage beast."

"Yes," I agreed, my heart beating as I thought about the way his fingers danced across the instrument. "I can see why Eve..."

He looked at me, his face red and wet. Dabbing his brow with a bandanna from his back pocket he asked, "Why Eve, what?"

"I don't remember," I lied.

Setting his guitar on the stool, he inched towards me.

He reached out his hands, our fingertips touching before interlocking. He was close enough that I could hear him breathing. Soon my breaths matched his and we stood, inhaling and exhaling in perfect unison.

He lowered his face close to mine, his warm breath creeping over the back of my neck, sending shivers up my spine. I let out a small moan. He lifted a strand of my hair and twirled it around his finger, drawing me into him. Our mouths were close. I could almost taste the salt on his lips.

"You're beautiful," he whispered, moving one hand down to the small of my back. "Your body, your spirit, your mind. You have a fire about you and it's sexy."

I had never thought of myself as sexy, but if he did, that was okay by me. I closed my eyes and tilted my head back...

"Look what we found!"

Eve burst through the front door and Paul dropped his hands, taking a giant step back. Eve was holding up two flashlights, one orange and one black. If she had seen how close Paul and I had been standing, she didn't let it show.

"For some strange reason, Mom's shop was out of candles, but she had plenty of flashlights," she said. "Like, hundreds of them."

Shane followed Eve inside, carrying an armful of cardboard boxes. "Yep. And here I thought witches used candles, not flashlights."

"Maybe she's a modern witch?" Paul said, busying himself again with tuning his guitar.

"Oh, Paul. You're so funny. Isn't he, Maggie?" Eve eyed me and I shifted uncomfortably. "...Well, the flashlights won't help with the atmosphere in here," Eve continued, looking around. "But I thought they might be nice to put in the goodie bags at the festival. They already have the emblem on them..."

Eve held up a flashlight, pointing at a picture on the handle, a white outline of a witch riding a broom against a full moon.

"I have a few candles in the very back," Shane said. "It's enough to get us through our maiden fondue voyage. We can place an order for more and in a few days we can head over to Linsburg to see what kind of supply they have. If you want to ride along, that is?"

"I'd love to," Eve gushed.

"Oh," Shane called out from the back room. "Sorry, I meant Maggie. We had such a good time on our last outing I thought she might enjoy another."

I could feel the eyes of both Eve and Paul on me.

"Cat got your tongue?" Eve said, when I didn't respond.

"I, uh..." This should be my new catch phrase, I thought.

"I don't have time to go to Linsburg anyways," Eve said, her voice light. "I've got to finish getting the shop in order. Finally got electricity in there and Aunt Dora found her old set of keys. By the time the festival comes, it's going to be the crown jewel of Main Street."

"And," Eve continued, moving towards Paul and looping an arm through his. "It gives me and this guy some time to practice our songs. I've been working on our Halloween Playlist. 'Black Magic Woman'. 'Witchy Woman'..." Her eyes flickered towards me. "...'Evil Woman'."

"'Monster Mash'?" Shane asked hopefully.

"Sure, why not? Really stretch my vocal talents."

"Okay," I said, trying not to look at Eve's arm that had somehow draped itself around Paul's waist. "Merry and June Bug should be here shortly. Let's set up."

Eve and I spent the next hour lighting candles, setting tables, and draping vines of fake ivy interlaced with white Christmas lights across curtain rods and shelves. Meanwhile, Paul and Shane went about their duties in the kitchen, bickering about which spices to use for the various cheese, wine, and chocolate fondues. After several taste tests, they settled on a French theme for the evening, then returned to chopping, slicing and stirring themselves into a Zen-like frenzy.

Paul had become a regular fixture in the Dip Stix kitchen by then, and he and Shane had begun a friendly rivalry of who could out-sauce who. Eve and I were both amused by their battle for the title of Kitchen King, teasing them about acting like two little old ladies.

I was running a strand of Christmas lights over the archway leading into the kitchen, when I noticed Paul removing his apron. His gray t-shirt clung to his thin body and I caught my breath, recalling our time alone together earlier. I chugged my entire glass of wine, and called for more. Shane appeared obediently, filled my glass, and then disappeared back into the kitchen.

"Not sure why we have to get the entire restaurant ready for tonight," I complained as I unwound yet another string of white lights. "It's just Merry and June Bug."

Eve glided from one table to the next, laying out silverware and adding fresh flowers to the crystal vases. There was a certain Magick about her when she worked towards making something beautiful, and I couldn't tell if it was witchery or just her gift as a woman.

"Shane wants to get a feel for the whole ambiance before we officially open to the public," she said, straightening one of the new paintings on the wall.

The sound of excited chatter outside the front door let us know our guests had arrived.

"They're here!" Eve called into the kitchen, removing her apron and placing it beneath the hostess stand.

Shane entered the dining area and placed his Ipod into a dock behind a potted plant in the corner. Prerecorded music of Paul playing an acoustic guitar soon echoed through the room. He then dimmed the overhead lamps, letting the candles and Christmas lights take over the task of illuminating the room.

The effect was beautiful––I glanced at Paul––and romantic.

"Places," Shane said, and Eve and I moved towards the only booth in the restaurant, a voluminous red one tucked away into the far back corner. We sat, wide eyed and smiling, waiting for our guests to come in.

At last, the door opened and two blond heads emerged wearing matching, crocheted pink beanies.

"Ooh!" June Bug said, removing her jacket and hanging it on the coat rack by the door. "It's beautiful in here!"

I smiled, tucking a strand of hair behind my ear as I waited for Merry's reaction.

"It really is," she said, offering Shane a grateful smile as she hung up her own coat and removed the beanies from both of their heads.

Shane took their arms and escorted them towards our table. "Ladies, this way."

"Aunt Maggie and Aunt Eve!" June Bug whooped like she hadn't seen us in months instead of hours. Eve and I scooted towards the center of the booth, allowing Merry and June Bug to settle in on either side of us like bookends.

"You two must have helped out," Merry said, nodding approvingly as she surveyed the café. "...I'm sure the boys didn't do this all on their own."

"Maybe a little," I admitted, feeling suddenly shy.

June Bug wound her arms around my waist, giving me a big squeeze.

"A little?" Eve scoffed. "We basically took over the place."

"The first course will be ready in just a few minutes," Shane said. "Sorry, paprika mix-up. Can I pour you some wine?"

Eve and I lifted our emptied glasses and Merry said that water would be fine for now. We listened to the music for a moment, sipping our drinks and swaying in the booths, taking in the ambiance of the place.

"Wanna dance, honey?" Merry said, leaning across the table to ask June Bug, who nodded at the invitation.

The two were up seconds later, waltzing in and out of the tables, Merry twirling and dipping her laughing daughter. I hadn't seen my older sister this relaxed in a long time and I felt happy knowing that I had been a part of it.

"Let's dance," Eve said, and I turned to see that she had slid out of the booth and was herding Paul––who had three empty wine glasses in his hand––towards a free spot near the stage. She took the lead and Paul obliged. I felt a fire in the pit of my stomach as they joked about something I couldn't hear.

"I guess that leaves us two wallflowers," Shane said, placing another bottle on the table. "Shall we?"

I didn't want to dance, but I didn't want to sit here alone either. I drank my newly-filled glass in one long swill and stood up, smiling widely.

"Sure, why the hell not?"

Shane routed me towards a spot near the center of the room,

spinning me beneath his arm then pulling me near. I was dizzy and I couldn't tell if it was because of the wine or the dancing. I peeked over the top of his shoulder, trying to catch a glimpse of what Eve and Paul were doing. They were locked in each other's arms, dancing close, and Eve kept throwing her head back to laugh as if he were the funniest man on earth.

"You like him, don't you?"

I looked back at Shane, surprised by the directness of his question. His face was soft and serious.

"It's okay," Shane said. "He's a good-looking guy. If I were a pretty young woman I'd probably like him, too."

I couldn't help but laugh. "Maybe you have a little of your Uncle Joe in you," I teased.

"I don't know about that," he said, pulling me tighter. "But a man can tell when he's got competition."

Competition?

I suddenly felt bad for him. He had been mooning after Eve these last few days and she was too busy chasing Paul to notice.

I stood on tiptoes and whispered, "We could work together. Pull them apart."

"Maggie, neither one of us would want that. And you wouldn't want the win. Not unless it was fair, right?"

He smelled good and I moved in closer to inhale him. I hadn't smelled a man in a long time and I was missing the scent. Even so, Shane confused me. Why was he always so concerned with rules and etiquette? Why didn't he ever just take what he wanted? I knew my experience with men was limited, but I had heard enough about them to know that they were all cave men at heart.

"Why are you so nice, Shane Doler?" I smiled at him, surprised by my own candor. But it was an honest question, even if it was wine-induced. He was too nice for me––too nice for any of us, except maybe Merry.

In truth, he shouldn't give us the time of day.

"Well," he said, releasing me with one hand so that he could scratch his jaw as he thought. "I wasn't always nice. It was something I had to work at."

"Really?" I said as he spun me. "I thought people were either born good or bad and that was that."

"First off," he said, smirking down at me when I was back in his arms. "I don't think there is good or bad when it comes to people. They just make choices and the choices can be good or bad. But, at any minute..." He stopped dancing, grabbed my shoulders, and peered intently into my eyes. "...At any minute, the coin can flip and what was bad can be good and what was good can be bad."

I sighed. "Boring! Spare me the philosophical lectures, okay? I just want to know why *you* are nice."

"My father, he uh, well..." Shane started choking and he turned his head to the side. The song on the Ipod ended and another began. Shane resumed dancing, not as smooth this time, more of a sway than a dance. "...My father was not what you would call a *good* man. He had problems with drinking, women, slapping..."

Shane's fingers dug into my back then released.

"You don't have to say anymore," I said.

As Aunt Dora had said, we didn't need to know everything.

"It's okay," he assured me, wrinkling his brow. "At any rate, he and my mother died. Got in a car wreck on their way back from a bar one night. DUI caused by..." He let it hang there, not finishing the sentence.

"I see." I didn't know what else to say.

"So, I went to live with my grandma. Got into trouble at school for all sorts of things. Mainly just being angry, I guess. They weren't too big into counseling in those days. Then Uncle Joe got involved in my life. Started bringing me here during the summers. Introduced me to books and Magick and..." His eyes fell on me. "...The Maddock girls. You know," he laughed, his shoulders relaxing. "Ironically, I learned more about being a *real* man from Uncle Joe then I ever did from my dad.

"...But, more than anything, I wanted to be like all those cowboys

I read about in his library," Shane added. "They were good guys, you know? Tough guys with big hearts. And even if I couldn't ride fences in the morning and gallop off into the sunset in the evenings, I could still be a cowboy. I could still do the right thing, make an honest living, even kiss a pretty girl or two."

A glint touched his eyes just as the last song on the Ipod ended and our dance was done.

"I think that's my cue to attend to the cheese," he said, bowing.

My sisters and June Bug had already gathered back at the booth and I joined them, sliding in next to Eve.

"You two looked like you were getting along," Eve commented, refilling her glass. "Shane always did have a thing for older women. I remember how he mooned after Ruth Anne. Kinda pitiful."

Before I could respond that there was nothing going on between Shane Doler and myself, and that if she wasn't so self-absorbed, she would see that it was *her* Shane was after, Shane returned with a small silver pot.

"Sorry I didn't give you time to order," he said, placing it on a large trivet in the center of the table. "I figured you would want the *spec-ial-ty.*"

He said the last word with a French accent and June Bug giggled.

We watched as he turned the dials on the pot and added chunks of cheese, spices, and a liquid. The cheese melted and we took turns stirring as Paul appeared with a platter of breads, fruits and vegetables. The two demonstrated how to spear the food and dip it in the fondue, while being mindful of the hot pot.

We took turns and it was so good I soon forgot my ire with Eve.

"This is amazing," Merry said, as Shane removed the cheese and replaced it with a pot filled with a clear broth. "Dip Stix certainly got a makeover. Now we need to get people in here."

"I've put ads in all the local papers and Maggie's made some amazing fliers that we've been handing out. I'd say we are well on our way." Shane twisted the lid on a bottle of cider. "Now for the wine sauce...all nonalcoholic."

He winked as he poured several bottles into the pot, raising and lowering his arms like he was leading an orchestra. I was impressed that he seemed to know exactly how much to put in without a measuring cup.

Paul emerged again, carrying a silver tray filled with an assortment of bite-sized meats and potatoes. "Tell me what you think of this," he said. "I don't eat meat myself anymore, but I still like to hear about it."

His eyes met mine and I blushed.

"Oh Paul," Eve said, and I knew that I had been caught. "Maggie doesn't understand cuisine. She's been living like a cave woman in that commune of hers, haven't you Mags?"

Eve turned towards me, fluttering her eyelashes innocently.

"She's right," I said, spreading my hand. "No fine dining there. Just raw meat and wild sex."

Paul's smile broadened and I fluttered my own lashes, just as innocently.

"Maggie! There's a child here," Merry reminded me.

"It's okay, Aunt Maggie," June Bug reassured me. "I wouldn't eat raw meat. It's yucky."

We all laughed, except for Eve, who was stabbing at a piece of pork on her plate.

"I can't wait to get back to New York," she said, lowering her skewer into the pot. "I miss places with atmosphere." She sighed dramatically as she watched her meat turn from pink to white. "There's this one place that is positively charming. It's so nice you can't get in without at least a two month's reservation. But the owner knows me, so, you know..."

"Would that place be Hooters?" I asked, nonchalantly nibbling on a potato.

Eve's head turned swiftly in my direction, her eyes narrowing. "No, it's not Hooters," she hissed. "It's a *nice* place, something you wouldn't know anything about."

Her face had paled to an ashen white, but I wasn't done with her yet.

"Does the whole crew go to this *nice place* after the 'show' or just you?" I said.

"What are you talking about?"

"The cast members of your shows. Do you all go together?"

Eve's response was measured and careful. "I go there on dates, Maggie. Another thing you probably know nothing about. How long has it been since you've been on a real date? One that didn't involve handing out religious tracts or shucking corn?"

I turned towards the kitchen, my eyes finding Paul. "It has been awhile," I admitted. "But I think that's about to change."

Eve's energy grew as hot as the liquid in the pot. She watched me, trying to figure out how much I knew.

June Bug pushed her empty plate away. "Are we still going to the mall tomorrow, Aunt Evie?"

Now it was my turn to be surprised. "I didn't know you guys were going to the mall?"

"Oh, didn't I tell you?" Eve widened her eyes. "I'm taking Merry and June Bug to the mall in Linsburg and then to the movies. Won't that be fun, honey?" she asked June Bug, who nodded. "Sorry I didn't invite you, Maggie." Eve flipped back her hair. "...But you've been so busy lately, pining for things, I didn't think you'd have the time."

"That's fine," I said as Shane removed the pot and replaced it with a small black cauldron.

June Bug clapped as Shane poured in pieces of chocolate, marshmallows, and graham crackers.

"...On Thursday, I'm taking them to the County Fair in Herston," I added to Eve. "We're going to eat lots of cotton candy and go on rides and have so much fun we may never want to come back. Doesn't that sound fun?"

June Bug nodded as she lowered a strawberry into the chocolate.

"Well," Eve fired back. "The next day, Merry and I..."

"No!" Merry's hands slammed down on the table. We all stopped what we were doing, including Shane and Paul. "No," she said again, her voice softer. "June Bug and I aren't going with either of you. Not while

250

you act like this."

"Act like what?" Eve and I asked.

"I'm not a thing. You can't fight over me." Merry shook her head, her eyes moistening. "I put up with it when we were younger because you were both kids and needed me." She straightened her back, wiping her eyes with her hand. "But, in case you haven't noticed, we aren't children anymore, and I have one of my own to worry about."

Merry pushed herself out of the booth and dashed towards the bathroom.

"She's going to be okay," I said, my eyes following Merry as I tried to comfort June Bug. "She just needs a minute."

"She cries a lot," June Bug replied, wiping her hands with one of my swan napkins. "Ever since daddy left."

Eve looked at me for confirmation and I nodded that it was true. I suddenly felt terrible, wishing I could take back my actions. Eve and I had been acting like spoiled children. After everything Merry had gone through, she didn't deserve to be caught up in this.

"Can you stay here while we check on your mama?" I asked June Bug.

She nodded and pulled out a coloring book and crayons from her mother's purse. Eve and I went into the bathroom, finding Merry sobbing over the sink.

"I'm so sorry," I said, wrapping my arms around her. Merry had always been the strong one and our protector. I couldn't handle seeing her like this.

"Me, too," Eve said.

"Well, you should be." Merry pulled away and turned towards the mirror, placing her hands on either side of the sink. I could see her reflection. Her eyes were puffy and her nose was running. "I can't handle this little feud of yours anymore. Not now. Not when I have other things to worry about. Why do you think I left Dark Root in the first place?"

I had always assumed she had left for the same reasons the rest of us had, to get away from Mother. But now she was saying that it was because of us. Eve and I looked guiltily at one another. We had driven our beloved sister away.

"I just can't do it anymore," Merry said, her words breaking apart as she cried. She turned to us and buried her face in our shoulders. We put our arms around her back, smoothing her hair and telling her everything was going to be okay.

"It's not going to be okay," she sobbed. "My life is a mess. My husband took off to Florida with some coffee shop barista. I'm all alone." She threw back her head, releasing a mournful wail.

My heart broke into a million pieces at the sight of my sister in so much pain––Merry, who had never done anything bad to anyone in her entire life. Eve deserved this. I deserved this. But not Merry. It just wasn't fair.

Eve filled a Dixie cup with water and Merry drank it.

She collected herself, then began again. "Now I'm a single mom living in Kansas. The bills are stacking up and I think I'm going to lose the house. I was hoping that by coming here, I'd at least have you girls, but I'm starting to think I'm on my own."

"I'm so sorry," I said. And I meant it.

"Me, too," Eve added, wrapping her arms around us both. "Everything's going to be okay. You'll see."

We stood there under the dim fluorescent lights of the Dip Stix bathroom, all of us crying. Merry for the life she had just confessed, Eve and I for the broken lives we were too embarrassed to talk about. I looked up, my eyes meeting Eve's. Maybe we would never be friends, but we would always be sisters.

"Sorry to interrupt you, ladies." Shane's voice said from the other side of the door. Eve opened it and he stood there with Paul by his side, a concerned look on both their faces. "Maggie, I think you have a visitor."

He pushed open the door fully and I could see a man standing off to the side, a man with gray desperate eyes.

I stepped forward. "Michael...?"

TWENTY

GO YOUR OWN WAY

"MAGGIE! THANK GOD I FOUND YOU!" Michael rushed towards me with such purpose that everyone except Paul moved out of his way.

"Who are you?" Paul demanded, barricading himself between us.

Though Michael outweighed him by a good forty pounds, Paul looked ready to fight.

"Is this your boyfriend?" Michael eyed Paul, clenching his fists. "Now I know why you left. You had this guy waiting for you."

I held my hand up to Paul. "It's okay." Turning to Michael with crossed arms. "That is not my boyfriend and you know the reason I left. Now why are you here?"

Michael looked from me to Paul then back again, trying to decide if he believed me. At last, his eyes softened. He moved inside the restroom with me and I stepped back at the same time. I could feel everyone watching, except for Merry who had brushed past us and was escorting June Bug out the front door.

"I love you, Maggie," he said, almost whimpering. He shook his head and held his palms out to me. "God knows, I'm sorry for what I did. I have no idea why I did it. It was like I was possessed."

I glanced at Eve. I hadn't told her the details of my departure and I was embarrassed that it was coming out this way. To her credit, her face remained stoic as she hovered protectively near, along with Paul and

253

Shane.

"Michael, you need to go," I said, pushing him to the side as I tried to leave the restroom. "I can't do this."

"Can't do what?" he said, capturing one of my hands and placing it on his heart. "Go back to the man you love?" Still holding my hand he took a deep breath and lowered himself onto one knee. "Maggie, I know I said that marriage didn't matter to me in the past but..." His free hand reached inside his pocket.

My eyes widened as I realized what he was about to do. "Michael. No. Not now." I turned to the others. Eve looked confused while Shane and Paul still appeared angry.

"...Will you marry me?" Michael continued, opening a box that contained a gold ring with a large pink-white diamond.

Eve let out a gasp. I motioned to the others that I needed a moment alone and they moved away from the doorway, ready to jump in if necessary.

"Michael..." I tried to swallow, but my mouth was dry. All those years of wishing he had asked me, and here he was, proposing in a cramped, public restroom.

Merry returned to the restaurant without my niece. "I ran into Marion next door at the candy store. She is going to watch June Bug for a while." She didn't acknowledge Michael kneeling on the floor or the box in his hand.

Michael did a double-take, but was not deterred.

"I'll be so good to you, Maggie. We don't have to go back to Woodhaven. We could go anywhere. Get real jobs. Live like normal people. You could pursue your art or whatever you wanted. We can make it." He lifted the ring from the box. It sparkled enticingly.

Images of Michael and I––riding off into the sunset in our white van––ran through my brain. We could start over. Start a family. Michael had driven all this way here and changed his views on marriage. It must mean something.

Merry came to my side. I could feel her eyes on me.

"I don't know..." I said, running my fingers over the diamond, feeling the smoothness of the rock between its rough edges.

Michael stood up, looking down at me, his gray eyes filled with promises. I felt dizzy, lost in that wave of love and affection I had once held for him.

"I just..." I looked at the floor, searching for the right words. "I want to, Michael. I want to say yes so badly, but..."

"Then do. It's that easy. You say yes, we pack up your stuff and get the hell out of here. You told me yourself how much you hated this town."

I glanced at Merry. Her face was tight, but otherwise emotionless.

"I wish it was that easy..."

"It is." Michael attempted to place the ring on my finger, but my hands curled involuntarily. "Dammit, Maggie!" he said, his jaw clenching. "What else do I have to do to prove that you are important to me? I spent a fortune on this ring and learned how to drive a stick shift for you. Doesn't that mean anything?"

I nodded. He was right. The 'old' Michael wouldn't have done either of those things. I started to speak, to agree that, yes, I would be his wife, when Merry finally interrupted.

"Maggie, can I have a word with you please?"

"Can it wait?" Michael said. "We are in the middle of something here."

"Yes, I see that. But no, Michael, it cannot wait." Merry turned and faced him directly. He towered over her by almost a foot, but she stood her ground, arms crossed. "If you give me five minutes with my sister and she still wants to marry you, I will give you both my blessing."

Michael narrowed his eyes, turning his head slightly to the side, trying to get a read on her 'angle.'

"Five minutes," Merry repeated. "If you are really supposed to be together, five minutes won't matter."

Michael exhaled and nodded. "Okay."

Merry grabbed me by the arm and walked me through the restaurant and out the front door, shutting it behind her. It was dark and cold and I could see my breath. I bounced in place, wishing I had brought my coat.

"You're not seriously going to marry this guy, are you?"

"Maybe. I don't know."

"I'm not sure what happened to you two down there, but I can tell you one thing, he doesn't love you."

As much as I adored my sister, I felt like she was crossing the line. She didn't know anything about Michael or me. She was long gone by the time Michael had come into my life.

"Of course he loves me. He drove all the way here to get me. Besides," I said, staring into the night, which was growing colder by the minute. "...I miss him."

"Maggie!" Merry shook my shoulders, bringing me back. "Stop being stubborn and listen to someone's advice for once. He––Doesn't–– Love––You. Period."

Her words felt like a slap in the face.

"Why are you saying that?" I said. "You might be able to sense people's emotions, but sometimes you are wrong. You were wrong about Frank, weren't you?"

She looked at me, expressionless. Now it was I who had crossed the line. I wished I could take back those words, but it was too late. I was sure she was going to really slap me, or worse, walk away. But she didn't.

"Stop being stupid, Maggie," she finally said, her voice kinder than her words. "I need to tell you something, so, okay here goes..." Merry drew in a long breath. "When you first disappeared, Eve called and let me know. I was so worried about you, Maggie. So, so worried. I did some research on the computer and tracked you down."

"How...?"

Merry ignored my question. "I found you guys in Kansas. It was only two hours away from where I lived. I tried calling and I got Michael on the phone. At first he denied that you were there and finally he admitted you were, but he kept saying you were too busy to take my calls. This happened about six or seven times. Finally, I couldn't take it any longer and I made Frank drive us to your town. When I got there, Michael answered the door. He wouldn't let me see you or talk to you. He saw that I was worried and seven months pregnant but he told me you didn't want to see me or any other member of our family again. I knew that wasn't the truth. I knew you would see me, but he wouldn't let you."

Merry paused, giving me the chance to digest what she was saying.

"I never knew..." I began.

"...I came back with the sheriff three days later," Merry continued. "But you had all already packed up and moved on. That's the last I heard about you until Aunt Dora let us know you were alive and well in California. I didn't try to reach you again for fear Michael would uproot you like before."

I stared at my sister, remembering how quickly Michael had ushered us out of Kansas. He had said the locals hadn't appreciated our form of religion and we needed to move before things got ugly. But he was really trying to keep me from my family.

Jillian's words came back to me, too.

Real love doesn't try and control.

I no longer had the urge to go to Woodhaven, or anywhere with Michael for that matter. I had nothing but anger––and pity––for the man, and neither emotion would make me get into that van.

"You still going?" Merry asked quietly, a streetlight illuminating her pretty but tired face.

"Not a chance," I said. I took her hand and we walked back into Dip Stix.

Maybe I would still leave Dark Root, but it wouldn't be tonight.

We returned to see Eve and Michael huddled close in the booth.

Eve was rubbing his shoulder and I was surprised that I wasn't jealous. If Eve wanted him, she could have him.

"There, there," Eve said, as Michael sipped from a white ceramic cup.

"I'm sure she'll have you. You just have to show her what an incredible man you are."

Michael nodded and took a long swallow, finishing off his drink.

I shot Eve a what-the-hell-are-you-doing look, but she only smiled. Suddenly, Michael pounded a fist on the table, slid out of his seat, and stood up.

"Thank you, Eve," he said. "I *am* going to fight for her!"

Merry gripped my hand and we readied ourselves, but Michael jostled past us and out the door.

"Where's he going?" I asked as I heard the van roar to life. I was certain he was going to turn around, remembering that he had forgotten me, but he drove away.

"Well, ladies," Eve said, straightening the sleeves of her shirt. "I not only know how to reel them in, I also know how to release them." She raised Michael's cup and winked.

"You used your special tea?" I asked, leaning forward to peer inside the cup. "The dose you were saving for…" I didn't finish the sentence on purpose.

Paul was standing in the entryway to the kitchen, watching us.

"Yes," she answered. "Well, that and the power of suggestion." She pointed to a picture of an actress on the cover of a magazine in front of her. "Michael is now off to find some slut that got the role that could have made me a star because she sent the producer naked pictures of herself." She shrugged, flipping over the magazine. "Karma's a bitch."

"Eve!" Merry said, aghast. "We don't want that man stalking some poor woman!"

"Firstly, she isn't poor. I hear she cleaned up with those photos. Secondly," she said, turning to me. "The effects won't last long. A week. Maybe two. Long enough for Maggie to see what a mistake marrying that guy would have been."

"I think I already did." I squeezed Merry's hand. "But Eve, what about you? Don't you still need the tea?"

Eve lowered her eyes. "No. If I can't make the person I love, love me back without witchery, then I don't think I'd be happy anyway."

"How my little chicks have grown!" Merry slid into the booth and I followed. Merry wrapped her arms around the both of us. "Now, let's have some real coffee. *Gaston!*"

Moments later, Paul and Shane appeared. Paul carried a coffee pot while Shane balanced a tray of cups, saucers and whipped cream in his hands. Paul served us, smiling at me while he poured my cup. I could feel Eve watching us as she sipped her drink.

"This is the best coffee I've ever had," I said, holding my cup up for a refill.

"That's an espresso blend," Shane informed me. "It's got chocolate in it."

"You should definitely serve these," I said, licking the cream from the top of my lip.

"Well, I'm not great at making them. It's more Paul's thing."

Paul smiled. "Maybe you should hire me or the secret will go to the grave."

"Maybe I will," Shane said.

Paul wasn't going to Seattle, I realized, as I glanced around the room.

He had found his home.

TWENTY-ONE

THE BOYS ARE BACK IN TOWN

IN THE PAST HALF HOUR, I had gone from grumbling spinster to respectable almost-married woman, then back again to spinster. Despite it all, I felt happy and alive. For the first time in my life, I wasn't under anyone's rule, physically or emotionally.

My future was really my own.

This revelation deserved a drink and so I had one. And another.

We stayed at Dip Stix late into the night––so late, in fact, that that I thought Shane was going to boot us out. But he kept the place open and the wine rolling. June Bug returned and we regaled her with tales from our childhood. She asked tons of questions, throwing us into fits of nostalgic hysteria.

"...Remember the time that Mother got into the fight with that old lady who used to rent the house down the road? Claimed the lady had stolen her familiar...?"

We howled at the memory of Mother shaking a finger at the poor, aged widow, threatening to make her go barren.

"...How about that time you two got into it over that carnie boy?" Merry added. "He was some prize."

"I won, of course," Eve said, blowing on her fingertips.

I laughed so hard I almost choked. "Yeah, and he stole your credit card. Lucky you."

"Hey, a win's a win. I only hope all those shoes that showed up on my bill that month were for his mother."

At last, June Bug's head hit the table, a signal that it was time to go.

Merry fumbled around in her purse for keys, found a lipstick instead, and declared that she was ready to take us home. We laughed raucously and Shane raised an eyebrow.

"Methinks the fair ladies have had a bit too much to drink," he said, shaking his head.

"I can drive you girls, and we can pick up Merry's car tomorrow," Paul offered, removing the keys in his apron pocket.

We thanked Shane for his hospitality, promised to stop by sometime in the next week to help him clean up, and then huddled up for warmth as we stumbled towards Paul's car.

"It's cold," I said, blowing frost circles into the air.

"No shit," Eve said, her voice teasing.

"Yes, Fall has come to Dark Root," Merry agreed, laying June Bug in the back seat. She crawled in beside her, leaving Eve and I to fight over who would get the coveted middle seat up front next to Paul. I was quicker and gave Eve a smug look as I put on my safety belt. Just because we had made our peace didn't mean either of us was going to back down on Paul. Eve should have saved some of her tea leaves.

She took the window seat and pinched my knee. I pinched hers back.

"I'm telling Mom," I teased. She stuck her tongue out at me.

"Maggie," Paul said. "Will you find us some good music on the radio?"

I nodded, fiddling with the cigarette lighter, disappointed that no music was coming out.

"It's not working," I said.

Paul moved my hand onto the radio knob.

"You're a genius," I said, playing with the hairs on the back of his neck. He patted my head and cranked up the heat.

"He's not only a genius," Eve cut in. "He's cute, too. A cute genius. How often does that happen?"

"Almost never," I agreed.

Eve leaned across me towards Paul. Looking up at him with large doe eyes, she said, "...And the funniest thing is, he doesn't even know it."

"That's one of the things that makes him so cool," I added.

Eve and I spent the next few minutes trying to outdo one another on the reasons Paul was so great.

Finally, Merry spoke. "I don't know about all of you, but I'm wide awake."

"Me, too!" I said. That was an understatement. I was so hopped up on sugar, wine, and caffeine that I could do most anything––swim a lake, climb a mountain, build a pyramid. If I had springs in my shoes, I could probably launch myself to the moon. Then I had a sobering thought.

"Aunt Dora's going to kill us if we stumble in like this."

"I have an idea," Merry said, who had consumed a little wine herself. "Let's go to Sister House."

Eve and I looked at each other, mouths opened. "Are you kidding?" I asked. "With the monster still in there?"

"That monster," Merry said, tapping my shoulder repeatedly from the backseat. "Is precisely the reason we go. Look at the moon!" She motioned towards the yellow ball that hung motionless in the dark sky. It wasn't full yet, but it was getting close. "Perfect night for an exorcism, don't you think?"

"What about June Bug?" I said, trying another approach.

"We can drop her off with Aunt Dora. Problem solved."

"I'm in," Eve said, surprising me. "It's about time we had some fun. Whoo!" she yelled, opening her window and sticking her head out to face the wind, begging Paul to drive faster.

He looked us over. "I think you girls need sleep more than anything."

"I've been sleeping my whole life," Merry said, her eyes still on the sky. "Please, Paul. For us?"

Paul shifted in his seat. "Well, two have weighed in so far. Maggie?"

I looked at Eve. Her eyes were closed and she was mouthing the words to the Bob Seger song playing on the radio. Behind me Merry was giving me her sweetest smile.

"I can't let them have all the fun," I said, reaching for the crystal around my neck. I should have given it back to Michael, and maybe one day I would. For now, though, it offered me comfort.

"In the words of our great sister, Merry," I said. "'Let's send that thing back from where it came.'"

Before we went to drop off June Bug, we made a quick pit stop at our mother's shop.

Paul waited in the car while the three of us plundered the store. I hadn't seen the place in over a week, but I could tell that Eve had made some real progress. For starters, there was electricity, for which I was grateful. If there were any rats running about, I wanted to be able to see them before they saw me.

"Nice job," I said to Eve, as I made my way through the store.

There were still a few boxes, but they were organized neatly against the walls. The shelves had been dusted, the floors swept and the windows cleaned. I wondered how she had found time to tackle all of this and help out at Dip Stix, too.

Merry dug through the bins beneath the counter, pulling out herbs and sniffing them. She frowned. "These are a bit old and diluted, but they will have to do."

"Too bad we can't schedule the exorcism for next week," Eve said, pulling several candlestick holders from a low shelf. "The new stock will start arriving about then."

I watched my sisters, unsure of how I could help. I had never been much for 'the craft,' but I was suddenly fascinated by the process.

"I've been reading Mother's book," I announced, lifting the spell book from my purse. "Especially the parts about getting rid of bad spirits."

Merry gave me a curious look. "Good. We might need that."

"I think we have everything." Eve's arms were full as she made her way outside.

We followed, flipping off lights and locking the door behind us. Eve beat me to the middle seat and whispered 'nanny-nanny-boo-boo.' I stepped on her toe.

"Good grief!" Paul shook his head. "I didn't know witchery was such an expensive hobby." He made jokes about witches having to take in laundry to support their candle habits. Eve and I laughed, trying to out-cackle each other.

"Think we can throw a curse on Frank while we're at it?" Merry snickered, climbing into the back seat. I did a double take to make sure June Bug was still sleeping. She was. But Merry's comment stuck with me. She had always been a 'turn the cheek' sort of person. Either exhaustion, the wine, or our run in with Michael had gotten to her. Maybe all three.

We arrived at Harvest Home, charging through the front door.

Paul carried a sleeping June Bug over his shoulder like a sack of potatoes. Aunt Dora was awake, watching Andy Griffith on late night TV. Her legs were propped on an ottoman and she had a wet towel over her forehead.

"Aunt Dora," Merry stroked her arm. "Do you mind watching June Bug for a while? We have things to attend to."

"I know what things ya have ta atten' ta," Aunt Dora said, removing the towel from her forehead. "Da circle is cracked and chippin' away. Ya better make sure ya know what ya gettin' inta."

"Aunt Dora," I said, taking a spot on the ottoman near her feet. "Please tell us what you know about the circle."

Aunt Dora's eyes turned to slits. She pulled her legs from the stool, pushing her feet into pink slippers. She raised herself to standing, reached for her cane, and drew an imaginary circle on the ground with its tip.

"Da circle has many meanings: unity, wholeness, eternity. It is wid'out beginnin' an' wid'out end." She stopped, checking to see if we

265

were paying attention. "But in dis case, da circle represents protection..."

Aunt Dora limped towards the window, looking out at the moon. The glass steamed over from her breath and she traced out another circle.

"Dark Root is a stronghold, one o' da few left in da world today. An' dat's only because of yer mama." She looked at me, her eyes birdlike. "An' da reason it's a stronghold is because of da spell we put o'er the town. A spell o' protection. Ta keep da..."

"...Dark at bay," I said, remembering the incantation of my dream.

"Yes! But it was also meant ta weaken da things dat are alrea'y in. An' now dat da circles breakin', things are gettin' in dat aren't s'posed to come in, and da things dat are alrea'y in, are gettin' stronger."

"Why is the circle breaking?" Merry asked.

"We ha'nt done da spell in a few years now. It needs a' least se'ev to keep it goin', but da more sayin' it da stronger it gets." She swallowed and tapped her cane three times on the floor. "A few ha' died. A few more are losin' der minds." She shook her head sadly. "Ev'rything's fallin' apart..."

I wasn't sure what she meant about stronghold, but it sounded too big for my wine fuzzy mind. "We are going to Sister House to take on one of those 'things' now."

Aunt Dora didn't look surprised. "Take yer totem," she said, pointing the end of her cane towards my purse. "Da owl from yer mother's shop will protect ya."

"How did you know about the owl?" I asked.

She pointed a finger towards her forehead and gave me a wry smile. "I'm ol'. I know lots a things. I jus' don' make a fuss about dem."

"Thanks," I said, giving her a grateful hug. I knew very little about totems but I was game to try anything.

"Now, ladies," Merry said, covering June Bug with an afghan. "I do believe we are set. Let's do this."

"After getting rid of Maggie's loser ex-boyfriend, this will be a piece of cake," Eve said, pulling a jacket off the rack and opening the door.

I opened my purse and peered at the spell book and glass owl inside.

"Yeah, cake," I said, wishing I had more wine.

Maybe then I would believe my words.

Sister House, by light of day, appeared despondent, like the face of a beautiful woman whose time had passed.

But at night, especially beneath the light of a yellow moon, its fading beauty changed to a visage that was almost sinister——a small mountain of a house, obscuring and devouring the forest behind it, a forest that threatened to take it back.

One day, the trees seemed to say as they bobbed and dipped in the wind. *One day that land will be ours again. Until then, we wait.*

"The witching hour will soon pass," Merry said, as we piled out of the car, scrambling up the dark walkway. Her eagerness to go inside was unnerving.

"Should I go with you?" Paul asked, catching up to us. "I don't like sending you girls in there alone. What if there are squatters?"

I smiled at his naïveté. "Squatters are the least of our worries." His face took on a look of alarm. "...We'll be fine," I added. "Just don't leave us."

"Never," he said, reaching for my hand, as Merry and Eve climbed the steps to the porch. "Call me if something happens. I'll be right here."

I noticed Eve's silhouette turn in our direction and I released Paul's hand.

Paul returned to his car and hollered, "If I don't bring all three of you back, Aunt Dora will have my hide. I'm more afraid of her than of any ghost."

"As you should be," I called back playfully, then turned towards the door where Merry was jamming a key into the lock.

"He likes you," Eve said quietly, folding her arms across her chest to shield herself from the wind.

"Yes," I admitted. "Though I don't know why."

"You've got spirit," she said. "I just have fake eyelashes and a boob job."

She gave me a weak smile before following Merry into the blackness inside.

TWENTY-TWO

YOU CAN DO MAGIC

THE HOUSE WAS COLD, a down-in-your-bones cold, and I wrapped my arms around myself, trying to fight off the freeze. I found one of Mother's old fur coats in the entry closet and put it on. It was itchy and musty, but it was warm.

"Where are the cats?" I asked. Aunt Dora had been coming by to feed them, but the house was uncannily quiet and I had no idea where they were caged.

"Probably hiding, afraid they will be turned into another coat," Eve laughed, inspecting me.

"Aunt Dora let them loose in the basement," Merry said.

Eve and I turned our attention to our older sister, watching as she sprinkled a white powder in the shape of a five-pointed star onto the floor. A pentagram. Next, she formed a powdery circle around it. "The star must be inside the circle but the two shapes must not touch," she said.

I nodded, remembering from Mother's book that this was the symbol for protection.

"Maggie," Merry said, not looking up. "Can you sprinkle sea salt around the outside of the house? It will keep your 'thing' from escaping."

I swallowed hard, peeking out the front window. Small black shapes twisted in the night.

"I'm on it," Eve said, and I mouthed a grateful 'thank you' to her.

"What can I do?" I asked, watching Eve through the curtains. She had no awareness of the small creatures that slid into the shadows as she approached.

"Find more candles. The shop was out. Light as many as you can. Mostly whites, but the other colors are okay, too. Just no black ones."

"Got it."

Mother's shop might be devoid of candles, but her house had dozens. I found them tucked into drawers and baskets, and scattered across shelves. Once they were lit, I put them in holders and teacups around the living room. I then took five white tapers and placed them in the spokes of the pentagram––something else I had learned from Mother's book.

Finally, I placed the crystal owl in the center of the pentagram, though I wasn't sure why. It just felt right. When I was done, I tapped Merry on the shoulder.

She inspected the room, smiling. "Just like old times," she said, cocking her head to the side. "I kinda missed this."

"No ritual Magick with Frank, I take it?" I reached inside my purse, pulling out Mother's book and the sage stick. I passed the bundle of sticks to Merry, who nodded approvingly then lit it from a purple candle on the dining room table.

"No magic of any kind, I'm afraid. You know," Merry said, fanning the smoke from the burning sage towards the kitchen. "I sometimes wonder what life would have been like, if we hadn't all moved away. I mean, it wasn't so bad here, was it?"

"Well..." I hesitated, not wanting to dredge up bad memories. "Ruth Anne left and we never talked about it. Some people might say that's pretty bad."

"Yes, but..."

"And Mom was going nuts. You know, the last year that Eve and I were here together, I can't remember her saying more than a handful of words to either of us." I recalled my mother, sitting in her rocking chair, staring vacantly out the window. "It was like she had given up on everything."

"Oh, Mags, I had no idea." Merry draped her free arm around my shoulder, squeezing me. "I shouldn't have left you girls. I'm sorry." She sniffed, rubbing her nose with the back of her hand. "...And I didn't mean what I said about leaving because of you and Eve. That was my excuse. The real reason was..."

She paused, looking around the house we had grown up in.

"It's okay," I said, my own nose beginning to run from the bitter aroma of the sage. I was half-tempted to wipe it on Mother's fur coat but found an old Kleenex in the pocket instead. "We all had to go."

"And some good things came of it," Merry said, brightening. "You got to see the country. I had June Bug. Eve got to live as a glamorous actress in New York."

"Yeah, about that..."

"Yes?"

I stopped. Only a few hours earlier, I would have killed for the chance to tell her about Eve's real life in New York. But things were different now.

"I didn't travel around the country so much as the West Coast."

Merry smiled. "It's all good."

"All done!" Eve returned through the front door, showing us an empty cellophane wrapper. "Now let's get rid of Maggie's monster."

"We need to keep the lights off," Merry said, as we moved single-file through the ground floor of the house. Merry braved the front of the line, waving the smoke from the sage stick before us. Eve held the middle, plunging her candle into the shadows around us.

I lingered behind, clutching Mother's book and glancing over my shoulder to ensure that we were alone.

"Spirit of Sister House," we called out. "We demand that you to make your presence known!"

We repeated the phrase in each of the lower rooms: the living room, the dining room, the kitchen.

"It's not really a spirit," I reminded Merry when we had cleared the floor.

"I don't have a word for what it is," she said. "Spirit will have to do."

"What about that room?" Eve nodded towards a door that had always been locked—Mother's secret room. It had been forbidden for so long I had almost forgotten it was there.

Merry nodded and I gave her a quizzical look. Unless she had a key, that door was not going to open. We stood before it. Merry said something under her breath, then tried the handle.

"Crap!" she said, stamping her foot. "I thought it would work."

"Thought what would work?" I asked.

"The incantation, *Door of steel, door that's locked, let me in with just a knock.*"

"Where did you learn that?" Eve and I asked.

"Well," Merry admitted. "When I was a kid and couldn't sleep, I'd sneak out here and hide on the staircase watching Mama and her friends. Twice I saw her go into this room after reciting the incantation but I never tried it myself."

"Maybe we should hold hands," I suggested, feeling foolish as I put the book down on the floor. Merry reached for one of my hands and I grabbed Eve by the wrist so that she could still hold onto the candle.

"Let's say it together," Merry said.

"Door of steel, door that's locked, let us in with just a knock."

We said the incantation, our voices one. The candle in Eve's hand flickered.

Merry tried the door again, but it wouldn't budge.

"We forgot to knock," Eve reminded us, rapping on the door. We heard the soft click of the lock and Eve twisted the knob.

We were in.

Eve pushed the candle inside and our heads followed. The space was the size of a small bedroom and was just as crammed with stuff as the rest of the house. But instead of boxes and bins, there were chests and picture frames and books and things that sparkled––a tiny dragon's lair. Something in the far corner glimmered and if I hadn't had to climb a small mountain to get there, I would have retrieved it.

"Mother's hoarding. The early years," Eve said.

Merry passed the sage stick inside as we asked the spirit once again to show itself, with no luck.

"We will come back," Merry promised, shutting the door. "There are secrets in there, I'm sure. But we have other things to deal with now."

She glided towards the staircase and we obediently followed.

"This floor is clean. Now let's go upstairs."

We ascended the staircase with only a candle to light the way, listening to the wooden boards splinter and groan, as if warning us to turn back.

"Spirit of Sister House," we repeated when we reached the top of the stairs. "We demand that you show yourself!"

The hall was long and dark, but we knew every inch of it by heart. We moved through the guest room, Mother's room, the sewing room and the bathroom. When every room had been cleansed, we made our way to the nursery.

"I can't," I said. My legs begin to tremble as I recalled my last visit.

Merry ignored me and opened the door. Eve and I moved in behind her.

"It feels empty," I whispered, hugging Mother's book to my chest.

Eve held out the candle and we scanned the room. Toys and books littered the floor, evidence of the last encounter. But other than the mess, it appeared perfectly normal.

"Maybe it went away?" I said hopefully.

This had all seemed like a good idea earlier, but now, as I stood sober and in the dark, I wasn't so sure.

"Maybe," Merry agreed. "...But I doubt it. It's been here too long to call it quits without a real fight."

"Remember," Eve reminded us. "Maggie says it's an entity from another plane. And this room..." She extended her free arm. "...Is where it ports in and out, just above us. I can feel it."

Eve lifted her candle and we gazed at the ceiling.

"Maybe it's hiding in its home plane then." Merry gritted her teeth in frustration. "Which means we may never catch it."

I removed my cell phone from my skirt pocket and looked at the time. "If it does choose to show itself, we may have the advantage. In fifteen minutes, the 'thing' will be weaker, once the witching hour is over."

"Yes," Merry said, scooting a porcelain doll head out of her way with her foot. "But so will we."

I clicked a button on my phone to create a beam of light, pointing it into every corner, letting the beam elucidate the darkest edges of the nursery. The light caught dolls and books and bedding thrown haphazardly across the room, but nothing more. I was about to put it away when I saw something––a small dark blob hunkered near the ceiling, sitting on a shelf like a child's toy. Its red eyes flashed and it scurried across the wall, slinking back into the shadows.

I screamed, dropping the phone.

"What!? What did you see, Maggie?" Merry took the candle from Eve and aimed it at the shelf. We caught its shadow just before it disappeared again.

"What the hell?" Eve said, almost tripping over me as I frantically searched for my lost phone on the floor.

"You fucker!" Merry called out into the blackness. "Come show yourself, you motherfucker!"

"Merry," I said, shocked. I had never heard her curse before. "We want to get rid of it, not antagonize it."

"The hell we don't." Merry lifted the candle and we caught a blur as it scampered across a wall, unhindered by gravity. The room suddenly dropped in temperature, so much so that I could now see my breath.

"Don't mind messing with little kids, huh? But you can't stand up to us?" Merry's face contorted, steam rolling from her lips as she struggled to keep the 'thing' in view. "You're not so scary. Show yourself, you bastard!"

A strong gust of wind hurled itself across the room and our candle went out. The nursery door slammed shut, leaving us shivering in the dark.

I redoubled my efforts to find the phone, my fingers groping at the cold floor. At last, I recognized its shape.

"Found it!" I said, tapping the 'on' button without success.

Its power had been sucked dry.

"Let's get out of here," Eve said, scrambling for the door.

I expected it to be locked, but it opened easily. Eve and I launched ourselves into the hall.

"Merry!" Realizing she was still inside, I ran back in, grabbing her arm. "We need to fight it downstairs."

My sister didn't move. Whatever was in here had a hold on her.

"It's me you want!" I called out. "I'm your power source. Come and get me!"

The room warmed for a moment, as if considering. Then Merry was free.

I yanked her out of the nursery as she yelled over her shoulder, "You don't have the balls to fight us!"

We ran blindly down the hall, tripping down the stairs, barreling for our safe spot in the pentagram.

"Stay here," I said, pushing my sisters into the center of the star. I rushed to the pantry, removing five of the small brooms that Mother kept for spells and incantations. I laid them out around the star.

"Added protection," I informed my sisters, but I wasn't sure. I was running on cracked memories and instinct now. Once the brooms were in place, I joined Eve and Merry in the center of the circle.

"Do you think it followed us?" I whispered.

"Yes," Merry whispered back. "But it knows we mean to send it away."

"We need to call it out by naming it," I said, flipping through Mother's book and pointing to the passage on returning an entity to its plane. "There are multitudes of these *implings,* all with names, but we have no power over it until we know who it is."

The chandelier in the dining room began to rock.

"It's listening," I said, shoving the book at Eve. "Find its name." I turned my eyes towards the chandelier, holding out my wrists like I was offering up my veins to have blood drawn. "I'm here," I said again. "You want my energy. Now's your chance. Feed on me."

The chandelier's tremors quickened, violently swinging left then right until it came unhinged from the ceiling. It erupted and crashed to the floor.

"Girls, I think we're in trouble." Merry turned, pointing behind us. One of the brooms around our circle hovered several inches above the ground, then fell back to the earth. "It's trying to get in."

"Any luck on the names?" I asked, as the other brooms joined in, flopping around us like dying fish.

"There are so many of them," Eve said, running her finger down the pages.

"Just say them all, but quietly, so we don't accidentally call in the others. Maybe we will get lucky."

Eve read through the list, asking each particular entity to show itself, as Merry swung the sage stick around in a wild circle, like she was holding back a pack of dogs with a torch.

"It's useless," Eve said.

"No. We have to find it. Keep going." I picked up the owl from the floor and wrapped my fingers around its cool glass body. Aunt Dora had said that the owl was my totem and now it was time to put it to the test.

"Here!" Eve pointed to a picture on the next page. An image of a small, goblin-esque creature stared out at us with two red eyes. "Its name is Gahabrien. He's a small entity, not very powerful. Limited abilities in telekinesis and possessions. He feeds off sensitives and the residual energies of fear, especially in older homes. His own plane is dying...that's why he wants to stay here."

"He picked the wrong house!" Merry's eyes sparkled menacingly. "Gahabrien! We know who you are. I command you to return to the plane from where you came!"

"There's an incantation," Eve said, her fingers sliding down to the words at the bottom of the page. "It's most effective when said by a coven of seven, but..." She shrugged and we read the words together.

"Through the portal, you have come..."

As we spoke the first line of the spell, the brooms on the floor quickened their fluttering.

"To take that which does not belong to you..."

The closet door opened and shut and we could hear the cupboards in the kitchen banging. Cups and saucers poured out, crashing onto the counters and floor below. We had gotten its attention.

"We send you back, Gahabrien. Into the blackness you will go!"

The room around erupted into chaos. The dining room chairs flew backwards, spiraling into the walls behind them. Knick-knacks toppled from their shelves, and a crack formed at the base of the living room window, working its way up the glass until it reached the top––at which point, the window exploded. The explosion sent shards of glass in all directions, landing just outside of the perimeter of the circle.

One by one, the candles in the room went out.

Then all was quiet.

We held our breaths and waited.

Finally, Merry exhaled. "We did it," she said.

"I think so," Eve agreed.

I could make out the smooth features of Eve's face by the moonlight that filtered through the glassless window.

"...That was too easy," she said. "Almost anti-climactic. I think we can turn on some lights now." Eve stepped out of the pentagram and scanned the room.

"Where do you think it went?" I asked, not as convinced that it was gone as my sisters seemed to be.

"Back home for good." Merry bent over to pick up a broom. "We will have to have another ritual, one to close up the portal, but for now..."

Our momentary peace was interrupted by thumping sounds near the dining room. We turned to see Mother's books flying off the shelves, streaming like missiles straight for us.

"It's not over!" Eve yelled. She stood just outside the circle, and I saw her duck a large, hardcover book. "Now what?"

There is power in numbers.

The words came back to me. "Quick, Eve, go get Paul!"

She stood frozen for a moment, then ran outside.

"Maybe we should get Aunt Dora?" Merry said.

The books had gotten through the first layer of protection––the brooms––and were dropping just outside the pentagram's spokes.

"Not enough time," I said, hoping that four of us would be enough.

Eve and Paul burst through the door. "Holy shit," Paul said, covering his head as the books continued to fly around the room. "This is really happening."

"Quick. Into the pentagram. I have an idea." I showed them the glass owl and had them form a circle around me. "Hold hands and don't let go," I whispered. "I'm going to try and capture it."

"Are you out of your frickin' mind?" Eve's eyes widened. "Is that in the book?"

"No. But I have a feeling."

Merry nodded, giving me the okay. I swallowed as another book whizzed by.

I raised the owl overhead, cupped between my hands. I could feel its energy course through my body. It wasn't glass, I realized. It was crystal.

"Totem owl," I said. "I call upon you to aid in my protection..."

"Maggie, your hands are glowing!" Eve exclaimed.

I looked up at the owl. A vibrant yellow light emanated from my fingertips. I interlocked my fingers around the owl, hoping to snuff out the light before Gahabrien noticed.

"I'm here," I shouted. "And I give up! You can have me. You don't have to go back to that dying world of yours..."

Paul looked up, vehemently shaking his head. Eve tightened her hand on his, letting him know it was okay.

The moon fell behind a cloud, throwing us into near darkness. I could sense Gahabrien's energy; he was close by, feeling out the room with invisible tentacles, as if making a decision.

"C'mon," I said, enticingly. "I'm giving myself to you. You can live inside me forever."

"Are you crazy?" Paul dropped my sister's hands and shook me by the shoulders.

"Trust me," I whispered.

He clenched his jaw but rejoined the circle.

"Last chance," I called out again. "After tonight, I'm never coming back into this house. Take it or leave it."

The books that had been swirling around us suddenly toppled to the floor. A loud boom sounded through the room, shaking the walls. I felt a bolt of electricity hit me, starting at my feet and coursing its way upward. My whole body reverberated, twitching and jerking as I struggled to hold onto the owl.

Gahabrien was inside me, filling me with his vile energy.

Spittle formed at the corners of my mouth and I wanted to howl, tear, and bite like a rabid dog. I gnashed my head left then right, nipping at my companions, barking out their names.

"Maggie," one of them called to me. I turned my head and growled.

Still, there was a voice inside me that remained my own. My fingers twitched but I willed them to tighten their grip around the figurine.

But Gahabrien's will was overpowering my own. I felt myself slipping...

I turned my head, catching the light of Eve's eyes.

279

"I love you," she mouthed.

My eyebrows softened.

Deep, deep down, beyond my own guard and in that place that Gahabrien could never touch, I knew I loved her, too.

With what remained of my strength, I pushed his energy upwards, through my belly, my heart, my neck, channeling it up through the crown of my head. In those moments, sick and twisted thoughts popped into my brain. I fought my way through them and continued pushing, up through my arms, into my hands, and finally, into the owl.

Crack!

The figurine burned my hands and I dropped it. It fell to the floor, bounced, but didn't break.

"Quick!" I said, bent over and near to heaving. "Get something to cage this thing! Something glass!"

Eve looked around the living room. Her eyes found one of June Bug's collection jars. She grabbed it, slamming it over the top of the owl. Merry retrieved its lid, quickly flipped the canister, and screwed it on. The jar vibrated in her hands and she carried it to the kitchen table.

We gathered around, watching as the crystal owl changed from clear to a murky brown.

"Good job putting a lid on that thing," I said to Merry, feeling my strength return.

"I've had lots of practice capturing icky things." Merry smiled, her damp hair clinging to her face. She looked wobbly and I helped seat her in a chair.

Eve, for her part, appeared as composed as ever as she picked up books and placed them back onto shelves. Paul stood in the middle of the living room, his mouth trying to form words, but never quite finding them.

I winked at him.

"That was un-fucking-believable," he finally managed.

"Yeah, it was," Eve said. "What a night."

We spent the next half hour casting protection spells around the house.

Paul followed us, scratching his head and muttering things like, "trippy" and "bitchin'."

When we had finished, we fed the cats, changed their litter boxes, packed up our belongings, and headed out to his Explorer.

"I don't know about you girls, but I've got one hell of a headache," Merry said, sliding into the backseat. "I may never drink again."

"But look at what good work we do on the hooch," I said, staring up into the sky. The sun was rising and I yawned in protest, wondering if Aunt Dora would let me sleep the entire day through.

"You were amazing," Paul said, opening the passenger door for me. "I've never seen anything like that."

"Me?" I said, wiping a wisp of hair from my face. "No, it was Eve who carried that show. She put the salt around the house, figured out Gahabrien's name, and kept up morale. Without her, we would have been screwed."

"Yeah?" he asked, looking at my sister with newfound respect.

"Yeah. Eve, sit in the front and tell Paul all about it. I'll ride in the back with Merry and the owl."

Eve gave me an almost imperceptible smile, straightened herself, then settled in next to Paul. "Well..." she began. "When we first went inside, no one knew what to expect..."

Her eyes lit up and she launched into her tale, regaling him with her heroics the entire ride home. I could see the curl of Paul's hair at the nape of his neck. I could smell his scent, a mixture of paprika and sage. I could I could hear him laughing as Eve recanted our adventure. But I couldn't touch him. He wasn't mine. He belonged to Eve.

He had always belonged to Eve.

My heart broke a little, just like Mother's circle.

"That was kind of you," Merry said, laying her head on my lap.

"That's what I'm known for," I said, smoothing her hair. "My kindness."

"There's a first time for everything." Merry smiled, then closed her eyes and drifted off to sleep.

Twenty-Three

Changes

It's amazing what a good exorcism will do for the soul.

The next two weeks were some of the clearest, happiest days of my life. I can't say if it's because I had finally let go of Michael, had discovered a newfound kinship with Eve, spent more time with Merry, or because the rains had temporarily subsided.

Or, quite possibly, it was because the entity that had haunted me since childhood was now encased in a clear glass owl.

Whatever the reason, I relished those long October days, bundling up in scarves and hats to combat the wind that whistled down Main Street as I sipped cappuccinos with Shane on the patio of Dip Stix *Café*. For the first time in my life, I felt like I was part of a family.

I wasn't the only one who was filled with this sense of renewal.

My friends and I strutted around town like primitive hunters who had landed their first mammoth. We walked up and down Main Street, handing out fliers, hanging up posters, and convincing the old-timers that Dark Root's glory days were still ahead.

"It's over," some would say, shaking their heads.

"No, it's just the beginning!" I was seeing this clearly now.

We explained our plan to modernize the festival for the younger crowd––new colors, new decorations, current music––while bringing back some of the traditions that made Dark Root famous for the nostalgic––the parade, the lighting ceremony. We *could* save this town. As long as there were people who loved this community, anything was possible.

One by one, the townspeople fell to our enthusiasm.

Shop owners restocked supplies, painted their walls, and kept their businesses open into the evening. We convinced the mayor to add orange bulbs to the streetlights, line the shop windows with bright twinkle lights, and hand out lunch sacks cut in the shapes of jack-o-lanterns to be used as luminaries down the sidewalk. Shane and Paul built a large stage just north of Main Street, where a band could play. And I spent hours learning how to use the internet, advertising our event to nearby communities and colleges.

In the days leading up to the festival, Dark Root came alive.

It wasn't the same old town I remembered. It was better.

"I can't believe we're actually doing it," Eve said, as we worked side-by-side in our mother's store.

We had created magic inside this shop, too. It no longer looked like a movie set from a 1970's horror flick, it was now a *hip* establishment–– both modern and mystical. We still sold the witchy items––talismans, herbs, and candles––but we also stocked hookahs, CDs, lava lamps and jewelry. Eve had set up a station where she offered henna art, a sort of temporary tattoo that many of the younger girls liked. She painted intricate patterns on the arms and legs of our customers, surprising me with her talent.

"I'm proud of you," I said one morning, as we were getting ready to open the shop.

It wasn't quite nine and there was already four people waiting at our front door. I pointed to Dip Stix across the street, indicating that the restaurant was open, and two of them headed in that direction.

"Maggie." Eve turned from her task. "I've never heard you say you were proud of anyone."

I considered this. "I've grown up a bit. Maybe we all have. Mother would be proud."

At the mention of our mother, we both returned to our work. Though things were going well in Dark Root, there was still the shadow of our mother, lying in the hospital while Merry fought with administration, trying to convince them to send her home.

"We need to order about five hundred mood rings," I said, checking an empty bin. Mood rings had become popular again and we had sold off all our old stock. "How much will it cost, do you know?"

"Do I look like an accountant?" Eve arched a playful eyebrow.

I went to the drawer where we used to keep our calculator. Not seeing it, I moved my fingers through the jumble of office supplies inside, unearthing a picture I had never seen before. It was a photo of a smiling young woman, posing in front of Mother's shop.

Leah.

Time seemed to stop and all I could hear was the rapid beating of my own heart. I looked at the picture again in complete and utter disbelief.

Leah? Here?

With trembling fingers, I turned the picture over, looking for a date.

It was blank. I scraped my memory for any information I had on her. She claimed to be twenty-four when she joined up with us. She looked a few years younger in the picture than the last time I had seen her standing over the railing at Woodhaven, watching me leave. My whole body shook and I tightened my fingers on it to keep from dropping it.

"Eve." My voice cracked as I made my way towards the henna booth where she was mixing dyes. I held up the picture. "Do you know who this is?"

"Sure. She was one of Mom's friends. Merry hired her to stay with Mom overnight when she needed a break."

"What?" I looked at the picture again.

Leah wasn't smiling. She was smirking.

"What's wrong?" Eve said, puzzled. "Why are you upset? Do you know her?"

I was still ashamed to admit that she had taken Michael from me. "She was a recruit back at Woodhaven. Her name is Leah. I found her

285

and Michael..."

I turned my eyes down, embarrassment washing over me.

"That son of a bitch. No wonder you got out of there! And you almost took him back!"

"Yes, I know. But that's not the point. The point is that this woman has been with our mother. I heard she disappeared right after I left. What is she doing here now?"

Eve put a hand over her chest, dropping her bowl of paint. "This is too freaky."

"I know." I looked at the picture again. "This had to have been taken a few years ago. Maybe she––"

"––was the girl Mom hired to help her with the store!" Eve's eyes widened. "We need to tell Merry!"

I was quickly on the phone.

"How could I have let this happen?" Merry was hyperventilating into the receiver. "I'm usually so good at reading people. Oh, Maggie...I was just so tired, I would have let anyone help. Forgive me."

"It's not your fault, Merry. Just make sure she doesn't come near Mother ever again, okay?"

"I haven't seen her in a few days. Maybe she is gone for good. But I will let the hospital staff and the police know." I heard the lump in Merry's throat and I assured her all would be well as I hung up the phone.

"We need to find that bitch and figure out what's going on," I said to Eve.

It was now several minutes past nine in the morning, and the line outside our store had nearly doubled.

"Damn right, we do," Eve said, dark eyes flashing. "She'll rue the day she ever messed with us!"

I put my arm around her.

"What's that for?" she asked, surprised.

"Just for being you."

286

I spent the morning on the phone, relaying the new information to Aunt Dora and the police. Shane stopped in to check on us and, upon seeing how frazzled I was, insisted I join him for tea the moment my shift was over.

At six on the dot, I walked across the street to Dip Stix.

Since the café's transformation, I loved spending time there. It had a warm, inviting feel and Shane always saved the small table by the window for me, where I'd eat muffins and read from Mother's spell book.

On this particular evening, Shane brought me a special chamomile blend to calm my nerves. I drank from the over-sized mug, lost in feelings of confusion and anger. At a few minutes later, Eve wandered in, nodded in our direction, then went to see Paul in the kitchen.

"They're cute," I said, watching them flirt. Since the night of the exorcism they had spent much more time together. There was electricity between them that was tangible; something had shifted in Paul's feelings for Eve since that night, and she was eating it up.

"Yes, they are cute, aren't they?" Shane responded.

Dip Stix was fairly empty; the dinner *crowd* didn't usually roll in until around seven, after the other shops in town had closed down for the night.

He placed a hand gently on one of mine. "And you didn't unleash anything on your mother. Sounds like Leah was in the picture before you even met her." He paused, his eyes finding Paul and Eve, who were snapping dish cloths at each other in the kitchen. "You're a good woman. You deserve happiness too."

I chuckled. "I appreciate you saying that, but I'm fine. Really. As far as happiness, I think I'm finding it. And you've helped." I offered him a warm smile. "What about you? Given up on the quest for love as well?" I recalled how he had looked at Eve a few weeks before.

"Me? A cowboy never gives up on love or anything else for that matter. I'm just waiting for the right lady."

"Oh?" I asked, amused. "What exactly does a cowboy look for? A gal with a nice horse?"

He laughed so hard he doubled over, almost knocking his head on the table. "You're a funny girl, Maggie Mae," he said, wiping the tears out of his eyes. "A horse would be a good start, yes. But really, I'm looking for a woman with a brain. Someone who thinks about things. Engages in the world. Reads."

"Tall order for Dark Root. Maybe you need to broaden your horizons."

"When I was a kid living with my grandma, we got very limited TV. Got to watch a lot of reruns of old shows though. I always loved *Charlie's Angels.*" He leaned in, as if he were about to confess a very juicy secret. "I know everyone liked Farrah Fawcett or Jacqueline Smith, but I always liked the smart girl...Kate Jackson. That's my kind of woman."

"Weren't they all too old for you?" I asked, a wry smile playing across my lips. The thought of young Shane drooling over Sabrina Duncan was even more amusing than him looking for a woman with a horse.

"I like older women," he said, tapping his fingers on the table. "You know Maggie, Eve wasn't the reason I hung out in your home all the time when I was a kid." He lifted his eyebrows and kept them raised, letting me digest this new information.

"Hmmm..." I thought. Older women who loved to read...of course! It was no coincidence that Shane and Ruth Anne both spent so much time in Uncle Joe's library together.

"Shane," I said. "I have a brilliant idea. Let's find Ruth Anne! You're great on the internet. If anyone can find her, it's you." I was so excited by this prospect. Why hadn't I thought of this before?

"What?" he asked, doing a double-take.

I had already put one couple together this month. Maybe I could do it again. Love may elude me, but I could make others happy. Maybe I would get business cards.

Maggie Maddock, Matchmaker Extraordinaire.

"Shane. Let's find her! Let's find Ruth Anne."

"Didn't Merry already try to locate her?"

"Yes, but Merry isn't The Great Shane Doler, Master of the World Wide Web!"

"Okay," he stammered, wrinkling his brow. "If that's what you want."

I nodded, grinning. He could pin it on me if he wanted to. "Yep. And think how good it will be for Eve and Merry and my mother. Might snap the old woman awake." I was inspired now, practically gloating. If we could pull this off...

"Alright." Shane pushed in his chair. "Write down her full name, birth date, all that stuff. Then we can do a background search. It's hard to hide nowadays."

Several customers entered the diner and he left to greet them. I wrote down everything I knew about Ruth Anne. She was born June 7th, 1981––a Gemini. She had brown hair, wore glasses, and liked books and blue jeans. She was wearing a worn, green T-shirt and blue tennis shoes the night she got into that grey sedan and drove away forever.

I caught a flash of lighting through the window. It wasn't close but it was on the horizon. The rains would certainly return, but I hoped they would wait another ten days, long enough to get us through the festival.

But the clouds were darkening, drawing others in, gathering over Dark Root.

"Just ten more days," I said aloud. "That's not too much to ask."

TWENTY-FOUR

YOU'RE SO VAIN

"You've made some pretty good progress, little ladies." Shane tipped his hat to Merry and me, showing off his newly whitened smile.

I rolled my eyes as I lugged a large box from one corner of the living room to the other. Shane was in full cowboy mode lately, even going so far as to don a hat and boots most days. I teased him about wearing his Halloween outfit too early, but he insisted this was his normal manner of dress back in Montana and he was just getting *in touch with his roots*. I suspected it had more to do with the flirty girls who had descended upon Dark Root these days, oohing and ahhing over his biscuits and gravy as he told them stories about his *home on the range.*

Merry blushed under Shane's praise, succumbing to his cowboy charms.

I wanted to launch a throw pillow at him, but restrained myself.

Merry was doing so well. Frank had finally sent a child support check, she had convinced the social worker that Mother should come home, and a few of the men who wandered into Dark Root had commented on her prettiness, something she probably hadn't heard from her husband in ages. Merry was thriving and if I had to put up with the ghost of John Wayne himself to keep her that way, I would.

"It's all coming together," I agreed.

"Yes," Merry said. "The house is clean and town is picking up." She looked at me, smiling. "I haven't seen this many tourists since we were kids. And it's not even Halloween yet!"

June Bug bounded down the stairs carrying the Maggie cat—–the only feline they hadn't found a home for. Apparently, no one wanted a lazy, self-indulgent, kitty-cat who wouldn't share her food. But I liked her.

Maybe, when I finally settled somewhere, I would send for her.

"I think that's the last of the angora sweaters," I said, placing a hideous Christmas-colored one in a bin marked 'winter clothing.' I looked around, wiping my brow. Except for Mother's locked room, we had scoured and scrubbed every nook and cranny of Sister House. I opened the curtains, letting the dim, October light settle into the living room.

The Maggie cat leapt from June Bug's arms and pounced onto a small beam of sunlight on the floor. She curled up on the same patch of floor then, and fell quickly asleep.

Merry wiped her palms on her corduroy jeans. "I couldn't have done this without you guys." She allowed her eyes to rest on Shane.

He blushed, shuffling his feet, and this time I did throw a pillow at him.

"Stop that," I huffed. "Your golly-gee-willikers act makes you look like a dork."

He flushed a little more, but grinned at me.

"Grandma's going to be so excited," June Bug grinned, revealing a missing front tooth.

Merry, Shane and I glanced at one another.

June Bug was aware that grandma was coming home and that she was still 'sleeping,' but she didn't know there was a chance she might not wake up. After discovering that Leah had been 'attending' to Mother, the doctors conducted tests and found that her blood contained large traces of jimson weed, a poisonous plant that could bring about violent behavior, hallucinations, and even death. The doctors insisted the jimson weed may have been the reason she was mad as a hatter for these last few years, but it wasn't the reason she was still in a coma-like state.

"She's going to get better," June Bug said when no one spoke. She walked over to the Maggie cat, crossed her ankles, and sat primly down beside her. "I will give her my healing energy when she gets here, just the way Mama taught me."

I was filled with love for my niece. She had that same, selfless, caring quality that Merry possessed. I also hoped she was right. June Bug had lost her father and her home; she deserved to have a grandmother.

"Well," I said, rubbing my hands together. "It seems we are clear of..." I looked up the staircase, remembering that night a few weeks before. "...Everything."

Merry nodded.

Since we had 'cleansed' the house, there hadn't been any signs of mysterious activities here. Gahabrien remained caged in a mason jar, locked up in one of closets at Harvest Home. Sometimes, when I walked by the closet at night, I'd hear the soft noises from within, scratchings and scuttlings, but I never opened the door to check.

Some doors were better left closed.

"Are you ready?" I asked Shane.

He was driving me to Linsburg to pick up something nice to wear for the festival, a reluctant concession on my part after a week of listening to Merry and Eve's pleas. I argued that it was Halloween and most everyone would be in costume anyway, to which Eve replied, "Then you are going as the town beggar?"

Shane took out his keys and tipped his hat goodbye. "Come by for dinner, okay? Don't tell anyone but there's no dipping tonight. Paul's grilling steaks out back. Should be fun." He turned to me. "...Meet you out front, Mags."

"Thanks for helping, sis." Merry wrapped her arm around my neck and whispered, "I swear, if you don't hurry up and nab that boy, I will."

"As I said before," I reminded her, "I'm done with men. Too much work and not enough payoff." I didn't tell her that he was earmarked for Ruth Anne. I didn't want to ruin the surprise, assuming we ever found our eldest sister.

"Suit yourself," Merry said, dreamily watching Shane get into his truck through the living room window. "Just remember, I'm a single woman now, with needs."

"What needs, Mama?" June Bug piped up.

"Yeah," I teased, crossing my arms. "...What needs?"

"Steak, baby. Steak," Merry said, winking at me as she shooed me outside.

"Uh-huh." I said goodbye to June Bug and made my way to Shane's pickup, slamming the truck door after I climbed in.

"What's wrong with you?" Shane asked as we pulled out of the gravel driveway.

"Nothing."

"Didn't seem like nothing," he said, scratching his head and turning on the country music station.

"Do we have to listen to this crap every time we get in the car?" I said, rubbing my temple. "And why do you have to smile at every woman we run across, including my sister? She has real problems and here you are playing cowboy hero."

"Why, Maggie Maddock," he said, a pleased grin on his face. "If I didn't know better, I'd think you were jealous."

"Don't flatter yourself," I said, putting my feet up on the dashboard. "I'm just looking after Merry, is all."

"Yes, Maggie, my dear. Your kindness knows no bounds."

"Besides," I said, looking gloomily out the window. "You are supposed to be saving yourself for Ruth Anne."

Shane removed both hands from the steering wheel, placing his palms together in a jerky, praying motion. He mumbled something under his breath then returned to driving.

"Okay, Maggie. I will save myself for *Ruth Anne*."

Neither of us said another word as we made our way towards Linsburg.

Despite my irritation with Shane, my mood improved once we got to Linsburg, a town nestled in the mountains and paradoxically both colder and sunnier than Dark Root.

I could see the frost of my breath as we exited the truck and meandered down Main Street. Everywhere, there were smiling townies carrying steaming mugs of chocolate, talking about school, the holidays, and *"Have you heard, Haunted Dark Root is returning?"*

The place was positively buzzing.

"This is how Dark Root will look in just a few years," Shane said, sliding on the black gloves he kept in his console. "Mark my words."

"Dark Root still has a ways to go," I said, noticing the array of colorful shops that lined the road. "But we're getting there," I added, before he could start in on his positive thinking lecture.

Shane pointed to a small restaurant across the street called Sammy's, which boasted the *Best Grilled Cheese Sandwi*ches in the Pacific Northwest. "Let's check that place out."

I readily agreed. Though I loved Aunt Dora's cooking and the new cuisine at Dip Stix, a plain old grilled cheese sandwich on a cold fall day sounded really good.

The restaurant was charming, a revamped fifties diner complete with an old juke box and a red and white soda fountain. We took seats at the counter and ordered the house specialty from a blue-haired waitress named Marge.

"This is really good," I said, dipping my sandwich into the rich tomato bisque. Shane took a bite, smiled, then made a note in the little black journal he carried with him everywhere. "We might have to add this to our Dip Stix fare."

I finished my lunch and thought about ordering pie––there was a piece of apple that had taunted me since we arrived. Had Shane not been sitting across from me, already teasing me about inhaling my soup, I would have.

"Where next?" I asked, looking out the window as the waitress cleared our plates. There were so many fun shops, and I wanted to hit them all.

"We'll have to do the whole tourist thing some other day. The plan for today is to get you pretty for your big night," Shane said, grinning. He had a small glob of tomato soup on his chin and I didn't tell him––his penance for teasing me.

"I still don't think I'm fit to be the Master of Ceremonies. I think you would do a better job."

"Probably." His brown eyelashes fluttered as he considered. "But we need one of the Maddock girls. Merry's shy and Eve's––"

"––Eve," I finished for him.

Had we given Eve the MC title, the theme would have changed from Haunted Dark Root to All About Eve, complete with a slide-show presentation. Luckily, she was satisfied with decorating and bossing Paul around.

I handed the waitress a Haunted Dark Root flier and asked where the nearest beauty parlor was, which Shane found uncontrollably funny. The waitress directed us to Sally's Cut and Curl across the street. I had never had a real haircut before and I stroked my locks protectively as we entered the establishment.

"Will it hurt?" I asked.

"If it hurt," Shane said, removing his hat. "Men would all have long hair. Haven't you heard we are babies when it comes to physical pain?"

"Good point."

"Besides," he said, flagging down the receptionist, who was watching a reality show in the back room. "You don't have to get it cut short. Just styled."

I swallowed. If we were going to resurrect Dark Root I had to keep my hair long. It was a well-known truth that a witch's power was in the length of her hair.

"Why, aren't you pretty!" said a lady, whose name tag read Cleo.

She was an older woman, probably closer to my mother's age than mine. I looked around for someone younger, more modern, but they were all occupied.

Seeming to sense my nerves, Cleo waved a manicured hand. "Don't you worry. I've been cutting hair for forty years. I'm sure I can tackle that mane." She examined my wiry strands, puckering her lips as she scrutinized what she would be working with. "...How about we layer, highlight, condition, and straighten?" she said. "Maybe add in some side bangs? I think it will really bring out your eyes."

I looked helplessly at Shane, hoping he understood what she meant. It was all a foreign language to me.

"Don't look at me," he said. "I just tell them to cut off anything sticking out from under my hat." He rubbed one of his ears. "Almost lost the right one that way."

He smiled again, said something about me being in good hands and that he was going to check some other stores while I got pampered.

"I'll be back in a couple hours," he said, when he saw the look of panic in my eyes. "I think you will keep Cleo plenty busy till then."

When he was gone, Cleo swooned. "Isn't he a little muffin? You're a lucky woman."

"Yeah," I said, as she pushed my head under a faucet. "Lucky me."

When the first lock of hair fell from my head––a shocking, two-inch chunk of coppery wire––I gasped, then squeezed my eyes shut for the duration of the process. Cleo complained about the thickness, dryness, and overall sorry condition of my hair. I apologized repeatedly as she yanked and combed out knots. At last, she tapped the side of my cheek with her comb, telling me that it was time to look. I opened my eyes and gazed in the mirror.

Was that really me?

I had grown up sandwiched between Merry and Eve, both of whom were beautiful, but I had never felt anything other than average myself. Now, staring into the mirror and noticing how the bangs framed my green eyes, the way soft wisps fell across my shoulders, and the new honey-colored strands interwoven with my natural red hue, I felt beautiful. My skin was still pale and freckled and my nose a bit too thin, but my features came together.

I was Maggie, improved.

"Thank you!" I said, almost falling out of my chair. "You're a magical woman, Cleo." I handed her a flier and gave her a quick hug. "If you come to Haunted Dark Root I'll hook you up with a free henna tattoo."

Cleo removed my bib and I ran my fingers through my hair. It was so soft I couldn't keep my hands out of it. I turned from one side to the other, checking out every angle of my face in the mirror.

A low whistle caught my attention and I turned to see Shane, standing in the doorway with a few plastic sacks in his hand. He removed his hat and sauntered in my direction.

"You're as pretty as a flower," he said. It wasn't very poetic but I blushed nonetheless. Then I remembered how he flirted with other girls that way and I socked him in the arm.

"Careful," he said, rubbing his arm. "I bruise like a peach."

"You're lucky I don't have any peaches on me," I replied. "Or I'd throw them at you, too."

"I can't believe how mean you are being to me, after I went out and bought you presents. Now you'll never get to see what's inside these bags." He dangled the sacks in front of me but I ignored him and went to pay my bill.

"I forget you're not a normal woman, Maggie," he continued, following me out. "And that you can't be bribed with stuff, but..." He opened one of his bags and pulled out a topaz-colored bracelet. "...I got you some baubles."

"Pretty," I admitted, snatching a rose-colored broach from his hand. "But you shouldn't have spent your money on me."

"It's costume jewelry," he said, pinning the broach on my shirt and stepping back to look. "Didn't cost much. Now, let's get you dolled up."

Shane took me by the arm, pulling me into a boutique next door. It was small but overwhelming. I had never been shopping in a store that didn't sell second-hand clothing, and I wasn't sure where to start. Shane grabbed a sales girl and before long, my arms were loaded up with colorful pieces to try on.

"Try not to get carried away," he said as I zipped in and out of the dressing room with piles of clothes. "We don't want to start you on the path to hoarding. I hear it's hereditary."

I stuck my tongue out at him as I took in another armful.

"How do I look?" I said, emerging with my first real *outfit*——a form-fitting turquoise sweater dress and chocolate brown, heeled boots.

"Wow!" Shane's jaw dropped. I spun around then curtsied. "I have never seen anyone so beautiful in all my life!"

"You say that to everyone," I said, appraising my appearance in the three-way mirror. The dress clung to me in the right places and was forgiving in the others. It also brought out the color of my eyes. I just needed a belt.

Shane scratched the back of his neck. "Yeah, but I mean it this time."

Looking at the price tags, I frowned. $85 for the dress and $70 for the boots. Though I hadn't spent much since returning to Dark Root, it was still a huge chunk of the money I had left.

"I wish Mom was awake," I said, ducking back into the dressing room to remove the garments. "She could probably make me something almost as pretty."

I heard him laugh from the other side of the fitting room. "No offense to your ma, but she didn't exactly dress you girls in the latest fashions. Most of the time, I expected to find you all in prairie dresses and bonnets."

"Yeah," I agreed, reluctantly putting on my old clothes. "The only shows she watched on TV were *Little House on the Prairie* and *The Partridge Family*. I guess that's where she got her design ideas from." I left the fitting room and handed the sales girl the clothing I didn't want. But I kept the dress.

"Well?" I asked. "Should I?"

"Tell you what…" Shane said, grabbing the boots back from the sales girl. "You buy the dress and I will buy these. They seem to go together."

"I can't ask you to buy me those!"

"You didn't. It's my gift to you, for all you've done. You'd be insulting me if you didn't take them." He grinned, holding the two boots out before him.

I huffed, then grabbed them out of his hands. "Okay, then. But you will probably see me in this dress every day for the next three months. If I break down the cost versus how often I will wear it, it works out to less than a dollar a day."

"Why, Maggie," Shane said as we paid the bill. "I never knew you were so good at math."

"I'm a woman of many talents." I smiled coyly, watching the sales girl wrap my dress in tissue paper before placing it into a lavender-scented bag.

"So I've noticed."

We walked back to his vehicle and Shane set the packages down on the floorboard of the back seat. "And now it's time to get down to business," he said. "Do you know what you are going to ask her this time?"

I nodded, but truth be told, I didn't know. I had even more questions for Jillian this time than I did the first time I had come to see her.

Twenty-Five

Fly Like an Eagle

"You're right on time," Jillian said, opening the door. She was wearing a fitted, blue jacket layered over a beige, turtleneck sweater. Her hair was neat and her makeup perfect. She looked nothing like the psychics I was used to.

"And I love what you've done to your hair," Jillian added. I spun so that she could see the entire makeover and she clapped appropriately.

"Please, have a seat," she motioned towards the chair opposite her desk.

I glanced around the room. Some of the furniture I remembered from before was gone and there were boxes strewn about. I raised my eyebrows as she sat down and folded her hands beneath her chin.

"You caught me," she said. "I'm leaving."

"For good?" Though we had only seen each other a couple of times, I felt a strong connection to her and wasn't ready to let her go.

"It's the nature of the beast, I'm afraid," Jillian said, rolling her chair closer to mine. "I promise to keep in touch, though, don't worry."

"Where are you going?"

"Maggie," she smiled. "I haven't told many people, but I will tell you. I'm going to be a grandmother soon! I need to get ready for the birth of my first grandson." She clicked a button on her computer and it powered off. "I was going to leave a few days ago, but when I got your call, I decided to wait. You are officially my last client."

"Thank you," I said gratefully, then added, "...And congratulations!"

"Now, what brings you to my neck of the woods, my dear?"

I told her the entire story of how my sisters and I had captured Gahabrien and put him in a jar. Jillian listened intently, nodding from time to time. I concluded the story by telling her that the being was now being stored at Harvest Home, locked in a closet, and I wasn't sure where to go from there.

"Oh, Maggie," she said, her green eyes amused. "You shouldn't go trapping goblins if you don't know what to do with them!"

She threw her head back and let out a musical laugh, though I didn't understand why, because the story didn't seem funny to me at all.

"Well," she said, taking a pair of glasses out of her desk drawer and popping them onto her nose. "I get the feeling you've weakened it, anyway. Gahabrien never could stand up to a real challenge. How did you know to use glass?"

"Intuition, I guess."

"He hasn't given up, of course. But it's a pretty safe bet that as long as he is inside both your crystal owl and the mason jar, he isn't going to be going anywhere. But you must relocate him. Someplace where no one might accidentally stumble upon him, okay?"

Jillian reached beneath her blazer and pulled out a cross on a chain. "Take this and put it around the jar before you hide it. It will help to keep him sealed."

"But why a cross? Especially if he isn't really a demon?"

"The symbol of the cross predates Christianity. It has been used since the dawn of civilization as a means of keeping the dark at bay."

"So, it's powerful?" I took the chain and felt the weight of it in my hand.

"Symbolism, like any form of Magick, is reliant on a collective belief system. So, in this case, yes. Against Gahabrien and lower minions like him, the cross will be very effective."

I put the chain in my purse. "Thank you."

"Speaking of symbolism," Jillian continued, as she studied me. "I find it interesting that you used a glass owl to capture the thing in the first place."

"It was in my mother's shop and I took it home. Aunt Dora said it's my totem."

Jillian smiled when I spoke my aunt's name. "Yes. I would never doubt Dora's abilities to name someone's totem. She has a strong link to the animal world. Did you know..." Jillian raised the finger with the large diamond on it, twirling it at me. "...That owls were revered in some ancient cultures, as the guardians of the underworld? They helped transport souls from this realm to the next. How fitting that the owl is your totem."

"I don't think I like that," I said, shifting in my chair. Why did every conversation about my magical abilities always turn to dead things? "I was just thinking it was because I was wise."

"Maggie, some day you will embrace your gifts. For now..." Jillian tilted her head and her green eyes shone prettily in the light. "...You just have to accept them."

"Thank you...I guess," I said. "There is something else."

I removed the picture of Leah from my purse and slid it across the desk, not wanting to touch it any more than I had to.

"Can you get a read on the woman in this photo?" I said. "Her name is Leah. I knew her and I just found out she was working for my mother. I think she's somehow tied to Mother's sudden illness."

I tried to appear calm, but there was a burning in the pit of my stomach as I asked the question. I sat, quietly waiting for Jillian's verdict.

"You're not going to like this," Jillian said, after studying the picture for several minutes.

My heart was racing, wondering what she was about to say. "Go on."

"She is Larinda's daughter. And..." Jillian stopped mid-sentence, her eyes flickering off to the side. "...Well, let me just preface it by saying that what you are about to hear is going to be difficult. You and Leah share the same father. So that makes her your..."

303

"No." My mouth went dry. I had three sisters, I didn't need another——especially one like Leah. Psychics weren't always right, and for all I knew, Jillian might be some nut job. I mean, who else laughs about exorcisms?

I shook my head, contemplating getting up and walking out the door without a word.

Jillian nodded sympathetically. "I'm sorry. There is no way to soften this. And the quicker you knew the better. The girl in this photo has a very bad energy. Like rotten milk."

I sat blinking in my chair, wringing my hands, wishing I had never found the picture. Leah and I couldn't have the same blood. It was impossible. But I had to ask.

"Jillian, who is my father?" I said.

She pressed her lips together, as if she had said too much, but she answered. "He was a powerful warlock named Armand. He was a member of the original council."

The pieces were arranging themselves in my head. "He was the warlock who tried to summon a demon?"

"Yes." Jillian smiled softly and patted my hand. "We lost a great power when he went dark."

"My mother banished our father from the Council, without even trying to save him?" I couldn't believe it. We had the opportunity to know our father, and our mother had taken that from us. If Armand had gotten the chance to know his daughters, he might have turned out differently.

We might have turned out differently.

"Now, before you go blaming Sasha, there is something you should know." Jillian leaned in, cupping her hands in mine. "Your mother was trying to protect you...protect all of us. She could see the circle breaking and you girls were the only means she had of protecting it."

"The spells around Dark Root," I said, remembering what Aunt Dora had told me.

"That is one circle, yes. And so much hinges on Dark Root staying a stronghold. The world as we know it is changing. Some..." she said, lowering her voice to a whisper. "...Some would even say it's ending. The town you live in, is...was...a small point of light in a dark world. And Sasha foresaw it all slipping away, if she lost you to your father..."

"Even if everything you say is true, that still doesn't change the fact she kept us from him."

I was close to crying. I stood and walked to the bathroom. I splashed water across my face and took a sip by dipping my head and mouth beneath the faucet. Returning, I paced around the chair, not wanting to believe what she was telling me.

"Dear," Jillian said, rising. "Your father wanted to use your talents to further his own goals. He and Larinda didn't care anything about the rest of the world. They knew the end was coming, and all they were concerned about was protecting their own. That's probably why they went and had a baby of their own, hoping for someone with even half of your abilities. But I'm guessing that didn't work out, or Larinda wouldn't have gone after you or Miss Sasha."

"My mother is the most selfish person I've ever met," I said. "She wouldn't care what happens to the world!"

"Stubborn, yes. Misguided, yes. Selfish, no," Jillian said, her words warm. "As long as there is light in this world, however small, the end will not come. Do you think that lighting ceremony every October thirty-first was just for show? No. It was a symbol...a sign to The Universe that there were still enough people on this planet willing to band together and fight back whatever dark things are thrown at it. There is power in words, and in numbers."

Jillian's tone had grown terse. She caught herself and took a deep breath.

"If Armand and the others remained in the Council," she added. "Miss Sasha knew that light wouldn't last long. Your mother is a good woman, Maggie, just not in the traditional sense."

"So, why did you leave? Why didn't you stay and help?"

"I was called to do other things. When spirit knocks, I answer."

I put my hands in my face and cried. It wasn't fair. None of this was fair. Leah was my half-sister and some crazy demon summoner was my father. I wanted to hit something, kick something, scream. I hated Jillian for telling me this. And I hated Aunt Dora and my mother for keeping it from me.

"Maggie," Jillian said softly, peeling my hands away from my face. "I know this is hard to digest, but you must be strong. As I've told you before, your mother is depending on you."

I sniffled and accepted the Kleenex she offered me. "But why me? Why does everyone keep acting like I can make some sort of difference?"

"Because, Maggie, no matter what you call yourself––witch, wilder, magician, prophetess––you are a woman of great power. As you grow, so will your abilities."

Jillian lifted a piece of my hair, looped it around her finger, and smiled.

"I don't want to...I can't..." I said. If the world really was going to end, maybe Larinda and Armand––my father––had the right idea. Forget everyone else and take care of yourself.

"You are loved, more than you know, Maggie Mae." Jillian pulled me close then wrapped her arms around me. I wept on her shoulder as she patted my back.

"What can I do?" I asked, still feeling sorry for myself.

"For starters, finish what you've begun in Dark Root. And remember, light begets light, dark begets dark. Every action moves you in a direction."

I nodded and gave her a final hug. "Please call me after you move. I need you."

"I need you too, Maggie. We all do."

I left her office in a state of post-traumatic stress.

I was embarrassed for Shane to see me like this and I immediately pulled my hair over my face. He got out of the truck and ran to me, taking me in his arms. I was about to tell him everything that Jillian said, but he shushed me, kissing me on the forehead.

"It's okay, Maggie. Whatever it is, it's going to be okay."

I wanted to believe him but I couldn't.

Not only was the circle breaking, the whole world was breaking. And for some crazy reason, everyone thought I could put it back together.

Shane led me to the passenger seat and even let me pick out the music on the way home. But all I wanted to listen to was track thirteen on his Steve Miller Band CD——'Fly Like an Eagle.'

Twenty-Six

Runnin' with the Devil

I spent the next two days locked up in Harvest Home, eating ice cream and watching old TV shows with Aunt Dora.

I knew what Jillian had told me was true, that my mother had banished my father and that I had a horrible half-sister somewhere—— Leah. I knew that Jillian was also correct about another thing: saving Dark Root would somehow save my mother. I was angry at my mother and wanted to resist, but I also loved her. Why couldn't my heart ever make up its mind?

As I was having coffee in my bedroom early on the third morning—— and feeling quite sorry for myself——I caught sight of a flock of ravens outside my window, gathering on and around the stone table in the garden. I regarded the way they cawed and pumped their wings, aiming their beaks into the sky like arrows seeking out the last slivers of sunlight before the long winter ahead.

"Caw!" they screeched, ignoring the approaching darkness. "Live for today! Live for today!"

I put my coffee cup down.

The birds were right. Pining for a life I couldn't have wasn't going to change anything. I had friends and family here who needed me right now.

I took a shower, got dressed, and headed back out into the world.

For the next week, I took to walking the mile-and-a-half path between Harvest Home and Sister House, pouncing on leaves and picking wildflowers along the way. That time alone with just nature and my thoughts rejuvenated me in a way that sleeping all day never could.

"You're definitely a Fall girl, Maggie," Shane said one day, as I crunched every leaf on the driveway up to Sister House.

He and Paul had had been patching and repairing the gate, the shutters, and the porch while Merry and Eve attended to the inside of the house. I agreed with him, offering him and Paul sandwiches and iced tea from Aunt Dora's kitchen. That is how I spent my afternoons: trading jokes, handing out tools, and pointing out the spots that they had missed.

Shane threatened to take the leaf blower after me, if I didn't mind my manners. I threatened him back with an old Weed Eater. We were at a stalemate.

When each day's work was done, I would rush for the old swing in the back, where Merry, Eve and I used to take turns as Ruth Anne sailed us into the stratosphere. Now it was my own legs that propelled me forward, and I soared higher and higher, feeling the glint of sun between the long tree boughs touching my face.

Once I soared so high that my legs threatened to go over my head.

I panicked and hurled myself to the ground, crying out as I hit the earth.

Within seconds, Shane was beside me, pulling me up, wiping the dirt from my knees and asking if I was okay. He gave me a ride back to Harvest Home and the two of us sat in the cab of his truck, listening to music and not saying a word.

And it was good.

"I dun know what ta make o' ya, Miss Maggie," Aunt Dora said.

It was two days before the festival and we were digging in her garden, picking out the best pumpkins to use for the event.

"...Yer up and den yer down. Yer like a see-saw."

I lifted a deep orange pumpkin from the ground and carefully cut the vine with the rusty garden scissors she had given me. I dusted it off, then set it in the crate behind us.

"It's just hard for me to believe that there is darkness in the world, when there are days like this." I surveyed the patch. We had taken most every pumpkin except for a few small ones.

"Maggie, e'erything runs in cycles," Aunt Dora said, removing one of her gloves. "Ders good, den ders bad. Ders light, den ders dark. We can plant all da gardens we like, but da winter will come. Dats why we got ta harvest while we can." She stopped her work to study me, the lines around her eyes deepening. "I guess ye'll be gone by da time da winter comes?"

Aunt Dora had been like a second mom to me and knew me better than even my real mother.

I was still planning on leaving when the festival was over and Mother was back at home, but not because I hated Dark Root.

I needed to find my father. I needed to find my roots.

"I am going to miss this place," I admitted, sitting on my knees and looking around the property. The backyard was vast, un-gated. If left untended, it would become part of the forest that surrounded it. Being out here, especially in the company of my aunt, filled me with a contentment I never knew I had.

"It's goin' ta be a shame ta see dis place go," Aunt Dora said, struggling to get to her feet.

It took a while and I resisted the urge to help her up, because I knew she wouldn't want me to.

"Maybe you could buy it?" I suggested.

Aunt Dora had said that Harvest Home would be put up for sale in the new year. A few people from 'the city' had already expressed an interest in purchasing it, when it went to market. I frowned. I couldn't imagine Harvest Home belonging to some stranger.

"No, dearie. I don' have dat kin' a' money. Besides..." She put a palm to her hip and I knew that it ached. "I'm too ol' ta be runnin' dis big ol' house alone."

Aunt Dora groaned, shielding her eyes from the setting sun as she headed back inside.

When she was gone, I went to the porch and retrieved the tote bag I had hidden under a bench. Checking to make sure I was still alone, I headed back to the garden, to a spot on the far end that got little sun. I took a spade and dug a deep hole, then removed the mason jar from my bag. I placed the jar in the bottom of the hole.

"Rest well, Gahabrien," I said, tossing Jillian's cross into the hole as well. I then covered them both with dirt.

It was odd, finally burying him. He was connected to both my childhood and my childhood fears, but pouring that dirt over the top of him wasn't as liberating as it should have been.

Instead, I just felt...sad.

"Where will you go when it sells?" I said, continuing the conversation with my aunt as I entered through the back door, wiping the dirt from my shoes and tossing the tote bag into the trash bin. There was something baking in the oven and the scent of it made my mouth water.

I washed my hands then set the table the table for two. Shane was on a supply run, Eve and Paul were *hanging out* and Merry and June Bug were at the hospital.

It was just me and Aunt Dora tonight.

"I s'pose ders a house fer ol' witches somewhere," she laughed, putting on her mitts and removing a baking dish from the oven. "Dis turned out better dan I expected." She placed the pan on a trivet and removed the foil, revealing the most beautiful lasagna I had ever seen.

I took a large piece, promising myself I would start dieting tomorrow.

"I hope whoever buys this place will love it like we do," I said, adding a helping of sliced garden tomatoes to my plate and covering them in Italian dressing.

"I do, too," Aunt Dora replied wistfully, dabbing the napkin to her chin. "I'm sorry ya aren't stayin'. Havin' ya back has done so much fer me...an' fer e'eryone."

I blushed, but knew she was just flattering me. It was the others who had transformed this town. I was just along for the ride.

"Ya could stay an' help Merry wit yer mother at Sister House," Aunt Dora said hopefully. "Be a shame ta let all dose rooms be empty."

"I can't," I said, finishing off my first piece of lasagna. It was even better than it smelled. "There are things I need to do."

"What kin' o' things do ya need ta do?" Aunt Dora held a forkful of lasagna to her lips, not opening her mouth.

I paused, wondering if I should tell her the truth.

"Auntie," I said slowly, knowing this was a delicate subject. "I know my father is Armand from the original Council."

Aunt Dora sat up straight as a board, dropping her napkin into her lap. "And?"

"I am going to find him."

Aunt Dora pushed herself away from the table so violently her plate crashed to the floor, causing tiny shards of ivory mixed with lasagna to spill across the linoleum. Her normally soft eyes flashed red with anger.

"Find him? After what he did?" Aunt Dora's hands balled into fists. She picked up her cup and threw it across the room, where it broke into a hundred pieces.

I sat in my chair, afraid to look up or down.

"He didn't really do anything," I began defensively. "True, he tried to summon, but from what I understand––"

"Dat's da problem. Ya don' understand anything!" Aunt Dora snapped. "Dat man ne'er cared about anybody but himself!" Her eyes were fixed on me, her gaze cold. At last, she turned and walked into the living room, her feet crunching on the porcelain from her coffee cup as she left.

"Mark my words, Maggie," she muttered angrily. "He won' care about ya. Only yer powers..."

I had never been chastised by my aunt in my life, and I sat there dumbly, unsure of what to do. Finally, I took a wad of dish cloths from a kitchen drawer and got to work cleaning up the mess. It took me an hour, but I was going purposefully slow, waiting for Aunt Dora to fall asleep in her recliner before tip-toeing past her, and into my room.

As I opened the door I sensed a presence inside.

I caught a glimpse of it in my peripheral, a small dark shape lurking in the corner. I walked past it and flung myself into bed, not bothering to switch on the light.

"Please go away," I said to it, exhausted. "If you want to play tomorrow, that's fine. But I can't do this tonight."

I felt a lightness in the room as my mind faded to black.

"A week ago, you're telling me you're thinking about staying, now you want to leave again?" Shane was bent over, wrestling with the legs of a fold out card table he was trying to set up in front of Mother's store.

Tomorrow was Halloween, the official opening of Haunted Dark Root, and Shane insisted we give early visitors a taste of what was to come. Apparently, this included Eve and I giving free ten minute Tarot Card readings on Main Street.

Eve had finished her shift. She was a natural, telling people exactly what they wanted to hear. 'Of course you are going to get that raise...' 'You just need to put a little vanilla behind your ear, then he will come running after you...'

She then sent them on their way, giddy and excited, and vowing to come back the following day for the main event. I wasn't sure I could follow that act.

"I need to find my father," I said, as I carried a chair from Mother's shop onto the sidewalk.

Shane had arranged my stand so that I would be in clear view of pedestrians, without blocking the walkway. I removed a new deck of tarot cards, shuffled them, and placed them face down on the table.

"I won't be gone forever," I added.

"But, isn't he dangerous? Are you sure that going after him is a good idea?"

Shane stood over me, dressed in tight jeans, boots, a button-down, plaid shirt, and his now-famous cowboy hat. I half-expected to see a lasso or a bull whip in his free hand. Whenever someone passed by he tipped his hat and smiled, pointing out all the fine amenities that Dark Root had to offer.

I had to hand it to him; he was a natural at public relations.

"I appreciate the concern but I'll be fine," I said.

"I'm not gonna try and stop you. If I had a chance to see my father, I'd take it." Shane took a drink of water from the Dixie cup on my table. "I just want you to be aware how much you've done for this town."

"Me?" I said, noticing that a group was already beginning to assemble at my table for their free readings.

I had never done a Tarot Card reading in my life, but I had seen my mother do enough of them to at least fake it.

"I've done practically nothing," I protested. "It's you guys who have made the difference."

"Are you kidding me?" Shane removed his hat and ran his fingers through his floppy brown hair. He returned the hat to his head. "People don't come here to see me. They come for this. They come..." he added, reaching into a large paper sack and pulling out a shiny, black, witch's hat. I shook my head violently as he placed it on me, pulling it down around my ears. "...To see Maggie Maddock and The Witches of Dark Root."

Shane looked to the crowd, raising his hands and encouraging them to applaud for me. I shot him a look that said he was in big trouble later.

"He's right," Eve said, looking up and down the street for the delivery man who was supposed to bring the candles for the lighting ceremony. "They come to see the women."

Shane propped a sign against my table that read FREE and the crowd grew larger.

I sighed, realizing I was going to be trapped here all afternoon.

"Are you done?" I asked. "Looks like I have work to do."

"Not yet," he said. Shane stepped back into the store and returned with an old-fashioned broom. He set it next to my table, framed the picture with his hands, and nodded approvingly. "...Now we're done." He dusted the corner of the table with his fingers and whispered, "Just think about staying. It would mean a lot to...us."

Then he crossed the street and headed for Dip Stix, maneuvering through the steady stream of pedestrian traffic.

"So," a voice at the front of the line said. "Are you going to read my cards, or what?"

I nodded absently, pointing to an empty chair across from me. I shuffled the deck until my hands tingled, my sign that it was time to stop.

"Tell me what you would like to know," I said, laying the cards out in a line, face down on the table. "Then pick three: one for your past, one for your present, and one for your future."

"I want to know how your mother's doing."

The voice was low, taunting and sarcastic.

I raised my eyes, peeking out from under the long brim of the witch's hat.

Leah.

The world spun and I searched the street and the nearby windows for Eve or Shane. Neither were in sight. I clenched the edge of the table with my hands, steadying myself.

Leah regarded me coolly, that same smug look I remembered pasted on her pinched face.

I took a deep breath, fighting back the urge to reach across the table and grab her. There were families watching with small children. I couldn't lose it now, no matter what she deserved.

"What are you doing here?" I said.

Leah smirked, her glasses threatening to slide off her stub of a nose.

"Oh, I was out and about," she smiled sweetly. "I thought I'd pay a call on some old friends."

"I'm not your friend." I could feel my lips twist into a snarl.

"Give me my reading or I'm complaining to management." Leah flipped over her first card: The Hermit.

"Too bad there's not a weasel card," I said, refusing to be rattled. The table shivered, betraying my calm face. "You'd better go. You saw what happened the last time I lost my temper..."

Leah tilted her head back to laugh, placing a hand on her chest.

"The candle trick?" she said scornfully. "Please. Level Two Magick, at best. You're nothing more than a neophyte when it comes to casting. My daddy could do that in his sleep." Leah licked her lips, flipping over the second card: The Devil. "Oh, I meant *our* daddy. He was a pretty neat guy. Too bad you never got to know him."

My fingers dug into the table. "That's about to change," I said, flipping over the last card: Death. I pushed the card in her direction. "...I'm going to find him."

"Good luck with that." Leah picked up the card, raised an eyebrow, then tore it in two. "He died a few years ago. Or hadn't you heard? I guess your psychic friend doesn't know everything, does she?"

"Jillian?" My eyes widened. "How do you know about her?"

Leah leaned back in her chair, that smug smile back on her face. "I know many things, *Magdalene*."

"You're a liar," I snapped, my eyes darting around to see who was watching...and listening. My father wasn't dead. He couldn't be. Not before I got to meet him. "My father sent you to Woodhaven to find me. That's why you were there," I said.

Leah snorted. "What an active imagination you have. You still think everything is about you. Woodhaven. Dark Root. Michael. *Daddy.*" Leah removed her glasses, wiping them with the hem of her shirt before she put them back on. "Daddy's dead. And your mother may be joining him shortly."

I'd had enough.

I stood, knocking my chair back. I reached for her then noticed a little girl about June Bug's age watching me.

"Reading's over," I said instead, squeezing my hands into fists. "And if you ever come near my mother, or anyone else in my family again, you will be sorry."

Leah rose, placing her hands on the table as she leaned forward, her mouth inches from my ear. "Daddy didn't send me. My mother did. Your family is in possession of an artifact that belongs to us..."

"Artifact?" I said, genuinely baffled that time. "What artifact?"

Leah paused, as if deciding how much to tell me. A smile cracked her thin lips.

"I tried to break the old hag first," she said. "But she was more stubborn then I realized. I almost got her to confess to its whereabouts, but she was stronger than the tea I gave her. She just kept saying your name. So..." Leah tilted her head to the side "...I went after you, instead."

"I knew it!" I snapped. "You *are* the reason she got sick! What else did you use besides the jimson weed?" I put my hands over hers, digging my nails into her flesh.

Leah flinched, but didn't pull away.

"Enchantments are my specialty."

I looked around me again for Shane or Eve. Still no sight of either of them. I moved my fingers from Leah's hands to her wrists, squeezing them tightly, holding her captive.

"What sort of enchantment did you use? And what's the elixir?"

"A little something I learned from your mother's book." Leah smiled like a cat who had finally caught its mouse.

At first, I wasn't sure what she was talking about, but then I understood.

"The missing pages in Mother's book. You took the spell and the anti-spell!"

"I learned so much from that little book." Leah's eyes sparkled, zeroing in on the crystal around my neck. "I learned about love. That was fun. Watching that pathetic little man of yours run around like a chicken with his head cut off, doing my bidding..."

She licked her lips, then sighed dramatically.

"...I never counted on you leaving," she said. "I honestly thought you'd stick around, put up a fight, and then give me what I was looking for in trade for your...boyfriend. And he was, shall we say, useful to me for a while."

Leah pulled her hands free, letting her words sink in.

My heart stopped as I put it all together.

She had been able to cast a spell on Michael just as easily as Eve had. Without thinking, I swung my hand back and slapped her, sending her head jerking in the opposite direction. I heard someone in the crowd gasp, but I didn't care. I was beyond caring.

"I suggest you stop," Leah growled, taking a step back beyond my reach. "*Wilder.*"

"Or what?" I asked, ready to charge her.

"Or else, you will never get the anti-spell." Leah smiled, her ferret eyes gleaming, knowing that she had me cornered. "I'll return tomorrow and trade you the artifact for the anti-spell."

She placed a dollar on the table and backed away.

I could chase her, I thought.

Beat her to a pulp and demand the page back from my mother's spell book. But my plan could backfire and I might never get the anti-spell. Besides, there were families everywhere and we had worked too hard for me to blow it now. I would just have to play along.

"What is this artifact I'm supposed to bring?" I called to her.

"The circle," she said. "I will find you tomorrow night, before the lighting ceremony."

Leah slipped into the crowd then, disappearing.

A plump woman with gray hair took her seat at the table. "Great performance!" she beamed. "It all seemed so real!"

"Thank you," I said, absently. "All part of the show."

TWENTY-SEVEN

AMERICAN PIE

DARK ROOT, OREGON
NOVEMBER 1, 2002

THE SUN WHITTLED ITS WAY THROUGH THE BRANCHES *and shone like a spotlight on the worn out path that Maggie and her family walked along. The first of November marked the passing of the Light Half of the year and the beginning of the Dark Half. It was tradition for Miss Sasha and her daughters to make one final pilgrimage into the woods on this day to take stock of what they had learned and plan for the winter to come.*

When the girls were young, it was a fun event, almost like a camping excursion. There would be stories told and even marshmallows roasted as they huddled around the fire and listened to the wildlife.

But the girls were growing up now and the feeling was different. It had been several years since Ruth Anne had left and now Merry was saying she was going too, as soon as she turned eighteen. Even the steady crunch of brown leaves beneath Maggie's feet couldn't lighten her mood. There was a cavity in her head and heart that no amount of her mother's banter could fill.

Maggie bent down to retrieve a leaf, so brown it was almost black. She crumbled it in her palm, letting the small bits sift through the cracks in her fingers. A wind blew, catching the fragments and sending them spiraling back into the woods. An owl hooted from one of the newly bare branches but Maggie didn't jump.

She wasn't scared anymore. Not of owls, or witchery. The only things she really feared were the dark and the feeling of loss, and she vowed to steer clear of both of them.

"Right here, girls," her mother said, removing her black pointy hat.

She only wore the costume on two occasions, during Halloween and the day after, when they gathered as a family for communion. The girls had once joined their mother in dressing up, as well, but this year they trudged along in worn blue jeans and sweaters that had seen better days.

Maggie took a seat on the gray rock her mother had designated as her spot, situating herself so that the sharp angles of the stone didn't cut her skin. Merry and Eve took seats next to her and the three faced their mother with somber eyes while their long hair whipped out around them. Merry eventually tucked the ends of her hair under her bottom, but Eve and Maggie let theirs fly.

Miss Sasha didn't seem to notice how miserable the girls were, or if she did, she pretended not to. Instead she reached into a paper sack and passed around finger sandwiches, keeping one for herself. A cloud moved in front of the sun and she peered at the sky, a look that said she knew time here with her daughters was growing short.

"What was your favorite part of the festival?" she asked Merry as she removed the wrapping from her sandwich.

In the old days, Merry would say the candy apples or the haunted houses or something equally spooky and fun. This year Merry shrugged and said nothing.

"Eve?" Miss Sasha shifted her gaze to her youngest daughter.

"When it was all over," Eve replied, cracking a near smile.

Their mother was undaunted and continued on to Maggie.

"I liked our float this year. It was nice."

Maggie could feel her sisters' stares turn to her.

Their 'float' was a ramshackle cart, haphazardly decorated with marigolds and leaves. It was the saddest float the girls had ever seen and Maggie had heard people laugh as it rolled through town. But Miss Sasha still sat at the head of it, waving her arms and smiling to the small assembly of people who had come.

Mother was losing not only her Magick, Maggie realized, but also her mind. And though Maggie was angry with her mother for many reasons, she couldn't stand to see the one quality in her mother she had always admired slip away––pride.

"The decorations were nice, too," she added for good measure.

"That's marvelous, Maggie. And thank you. I worked very hard this year." Miss Sasha paused, licking her lips. "Maybe we could work together on one next year. Wouldn't that be fun?"

Maggie swallowed, wanting to cry. By next year, Merry would be gone.

"I don't think I want to be involved in the festival anymore." Maggie looked at her lap, surprised by her words. She was used to arguing with her mother, but this plain truthful confession made her feel very exposed.

"I'm not sure what you mean, dear," her mother said, taking another bite of her sandwich.

Maggie couldn't tell if she was genuinely confused or just playing one of her games.

"Our sister left," Maggie said, careful not to mention Ruth Anne's name. "Aunt Dora hardly comes around anymore. And now Merry's leaving. The festival gets fewer visitors every year. We aren't The Witches of Dark Root anymore. We are just..." Maggie choked, trying to get out the last embarrassing word. "...jokes."

"I didn't raise you like that," her mother snapped, her voice as cutting as the winds.

"None of this is real." Maggie shook her head, hoping to catch her mother in one of her few lucid moments. "Witchery isn't real."

"You can't mean that!" Miss Sasha said. "After all you've seen?"

323

"Even if I did think that it was real, what use is it?" Maggie said. "I want a normal life, with a normal family." She bowed her head, burying her face in her hands. Surely, her mother had to understand. She bit her lip so that she wouldn't cry, then faced her mother again.

"Our life is a joke," she finished.

"I'm sorry you feel that way." Her mother crossed her arms, her face and shoulders drooping.

Maggie was prepared for her mother's anger, but not her disappointment. She wanted to crawl under the rock she sat on.

Miss Sasha studied her other daughters. "Do you feel the same? Is our life is a joke to you, too?"

Eve looked down and Merry said nothing.

"I see," their mother continued, far calmer than Maggie would have expected. "Well, I release you all, then. Maggie and Eve you are absolved of any future festival activities. You shall stay, go to school, and help out in the shop until you are of age. After that, do whatever you like. Merry, I wish you and Frank the best."

Miss Sasha stood and gathered her skirt.

"...But don't come crying to me." She looked at each of them in turn. "When the darkness comes. Remember you were warned."

With that, Miss Sasha disappeared down the path they had all come from.

Alone.

Harvest Home, Dark Root, Oregon
October 31, 2013

I was up with the ravens, watching them through my bedroom window as I slipped off my robe and pulled on the long, dark dress Eve had purchased for me.

The birds pecked at the table, fighting over invisible crumbs. When they felt me watching them, they turned, twelve black, unblinking eyes boring into me. I stared back, me against them, until a gust of wind ruffled their feathers and sent them flapping away. The smallest one turned his head, mid-air, as if to say it would return.

I shivered and closed the curtain.

The dress Eve had bought was several inches too wide and a foot too short.

I resisted the urge to grumble. I would only have to wear it today, then I could send it back to whatever thrift shop Eve had found it in. I pushed my feet into my black, satin slippers, then went downstairs.

Aunt Dora was standing in the kitchen entryway, waiting, arms crossed.

"Maggie, can I have a word wit' ya?" she said.

I nodded, but I wasn't exactly looking forward to this conversation. We had not spoken since the incident two days earlier, and I had no idea what she wanted to say. I followed her into the kitchen and sat down at the table. There was a stack of pancakes waiting for us along with two jars of her homemade preserves.

"Eve must be gone already," I said, trying to make small talk as I placed a pancake on my plate. "I was going to talk to her about this dress, but..."

"Aye, dat she is. She wanted ta get up early an' work on da float." Aunt Dora's eyes fixed on me, feeling me out. "I thought dis would be a good time ta catch ya, before ya head out."

I moved my food around on my plate, listening.

"I shouldn' o' got my ire up wit' ya. It wasn't right. It's just...well, Maggie. Der are things ya don't know. Things we kep' from ya. From all o' ya. Not ta be mean. But because we had ta. 'Til da time was right."

I took a bite, chewing slowly.

Things they wanted to tell us when the time was right?

Aunt Dora poured herself a cup of tea. "Ta calm my nerves," she said, her smile tense. I watched her add a long pour of honey to her drink. "...I can't tell ya e'erything. Dat's not my place. Dat's yer ma's." Aunt Dora nodded, as if to confirm to herself that a chain of command had to be followed, no matter what her personal opinion on the matter. "...But I can let ya in on a few things."

A tremor reached her hands and fingers, and the tea sloshed out of her cup.

I gently took the tea from her and placed it on the table. "Go on," I said.

"Ya girls were all special," she said, wringing her hands, her eyes darting around the room as if she thought we were being watched. "We knew dat, from da moment each o' ya was born. But ya, Maggie Mae... ya were a force. Had da stronges' powers o' dem all. Yer ma thought she could tame ya, channel it. But like all children do, ya had yer own feelings about things. Ya were a wilder, and no matter what anyone says, dat's not a bad thing. Ya just wern't tamable."

Aunt Dora's eyes drooped and her face followed.

"I was a handful," I agreed.

"Ya certainly were. Gave us fits! But ya were loved." Aunt Dora paused, fanning herself with her hand. A fly landed on her plate and she shooed it away. "Ya were yer mother's favorite. Maybe it was because da two o' ya are so much alike. Full o' pride and stubbornness, not wantin' anyone' ta tell ya what ta do."

I had never considered myself to be like my mother. The thought made me uncomfortable and I pushed my plate to the side of the table.

"Yer mother was jus' in o'er her head. It's always easy ta raise da little ones but when dey get ol'er, dat's a whole other story. She tried, best she could. But when Ruth Anne left, it almos' broke da poor woman. Ev'rything she worked for, gone. We're lucky she had any sanity after dat..."

"She wasn't the only one hurt when Ruth Anne left," I said. "In one day, we lost a sister and our mother."

Mother had never been a traditional parent, but at least while Ruth Anne was with us, Mother was engaged in our lives. I could forgive my mother most anything, but not her emotional absence.

Aunt Dora appraised me. "E'er seen me do any Magick?" she asked.

"No." I had rarely seen any of them perform actual Magick, aside from the rituals that may or may not have worked.

Aunt Dora laughed, her body jiggling. "I'm about ta show ya something. Something I probably shoulda shown ya a long time ago. But ya weren't ready den."

"Am I ready now?"

"No, but time is short. Da layer between living an' dead is lifted ta'day. Ta'morrow begins a long col' winter."

I nodded. I knew the legend. During this time the veil between worlds was lifted. Spirits moved freely between planes, spells were stronger, and a witch's power was doubled.

"What does this mean for us?" I asked, still not following.

"Take my hands, Maggie. An' whatever ya do, don' let go. Don' be afraid." Aunt Dora's eyes took on an ominous look that frightened me.

But I obeyed and reached for her hands across the table. We closed our eyes, listening to each other breathe, until our breaths synched up and we inhaled and exhaled in unison. My head dropped forward as I let go of the world. All I was aware of was my own breathing and that of my aunt's.

I was suddenly transported to a green meadow, where the sun was shining. I laid on the grass and felt the earth beneath my body.

Feeling heavy and tired, I went to sleep.

"Maggie, wake up." It was my aunt's voice.

She was standing over me, dressed in a suit of white feathers. She reached for my hand and as our fingers touched, I felt a jolt of electricity so painful I cried out, trying to pull away. She held tight.

"...Stay with me, Maggie," she said. "It will pass."

The pain racked me, pulsing through my body, lighting up certain parts of my nervous system, shutting down others.

"Stop!" I tried to scream, but nothing came out of my mouth. The sensation was so excruciating that my mind began to go black.

Just as suddenly the pain subsided, and I was back at the kitchen table, floating up from my chair, slipping through the barriers of the roof, ascending into the clouds. I twisted and turned, taking in the sights of my house and then my town, both of which became specks of dust as I rose. I became aware of two heavy appendages at my side. Wings! Wings covered in gray feathers. I called out to my aunt, but the words emerged as a long, baleful whistle.

"I'm with you, Maggie," Aunt Dora said, her voice emanating from a large white owl. She stretched her wings, sailing past me and looping through the universe.

Was I an owl, too?

I felt myself begin to drop, so I copied her moves and followed.

At first the feeling of suspension was terrifying, but as I worked at it, I discovered that it was also exciting. We were soaring, swooping, diving, looping, and screeching at the other birds we passed. We owned the sky.

Aunt Dora pointed her beak towards the sun and flew straight upwards. I chased her. When she reached the appropriate altitude, she stopped, hovering in the air. I was quickly beside her and we stayed there, quietly flapping our wings. We were too high up for the wind. We were too high up for anything.

She spun her head in an almost full circle as a large raven passed, its beady eyes mocking us, as if it knew we didn't really belong.

"Remember, Maggie," Aunt Dora said, her thoughts in my head. "Ravens are scavengers, but owls are hunters."

I wasn't sure what she meant and I was about to ask, when Aunt Dora pointed a feathered wing towards the earth. I opened my mouth in horror as I witnessed a wave the size of a skyscraper rolling across the ocean before crashing over the shore.

Buildings shattered like children's toys. Cars were swallowed. People screamed, trying to run but unable to escape. The water took everything.

I pumped my wings, ready to dive down and pluck someone from the ocean, but the water receded just as quickly, leaving nothing behind.

"There is more," Aunt Dora said with her unmoving beak. "This is only the beginning."

We zipped through space, watching as storms and tornadoes and earthquakes claimed one piece of the world after another. So much pain and desperation.

A shadow slid over the earth.

"Make this stop!" I begged, as a tear slid from my eye and dropped a million feet onto the ground below. "Please!"

She bowed her head and barreled towards the earth. I followed, unsure if we would crash. I didn't care. I just wanted to be out of the nightmare.

Within seconds, I was back in the meadow, waking up from my nap. The sun was shining on my face. It was as if the bad had never happened.

"Maggie, ya okay?"

I blinked. This wasn't the meadow. It was the kitchen at Harvest Home. We were both back. The world hadn't ended. The tea was still hot. Aunt Dora released me.

"That was just a dream, right?" I said. "Or a bad trip? Please tell me that's all that was?"

Aunt Dora shook her head. "Da future, Maggie. One version anyway."

"But, how?"

"Da darkness comes, Maggie. It's already pullin' itself o'er da earth, devouring it up, piece by piece. We help keep da light." She smiled, almost shyly, brushing a gray curl out of her face. "Dark Root is a stronghold. One o' only a few."

"What I saw isn't for certain?"

"I think it will all happen one day, but we can push it back. A year. Two. Twenty. A hundred. No one knows. An' da torch is being passed on ta ya, Maggie."

How could this duty fall to someone like me? Why wasn't Merry chosen? Merry, who was all good? "I'm glad you kept this from us, really," I said. "...I had enough nightmares when I was a kid. But I'm not sure what keeping the light means, or what we can do about it."

"It's a tall order, Maggie, but ya start small. One light lights another, an' pretty soon ya have a whole world o' light. An' remember. Ya aren't alone. Ya have yer sisters and yer friends." Aunt Dora stood, patted me on the shoulder and placed her tea cup in the sink. "Now, if ya will excuse me, I need rest. Dat took it outa me."

"I will do my best," I said.

"I know ya will. Now I think it's time ya went an' saw yer mother."

"I will," I promised. "Very soon."

Twenty-Eight

GYPSIES, TRAMPS, AND THIEVES

"AUNT MAGGIE!" JUNE BUG RAN TOWARDS ME, arms waving overhead as I entered Dip Stix Café. "You made it!"

"Of course I made it," I said, looking apologetically at the others for being late.

It was already a few minutes past nine and I had spent the last hour shopping in Linsburg with Shane's credit card, filling the cab of his pickup with as much candy, chips, and party supplies as it would hold. Now that Aunt Dora had shown me the possible future, I wanted to do everything in my power to help Dark Root prosper.

"Can you all help me unload?" I asked. "I had to park two blocks away. It's hard to believe, but there's not a single parking space left on Main Street."

"That's not a bad problem to have," Shane said, locking the diner.

He, Paul, Merry, Eve and June Bug followed me out the vehicle. We dodged a boy chasing a white balloon that had gotten away.

"Looks like things are going pretty well," I said, opening the truck door and passing out the supplies.

"You weren't here for the apple riot," Merry joked. "Things got ugly."

"Yep, but fortunately Paul calmed the crowd with his sweet music," Eve said, smiling at him over the brown paper sacks in her hands.

"I love The Eagles as much as the next person," Paul sighed. "But if I get one more request for 'Witchy Woman,' I'm turning in my Don Henley Fan Club card..."

"Judging by the amount of people here already, I do believe we're going to pull this thing off," Shane said. "It may not be enough revenue to get us through the year like it did in the old days, but it's a really good start."

We dropped the supplies off at Dip Stix. There was already a line forming for Shane's advertised Boo Biscuits and Ghoul Gravy brunch special. He sighed dramatically as he surveyed the work ahead of him.

"I guess I'll have to do this without Paul," he said. "Since he is going to be playing in the square all morning."

"I can help," June Bug said enthusiastically.

"Me too," Merry chimed in. "I was married to Frank for eight years. I know how to serve people."

Shane smiled and handed them each an apron. They put them on and vanished into the kitchen.

"Need me?" I asked, noticing how tall he was, a good six inches taller than me.

"You have other duties." Shane pointed towards Miss Sasha's Magick Shoppe. Eve was already there, changing the sign to 'open.' About two dozen women of all ages and shapes pushed their way inside.

"Palm reading duty. Got it."

"Remember," he said, handing me a pair of scissors. "The mayor's going to call you out at some point for the ribbon cutting ceremony. Try and smile for the pictures, okay?"

I made a silly face and dropped the scissors into the deep pocket of my dress.

"Now put on your pointy hat and be a good witch," he added.

I walked to my designated spot across the street. An A-frame chalkboard read: *Free Palm Readings*. I added: *Tips Strongly Encouraged*.

I groaned as I noticed the crystal ball on my table. Shane left no detail to the imagination.

I sat down and folded my hands, pausing for a moment to take in the town. Main Street was draped in twinkle lights and multi-colored balloons and streamers of orange and yellow. Small children trick-or-treated at the colorful booths that lined the sidewalk. Teenagers paraded around in outrageous costumes, trying to out-shock one another. Women sampled sweets from food carts and old men sat on benches, enjoying the cold air while talking about times past. The shops were all filling with customers.

"The Haunted House is now open!" the shop owner next door called out.

Passersby wandered into the bookstore that had been converted to a spook-house with a few cobwebs, candles, and paper ghosts.

Across the street, a shop owner was setting up a pie-eating competition and there were already three people lined up who looked like they would be strong contenders. A large bouncy house was set up near the bandstand and the shrill of children's laughter filled the square. Pony rides were offered a few dozen yards off the street, the sickening-sweet smell of manure trying to overpower the pies. No one seemed to mind.

Eve came outside to tape up a large sign on the window that read, 'Out of Mood Rings.'

I was filled with a sense of pride for my family, friends, and community.

But it wasn't over.

Leah had promised to come with the anti-spell today. I had spent the previous evening searching for the 'circle' she was looking for, but still had no idea what she meant. It didn't matter. I would get the spell from her one way or another.

To my left, I saw the Mayor ascend the orange-painted platform and take the microphone. He talked at length about our journey to bring back the festival and said that we would be having our official ribbon cutting ceremony in just fifteen minutes. In the meantime, he said, Paul would be playing us a few songs.

"Play 'Witchy Woman!'" someone hollered.

Paul sighed and strummed on his guitar.

By three o'clock, I declared my booth officially closed. I folded up the card table and wiped down the chalkboard. The good news was that I had made over three hundred dollars in tips. The bad news was that I doubted I could ever touch another sweaty palm again.

"You have a knack for that," Eve said, joining me on the sidewalk while she kept an eye on the shop. There were only two customers inside––older ladies we had known since childhood––and I was pretty sure Eve could overtake them if they tried to get away with any of her merchandise.

The day had passed without any sign of Leah.

Though I dreaded my confrontation with her, I was also afraid she wouldn't show up. Without the anti-spell, Mother might sleep forever. My anxiety grew with each passing hour.

"You okay?" Eve asked, following my eyes down the road. "You seem more distant than usual."

I felt guilty for not letting my sisters in on what had transpired between myself and Leah yesterday, but it would only worry Merry and anger Eve. Leah was my problem and I was going to handle it.

"I'm just getting hungry," I said, sniffing at the air.

The scent of pumpkin pies, cinnamon apples, caramel corn and Shane's ghoul gravy made my stomach growl. A little girl walked by carrying a big fluff of cotton candy and I was about to ask her where she found that when Shane showed up. He was carrying two Styrofoam food containers. He handed one to me and the other to Eve.

"Compliments of the chef," he said.

I bit into a biscuit that was so hard I was afraid I'd chip a tooth. "It's like eating a rock."

"Sorry, that's all we had left."

Shane scratched his head and regarded the town. The streets were quieter now, with just a few people milling about. But that would change at dusk when everyone returned for the parade, the dance, and the lighting ceremony.

"I ran out of candy about an hour ago," he added, turning back to us. "...And I've been giving the trick-or-treaters complimentary menus and napkins. I'm surprised my place hasn't been toilet-papered yet."

"That's nothing," Eve said. "I've been giving the little ones makeovers. Twenty bags of fun-sized candy bars doesn't go as far as it used to."

"All in all, a pretty good day," I said, not admitting that I had been pilfering from her candy bowl whenever she used the restroom. "The candles get here yet?"

"No." Eve threw up her arms and slapped them down at her side in frustration. "I did some scrounging and we have around thirty white tapers, but I'm guessing we need at least three hundred."

A female shop owner I recognized waddled towards us.

"I just wanted to thank you young people so much for getting this started," she called out. "I've made more money today than I have in the last year. Albert is very happy." She held up a fistful of cash, looked longingly at the biscuits, and crossed the street to spend some of her newly acquired money at Dip Stix.

"Good work, ladies," Shane said.

"I can't wait to be done with the parade," I tugged at the black dress that was shrink-wrapping itself around my body as the day grew more humid. "I need to get out of this thing."

"I can't wait, either." Shane's eyes twinkled like the lights in his window. "I want to see you in that sweater dress again."

I felt my face redden to the color of my hair.

"Oh?" Eve raised an eyebrow.

I was sure she was going to say something catty. I hadn't shown her the dress for fear she would make fun of me.

She surprised me by saying, "I'm sure you are going to look

beautiful."

And I think she meant it.

The sun set behind the trees as we assembled for the parade.

Our float, *The Witches of Dark Root,* was traditionally the last one in line, signaling the beginning of the evening's activities. But Paul and Eve thought we should go first this year, so they could be done in time to change costumes for their Sonny and Cher extravaganza. We would be followed by the Mayor's car and the Home School marching band.

I wasn't happy with the lineup, but it did mean we could be done first, allowing me to keep an eye out for Leah.

Our float was an old wagon decorated with chrysanthemums and drawn by two black horses.

I stood in the center, pretending to stir a black cauldron as my eyes looked out from beneath the brim of my pointy hat, scanning faces in the crowd. Shane sat up front with the driver, seemingly at home and still in his cowboy gear. Merry, Eve, June Bug and Paul sat on bales of hay along the edge of the wagon bed, waving to the crowd and throwing out plastic spider rings. Some older kids ran behind them, begging for lollipops while Eve lectured them on the dangers of eating too much sugar.

We were nearly at the end of Main Street when I spotted Leah, lurking near one of the shops. She was dressed in a jacket, jeans and sneakers, easy to spot in a crowd of costumed spectators. I gave a quick glance to my companions, hiked up my long dress and side-stepped to the side of the wagon.

"Maggie!" I heard Shane call out as I leapt from the cart, wincing as my slippered feet crashed down on the hard pavement. My hat flew from my head and was immediately snatched up by a young mother in the front row.

I gave them a perfunctory curtsey then took off after Leah.

I fought my way through the crowd, almost tripping over a kid carrying a jack-o'-lantern and pushing through a couple dressed as John Lennon and Yoko Ono.

"Leah, wait!" I called, but she kept running.

She neared the edge of the bandstand. For a second, I thought I'd lost her; the crowd near the bandstand was as thick as Shane's gravy. Leah was small and quick, able to squirm through narrow openings through the wall of people.

"I have the circle!" I lied as she weaved in and out of the folding chairs by the stage.

Why had she wanted to meet me if she was just going to run?

Someone grabbed my wrist. Startled, I turned to see Shane.

"Where are you going?" he demanded, pulling me to a stop.

I pointed to Leah, "That woman has the spell we need to wake up Mother."

Shane looked at me with a blank face.

"Please," I said. "Just trust me."

He nodded and bolted after Leah, pulling me along behind him. We raced along together, dashing after Leah as she wove skillfully through the horde. She had the advantage of not needing to be careful, knocking into old women and pushing over children in her desire to escape. Even so, Shane and I were gaining ground. Leah looked back, her face ashen, then quickly changed direction, running for the bouncy house.

"We have her," I said, knowing there was only one entrance. But when we looked inside, I was surprised to find only two young children playing.

I shook my head. How could she have just disappeared?

"She probably didn't have the anti-spell anyway," I muttered, still scanning faces in the crowd. "...Or she wouldn't have run."

Shane closed his eyes, squeezing them shut. Within the span of a breath he said, "I know where she is."

He grabbed my hand and we headed east, down a long dirt road that led into the woods. I checked the ground for Leah's footprints, but the earth was dry and kept her secret.

"I don't think she's here," I panted. My lungs burned. My heart raced. The trees closed in, shutting out what was left of the light of the waning moon.

"Now it's your turn to trust me," Shane said, turning onto a branching path, almost invisible through the undergrowth.

I gripped his arm and followed closer.

Soon we reached a clearing, a large round area illuminated by the sliver of moon. I squinted, trying to pull up a memory. This was the clearing I had run to when I was a kid, the clearing where Merry and Shane had found me crying. And here was Leah, standing in the center of it.

We stared at each other, our mouths agape with disbelief.

"So, you found a tracker," she said, eyeing Shane with a look that rested somewhere between admiration and loathing.

"I prefer the term, 'remote viewer,'" Shane answered.

I looked at Shane, confused. Tracker? Remote viewer? I had no idea what any of that meant.

"You didn't bring the circle." Leah turned her attention to me, sneering, "...I would feel it on you."

"Leah," I said. "There is no circle. If you could really *feel* it, you would know that. It's just a metaphor."

"You're lying!" Her hands turned into claws and her mouth twisted with rage. Her hair seemed to stand on end.

"It's over, Leah," I spat. I was tired, done with games. "Give me the anti-spell."

"It's *not* over! It will never be over!"

Leah charged at me, nearly flying across the space between us. She was on me in a moment, knocking me back and landing on top of me. Her hands clamped around my wrists. We wrestled on the ground and I fought to break free.

Shane rushed to intervene. Leah let go of one of my hands, aiming a bony finger at him. A translucent blue orb flew from her fingertip, crashing into his chest. Shane went immediately stiff, his entire body frozen in place. Leah kept her hand up, raised and steady, maintaining the spell as she watched me out of the corner of her eye.

With her attention divided, I grabbed her raised hand and pulled her across my body, slamming her into the ground. Now I was on top, straddling her. Her glasses toppled from her face and she clawed at the dirt, searching for them.

"You bitch!" I said, taking her tiny wrists in one of my hands.

Her legs kicked but couldn't quite reach me. I took a handful of her hair with my free hand and slammed her head down in the dirt.

"Maggie, stop!" Shane was now free, disorientated and reaching for us.

Overcome with rage and not thinking, I thrust out my hand. A silver spark shot from my palm, hitting Shane and launching him back across the glen.

I returned my attention to Leah. "Give me the goddamned anti-spell!" I lifted my arm and slapped her hard across the face.

Who did she think she was? How dare she mess with me and my family and think there wouldn't be consequences? I was taking that anti-spell from her, one way or another.

"Tell me!" I hit her again, striking her nose. Blood gushed across her face. Leah squirmed beneath me, kicking and clawing, trying to bite at my arm that still held her wrists.

I hated her, hated her for all she had taken from me. Michael. My father. And now she was trying to take my mother.

"You can't have her!" I shouted. I pinned her hands over her head, holding them against the ground.

"Please stop," she begged, twisting and turning.

"Tell me where it is!"

"I don't have it!" she said. The blood from her nose had reached one of her ears, trickling in.

"You're a liar!" I moved my free hand to her neck, squeezing, feeling the veins pump against my palm. She flounced, gasping for breath.

I might burn in hell for what I was about to do, but she would be there with me.

My free hand slid down my side, into my pocket, and around the cold blades of the scissors. I didn't need magic. I pulled them out, letting her see the glint of moonlight on the steel. My soul felt as cold as the weapon in my hand.

"Maggie, stop!" Shane called, trying to pull himself to his feet. "You don't want to do this!"

My eyes flickered towards him, then back to Leah. He didn't know anything about her. He didn't know how she had used me, hurt me, stolen what was mine.

Leah managed to tuck her face into the crook of one of her arms, whimpering. "I don't have the anti-spell. I swear. That page was missing when I found the book."

"I don't believe you!"

"I promise! We were just so desperate..." Leah's wet eyes widened, tears mixing with blood. "You can't do this. We're sisters!"

My grip tightened and I yanked her by the hair, forcing her face sideways and planting a knee on her bloody cheek. I lowered the scissors, letting them hover just centimeters from her ear.

"You had your chance," I said, pulling the blades apart as she screamed.

Snip.

Her long brown hair fell into the dirt, separated from her head. I used the scissors again and again, until all that remained were uneven chunks of darker brown, closely cropped on her head.

"Go!" I said, rolling off her when I'd finished and tossing the scissors into the trees.

Leah scrambled to her feet, looked at her shorn hair on the ground, and then ran for the dark path opposite the way we had come in.

"Maggie!" Shane reached me, swallowing me in his arms.

"I couldn't get the anti-spell," I sobbed, wiping my nose on his shirt. "Mother isn't going to get better. I failed."

"No, you didn't fail. You passed, Maggie," he said, pulling me closer. "It's going to be okay."

"But nothing's changed," I said, taking one final glance at the path Leah had gone down.

I could have followed, but I knew that wouldn't save my mother. It wouldn't save me, either.

An owl hooted somewhere in the woods, a comforting sound as Shane wrapped his arm around my shoulders and escorted me out. He kicked the brush out of my way and carried me over the rougher spots. At last we emerged and a million twinkling stars greeted us.

"I'm sorry about throwing you back," I said, still in shock. "I was just so filled with anger. I have no idea how I did that. I didn't know I had that kind of power."

"I did. And don't apologize. It was actually kind of sexy. Dominated by two women in one night!"

I slugged him in the shoulder, then remembered something. "You knew exactly where she was. You knew where I was that night I got lost when we were kids. And you found me at the bus stop the night I came to Dark Root. You're a warlock!"

"Again, I prefer the term *remote viewer*. A gift I inherited from my mother. She could find anything. The only woman I ever met who never lost her purse."

I let him lift me over a pile of mud or manure, I wasn't sure which. "Why didn't you tell me?" I said.

"After the original council splintered, your mother had some reservations about a man's role in witchery. Uncle Joe trained me on the sly. Besides," he said, dusting off the back of my dress. "You weren't really sold on the magic thing, then. But after what I just witnessed, I'm guessing all that's changed."

"A tracker huh? I could really use you." I thought about all the things I'd lost.

"Use me all you want," Shane replied, as we stepped into the lights of downtown Main Street. Eve and Paul were singing, 'I Got You, Babe,' to a crowd of several hundred people.

Merry spotted me and ran over, whispering that we still had no candles for the lighting ceremony.

I waved her off. "We'll figure it out. We always do."

Shane and I crossed the street towards Dip Stix. "Now let's get you cleaned up," he said, unlocking the door and flipping on the light.

It took a second for my eyes to adjust and to see the figure sitting at the corner booth.

"Ruth Anne!" I almost chocked as I raced towards her.

"Surprise!" she said, her mouth forming a half-smile as she stood to hug me.

We cried, holding each other so tightly, I wasn't sure whose tears were whose anymore.

I looked at Shane, once again surprised by his ability to keep secrets. He grinned and stuffed his hands in his pocket.

"I told you I was good at finding things," he said.

"He's a frickin' genius," Ruth Anne admitted. "I had even changed my name."

"The internet is a powerful tool. I'm not sure what we warlocks did before it came along," Shane joked.

"You can tell me the details later," I said, not letting go of my sister.

Her hair was still short, wisps of brown hitting just above her shoulders. And she still wore the same large glasses she had always worn. She looked absolutely perfect.

"The others know you are here?" I asked.

Ruth Ann nodded. "I got in this afternoon. Shane thought we should wait and surprise you after the parade. If I would have known it was going to take you two this long to get here, I would have brought a book."

"Sorry." I bit my lip and gave Shane a knowing look. "We were a little delayed." Then, remembering the day Shane had confessed to liking older, intelligent women, I suddenly felt like I was intruding.

"I, uh..." I stepped back, almost without knowing I did it. "...I should probably leave you two alone. I need to get ready for the lighting ceremony."

Ruth Anne grabbed me again, whispering in my ear. "Don't be an idiot. He's not interested in me." She kissed me on the cheek, then winked. "Now, if you'll excuse me, I've been confined to this restaurant for most of the day. I'd like to get some of that caramel popcorn I've been smelling through the window for hours..."

"We'll catch you out there after Maggie changes," Shane said. "Thanks for being such a good sport, Ruth Anne."

I gave my sister a final smile and headed towards the restroom to get ready for the lighting ceremony. After all these years, I couldn't believe I was seeing her again. No matter what I may have believed before, I was now a firm believer in miracles.

As I carefully applied my makeup and straightened my hair, I studied my face in the mirror. It was almost imperceptible, but I could see that in the last few months it had changed. It was softer now. And older.

"You almost ready?" Shane called to me, knocking on the bathroom door. "The natives are growing restless."

"Yes," I said, blotting my red lips on a piece of toilet paper.

I still wasn't sure how we were going to manage the lighting ceremony. We'd probably need at least three hundred white candles. Everyone was counting on me to supply them. I stood at the sink for several moments, staring at my reflection and racking my brain for a solution, but I came up empty. After everything we had been through. I couldn't believe that Haunted Dark Root might fail because of a candle shortage.

"Damn it!" I hit the sink with my hand in frustration.

A light bulb popped above me, then went out.

And I had an idea.

Twenty-Nine

Don't Let the Sun Go Down on Me

Shane and I walked into the night, down the now-empty sidewalks and towards the bandstand at the edge of town.

The number of spectators had nearly doubled in the half hour we were inside Dip Stix, preparing. Paul was serenading the crowd sans Eve with an acoustic version of 'Love Potion Number Nine.' The crowd clapped along, but there was a feeling of restlessness in the air. They were all waiting for the moment when they could take part in the traditional lighting ceremony, helping to 'ward off evil' for another year.

"You look beautiful, sis," Merry said, as I made my way up the back steps of the stage, joining her, June Bug and Ruth Anne.

"Thank you," I said, pulling at the blue-green sweater dress. It felt tighter than the last time I tried it on. No one seemed to notice; they were too busy focusing on my *transformation*.

"I can't believe you got that hair to behave," Eve said, touching a strand that had been highlighted a honey-yellow during my trip to Linsburg. "And check out those boots! Are they real leather? I can't believe you've been keeping them from me! I might have to borrow them."

"You'll have to pry them off me, first," I said.

Eve gave me a sly smile that said *that can be arranged*.

"I'm glad you're here," I said to Ruth Anne. She had never enjoyed

345

these ceremonies as a kid, but now she seemed relaxed as she munched on a corn dog and swayed to the rhythm of Paul's guitar.

"Yes," she agreed. "We have so much to catch up on."

"I'm a bit worried," Merry said, looking out at the hundreds of people assembled before the stage. "I hope you're right about this."

"Me, too." I swallowed.

"There's only one way to find out," Shane said. "Shall we?"

He took my hand and led me towards the center of the grandstand. As we passed in front of Paul, he stopped playing to stare at me. Eve took her seat next to him and grabbed his jaw, forcing his gaze onto her. He grinned and the two exchanged Eskimo kisses. Ruth Anne made a gagging gesture behind them and we all laughed.

I walked into the spotlight, aware that hundreds of eyes were now watching me. I lifted the microphone with shaking hands, not used to being the center of this much attention. Ruth Anne, Merry, Eve and June Bug joined me in the front row, standing off to my right. We waved out at the crowd and they cheered in response.

The next generation of Dark Root witches had risen.

"Good evening, everyone," I said, when they had at last quieted down. "And welcome to the Annual Haunted Dark Root Lighting Ceremony."

With that, the crowd broke into another round of applause.

"I realize our little coven's been AWOL a few years," I said, brushing a piece of hair out of my face. "But we are back now and here to stay."

The crowd went crazy––clapping, cheering and stomping their feet. It reminded me of the revivals back at Woodhaven, only bigger and louder. I stepped forward, the spotlight still following me, my eyes resting on a young woman in the front row.

"Legend says that over a century ago, a woman named Juliana Benbridge lost her husband, Charles, when he jumped to his death from one of the tallest bridges in Portland. By all accounts, Charles had every reason to live. He was young, wealthy, a sought-after architect, and married to the most beautiful woman in the city. Still, one fateful evening while out for a walk, several witnesses saw him suddenly stop, and then——as if under a spell——walk to the edge of the bridge and hurl himself into the icy water below. His body was never found. Later, a maid confessed to hearing Juliana complain of her husband's bad habits, just that afternoon...

"Now, that in itself shouldn't have aroused much suspicion. But Juliana had been a mystery ever since she had moved to Portland at the age of sixteen. It was said that flowers bloomed or wilted in her presence, depending on her mood. A cock that crowed too early one morning, interrupting Juliana's beauty sleep, suddenly fell over dead. And a neighbor claimed her pitcher of milk had soured, just because Juliana had touched the pitcher.

"But, the biggest reason Juliana was under constant scrutiny had less to do with sour milk and more to do with her unusual ability...an ability that caused a lot of distress among the elite of Portland. Juliana could make men fall suddenly——and violently——in love with her. Husbands left their wives. Clergy left the church. Fathers left their families. All of them claimed they were under a spell.

"And so, shortly after her husband's passing, Juliana received a visit from her neighbors, advising her that if she did not leave immediately, they were going to get rid of her themselves. Juliana——being a practical woman——left the city with her two daughters and moved to Salem, where the family commissioned a company to build them a new house deep in the forests of Central Oregon. From there, Dark Root was founded.

"It is said that Juliana's magick followed her into the woods and that it still runs through the blood of her descendants, growing stronger with each generation. She was the original Dark Root witch and we," I said, waving towards my sisters. "Are her great-granddaughters."

I caught my breath and smiled at Ruth Anne, Merry and Eve.

They smiled back. We joined hands and curtsied as the crowd cheered for us. It was a strange feeling to be openly embracing my roots like this, but I wasn't alone. I had never been alone, I now realized. I had always had my sisters.

I took the microphone and knelt down, speaking to a little girl in the front row.

"Some people think that all witches are bad, but that's not true," I said. "Since the time of Juliana, we have been using our powers to push back the dark spirits that threaten to take over the world. Even though our Magick is at its strongest on All Hollow's Eve, we can't do this alone. Can you help us?"

The little girl nodded eagerly. I winked at her and stood up.

"I now invite you all to join me in the traditional lighting ceremony. Please gather tight around the stage."

Those who had attended the festival in years past quickly made their way to the front, forming a tight ring around the stage. Others followed suit, closing in around them. Parents in the back rows placed their children on their shoulders, giving them a better view.

We kept our places on the platform and watched.

"Now," I said, when everyone had arranged themselves the way they wanted. "Did everyone get an orange goody-bag today?"

I lifted mine up so they could see what I meant. Most people held theirs up in response, but a few shook their heads.

"Please raise your hand if you do not have one and someone will bring one by," I said.

Shane and Paul hopped down and began distributing the extra bags.

"Still three to spare," Shane said, when he returned a few minutes later.

I sighed in relief. Part one of my plan had at least worked.

"Inside your bag, you will find a flashlight. Please pull it out."

As they rifled through their sacks, Shane dimmed the stage lights.

"They say that one small light, if passed on, can illuminate the world. And so I ask you, this Halloween night, that as your lantern is lit, you pass it on to the person next to you."

"There's no batteries," a boy called out, shaking his flashlight and flipping the switch as others did the same.

"Patience," I said, as I showed everyone that my flashlight was also without batteries. "Even a witch needs a little time."

"Time to get wild, my little wilder," Shane whispered, returning to my side.

"I'm not sure I can," I whispered back.

It was a good idea in theory, but I had my doubts that I could pull it off. I wasn't a magick-on-demand type of witch.

Shane took my hand and squeezed it. "I've seen you do great things, Maggie Magic. You can do this."

I took a deep breath, still unsure of how to tap into my powers, but no longer doubting they existed. Aunt Dora believed in me. Jillian believed in me. My sisters believed in me. Even Shane believed in me. Now I had to believe in myself.

Closing my eyes, I raised the flashlight above my head, concentrating on the object in my hands. I imagined a stream of light rushing through me, emanating from the balls of my feet, moving through my body and head, then into my arms. I felt calm and tingly all at the same time, almost giddy. My fingertips tingled as I poured my energy into the dead flashlight.

A gasp from the crowd forced open my eyes. I gasped too when I saw the beam of light that shot up from my flashlight and into the dark sky. A small beacon in the night.

I looked to Shane who nodded encouragingly. He knew the hard part was still to come.

"Join hands," I told my sisters, offering Ruth Anne my free hand as I continued to hold the flashlight in the air with the other. "I need to draw from you."

We stood in a line across the stage. Everyone was quiet as they waited to see what would happen next.

I reached deep inside my soul, searching for that door that had been locked up like Mother's secret room. It was open now, gaping and raw. I turned my thoughts to that happy place of my childhood, running in the garden with my sisters. There was no rain there. No darkness. Only love. And light. Enough to fill the entire world.

I focused our collective energy as I dipped my flashlight onto Ruth

Anne's, mentally pushing it through. Her flashlight lit up, eliciting an 'ah' from the crowd.

Ruth Anne turned to Eve, tapping her light to her sister's, and a white halo elucidated her face. Eve touched her flashlight to Merry's, then Merry transferred her light on to her daughter. June Bug gasped as her flashlight lit up; she waved it like a sparkler on the Fourth of July.

"Now, go light theirs, honey," Merry said, directed June Bug to the crowd.

June Bug tottered carefully down the steps, and tapped her flashlight against a little girl's in the front row.

"Mom!" cried the girl, her eyes gleaming. "Look!" She touched her mother's flashlight and smiled. On and on it went, four hundred flashlight beams aimed at the heavens.

A tree cracked behind us. A raven cawed. The veil between the living and dead was almost non-existent tonight, but nothing was going to break through. We had helped to seal the circle around Dark Root, making a statement that we weren't ready for things to end. There was still light in the world and we weren't giving up.

"You did it!" Shane said, taking my flashlight and kissing the tips of my shaking hands.

The act had taken all my strength and I looked around for somewhere to sit. Shane escorted me to a stool by the microphone, pressing his palms to the small of my back, so that I wouldn't fall over.

"I'm still not sure how doing this is going to help Mother," I said, watching the world spin around me.

"Maybe it's all in the symbolism," Shane said, scratching his jaw.

I nodded thoughtfully. Maybe he was right.

I had finally accepted that I was a witch's daughter and a witch myself. My sisters and I had all returned to our childhood home. And we had performed the ritual Mother believed would help stave off a cataclysm. Maybe symbolism was enough.

As I sat on the stool, replenishing my energy, I watched the flashlights turn off one by one. Even so, that didn't put an end to the excited chatter,

"How did they do that? Was that a trick?"

I managed a weak smile. I didn't know the answers.

Magick was at work and I would never doubt it again.

"Okay," Eve said into the microphone. "I think its party time!"

Eve and Paul took the stage again, performing a rousing rendition of 'Superstitious.' Eve's voice cracked on a few notes, but no one cared. Everyone was too busy having a good time.

"You're a real witch now," Ruth Anne said, coming over to me and mussing up my hair.

"Shhh, don't let that get out," I said, trying to salvage my hairdo. "I have a reputation to protect."

Shane helped me to my feet. "You look pretty weak. I think some biscuits would fix you right up."

"You sure you wouldn't rather eat biscuits with one of my sisters?" I asked.

"All wonderful women," Shane admitted. "But I've had my eyes on another one, ever since our first game of hide and seek."

"You!" I stomped my foot. "All those games of hide and seek you talked us into and you were cheating!" Another thought occurred to me. "You never used your, what did you call them, remote viewing abilities to watch us girls doing other things, did you?"

"Only the good things," he smiled.

The music changed and Eve launched into 'Purple People Eater.' The crowd sang along as she worked the stage, completely in her element.

June Bug ran to me. "I love you, Aunt Maggie," she said, laying her head against my hip. The moon hit her hair, casting gold reflections all around us, more poignant than any light I could produce. "This is the best Halloween ever!"

"Yes," I agreed. "I think so, too."

It was just after nine on the morning of November first, the day our mother had always referred to as *The Day of Taking Stock*. We were bringing her home from the hospital today, and we gathered outside her door.

"I just need a few minutes alone with her," I told the others.

They nodded and I tiptoed inside, closing the door behind me.

"Mama?" I said, lips trembling as I stepped in.

She was still in a coma, hooked up to tubes and machines, looking even more frail than when I had last visited her, over a full month ago now. If resurrecting Haunted Dark Root was supposed to help her, it wasn't showing.

"Oh, God, Mama," I said, moving closer. "Maggie's here." I took her hand, almost a translucent gray, and squeezed it. "...And I'm not leaving this time, okay?"

Her breathing hung for a moment, and then continued.

I squeezed her hand again, wondering if she had heard me.

"I should have come sooner," I said. "I know that now. I haven't been a very good daughter. I have no excuses." I paused, rubbing my temples with my free hand.

"I was just...just so angry with you. Angry that that you never told us who our father was. Angry that I...I...I thought you were using us to gain attention for yourself. Angry for...for Ruth Anne and Merry leaving." I couldn't hold back the tears. "I never knew that you were trying to protect us. I wish you had told me..."

Her monitor started beeping.

Was I squeezing too hard? I relaxed my grip and took another breath. For the first time in my life, I was seeing her, not as the high and mighty Miss Sasha Shante for whom all of Dark Root bowed, but as the human woman she really was. A woman who made mistakes and had regrets. I wiped my eyes with the sleeve of my dress and continued.

"I shouldn't have left Dark Root without telling you," I said. "It was wrong. And I'm going to make it up to you. I promise. I'm staying this time. Maggie's home."

I opened my purse and removed the bus ticket I had purchased when I had first come back to Dark Root, the ticket that expired today. My father could still be alive, and if so, I wanted to find him. But for now, I had everything, and everyone, I needed. I ripped the ticket up into tiny pieces and dropped them into the wastebasket.

Mother's breathing remained ragged. I pressed her hand to my lips and then set it on the bed beside her. It slipped, flopping over the edge, and the crystal band on her thin arm slid to the floor. I picked it up, about to place it back on her wrist, when I noticed that it was cracked.

I held it to the light. There wasn't just one crack, but many––small rivulets embedded deep within the glass. How could it have cracked inside?

The circle.

This was the artifact that Leah has been looking for, I was sure of it. And it was on Mother's wrist the whole time.

I inspected it again. The circle was cracked, but it wasn't broken yet.

"I'm taking this now," I said, putting on the bracelet.

It pulsed on my wrist, tightening with every squeeze. I felt a series of tingles, like tiny currents crawling up my arm. My fingers twitched and I lifted my hand to see sparks of amber, violet, green, and yellow. I lowered my arm, willing the energy to dissipate. The colors faded out and I was left feeling nauseous. Still, in that moment, I felt connected to...

Everything?

I looked at the bracelet again. There was still so much I had to learn.

"Aunt Maggie, can we come in yet?" June Bug asked from the doorway.

I nodded.

"Ah, I see you found the bracelet," Ruth Anne said. "Be careful with that thing. I hear power can go to your head."

"We can discuss Maggie's impending insanity later," Eve said, taking my hand.

Ruth Anne and Merry joined us and we encircled our mother. June

Bug stroked her grandmother's face while Shane stood behind me, touching my shoulder. Paul sat down in a chair and began playing the first few riffs of 'Maggie May' on his guitar.

"There is power in words," I said, reciting the lesson from my dreams, then remembering my conversation with Jillian. "...And in love."

"You're right about that," Merry said, her face soft as she took in the picture of June Bug attending to our mother.

As we held the circle, I reflected back on the six weeks since I had returned to Dark Root. In that time I had learned that magic was real, but it wasn't just reserved for witches. I could see it in the changing seasons and hear it in the lyrics of a song. I could feel it every time someone kept a promise, or made a sacrifice. Magic was there whenever someone performed an act of kindness––or forgiveness. Magic could be found through music and laughter and love and, above all, family. This everyday magic was more powerful than any incantation or spell or working of the craft. This was the magic that lit up the world.

"Look!" June Bug called.

Mother's blue eyes fluttered open. Her lips were cracked but she managed a weary smile before falling back to sleep.

"I think Grandma's going to be okay!" June Bug beamed.

"I think so too," I said. "As a matter of fact, I think we all are."

"You're a good daughter and a good auntie, Maggie," Merry whispered, placing a hand on my belly. "And you're going to make an even better mother."

"You mean..."

"Yes," Merry smiled. "The circle continues."

ABOUT THE AUTHOR

April M. Aasheim was the second-oldest of six children, and spent her childhood living with her mother and her stepfather, traversing the Southwest, and following one 'get rich quick' dream after another. Though her travels were interesting and often brought her into contact with colorful and fascinating people, April longed for a *normal* life. Her early adult years were spent working as a preschool teacher, a social worker and a community activist. She was also a wife and a parent. During this time she started writing about her life and the people she met. She also realized that there was no such thing as a normal life.

April currently lives in Portland, OR, where she is happily married and is trying her hand, unsuccessfully, at gardening. She has published several short stories and is the author of the humorous and well-received contemporary women's fiction novel, *The Universe is a Very Big Place*. She is currently working on her third novel, *Mama's Not Home*, which will be available in early 2014.

April maintains an active blog about her adventures as a suburban housewife at aprilaasheim.blogspot.com

41117939R00218

Made in the USA
Lexington, KY
29 April 2015